HITTA'S TEA MAKER

Hitta and Angel's Tale

EDWINA FORT

Hitta's Tea Maker/Edwina Fort. – 1st edition

ISBN

HITTA'S TEA MAKER

First and foremost, I would like to thank The Heavenly Father for once again using my hands as a tool. I would like to thank Team 2019 for putting in that work and helping this book to come about. And finally, I'd like to dedicate this book to my little Cousin Angel, who is out there grindin'. The world sees you, boo…do yo' thang! I am so proud of you!

When I was little girl, my mama told me that God is a Master Weaver and that life is His tapestry. She said no one knows what in the end the picture will unfold, but that we are all threads intertwined in His divine masterpiece. Some threads are dark, and some are bright, but one can't exist without the other because then the picture wouldn't be precise. She says balance is needed in order to bring God's plan into sight, but that in the end, everything will be alright. For it is written that Yah spoke into the darkness and said, let there be Light.

Edwina Fort

Chapter One

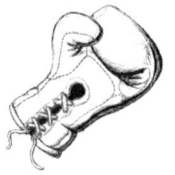

THEY MET...

> *I Knew from The First Moment We Met. It Was... Not Love at First Sight Exactly, but more...Familiarity. Like: Oh, Hello, Hey It's You...It's Going to Be You.*
>
> Mhairi McFarlane (via 5000Letters)

Angel

For as long as I can remember, I've had nightmares. Not your average nightmares with monsters and such. No...

I dreamed about a world depleted of all life. A world on fire...

A world ravished...

These dreams I kept to myself. Coming up in the foster system you learn to keep a lot of things to yourself. I don't think I've ever had a good night's sleep. I am the only one with a case of insomnia that my teas cannot fix.

People come to my shop from all over the city to get teas that will help cure whatever ailment they suffer from naturally, and so far, I am the only one my teas did nothing for. I don't know if I've become immune to the herbs because I've consumed so many of them, or if… and this is what I suspect it to really be, I'm meant to have these dreams.

For some reason, I think God wants me to see the world the way that I see it in my sleep. It does help me come up with tea recipes. LOL! I know that sounds strange, but it does…

However, I didn't start off my tale by telling you guys about my nightmares for no reason. I did it because although my nightmares scare the heck out of me, it's nothing compared to the fear my foster brother's boss causes me to feel.

Westly, who is my foster brother, does maintenance work at the neighborhood gym, a job he's had for the past six months. It really is bittersweet. Sweet because for Westly having a job for six months is a huge improvement to his record. Over the last ten years, I doubt if he'd held a job for longer than two weeks, let alone six months.

Westly has two major habits that keep him from being a reliable employee. One, he's a heroin addict and two, he often steals to support his heroin habit.

So the fact that he's held this job for six months is amazing. He's even for the most part, been able to pay his half of the rent. Well… until recently, but I'll come back to that.

The bitter part about him having this job is that he works for a goon. There is no other word that can describe him.

Okay, maybe…Heathen, Thug, Savage, Animal, Bear, Lion…Brute!

Yes…Brute is a better word.

The man is a complete brute. When he walks down the street, people scramble to get out of his path. He's a bad man and his bad vibes go out ahead of him to clear the way.

I bet he kills people. He looks like the type. He's probably beat somebody to death with those huge, scarred monster paws he calls hands.

Anyway, the man is completely uncivilized.

But what makes things so much worse is the fact that he's attracted to me for some strange reason. I was nothing like the kind of woman he should be attracted to. I wasn't a fancy dresser or a partier…I wasn't bold or even brave.

I am a boring tea maker. A boring tea maker who blends so well into the background that folks barely notice me. When people come to my shop, their eyes are drawn to the many jars of herbs and my tea displays that I have worked so hard on.

Although I'm standing there taking their order, very seldom do they stop and really take me in. My beautiful teas are truly the stars of the show.

This doesn't make me feel bad. It has always been that way for me. In fact, I love it that way. I don't like drawing attention to myself, which is why I dressed in boring, loose-fitting clothes that take away from my looks rather than add to them.

It's an old trick I learned early while growing up in foster homes, you didn't want to attract the wrong kind of attention to yourself, things could get really nasty. So many times, I'd almost fallen prey… But thank God for Westly, who protected me in those days.

Anyway, I'll tell you more about that later as well… First, let me finish telling y'all about my amazing ability to go unnoticed.

Well…to everyone but Hitta.

The first time I came to the gym to pick up rent money from Westly, Hitta was standing at the front counter, where the cash register was, talking to the person that I assumed was his cashier.

When I came in, they both looked up, the cashier with a warm greeting smile and Hitta with a fierce scowl that almost made me turn around and run back out the door, but I didn't because our rent money was very late and the landlord was once again threatening to put us out.

So…I pressed on, but my eyes as if they had a mind of their own took in the monster of a man in front of me. His muscles were very hard and defined. I don't think he had an ounce of fat on him…anywhere.

This I was able to see because he wore a white wife beater that fell on him in a way that could be distracting to a woman weaker than I.

He had several tattoos, but what really stood out were the two words that were angrily slashed up each of his forearms.

The right arm had the word Hard slashed up it, describing that forearm perfectly. And the left arm had the word Hitta slashed up it… no doubt describing those monster fists perfectly. There was another tattoo on his right bicep, but I wasn't close enough to see what it was. And it looked like another that began somewhere under his tank top and went all the way up to the left side of his thick neck.

Gracious!

In his ear, he wore a diamond earring that wasn't really big, but big enough to let the onlooker know it wasn't cheap. Around his neck, he wore a gold necklace that had a pair of diamond-encrusted boxing gloves hanging from it.

My gaze continued down his body. He wore a pair of brand name black sweatpants on his muscled legs that fell on his tampered hips as if he was modeling them and a pair of black Jordan's on his feet.

The fact that it looked as if he was fresh from the barber with the low-cut hair and full beard that was lined perfectly, did little to take away from his fierceness. In fact, if you could get past the frown that looked as if it may be permanently fixed on his face, he was a really handsome man in a very rugged kind of way.

The closer I got to the giant, the more I had to strain my neck to look up at him. And the closer I got to him, the more it felt as if he could just pick me up with one hand and snap me in half.

Gracious! The violence that was pouring off him was suffocating. You ever met someone and thought…this person is very dangerous? You look in their eyes and can tell they won't hesitate to hurt or kill… In Hitta's case… Smash!

I had to change my thoughts or else I was going to lose my nerve and go scurrying back out that door making a complete fool of myself. So I decided to do my best to ignore the big frowning giant to the right of me with the cold deadly eyes.

It wasn't easy though. First of all, he didn't move to the side like a normal, civilized human being would have done so that I could speak with the receptionist privately.

No… he just rudely stood there, forcing me to stand closer to him than I was comfortable with. He smelled like power. Instead of cologne, he smelled like whatever soap he'd used to wash his clothes and rage.

And I know you're saying, what the hell does rage smell like...?

And I'm telling y'all, it smells like Hitta.

Anyway, so I'm standing there trying to ask the receptionist if he'd get Westly for me and Hitta is staring at me as if I'm an ice cube and he's a man that's been lost in the desert for thirty days. I give him a look that says it's rude to stare...

And would y'all believe the heathen found that amusing? He even cracked those intimidating lips of his into a smile. I shivered because I didn't know what was more frightening, his smile or his scowl.

However, that wasn't the worst part. The receptionist then left to go and find Westly, leaving me alone with the brute.

Y'all, the gym was huge. Who knows where Westly was? So I take a few steps back and pretend to read the postings on the cork board that were there. The whole time he was watching me. He hadn't moved his big body from where he leaned on the counter.

And then he opened his mouth and spoke, the sound of his deep voice nearly caused me to jump out my shoes. I kid you not, a squeak of fear left my throat.

Don't shake y'all's heads at me, I told y'all I'm not that brave. I had a tragic childhood. I hate that I'm this way, but I am very squeamish.

Anyway, so he spoke.

"Why you dress that way?"

My mouth dropped open at his rudeness. "Excuse me?!"

"I don't like to repeat myself."

At that moment I was thanking God for my brown skin because if I had been a few shades lighter, I would be beet red right now.

Not only was he a rude brute...he was bossy and mean.

I held my head up as if he was nothing. "Dress what way?" I wanted to say heathen but changed my mind.

"Like a homeless person."

My mouth dropped open again.

Oh, my God! Did the man just tell me I dressed like a homeless person? I was so insulted that at that point, my fear of him faded for just a bit. I put my hand on my hip.

"For your information, this style is called Boho."

He lifted an eyebrow and I could tell by the little evil smirk on his face he was enjoying himself at my expense. "Hobo?"

"No! Boho…It's a difference." I nearly yelled. I started to begin that sentence with, are you deaf! But then thought better of it. This guy felt dangerous, like make you disappear dangerous.

He grunted, letting his intimidating gaze roam over my body.

Okay, so maybe I didn't wear the brightest of colors. That day I believed I had on my long maxi black skirt that fell to cover my feet completely and a grey oversized sweater that hung off one shoulder. I'd partnered that ensemble with my black hand beaded tasseled purse. I'll admit it wasn't the prettiest thing in my closet, but I didn't look homeless either.

His intense gaze was starting to unnerve me. He had yet to look away from me since I walked through those doors. He studied me so intensely it felt as if he could see under my shabby clothes to the figure I worked very hard to hide.

After his insulting words, he didn't say anything else, he just stood there watching me. And the way that he did it was so unnerving. People walked past and said goodbye to him, but he never looked away from me. He just nodded his head to whoever it was and mumbled something in a language that was purely his because I don't think it was English.

I know he was a brute and probably uneducated…but even he had to know that it was rude as hell to stare at somebody like that. It was almost as if he knew he was making me nervous and was enjoying it.

Although Westly and I were fairly new to this neighborhood, I'd heard enough from the girl who lived across the hall from me to know that he was something of a big shot around these parts. She said he used to be a professional boxer and was doing really good until an injury forced him to stop.

Of course, I was very curious as to what the injury was, there weren't many ailments my teas couldn't take care of. There were some…

But not many…

However, he was such a brute we will never find out. If he had been civilized, I would have tried to reach out to him. There was no way that was happening now.

I was so relieved when I looked up and saw Westly walking towards me that I nearly ran to him and threw myself into his arms. Although an addict, my brother has always protected me. The giant frowned when he saw this…

"Hey, Bo…" His deep voice seemed to rumble through the floor. "This yo' girl?"

He still hadn't moved from where he casually leaned against the counter.

Westly seemed shocked that his boss was actually talking to him. I would later find out that was the first time he'd ever said anything to him.

My brother chuckled in that way that let me know he was freshly high. In another few minutes, he would start the nodding.

"Naw, bossman, this here my little sista."

The giant grunted again as his gaze once again raked down my body. "This the sista that stay with you?"

Westly was now beaming like a small child whose hero had noticed them. "Yeah it is…I—I didn't think you knew anything 'bout me."

I rolled my eyes. I wanted to kick him for being so infatuated with the brute.

At one time y'all, my brother was so very strong and handsome. Girls used to line up at our foster parents' door to see him. Of course, I would get nervous whenever he went out because that meant I would be home with Kirk without Westly's protection.

Scary times…

Very scary times…

Anyway, back in those days, my brother was the man to know. Now, the heroin and whatever other drugs he liked had torn his body down. He was only a tenth of the man he used to be. Of late, he's been scratching big sores on his arms and face.

I pray he hadn't started doing meth, but I fear that he has. I have paid for him to go to rehab more times than I can count, but so far, nothing has worked. However, I can't turn my back on him. Had it not have been for him putting the fear of God in Kirk's heart, I would have been brutally raped many times.

No, I can't turn my back on him. I take comfort in the fact that although he steals like nobody's business…he's never stolen from me.

Not once…

"I know about everybody working for me." The giant spoke again, drawing my attention back to him. "Including the fact that you like to suck on that glass dick…" His intense gaze fell back to me.

But I was too busy trying to pick my mouth up off the ground for the third time. He'd just put my poor brother on blast and brought up his ailment in the most vile way. The guy at the register pretended to shuffle around some papers.

"You sure are rude…" I finally hissed. I'd had enough of his horrible personality.

"Baby, I don't sugga coat sh*t."

Westly gave a nervous laugh. "I'll be right back, boss, I just need to talk to my sista outside for a minute."

His hands shook as he led me away. I looked back over my shoulder at the animal man and I swear, what he did next nearly made me trip, had Westly not been holding my arm so tightly I would have.

He slowly licked his lips and then kissed toward me, but that wasn't the shocking part. The shocking part was my body's response to that scandalous gesture. I felt a spasm between my thighs that stole my breath.

That was the first time anything like that has ever happened to me. When I frowned at the brute's vulgarness, he had the nerve to wink at me with that evil grin on his face, as if he was very much aware of what his vulgar gesture had done to my body.

Needless to say, after that day, I did my very best to avoid going to the gym for anything, but then I started seeing him in the oddest of places.

Like the bus stop when I'm on my way to and from work. It isn't every day, but some days he'd be sitting there watching me in that big black Hummer with the tan leather seats that my brother thought was the best vehicle to have ever been created under the heavens.

He never said anything, just sat there and watched me get on the bus or get off. For my own sanity, I'd convinced myself that he wasn't sitting there for me. The gym was right across the street. He could be sitting waiting for someone to come out or just waiting to go in.

And then it was that time he'd shown up at the carnival that I'd taken my six-year-old niece to. She'd dragged me all over wanting this and that. And well, I was on a serious budget and could not afford to get any more tickets to get on any more rides.

My God, the tickets were nearly five dollars apiece, and you needed at least three to get on each ride, which meant every ride was costing a whopping fifteen dollars for four minutes. And of course, like any kid her age who didn't understand money, she started to have a fit on me.

I know I need to be firmer with her, but the truth is, I didn't have it in me...Both of her parents were drug addicts. The only time she got to be a kid free of worries is when she was with me.

So there I stood in the middle of the carnival checking my bank account with my phone trying to see which account I could get away with pulling a few more dollars from when suddenly she went quiet and started thanking someone like crazy.

I looked up to see her happily holding a hand full of tickets, so many tickets that it would take us the rest of the night of riding rides to use them all. My gaze rose to the crowd to try and see who the hell had just given her so many tickets when I saw Hitta's muscled back walking away from us. And just like always, the crowd just automatically parted for him.

Once again, I'd convinced myself that it was a coincidence and he was not following me. But I knew deep down that he was, which was confusing because he thought I dressed like a homeless person. Surely he wasn't attracted to me. So why else was he following me?

Anyway, I'd managed to avoid the gym and was doing a damn good job at it till today. Westly had been late on his half of the rent for the last three months and I'd had to pay the whole thing. Because of this, I'd fallen behind on a few things to do with my shop, like the insurance.

Well, actually I'd lapsed on my insurance policy a few times, but it had never been an issue till now. My shop is in a very old building, only God knows when the last time the electric wiring had been updated.

The fire started in the walls and did quite a bit of damage to my west wall. Because it happened during the time I'd let my insurance lapse, I was paying for the repairs out of pocket. With paying for that plus the rent on both the apartment and the shop, plus footing the bill for my niece's schooling, because neither of her parents could do it, and I didn't want her going to the school around her mother's house, because it was a death trap. Just last week, three kids had gotten shot standing in front of the school...

My money was extremely funny and for the life of me, I couldn't figure out why. The tea shop wasn't doing too badly. I was blocks away from a college campus, so I had a steady stream of customers... It was only me working there because I couldn't afford to hire anyone, so it wasn't like I was paying for labor...

And yet here I stood outside my brother's job broke and needing him to come through with some major funding.

It was bad...

Not only was my wall half repaired, but I was also behind on the rent for both the apartment and the shop...not to mention Jessie's tuition that will be due at the end of this month.

I paced back and forward in front of the gym, trying to work up enough nerves to go in. The members who went in and out looked at me as if something was wrong with me, but I didn't care, I was a nervous wreck.

What if he was in there?

What if he was standing right by the desk again?

After a group of three guys came out, I walked to the door and stood on my toes to try and look into the round window. I had to clutch the handle and try and hoist myself up because I was still too short to see.

As you guys may have guessed, I am vertically challenged in a world where everything was made for tall people. I think I stopped growing at twelve and a whopping 5'2.

My arms strained as I finally got myself up high enough to peep in the window and smiled when I saw he wasn't standing at the front desk. There was a pretty girl behind the cash register today.

A squeak left my throat when right then my arms gave out causing me to fall back. I braced myself for the impact with the ground, but it never happened.

I was caught by something hard, but it wasn't the ground. My eyes widened when I saw that the muscled arm that was wrapped around my waist shamelessly holding me against an equally muscled body, said Hard. The other arm slowly joined it securing me completely, said Hitta.

Dear God! I had fallen right into the brute's arms. For a moment I didn't move. He tightened his arms as he brought me even closer gently burying his face in my long braids at my neck. My lips parted in a gasp when I felt his mouth lightly brush my skin.

The caress was barely there, but because I was super sensitive at that moment, I'd felt it. His lips made their way up to my ear.

"Man, shawty...I want to f*** you so bad." He whispered.

His words that should have angered me caused an answering response in my center that surprised me.

The emotions that were racing around inside of me were all brand new and for just a moment, I paused to try and understand them.

Arousal I understood. Although it was true, I'd never felt it to this extent, it was a feeling I understood. It was the other thing he caused me to feel that stunned me.

It felt really good being held in his arms. The top of my feet rested on his bigger ones... For the first time in my life, I felt... safe.

I know I said earlier that Westly always protected me and he did, but his protection was as shaky as him. Even though he protected me from Kirk, I was still afraid. I was always afraid. The feeling that I felt now was different.

I felt safety in Hard Hitta's arms. That thought frightened me right out of the stupor I had fallen in and I scrambled away from him.

"I'm so sorry!" I told him staring at the ground because I was not brave enough to look into his face.

"You looking for somebody?" His voice was so very deep.

I nodded pushing the braid that had fallen in my face back behind my ear. "Yeah, my brother."

"Why?"

That made me look up at him startled. I can't believe how rude he is. I opened my mouth to tell him off but changed my mind. Instead, I cleared my throat.

"Nothing important, I just have to tell him something."

He took a step closer to me and I took another step back.

"This the only time I'm going to let you lie to me. Consider this a warning. You lie to me again and I will have to punish you. You hear?"

He growled those words at me. And I'm not going to lie, they scared the hell out of me. He'd just threatened to punish me. What the hell did that mean?

He is so freaking mean!

Not able to take his intense angry gaze any longer, I turned my head and nodded, looking at the cars that were passing. He was too intimidating. And to top it off, he was not moving to walk away, not getting the picture that I didn't want to talk to him about it. He just stood patiently waiting for me to tell him my business.

Tough Titty…I ain't telling him nothing. I may not be brave enough to tell him off to his face, but I can give the silent treatment like nobody's business.

I folded my arms and looked down at my foot that I was using to gently kick a rock around. He chuckled before his muscled arm came toward me. I jumped away from him as if he was holding hot coals, but exhaled in relief when I saw he was only opening the door. He held it open for me and gestured for me to proceed.

I did so quickly, practically running to the counter to ask the pretty girl if she could tell my brother I was here to see him, but she was only half listening to me. Her attention was on the big man that had followed me in.

He walked behind the counter and picked up a pile of mail and began to look through it. He must have just gotten here because he carried a gym bag on his arm. She walked over to him and began to tell him something with a big flirty smile on her face, but he stopped her.

"Get over there and help the lady standing there?" He grumbled in his truly rude fashion.

She turned red with embarrassment, for just a moment her mouth opened as if she couldn't believe he'd talked to her that way. There was no doubt in my mind they were sleeping together.

"I'm sorry, how can I help you?" She nearly snapped those words to me. She was not happy with me.

Great! Now she hated me because of him. I smiled kindly at her, hoping to extend an olive branch. I didn't want to make anything tough around here for Westly. He was doing so good.

"Yes, may I speak with Westly Baker, please?" I repeated for the second time.

She rolled her eyes and walked away to get him. This time I will not make the same mistake and stand here to be harassed by the mean guy. I turned and walked back out the door, Westly will know to look for me outside.

A few minutes later he came out. "What's going on, baby girl?"

I groaned because he was high. I really wished he was sober so that he could know the severity of what I had to tell him.

"West, I need your rent money for the last three months. Ms. Armstrong came by the shop again today. She's threatening to put me out. Although the fire happened because of the wiring in her building, she still blaming me. She wants me gone! With me not having her rent money, this will be just the excuse she needs to put me out! West, you know I will go crazy if I lose my shop! Working with my teas is the only thing that brings me comf---"

"Whoa! Whoa! Whoa! Angel, Damn! Calm down!" He took my arm and pulled me away from the gym doors. "Just relax, I'm going to have the money for you tonight."

Y'all see what I mean? That was the drug talking.

I folded my arms across my chest. "Westly, I'm serious!"

He chuckled, his eyes blinked so slowly it looked as if he was going to nod off any second. "And I'm serious too, baby girl. I'm going to have the money tonight."

"Where you gon' get that kind of money from?"

"A patna of mine just got back into town. He owes me some money from a job he and I did a few years ago."

See what I'm saying? I was in no mood for his crap. My brother may not steal from me, but he had no problem lying to me.

"Westly, don't you understand what I'm saying?! I'm getting ready to lose my shop!"

"Hey! You ain't gon' lose nothing! Don't I always come through? Now I told ya, a patna of mine is going to drop off a package to me tonight. I'm going to bring it home, just relax. You'll be able to pay Ms. Armstrong worrisome a** in the morning."

I gave him a long look. He smiled at me with droopy eyes. "Relax…"

Chapter Two

YOU BELONG TO ME

Angel

"Oh, my God, West! Where did you get all of this money from?!"

My brother had just walked through our front door and dumped about ten thousand dollars onto my lap. He chuckled as he headed into his bedroom. Our apartment wasn't that big. The kitchen and living room were all in one space. My brother's room, the bathroom, and my room were three doors connected to this space.

There were no hallways or anything, so I could see him from where I sat on the couch clutching the rolls of money he'd just dropped in my lap. He had a nervous grin on his face as he hurriedly pulled some of his clothes out of his drawer and threw them into a plastic bag.

It was that grin that concerned me. It said I can't believe I've done what I just did.

"I told you, a patna of mine came into town and paid me for a job he and I worked on together a while back. That should be enough to cover our rent, your shop rent, and a couple of months of Jessie's tuition. When I get back into town, I should have enough to cover a few more months."

I frowned as I watched him put his brush and pick in the plastic grocery bag.

"Where are you going?"

"My patna has another job for me that should pay as well as that one. But I have to leave out tonight."

Every cell in my body told me that he was lying to me. The fact that he has yet to make eye contact only verified it.

"What kind of a job?"

"He builds houses," was all he said.

I sat and waited for more, but nothing else came...

Now the ball was in my court. I could do two things, return this money to him and demand he take it back to whoever he stole it from...and then lose my shop, thus losing the only perfect thing I'd ever done in life. I would also lose my apartment and wouldn't be able to pay Jessie's tuition, at which point, she would end up in the public school down the street from her house.

Orrrr....

I could turn a blind eye and take this money. West said he got it from helping his partner, whoever that was, build houses. Why not just believe him? Thus, keeping my shop, my apartment, and Jessie's spot in that amazing school where she doesn't have to worry about dodging bullets on the playground.

Hmmmm...What is a girl to do?

I grabbed Westly's arm as he went to walk past me to the door. "Just promise me you didn't take this from an orphanage or a hospital and that nobody is going to kick down my door looking for this money and blow my brains out because of it."

He squatted down next to me and smiled...and I remembered a time he was so handsome that it hurt to look at him. Now, he was only a ghost of the man he used to be.

"Come on, baby girl... You know I wouldn't put you in that situation. The money is good. I earned it...Every cent of it." He leaned forward and kissed me on the forehead.

"I have to go...I'll be back in a few weeks."

"Be back from where?" I asked as he headed out the door.

"California."

And then he was gone…

I tossed and turned all night, conflicted. The next morning, I lay in bed and the battle I'd fought within myself continued. I knew the money was bogus. Westly ain't ever had a job that paid that much. So, the fact is, he'd stolen the money. If I partake, then I'm stealing it too.

But I also knew that if I didn't pay the things that needed to be paid today, I would not only lose my livelihood but because my livelihood supported so many others, they would lose as well. Damn Westly for putting me in this situation.

I thought about Jessie. I loved her like she was my own child. There is nothing that I wouldn't do for her. If I lose the shop I couldn't pay for her schooling, her clothes, hell…her food because God knows her mama and daddy borrowed from me often enough to feed her.

By the time I'd finished my morning cup of tea, my mind was made up. And after praying that God forgave me, I paid the rent for my shop. I'd tried to get Ms. Armstrong to take one month's rent, although I was behind on two, swiftly approaching my third.

If I paid her for the two months, it would suck up more than half of the ten grand and I will still be in a tight spot once everything was paid.

"Absolutely not!" She screeched. "I've been more than patient with you. First, you cause a fire inside my building—"

"That fire was not my fault. The fire chief said it was because of the old wiring. Technically, you should be paying for the repairs."

She opened her mouth as if I'd slapped her. Ms. Armstrong was an old white woman, who believed in the traditional way…if you know what I mean. And you're going to think I'm kidding, but she looked and acted just like the woman in the movie Driving Miss Daisy.

Her racism wasn't overly noticeable. Well, …at least not to her. She was what my great, great…heck, I don't know how many greats, grandmother Tabitha would call an undercover racist.

Now, I know you all are wondering how the world I knew what my great, great…I don't know how many greats grandmother would call Ms. Armstrong. And the answer is simple…

She told me.

What I've just said has thrown many of you for a loop… But no worries, I will come back to this topic and explain that phenomenon a little later. Just know that it was because of Tabitha that I'd opened the tea shop at nineteen. It was she who taught me how to use the herbs to make teas for healing, taste, and overall well-being.

"You don't need to be talking to me that way, girlie! I've always been good to you people!" She was good and worked up into a frenzy now.

"What way? I was just trying to explain…" The look in her eyes brought my explanation to a halt. It was time for my lease to be renewed, the last thing I wanted to do was get on this woman's bad side.

I exhaled.

Well, that and…for some people, it was just a complete waste of time to try and reason with them. The sad part about the whole situation was that she didn't even realize just how racist her statement was. She truly believed in her heart that she was a good person because she'd been good to us people.

"You know what? You're right, Ms. Armstrong, I will write you a check for both months' rent. I owe it, it's only right that I pay it. I really appreciate your being understanding these last few months."

She huffed as she held her head up as high as it would go on her little wrinkled neck.

"That's more like it. I don't know what has gotten into you talking back to me like that. In my day, such a thing would have never been tolerated. My mother raised us to be kind to the colored…but it's only so far kindness can go. I took a chance on you and let you rent this place because you seemed to be more put together than the rest--" She actually caught herself and after clearing her throat, continued her tirade.

"I believe I've been more than patient with you."

"Yes, you have."

I ground down on my teeth and wrote her a check for seven thousand dollars. Remember Angel, you need her to agree to another two years on your lease.

The things that we as a people had to put up with in order to compete in the race. I learned long ago that it did no good to complain. Complaining only gave folks an excuse to call you lazy and say you wanted a handout. The fact is, I owe her the money and I needed to pay it.

She took the check and had the nerve to ask for a half pound of my healthy heart blend that I'd been making for her since I'd opened the place, a hundred- and twenty-two-dollar order that she never once offered to pay for. Of course, she didn't look at that as a handout, instead, she saw it as something she was owed for allowing me to exist in her realm. She always took the tea without even a thank you…today was no different.

"And don't be long getting that wall finished. There's a draft coming in through that hole." She shivered for good measure and then turned and marched on out the door, causing the little bell over it to ding angrily.

I had to bite down on my tongue so that I didn't call her an old hag. Instead, I reminded myself why I put up with her crap by letting my gaze take in my amazing tea shop. Ms. Armstrong was a slum lord, but she had a treasure of a building buried here in the heart of Oak Park.

When I stumbled upon this place, it was just sitting empty and abandoned. She was doing nothing with it. I found out from the city that it was her father's general store some years back and had been willed to her after he died.

She'd never done anything with it, practically forgetting it existed. When I finally hunted her down and asked to buy it, she told me she would get back to me after she'd talked to the family lawyer. Of course, she never got back to me, so I had to hunt her down again.

She then quoted me a ridiculously expensive amount.

"But the building is abandoned…" I reminded her.

"Do you want it or not, missy?"

That's when I realized what I was dealing with. My shoulders slumped and I almost gave up. That night, I stood outside the shop looking into the dirty windows, just imagining what could be.

"Be a shame if that old biddy's greed keeps you from having this gem."

I smiled at the sound of Tabitha's voice…her just seeming to appear out of nowhere no longer surprised me. She cupped her eyes with her hands and looked through the dirty glass into the shop.

"Going to need a lot of work though."

"Yeah it is…but it won't be me doing it. I can't afford what she's asking for the place, let alone fix it up."

Okay…really quick, just so that you guys are not in the dark, let me explain a few things about my great, great---you know what, skip that. From now on, I'm just going to refer to her as Greatie, that's what I'd taken to calling her years ago.

For a long time, I thought she was a figment of my imagination. The first time I could remember talking to her, I was five…still living at home with my mom, who was strung out and still is on every drug beneath the sky. She used to leave me at home by myself sometimes without any food.

It was during those times when I saw Greatie the most, she would come and see me and bring me food. That's when she first started teaching me about teas. She would bring several plants for me to study and while I experimented with them, she would sit and embroider. When I told my mom about her, she laughed and said I had an imaginary friend.

She had even convinced me it was true. So, after that, whenever Greatie showed up, I'd just assumed she was from my imagination, except my pants that had once had a hole in them was now sewn up. And the skirt that had been too short, was longer…and not to mention the pretty pink sweater she made me with the word chosen stitched over the heart, that I still had to this very day. Sometimes, I let Jessie wear it when she was over my house.

Anyway, …my mom never noticed these things, because like I said, she was always too high. Greatie didn't show up every day…She didn't even show up every month. Sometimes years would go by in between her visits.

But I always remember her showing up at pivotal points in my life. The day they took me out of my mother's home, she came and saw me before the police showed up, telling me my life was getting ready to change. And the day I moved in with Westly and his family, she came and warned me about Stan, Westly's stepdad. She said that he was a predator and I had to always sleep with one eye open while in his home.

By that time, I'd already been to several foster homes and knew well how to sleep with one eye open. But she told me that I would find a temporary protector in West...but that he wouldn't remain so. She told me not to worry because the Ancient of Days never left his children defenseless...and that he would send me a true protector that will slay all of my monsters.

It was during that time that I realized that she wasn't a figment of my imagination. Westly came in the kitchen one day while I was trying out a new tea recipe and she was sitting at the table working on my eighth-grade graduation dress.

"Who are you?" he asked.

I whipped around from the stove. "You can see her?"

Both he and Tabitha looked at me as if I'd lost my mind. And at that point, I thought I had. You see, if Tabitha wasn't a figment of my imagination and was in fact real, then that meant she was really my great, great, great...only God knows how many greats grandmother.

My mom's mom died when I was five. I remembered going to her house a few times, but not many because she didn't support my mom's way of life. I remember seeing pictures of my great grandmother on my grandmother's walls, although they favored her, neither of them was Tabitha.

Greatie said that my mom's mom was her great, great, great, many greats granddaughter.

So, you guys may ask the question, how do you know she's not just some crazy old woman lying to you?

Well...because I look just like her. I mean almost identical. She's short like me, her skin is the same shade of brown as mine. Her hair is white now from age...but it's the same length and even the same grade as mine. She has the same birthmark I have on my shoulder. It's a brown mark that resembles the continent of Africa...I kid you not.

Although she's clearly much older than me, her skin barely has any wrinkles, just a few laugh lines around her eyes and lips. She said it's that way because she drank herbal tea her whole life. Her love for tea passed down to me. Although technically, she's a seamstress…and I can't stitch to save my life, she is definitely my kin.

It was then I learned and accepted that there was more to this world than what we were being told. It was also then my nightmares started…However, I'll tell you guys about those a little later.

Anyway, so she and I are standing there in front of the shop that at the time, was abandoned when she came up with a beautiful idea.

"Well, if it's too high to buy, how much do you think she'll charge you to rent it?"

I turned to look at her with a big grin on my face.

"That's a wonderful idea, Greatie!" And then threw my arms around her and gave her a huge kiss on her cheek that caused her to chuckle.

That next week, I was signing a two-year lease on the tea shop. Ms. Armstrong's rent was still a little high, but this was Oak Park, everything was high in this area. Plus, this place was so worth it.

The hardwood floors were very old, but when I'd first rented the place instead of tearing them up, I had them waxed until they shined brightly, highlighting their uniqueness. The walls were all various shades of brown cobblestone that really added a homey feel to the place.

I'd lucked up and found an antique sectional couch that was quite big and comfortable at a storage auction a few years back. I got it reupholstered in Ankara African fabric that blended in perfectly with the walls and the floors.

I'd used the same fabric on the two big claw foot chairs that sat in front of the fireplace that I kept lit in the wintertime. Between the two chairs sat an oak table that had a chessboard carved into the top. Each of the pieces had been carved out of oak wood as well. That table had been a gift to me from one of the charities I did an annual fundraising for.

On the walls, I had a few paintings and some of my favorite quotes from the book of Proverbs. I had several bookshelves that had every book I could find about herbs and teas on them. I'd managed to get fifteen tables in my space without making it feel overcrowded. The tables were all old wood that I allowed my customers to autograph…I felt it added a little character to the place. I wanted them to feel that they will always be a part of it.

I had a few plants scattered in the mix for color and also because Greatie says one should always have plants in your environment because they helped to purify the air.

But as amazing as my dining room was, the coup de grace was my tea collection. One of the main reasons I'd chosen this place for my shop was the deep mahogany wood wall of shelves that were behind the L shaped counter.

Whoever had designed them was simply brilliant. They'd carved them out of the wall, and they went from floor to ceiling. Somehow, they'd managed to get them to form a curve. I had exactly eight hundred jars in varies sizes, of herbs, roots, and flowers lined up on them that I was very proud of.

And you already know because I was short as all get out, I had me a step ladder on wheels that I used for the top three shelves.

On the counter, I had two big golden antique steamers…another storage auction find. Even though I only sold tea…I could make it several ways. To give my coffee addicts the full tea experience, I often steamed it with a bit of milk and cinnamon. I am proud to say that I have successfully converted hundreds of coffee drinkers to tea drinkers.

I smiled as I gently nodded my head. I've created my own little slice of heaven in this shop. It made putting up with Ms. Armstrong's ignorance well worth it. Inhaling deeply, the smell of herbs filled my nose comforting me.

However, my gaze fell on the huge hole in my wall covered by the thick plastic and I cringed. She wasn't lying, there was a draft coming through it. Chicago in the winter was a very brutal place. I threw a couple of logs in the fireplace, that hole was really killing my vibe. I'd tried to conceal it the best way I could, but there was no covering it up.

I'd thought I was going to have enough money left over from the ten grand to get someone back out here to work on it, but after I pay our back rent for the apartment and Jessie's tuition, there won't be much left.

I was just going to have to find another way. Maybe I can try and take out a small loan. I'd taken out one to get this place fixed up when I'd first gotten it and after two years, have almost paid it back in full. Of course, my payment was well overdue at this point, in fact, the bank's letters have begun to pile up on my junky desk in the back with the rest of my bills.

I shook my head…I was going to have to find another way.

As I walked around the shop turning on the display lights that I have highlighting my beautiful mahogany wood shelves, the phone on the wall rang. I smiled because I already knew who it was.

"Why aren't you in school?" I asked as soon as I picked it up.

"My mama and her friend still sleep."

I rolled my eyes. Goodness, I wish I could just take my niece from her trifling parents. I asked Trina, who is my niece's mother if I could adopt her years ago, but of course, she angrily said no. My niece is nothing but a check to her.

"You still coming to pick me up Friday?"

"Of course, Flower Bud. Don't I come to pick you up every Friday?"

I could hear the phone move from where she nodded. "I just don't want you to forget me."

Tears came to my eyes. Dear God, give me strength. "Baby, your Tee-Tee ain't gon' never forget you, you hear me?"

The phone rustled from where her hair beads rubbed against it as she nodded. I took her to get her hair braided every time I got mine done. I liked going to that braid shop because they braided our real hair just as good as they did when adding hair. Neither Jessie or I needed to add hair because our natural hair was thick and long.

"Do Tee-Tee a favor and go wake your mother up and tell her you need to get to school. Are you dressed?"

Her beads rubbed against the phone as she nodded.

"Did you take a shower and brush your teeth."

"Yeah! I used that toothpaste you got me that taste like bubble gum!" In her excitement, she screamed that at me.

"Jessie, you didn't eat the toothpaste, did you?"

"Only a little bit, but I didn't mean to…"

I smiled. When I first got her the toothpaste, I had to explain to her that although it tastes like bubble gum, toothpaste was not good to ingest because of the fluoride in it.

"Alright, Flower Bud, go wake your mama up. And don't forget to call me when you get in from school."

I had her call me every day when she got in because a few times, Trina had forgotten to pick her up from school. I gave the school my number so that they could call me when that happens. I shook my head as I finished getting the shop ready for opening.

I have begged my brother to file for custody. If he gets custody, then I can take care of Jessie. I'm the one taking care of her anyway. But he refuses. He says Trina ain't that bad and Jessie needs her mama. The only reason why I haven't called the Department of Children and Family Services on her is because... maybe he's right.

My mama gave me up when I was very young. And I often think I would have liked if she would have kept me. I could have survived her drug habit or whatever, just as long as I was with her. It would have been a far better life than the one I had in the three foster homes I ended up in.

There was a knock on the door. I looked up and smiled when I saw the young man with my daily boxes of baked goods. Because I was no baker, I'd worked out a deal with the bakery around the corner. Every morning they dropped me off a variety of pastries.

While he arranged them in the glass display case, I prepared the daily tea for his aunt, who owned the bakery. Before she started drinking my teas, she suffered from arthritis. Years of rolling dough had been the culprit.

The medicine the doctors prescribed for her had terrible side effects. I made her a tea with grounded up turmeric and ginger, I added a few other things to it, but the turmeric and ginger were the true powerhouses. After a week of drinking my tea, she was able to straighten her fingers after not being able to straighten them in years.

She was so thankful that she gave me several boxes full of bake goods every morning at only half the price she charged her other customers, but only if I continue to make her tea.

After I paid him for the pastries, he handed me a receipt. I took it back to my little office and threw it in the drawer with my many other receipts. Maybe I'll finally get around to arranging them today...

Ha!!! Every morning I told myself the same lie, knowing very well I was not going anywhere near that receipt drawer.

As soon as I turned the closed sign to open, my day got to rolling and didn't stop till I served my last customer at seven that evening. I really could not understand why I was struggling for cash although the tea shop did such good business. I probably should talk to someone about it and see if they could help me figure it out.

After cleaning up everything, I put the left-over pastries in a few bags. On my way to the bus, I walked past the soup kitchen and gave them to Minnie, who ran the kitchen so that she could give them out to whoever wanted them.

As soon as the bus got close to my stop, I started straining my neck to see if that black Hummer was sitting outside. When I didn't see it, I exhaled, only... I didn't know if it was from relief or disappointment.

Although Hitta was not my type...not even close, it still did something to my insides to know that I'd somehow caught the eye of a man like him. He seemed like the type that would be attracted to the kind of girls like the one who was working at his register yesterday.

She was the kind of beauty you turned on the television and saw, the kind of girl like the Kardashians, who had nice clothes, hair and nails always done up...probably wore expensive high heels. I was the complete opposite of that.

I wore my hair in braids that fell to my butt. As you know most times, I wore baggy clothes because thanks to Stan and his exploring fingers, I was very self-conscious about showing off my figure in any way.

My idea of a good time was grabbing a good book and lying flat on the grass at the park and reading it. A great time would be if the sky was clear and a gentle breeze was blowing. Several times, I'd done just that at the park around the corner from the tea shop and ended up falling asleep.

Hitta's idea of fun was going to the latest night club where everybody worshipped the ground he walked on, at least according to Tasha, the girl who lives across the hall from me. Several times, she and

I have ended up in the basement doing our laundry at the same time and in those short visits, she'd managed to fill me in on most of the neighborhood gossip, including the fact that Hitta and his crew were very dangerous, just as I had figured.

Tasha told me story after story of people that had come up dead after having a run-in with him, people who placed bets on a fight and couldn't pay. She said it was no secret that Hitta was a well-known killer, who had managed to become a famous boxer for a little while.

According to Tasha, other fighters were afraid to fight him, not just because he was the champion…but because he had taken his street ways to the big leagues with him. As I stepped off the bus, I decided that it was relief I felt at not seeing his Hummer across the street tonight. I had no business even thinking about a man like that.

"Hey, baby girl." The sound of my mother's voice brought me up short. She was sitting waiting for me on my porch.

I exhaled…so glad I'd stopped by the apartment management office and dropped off the rent check.

"Hey, ma…"

She stood from the steps to give me a hug. I held my breath because she reeked of alcohol and body odor. Her thin body shook so badly it felt like she was going to fall over.

"Where have you been?" I asked as I sat on the porch. There was no way I was inviting her upstairs. My mom had stolen from me so many times it wasn't funny.

She sat back on the porch next to me. "Them bastards threw me in jail."

I didn't even bat an eye…There was nothing new in that department.

"How long were you locked up?"

"Six months…"

I nodded as I watched the cars drive by. I knew why she was here—

"Baby, mama need a few dollars."

Dang, that was quick. She didn't even ask me how I was doing. Normally, she would at least try and pretend that she cared. I shook my head…I was surrounded by crackheads.

"How much?"

"Two hundred dollars…"

I reached in my purse and pulled out a twenty before coming to my feet handing it to her. "That's all I have."

She took it with dirty hands before smiling up at me with teeth that had begun to rot… "Thank you, baby, you gone upstairs and get some rest, mama will talk to you later."

Surprisingly, she got up and slid into the passenger seat of an old beat up Honda. When it rolled past, she waved at me with a huge smile on her face. The man that was driving was in no better condition than she and I couldn't help but wonder if they had stolen that car. I stood for a minute and watched them go.

Would this be the last time I saw my mother?

Will she end up in jail?

Will she end up dead?

All questions that I've asked myself a million times over the years. Even though I was in foster homes, I'd kept in contact with my mom. When I was younger, she made me believe that she was going to get herself together and come back and get me.

Every time my caseworker set up a visit for us, my heart would swell with excitement. I couldn't wait to see her, to see if she had kept her word and gotten clean. Many times, she came to our visits high… and then there were the times she'd forgotten all about the visits.

By the time I'd turned fifteen, I stopped hoping. I'd been let down in life so many times, I'd become jaded. Many folks gave people the benefit of the doubt. I doubted people *benefitably*. If folks turned out to be good, it came as a surprise to me…because the majority of the people in the world are bad.

By the time I got upstairs, I was so tired that I shrugged out of my coat and kicked off my shoes at the door. My target was my bed that I saw beckoning me as soon as I walked in. With tunnel vision, I crossed the space that was separating me from my pillow, only managing to step out of my black slacks on the way.

Still dressed in my thigh high stockings, panties, and my halter sweater, I crawled into the bed and collapsed. I didn't move from that spot until the first wave of my nightmare hit.

I was lying in the grass in the park around the corner from the tea shop. I held a book in my hand, but I wasn't reading it. Instead, I was looking up at the sun that looked strange. It seemed to be getting closer to me…

I reached up and wiped away the sweat from my brow. The sun got closer…other people in the park had stopped to look at it. The closer it got, the more afraid they became…the heat coming from it began to be unbearable. Steam came from the cup of water on the ground next to me. It looked as if something broke away from the sun and it was heading our way quickly. People began to run, but I knew there was no place to go. And then all of a sudden--

BOOM!

Crying out, I jerked up in the bed just as my front door busted off the hinges. For a second, I thought I was still dreaming when Hitta's big body filled the frame. His angry gaze came to mine and I realized it wasn't a dream.

There were more men with him, but it was his gaze that held me prisoner. I felt frozen in fear until he began to come towards me. Seeing him charging my way like an angry bull snapped me out of my panic induced coma and I scrambled out of my bed.

"Find that f***ing crackhead!" I heard him growl to his men before he barreled into my room. I grabbed the nearest thing to me, which was a big herbal book I'd been reading and threw it at him. Using his powerful hand, he angrily punched the book sending it flying back across the room.

I screamed as I tried to run past him, but his big warm hand palmed my belly before he slammed me back against the wall. It wasn't hard enough to hurt, but it was hard enough to get my attention, not to mention the fact that he was crowding my space in a very threatening way.

He was so strong, his hand still flat against my stomach was holding me against the wall while his other arm rested on the wall just above my head. He leaned in close, trapping me with his big stout body.

Tears filled my eyes when his raged filled face got close to mine. I wanted to scream for help, but I was so terrified the only thing I could do was stand there shivering.

"Where yo' f***ing brother?" He growled.

And...

Oh, my goodness!

The force of his words had my knees knocking, if his hand was not there on my stomach holding me in place, I would have slid to the ground.

"I—I don't know," I cried. "Please don't hurt me!"

"He's not here, boss," someone said behind us.

"It's cool, go downstairs and wait for me."

Although I couldn't see anything past Hitta's big body, I heard the other men as they filed out, leaving me alone with this...this...

Force of nature!

"Please don't hurt me..." I repeated through trembling lips as his gaze raked over my face. He moved back a few inches so that he could look down my body and I saw something change in his eyes.

I bit my lip wanting to cry out again when I realized I was standing there in nothing but my black thigh-high stockings, black panties, and my black halter sweater...his big warm palm was still pressed against my naked stomach.

"Damn..." I heard him whisper as he took in my body.

"What do you want?!" I yelled, not able to take it anymore.

His heated gaze came back up to mine. "Yo' crackhead a** brotha stole money from me yesterday."

I closed my eyes...

No, Westly! No!

Oh God! No!

Out of all the people in the world to steal from.

Please, God, ...don't let this be true!

When I opened my eyes again, he was biting his lip looking at me with that hungry gaze of his. I've never had a man look at me like that before. His gaze took its time taking in my body as his thumb rubbed against my soft stomach.

"Please tell me that wasn't your money?" I whined.

"Where the f*** is it?"

My shoulders slumped. *I give up...* this was just too much.

"I—I spent it."

I don't know why I told him the truth. Maybe because I didn't want him to kill my brother and I knew he wouldn't kill me. As if to confirm my words, a deadly grin slowly spread across his face.

"You spent my money, Teacup?"

Although it was the last thing in the world that I wanted to do...I nodded. The look that came into his hard gaze as it once again took its time raking over my barely clad body was that of a conqueror. When his eyes settled on my trembling lips, there seemed to be some kind of hidden pull between us, his head came closer to mine and it looked for a moment as if he was going to kiss me.

I held my breath, terrified, yet...and I really hate to admit this...excited.

"Well now..." he muttered, his lips only inches from mine. "It looks like you... belong to me."

Chapter Three

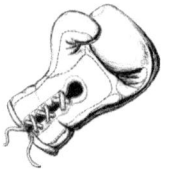

MY OBSESSION

Hitta

Everything about this little woman called out to me, it has since the first day I saw her. It was like the cells in my body just knew that she was meant to be mine. My boy, Rome joked that I had become obsessed with her, but the truth was, my feelings for her were far past obsession.

Angel had become the reason behind all of my actions in the last three months. I have never felt this way about another human being... ever. Sh*t, I think she is my first crush.

Naw...I take that back. This was more than a crush.

I've sat in my truck and watched her, imagining how her skin would feel under my hand, how it would taste against my tongue. Leaning in, I inhaled her scent...she smelled like flowers and something else that was uniquely her and a heady aphrodisiac to me.

She was mine!

Finally... mine!

I stepped back just a bit so that I can see this beautiful body she hid under her homeless clothing. I knew she was banging under all that sh*t. When she jumped out of the bed and I saw that she was dressed like a sex kitten in only a pair of thigh high stockings, black panties, and a halter sweater that left the lower half of her stomach exposed to my greedy gaze, I signaled for my men to search the other room...because God knows, had one of them laid eyes on her, I wouldn't have hesitated to put a f***ing bullet in their heads.

Her body was mine...My word, no man but me will ever see it. She had the kind of body that all of these Hollywood broads were paying a grip for. Thick, beautiful brown hips flowed up into a slim waist that connected to a pair of full, plump breasts that I couldn't wait to taste, giving her that iconic pop bottle figure. I wanted to palm her plush behind and see how well it filled my hands while I pulled her close so that she could feel how much I needed her.

I wanted to lift her into my arms until she wrapped those thick thighs around my waist and drive into her heat. I wanted to hear her scream my name as I made her lose herself in pleasure. I bit my lip... Hell yeah, I wanted to make her lose herself.

Gently, I moved my thumb across her softly curved stomach and felt it quiver under my touch. I wanted her so bad I damned near groaned. My body was reacting to her in a way it has never reacted to another woman. Seeing her jump up out of the bed scantily clad gave me an instant erection, an erection that was growing more painful by the minute.

I needed to sink into her moist heat like I needed to breathe. Her fear caused her to breathe rapidly, which caused her luscious breasts to brush against my arm.

I licked my lips, needing to taste them. As if it had a mind of its own, my palm began an upward caress along her stomach, but before it could go farther, her soft hand came to rest on my arm.

"Are you going to hurt me?"

Even her voice...it was like cool water to my burning soul. Gently, I rubbed my thumb against her belly, wishing it was my tongue instead. She looked at me as if I was a monster, a big f***ing brute, who wasn't good enough to breathe the same air as one so pure.

Maybe I wasn't... But the fact was, I am her monster now, her brute. And she was mine, so she needed to get used to that.

"I'll never hurt you, Teacup." I shook my head. "Not ever...baby. That's my word."

She licked her lips and I groaned, wanting to taste them so badly, I was barely controlling myself. I didn't want to mess this up. I knew she thought I was a brute and I am, I ain't gon' lie. But for her, I can be gentle. For her, I will be gentle, even if it killed me.

I ain't never gave a damn what a woman I was messing with thought about me or the way I ran my sh*t. If they had a problem, they can move around...that's the way I always saw it. Women threw themselves at me, always have. There were too many for me to get caught up on what one of them thought.

But Angel was different. I ain't never met another woman like her. And if I messed this up and scared her away...I will never find another like her. It felt like she was made just for me. Everything about her... just for me.

"What are you going to do with me then?" Her question was quiet as if she was terrified of the answer.

My gaze fell to her plump lips that begged for my kiss. "I'm going to keep you."

She frowned and it was the cutest thing. I loved it when she got huffy with me. And yeah, I know I'm a sick mutha f**** for that, but it was true. When she frowned at me or gave me that look that said, I'm an uncivilized mutha f****, it did something to me... turned me on.

Yeah...She was my obsession. Rome was right.

"What do you mean keep me? You can't just keep people."

I tilted my head to the side as I studied every detail of her beautiful face, from her smooth mocha skin to the gentle slant of her eyes. She had beautiful eyes...encased with long eyelashes, another thing chicks paid a grip for that she had naturally.

"Who gon' stop me, Teacup? Yo' crackhead a** brotha?"

She bit her lip, wanting to reprimand me for calling her brother a crackhead, but she was afraid. I wanted to tell her that she didn't have to be afraid of me and if she wanted to curse me out, all she had to do was do it.

But I didn't want her fear of me to go away before I got her moved into my house. And then once I got her there, I will show her that she was the one person in the world that didn't have to fear me because she was the one person I will never hurt.

"I'm sorry I spent your money." She whispered, looking away from me.

She was so f***ing timid. Rome had done some digging into her background for me and shawty had a really messed up life. The state took her away from her mother when she was seven and she ended up in the foster care system.

Although I didn't end up in the foster care system, my mother wasn't sh*t either. It was tough scrapping my way out the gutta and I'm a mean SOB. I could only imagine what it must have been like for her, being so gentle, soft, and so pure... And yet, she made it out and started her own business at nineteen years old. She was a warrior, she just didn't know it.

"Yo' apologies ain't enough, shawty. Ten G's ain't no lil money. Somebody got to pay for that sh*t." I put my finger under her chin and gently turned her face till our eyes connected.

"Yo' brotha got to die for that sh*t."

Her eyes widened and she clutched my arm again, shaking her head fiercely. "No, Hitta! Please don't kill him! I'll pay for him...It was me that spent the money anyway. You can keep me! I swear I won't give you any problems."

Satisfaction rushed through my veins like blood. *I know damn well I can keep you. I'd like to see a mutha f**** try and say different.*

"You sure? 'Cuz I can find him tonight and handle this business."

Her fingers tightened on my arm as her beautiful eyes filled with tears. "I'm sure, Hitta. Whatever you want," she muttered.

And that sh*t tore at my heart. Something became clear to me at that moment. This girl was my f***ing kryptonite. Seeing her in tears was not something I liked. I would do anything to bring a smile to her face, but I also knew that this process had to happen. She didn't know she needed me as much as I needed her, so yeah, this seemed hard for her.

But I'd been planning for this moment for the last three months. I was ready for her. I'd studied everything about her. I knew what she liked and what she didn't. I knew what she needed...I was going to take care of her. I felt like that is what I was put here to do.

I lifted my hand and gently wiped away her tears with my thumb. "Don't cry, Teacup. I'm going to take care of you."

What she did next surprised the sh*t out of me. She lifted her head and took me in before she laughed bitterly as if she didn't believe me.

It was my turn to frown at her. "What? You don't believe me?"

She exhaled. "Look, I'm tired. It's been a long night, can we pick this back up tomorrow? I can come by the gym and we can work something out. Don't worry about the door...I'll fix it when you leave."

See what I mean? She was so f***ing adorable. Even though she was scared out of her mind, she was standing here trying to dismiss me. She still gave me the benefit of the doubt. She spoke to me like I was a reasonable mutha f****, that will do the right thing and turn and walk out this door without her.

I smiled...Damn! She spoke to me like I wasn't what I was. She didn't know yet that I'm a f***ing savage. It's alright though...I am a patient man. We had all the time in the world for her to learn.

"Naw, shawty, you must have misunderstood. This ain't yo' spot no mo'. Grab yo' sh*t, you coming home with me."

————

Angel

Because of my nightmares, I didn't get nearly enough sleep to function most times, so, I figured my tiredness had caused me to hear him wrong.

"Excuse me?"

He chuckled. "You heard me."

Oh my God! I can't believe this was happening to me. Was he getting ready to rape me? And what the hell did he mean this ain't my spot no more. My mind raced trying to figure a way out of this. I've never had sex before. Thanks to Stan, I'd been too afraid to ever go there with any of the guys I'd ever dated.

And it wasn't that I didn't want to lose my virginity, I just wanted to lose it to a gentle guy...A safe guy. A guy I have yet to find. However, that guy was definitely not this brute of a man standing in front of me.

Damn you, West! Look what you've gotten me into. There had to be another way out of this. Maybe I could find a way to get the money back...

Hell...who was I fooling? I couldn't even get the hole in my shop's wall fixed. Where did I think I was going to pull ten-thousand dollars from? I had to do something though, there was no way I could go home with Hitta and do what he wanted me to do. The thought of it made me want to fold up into a ball and cry.

"I can't go with you tonight." My voice sounded desperate.

He lifted an eyebrow. "Why not?"

I licked my lips and his hungry gaze followed. "Because, I—I."

I can't go with you, sir because I'm a virgin and I'm afraid a man as big and vicious as you will tear me in two.

Damn it! I couldn't think of a good enough reason that wasn't embarrassing as heck.

"Because—"

"You're afraid," he interrupted, saying the words I was struggling with.

I nodded. "Yes, I am terrified."

There was no use in lying at this point. Plus, it would do no good, I knew I looked terrified.

His gaze raked over my face, studying me before he nodded, stepping back. I exhaled in relief, but when he moved his warm hand from my stomach, I felt a sense of loss that confused me. He grabbed my robe off my chair and put it around my shivering shoulders.

I slid my arms through the sleeves before tying the belt tightly around my waist while keeping a wary eye on him. I didn't know what he was going to do next. It felt strange having him in my room.

Heck! It felt strange having him in my apartment, he didn't fit. Even though he was a brute, it was clear he was a wealthy brute.

Today, he sported a black t-shirt and a pair of designer black jeans. On his feet was a pair of black Timberlands.

I wasn't learned in the art of spotting name brand watches, however, one didn't need a Ph.D. to know that his watch cost more than everything in my little pulled together apartment. It was silver or maybe white gold, but the bling in it, although not done to the point of tackiness, was blinding.

In his ear was a diamond stud that also flashed startlingly in the dim lighting of my room. Now that he was a little closer, I was able to see the tattoo that went from the right side of his neck to disappear inside his shirt was some kind of fancy script, although I couldn't see what it said.

I inhaled… even his spicy cologne smelled expensive. Delicious… but expensive. He was definitely what Tasha would call a baller.

He took my hand and pulled me toward the bed. "Come here."

The bed! Oh God!

My heart started racing really fast…so fast that I thought I was getting ready to have a stroke. *Was he getting ready to rape me now?*

"Sit down for a minute."

I sat down on the very edge of the bed, my body stiff as a board, my knees were squeezed together so hard they hurt. He squatted his powerful form down in front of me so that we were at eye level and I inhaled sharply.

What was he going to do to me? Tears filled my eyes again, but they didn't fall.

"Look, Angel…I know that you think I'm a brute." He muttered, his eyes falling to my feet.

Slowly the breath I'd been holding left my body. For the first time since I've known him, he appeared human, a human with feelings. For the first time, it crossed my mind that I may have hurt said feelings with the way that I've looked at him and acted around him up until this point.

"I can't help the way that I am," he continued. "I'm a product of my environment."

My hands twitched in my lap. For some strange reason, I just had the impulse to rub my fingers through his beard and tell him he was perfectly fine the way that he was. I'm going to chalk that up to lack of sleep because surely, I was not developing nourishing feelings toward this man.

"Yo' brotha stole a lot of money from me. You don't want me to kill him... so I won't. All I ask is that you come live with me. Be my companion."

"You mean, like friendship?" That wasn't that bad...

He grinned, shaking his head. "Hell naw...I don't want to be yo' friend. I want to be yo' man."

He didn't say anything else, he just waited for me to respond to that. I lifted my hand and rubbed my temple. There was a lot of pressure behind my eyes. How in the world was I supposed to respond to that?

"We don't even know each other. What if I move in with you and then we decide we don't like each other?"

"If that happens, I'll get you another place to stay. Just give it a chance."

I thought about his words. What was his deal? Most guys like him didn't even want a girl to leave a toothbrush over at their house, let alone move in with them. He probably thought that's what he wanted now, but will change his mind shortly after I move in.

Guys like him weren't used to rejection. According to Tasha, women threw themselves at him. She said he was hood royalty. The fact that I had rejected him must have triggered some kind of hunter's instinct in him or something. He set out to prove to himself that he could get me.

By taking that money, I'd played right into his hands. And now he would be able to pat himself on the back and say, I got the girl that rejected me. And in order to assuage his pride, I was going to have to be his live-in *companion*...

"I don't even know your real name." Everybody called him Hard Hitta...but surely his parents didn't name him that. How can I move in with a man whose name I didn't know?

His gaze went back to my feet before he chuckled, shaking his head a bit. I could tell he didn't want to tell me.

"You can't laugh at me, alright?" I nodded.

With a grin on his face, he shook his head again as if he couldn't believe he was getting ready to tell me this.

"William…William Taylor. When I was a kid, everybody called me Willie."

Oh… wow!

Okay…did not expect him to say that.

"Willie?"

He nodded waiting on me to laugh. And I'm going to be honest, if I wasn't facing this crisis, I probably would have chuckled. However, it was hard to laugh at anything when it felt like your world was being torn apart.

I looked around my little apartment, although… I don't think losing this place will be such a hardship. I never took the time to make it home, because I spent all my time and energy at my shop. The few little pieces of furniture we had were Westly's parents' old furniture that they let us have when they got new stuff.

My bed was the same one I'd had since I moved in with them at thirteen. If I was being honest with myself, I could walk away from all this stuff with no problems. I'd fought Stan off of me more times than I could count on this couch and my bed, so I definitely won't be shedding any tears over the loss of them.

However, if I let this place go, I needed to be ready to start over when Mr. Willie here got over his little infatuation with me. Heck…I don't even know how long he was talking about.

My gaze fell back to him and I inhaled when I saw how intensely he studied me. I frowned, I didn't know how I felt about that. When he looked at me like that, he made me feel like he could see inside me…Like he could see a part of me that was not open to the public.

I cleared my throat. "How long?"

He grinned and for a second, I felt like Little Red to his Big Bad Wolf. "Six months." He muttered. "If at the end of six months you don't love me…You find wherever you want to live and I will pay for it."

It was my turn to grin. "Love?" My voice was laced with amusement.

He nodded… "Love, shawty." His was laced with confidence.

Ooookay…Somebody really thought a lot of themselves. I wanted to tell him he was shooting pretty high for love. I didn't think I really liked him. I mean…yeah, he's handsome and got the kind of body that can cause a girl to drool a little, but he was uncouth. He was brutally honest to a fault. He said what was on his mind and didn't care what anybody thought about it.

And according to Tasha, he killed people. Not my idea of boyfriend material at all.

I wanted a guy who I could talk to about my teas, a guy that will lie in the grass with me and read. A guy that is faithful to me and kind.

I exhaled…Still, if being his girlfriend for six months will keep him from killing my stupid brother, I guess I can do that. Except--

"Are you going to want sex?"

He grinned again and I realized he had dimples.

"Hell yeah…"

I stiffened and he placed one of his big hands gently on my leg. "But I won't force you or nothing. I ain't no rapist. We can do it when you're ready."

"Really?!" I asked, beginning to feel like there was a light at the end of the tunnel. If that was the case, I'll never be ready, surely not by the time my six months were over.

He frowned. "Damn, *Teacup*, did you think I was going to rape you?"

Relief flooded my body like a cool wave.

"How the heck was I supposed to know? You came bursting in my door like the freaking Incredible Hulk, scaring me half to death. What is wrong with you, William?" I admonished him, using his real name to get under his skin, now that I knew my life and my virtue was not at stake.

He chuckled. "I'm an uncivilized bastard."

I wish I could explain to you guys what it was like talking to him. I swear he had his own way of using the English language. His deep voice was confident and smooth…when he looked at me the way he was doing at that moment, he made me feel as if he knew a secret as if he knew my secret…and he was using it to control me.

Yeah…that's what it is. It felt as if he was effortlessly controlling me somehow…

With my lips pressed tightly together, I shook my head. "You should work on that…"

"Yeah…Won't you teach me then."

"What? To be civilized?"

He nodded. "Why not? It'll be fun."

I looked down at the belt of my robe that I played with between my fingers. "It's just that…"

"What?"

My gaze came back to his face. "I'm not a miracle worker. What you're asking would take a doctor…or a priest."

He stared at me for a moment before he held his head back and roared with laughter. I grinned, pleased I'd caused the brute to laugh like that. I didn't even think he was capable of laughter.

"I see you got jokes…" he said around his mirth as he came to his feet. For the first time since he kicked in my door, he looked away from me to take in my place.

"How much of this sh*t you want to keep?"

I held up a finger. "First lesson, how about you not call the furniture of your girlfriend for the next six months sh*t?"

My words pleased him. I could see it in his eyes, before he put his hand on his chest, looking at me with mock surprise. "Was that rude?"

It was my turn to laugh. "You know doggone well that was rude."

He shook his head. "My bad…let me try again." He cleared his throat. "How much of this crap would you like to take with you?"

I held my head back and laughed so hard I snorted. I put my hand to my lips…Oh my goodness! It had been a long time since I laughed that hard. I'd forgotten I even had that little annoying habit.

He held out his hand for me. "Come on, Angel, let me take you home."

My laughter died as I stared at his big hand. Slowly my eyes rose to his. His gaze was so intense it stole my breath. There was so much there. Hitta was uncouth, that much was true, but he was also a real man, a strong man.

There was so much strength in him, it poured from him like water.

Something told me that if I took his hand, my life will never be the same. Hitta brought change with him. Suddenly my fear was back.

Was it change for the better…or will this change leave me broken?

I'd been through so much and I was still standing…but just barely.

Hitta, with his strength, there was no way he would break me gently. He would break me in a way that could never be fixed.

"You have to trust me, Teacup."

See what I mean about the way he studies me? How did he know I was fighting a battle in my head?

"Why should I trust you? What makes you so special?"

"That answer is simple. You should trust me because I will protect you with my life…even from myself if need be. That's my word, shawty."

My Greatie's words that she'd said to me all those years ago came to me as clear as day, as clear as if she was standing here saying them to me right now.

"Don't worry none, child. The Ancient of Days never leaves his children defenseless. He's going to send you a protector so fierce he will destroy all your monsters. Just wait and see…He's going to destroy them all."

I slowly slid my hand into his bigger one…

Chapter Four

MOVING ON...

Angel

"Wow, where did the moving truck come from?" I asked Hitta when I walked out of my apartment building two hours later.

To say that said two hours have been breathtaking is to say the least. Once I got dressed, Hitta put in a call and a group of guys that were mountains like him came through my door a few minutes later.

"Show them what goes and what stays," he muttered as he headed out into the hall to take a call.

These men were on a mission. It was like a whirlwind, they moved with precision and determination. A few packed things into boxes while others took those things downstairs, the rest were on trash duty. Everything that I said that I didn't want, they took to the trash...

Speaking of which, all of my brother's things were now amongst the number of things that got trashed.

Hitta came back in while I was instructing his guys to pack West's items, I was going to see if he wouldn't mind taking me to my shop so that I could store them there.

"Why y'all packing this sh*t?" he grumbled.

I turned around startled because I didn't hear him come up behind me, for a big fella, he moved silently.

"Oh, these are Westly's things. I was going to see if it's a way we can drop this stuff off at my shop and I can just keep it there till he gets back."

He frowned down at me… "Hell naw!" His gaze rose to his men. "Trash this sh*t."

"Wait! You can't throw my brother's stuff in the garbage. He'll be back for it, it's bad enough he's going to have to find someplace else to stay."

"What are you? His mama? F*** him!"

I opened my mouth to dispute him, but he continued talking right over me.

"Is this the same nigga that stole money and got you framed for it, then left you to take the heat by yourself? He don't know sh*t about me…You could be floating at the bottom of the river right now for all the f*** he cares…" He looked up at his men.

"Trash this sh*t!" And then he turned and walked back out of the room when his phone rang again.

The conversation was closed because at that point, it didn't matter what I had to say, his men carried out his orders with no questions. I stood for a minute dumbfounded as they did…

I think it was at that point that the change Hitta was bringing in my life settled in. It was at that point that it became clear that he was taking over things with a mighty arm and I didn't know how I felt about that.

In a way, I agreed that it was lowdown what Westly did to me, but I also knew my brother, he was trying to help. He knew how much my shop meant to me and he came through with the money to save it. Yeah, he'd stolen from the king to do that, but he didn't believe it would fall back on me, he probably thought the heat would be on him, which is why he left town.

At least that's what I prayed he'd thought…

Either way, I felt horrible that all of his stuff had gotten thrown away. I'd already been trying to figure out a place for him to stay when he gets back. He wasn't going to like it, but maybe he could sleep at the shop for a little while. I knew he was trying to help by stealing the money from Hitta, but that didn't change the fact that there were repercussions for our actions. I wasn't going to be the only one paying for it.

Hitta asked if I was my brother's mom…

The truth is, even though West was older than me by ten years, I still felt responsible for him for several reasons, one being like I'd said earlier, he'd kept Stan from hurting me to the point of no return. Although my foster dad did some pretty messed up things to me when I was a little girl, I still had my virginity because of Westly.

He'd threatened to kill Stan several times. They'd even gotten into a brawl a time or two because of me. Of course, Diana, Westly's mom blamed me for the divide that happened in her home, because she simply refused to believe that her fancy doctor husband was touching me inappropriately.

I was under a lot of pressure and didn't tell Westly every time Stan touched me because I too didn't want to see them fighting. Because of this, Stan had learned to skate the thin line. He never went overboard with his assaults, a stolen kiss, a breast grab, a grope to my butt…

One night, I woke up and he had his finger inside of me, hurting me…That night we thought Westly was going to kill him. Diana had gotten so upset she kicked both Westly and me out for almost two days.

After that, Stan never went so far again. However, his searching fingers never stopped. Even to this day, I hated going around them, but because they were Westly's parents, our paths crossed whether I liked it or not.

Just the other day, Stan had come by my shop looking for West. He said my brother had stolen forty dollars out of Diana's purse. I told him I hadn't seen him, but of course, he didn't leave right away…

"I dreamt about you last night," he'd said as he began to walk around the counter.

"Don't start, Stan, this is my place of work. You have to go!" I told him, recognizing the look in his eyes.

Unfortunately, at the time, the shop was empty, which left me at his complete mercy. However, I wasn't a little girl anymore and was prepared to do whatever I had to do if he put his nasty hands on me. I took a few steps back and grabbed a kettle of hot water.

"What are you going to do with that? Why are you so mean to me anyway? If not for me, you wouldn't have been able to get the loan so that you could fix this place up. Don't you know by now that I love you?"

I rolled my eyes. He was always spewing this nonsense and he never let me forget that it was because he's Dr. Stanly Baker that I was able to get this place. I didn't even want to ask for his help, it was Westly who went to him and asked him to help me get the loan.

"Get out!"

My voice quivered in a mixture of fear and rage...Because of him, I was broken. I just wished he would leave me alone.

"You'll never be rid of me, sweetheart. You and I are meant to be."

"You and *Diana* are meant to be...that is your wife!" I snapped, trying to hold on to the scream of rage that was always inside of me when he was around.

Everything about him disgusted me... The way he looked in his expensive suits and loafers, the way he always smelled like hospital soap, even when he wasn't at work, and the way his eyes roamed over my body, leaving my skin crawling in their wake.

At the hospital, he was a catch. Many flirting nurses have given Diana the blues over the years. However, to me, he looked like an evil troll and I hated everything about him!

He chuckled as he took another step toward me. I tightened my hand on the kettle.

"You know, she'll be dead soon. Everything I have can be yours."

"How can you say that about her? She's going to beat the cancer. You should be supporting her!"

"Oh Angel, you've always been such the optimist. However, I'm a doctor, I see these things all the time. She has stage four bone cancer; she will not survive the year." He didn't sound sad in the least that his wife was so deathly ill.

The sad part about his words is that they were true, Diana was dying. Many times before her cancer had spread like it has, I'd offered to make teas for her that would strengthen her bones and help to alkalize her body, but she refused my help…she was married to a doctor and thought my faith in herbs was hocus-pocus, whatever the world that meant.

But I knew the real reason she refused my teas. For some sick twisted purpose, she was jealous of me. Instead of her helping me when her husband tortured me, her hate caused her to turn a blind eye and pretend nothing was happening.

"Just let me put my face between—" Stan began, but mercifully, a group of students walked through the door causing the creep to slink out like the snake he is. I didn't release my grip on that tea kettle until I saw his BMW pull away from the curb.

He is the bane of my existence and for the most part, Westly had protected me from the worst. I don't know where I would have been without him…

The second and main reason I felt like I had to look after my brother is because I blame myself for his drug addiction. It was my mother who'd introduced him to heroin. When I was fifteen, I begged him to take me to visit her. During that visit, she'd flirted with Westly shamelessly. For a little while, even though I warned him against it, they dated. When she broke his heart, she left him penniless and addicted to heroin.

If only I'd faced the facts about her sooner instead of holding on to the childhood fantasy of being reunited with my mom, I would not have been so dead set on going to visit her that day. It was all my fault this happened to him. The least I could do was be supportive of him…

Hitta will never understand that. I could see it in his face when he told his men to throw Westly's stuff away. It served as a reminder of just how ruthless he is…Something I already knew from the beginning.

Anyway, two hours later, my apartment was empty, and that portion of my life forcibly closed. When I got downstairs with my purse and my favorite pillow in my hand, I was surprised to see a moving truck sitting there.

"U-Haul is right around the corner, didn't take much to rent a truck," he grumbled as he held the passenger door of the Hummer open for me.

"Yeah, I know...I guess I'm just surprised to see it."

I was, although I didn't know why. It just seemed as if this was all well-organized instead of a last-minute thing. When he'd kicked in my door a couple of hours ago, he'd done it with the idea that he was going to find Westly.

At the last minute, he decided to take me instead... Two hours later, here I stood with all of my stuff neatly packed into boxes, loaded into a U-Haul and my keys back into my landlord's hand, who surprisingly let me out of my lease with no problem...

It probably didn't hurt that Hitta had paid him a healthy sum of money for the broken door.

Anyway, all of this happened in a matter of two hours...

"Don't stress over it, *Teacup*." He opened the passenger door of the Hummer. "Hop in, let's roll."

I squeaked when he suddenly dipped, lifting me up in his arms. My startled gaze went to his...

"What are you doing?"

"Helping you in, you're a little short."

I grinned. "You can't call people short anymore...it's politically incorrect. You have to say vertically challenged."

This caused him to laugh as he gently placed me on the seat. It was true, it was a big step up into his truck. It didn't help that he had huge meaty tires on it that lifted it up a few more feet into the air.

He stood for a minute next to my seat as he thought about my words. There was a quiver deep in my belly at having him stand so close.

"I had a retarded guy tell me that the other day..." he said as he reached over me to grab my seatbelt and put it on.

My mouth opened in shock. "You can't say retarded anymore!"

"Why not?" he asked with a grin on his face. Again, he was looking at me as if he knew a secret and was getting ready to effortlessly control me with it.

"Because it's politically—"

"Incorrect...Yeah, I know. The thing is, the definition of retarded is one that is less advanced in mental, physical, or social development than is usual for one's age. The guy I was talking to was forty...and that retarded mutha f**** was trying to wax my truck with dish-washing liquid."

Oh my God! Laughter exploded from between my lips...And before I could stop it, I was snorting like crazy.

Tears came to my eyes as I tried to control my laughter, but no matter what I did, I couldn't stop. Just imagining an angry Hitta chasing some little guy around his truck for trying to use dishwashing liquid for wax was too much.

He stood and watched me laugh and snort with a pleased look on his face... I tried to cover it up, but it wouldn't stop. See what I mean? Effortlessly.

When my laughter finally died down, he did something that surprised the heck out of me...he leaned in and gently placed a kiss on my lips.

Y'all know what?

It was surprisingly pleasant. Because of Stan and the many times he'd forced his nasty lips on me, the thought of kissing has always terrified me, which was why I'd managed to avoid it with all the guys I'd ever dated...which weren't many.

Hitta's kiss although a quick gentle caress, was nice...I'll even venture to say that I actually liked it and wouldn't mind doing it again.

"Now, wouldn't you call his retarded a** retarded?"

I grinned as I reached out and wiped my lip gloss off his lips...an action that felt so natural. I didn't realize what I was doing until I was actually touching his soft lips with my thumb. His gaze darkened.

"Although what he did was a bit stupid, you still can't use the word retard. Like the word short to describe vertically challenged people...it has been buried for kinder words." He stared at me for a moment, trying to determine if my words were in fact true.

Then he grinned. "Bullsh*t..."

"I'm serious," I told him around my laughter.

"Yeah okay...political incorrectness my a**. You short and Jerry's retarded a** is retarded. Case closed."

And then he kissed me again, just a quick gentle brushing of his lips against mine. Just like the first time he did it, that little caress caused an answering quiver to happen deep inside my belly.

I touched my lips amazed as he shut my door and strolled around to the driver's side of the truck. What did it mean that I liked his kisses?

I thought about him giving me the definition of the word retard and something else about this mystery man's character became clear to me. Although he completely slaughtered the English language when he spoke...He was very intelligent.

Heck, I couldn't even give such a thorough definition of the word retard and I prided myself on being something of a word guru. I am the undefeated champion of Scrabble after all.

Now, on a serious note...I guess that age-old saying is true, you shouldn't judge a book by its cover and I'd mistakenly judged Hitta as an uneducated, uncaring, coldhearted brute, that had nothing to offer the world but his rage and his fists...

And yet, here in a matter of hours, he's managed to surprise me, arouse me...and make me laugh harder than I'd laughed in years, reminding me that I had that embarrassing snorting habit.

"Are you hungry?" he asked as he adjusted the heat settings making the inside of the luxury vehicle nice and toasty.

I shook my head, now suddenly feeling shy for some reason. It was different when I thought I was dealing with an intellectually inferior human being. But now that I knew I wasn't and that he was probably smarter than me, I felt intimidated in a way that his physical strength could never make me feel.

The feeling I got when talking to him that made me feel as if he was somehow effortlessly controlling me didn't seem so farfetched now.

"What did you eat?"

"Ummm..." I thought about it. The last thing I ate was a half of a muffin with a cup of tea around lunch time, I haven't had much of an appetite with all the stressful things going on in my life at the moment.

"Yeah, you thinking too long. We're going to grab something to eat on the way in."

I didn't respond, his mind was already made up, plus my stomach was a bundle of nerves. Now that we were headed toward my new home for the next six months, I tried to imagine what to expect.

I stole a glance at the powerful man sitting beside me…What would his home be like?

Would it be like his truck?

My gaze took in the tan leather seats that looked nice and conditioned. The shining wood framed dashboard that looked like something that belonged in a spaceship. In fact, the truck was so nice on the inside it felt like I was gliding in a luxury plane. It smelled expensive…

Would his place be like that? Luxurious, expensive, and cold… I exhaled. Whatever it was like, I only had to put up with it for six months, most of that time I would be at my shop anyway. My real home…

We drove for a good while. I was surprised when we drove into the Oak Park area…and even more surprised when he brought his truck to a stop in front of my favorite Indian restaurant. They stayed open till two because there was a little neighborhood bar attached to it as well, but they had the best curry lamb to be found in the Oak Park area.

"I love this place," I told him as he helped me out of the truck.

He smiled. "I know…" was all he said, still holding my hand and leading me inside.

How does he know? Was it true then that he'd been following me? When he showed up at the carnival and gave Jessie those tickets, I'd convinced myself that it had been a coincidence, even though I knew the truth.

"I own a tea shop that's not too far from here," I told him after we placed our order.

This was a test…I wanted to see if he was going to pretend like he didn't know that, but right then something else came to mind. *He's been calling me Teacup all this time.*

"I know…" His smooth deep voice cut into my thoughts.

Once again, he was giving me that look that said he was going to effortlessly control me. It was like he knew what I was going to do next and he was ready for it.

"How do you know?"

He turned to face me fully then, seeming to block out the rest of the restaurant. When he looked down at me with that intense dark gaze of his, he made everything else disappear…it was just him and me in the whole world.

"You intrigue me, Angel. And when something intrigues me, I have to know everything about it…" He paused for just a moment as he took a step closer, effortlessly pulling me deeper into the web he was casting around me.

"It becomes an obsession."

I inhaled when he wrapped one of his strong arms around my waist pulling me close. My hands, as if they had a will of their own, gently clutched his hard biceps before they traveled farther up his arms and came to rest on his big pecks. And I realized that I'd straight up just felt him up, something I'd secretly wanted to do since the first time I saw him standing in his gym in that tank top.

Goodness, he felt amazing…

This man's body was just that…simply amazing. However, he was so tall I had to hold my head back to look up into his eyes.

"Are you obsessed with me, Hitta?" My words were barely over a whisper.

He nodded… "I am."

"Why? I'm nothing like the kind of girl you're supposed to want."

He grinned. "And what kind of girl is that, shawty?"

I bit my lip as I thought about it. "You know, the kind that can handle a man like you."

My statement made him chuckle. "And what kind of man am I?"

One that was continuing to surprise me. "You're a hard man, a man from the streets."

And I wasn't. Although I'd been born in the ghetto and lived there as a little girl, most of my life, I have lived with the Bakers in their posh suburban home. I'd gone to a really good school and lived in the kind of neighborhood where one could sleep with their front door wide open should they choose and not worry that they'd be robbed or murdered in their sleep.

I was back to living in the ghetto because it was all I could afford right now with all of the people and the things that I was supporting.

And quite frankly I would rather stay in a cardboard box that continue to live under Stanly's roof.

Hitta nodded. "I am that, but it's more to me, you know. Something about you called out to me, real strong. Now, you all I can see... I think you will be able to handle me just fine."

His words made me feel good and that confused me... What was it about him that was changing me, causing me to like things that I thought I wouldn't and probably shouldn't? The man had just told me that he was obsessed with me and instead of running for my life, I wanted to be closer to him.

How could a ghetto superstar like him become obsessed with a little nobody like me? I've been invisible my whole life, only seen by someone that I'd thought was a figment of my imagination most of said life.

"What's happening?" I whispered, still drowning in his gaze.

He grinned down at me. "I don't know, *Teacup*, but whatever it is, I like it."

My gaze fell to his soft lips as his head began to lower. He was going to kiss me again, but this time, it would not be a quick peck. As if it had a will of its own, my head tilted back bringing my lips closer to his. And right when our lips were getting ready to touch, the man behind the register called our number.

I blinked rapidly, looking around me when suddenly the sounds and sights of the restaurant all at once came back into focus.

What the world?!

Hitta had the power to make everything else around me disappear. I've never experienced that before. The few guys that I've dated were alright, but nothing spectacular. They had all been artsy like me, the kind of guys that I always thought I wanted to be with. And yet...

Not a one of them had ever made me drown in their gaze until the sights and sounds around me disappeared into blackness...

No, it was the brute who caused this... The thug that I'd prejudged and was now being made to feel like a giant a** for doing so.

I was so troubled with my thoughts that I didn't notice he'd brought the truck to a stop a short distance after leaving the restaurant until he killed the engine. We were still in Oak Park. He'd pulled into a long driveway and came to a stop behind the U-Haul truck that sat in front of a big beautiful home that was lit up nicely against the night sky, a few of the guys that had helped me pack were carrying my things inside.

My mouth dropped as I sat up in my seat staring out the window.

This was the kind of house I'd always dreamed of having but knew I never would. It looked like it had been featured in the Home and Garden magazine, the kind of house Martha Stewart held her cooking shows in.

I loved Oak Park. Before I'd opened my shop here, I'd come here to escape my home life for a few hours. All of the houses and the stores in this town had an old-world charm about them that made me feel warm on the inside.

I swore that when I bought my first house, it would be here. But this house…

This was one of the better homes in Oak Park… The fact that it sat on about five acres of land testified to that. I had yet to see inside but I was already in love with it because of the huge wrap-around porch that was lit so beautifully.

A WRAP-AROUND PORCH!

"Oh my, God! Is this your home?" I said, not able to take my eyes away from it. It was simply amazing.

"It's *our* home." His quiet words caused me to look at him. He sat back in his seat looking like the street king he was, relaxed, watching my reaction.

Suddenly, I was very sad that I was only going to be here for six months. I would have loved it if his words were true. I would have loved for this place to really be mine. But just like everything in my life, it was only temporary.

I smiled… "Your home is beautiful."

He studied me in that way that he does for a moment before he jerked his head toward the door.

"Let's go in and take a look around."

I didn't wait for him to come around to my door, I was so excited I opened it and hopped down out of the truck.

He chuckled. "Going to have to get a step put in over there."

Since it sounded like he was talking more to himself than to me, I didn't respond. Instead, I let my gaze take in as much of the beautiful yard I could see in the dark. There was a big tree off to the side of the house, I wondered what kind it was. Because it was winter, there were no identifying leaves on it.

"Do you know what kind of tree that is?" I asked as we walked up the three steps to the porch of my dreams.

"Yeah, I think the realtor said it is an apple tree."

I looked at him startled. "You don't know?"

He shrugged. "I just moved in last week."

"What?!" I asked, but right then we walked into the front door and all my thoughts faded.

Although it was empty except for the few pieces of furniture I'd brought, it felt like I'd just walked into a bigger version of the Tea Shop. The floors were a beautiful hardwood like the ones at the shop, but far better, they looked brand new and were so shiny I could see my reflection in them.

The walls were made of various shades of brown cobblestone, but where the stones on the shop walls were clearly a budget buy kind of thing, no expense had been spared on these. To the right of the foyer were a grand set of stairs, I wanted to go up them and see what was up there, but I needed to finish my tour downstairs first. I felt like a kid in a candy store, there was so much awesomeness to see.

The house was completely empty. The guys walked back and forth past us carrying my boxes upstairs and to the back, probably to the kitchen.

"Wow!" I gushed when we went into the living room.

There were eight huge bay windows, in front of them was a padded bench that ran along the length. Because I had a little thing for designing, I could see these windows surrounded by a few plants and a beautiful set of curtains…nothing too heavy, maybe sheer or linen.

My gaze went to the big fireplace that would look great with a fire roaring inside of it, I could see a pile of logs sitting off to the side and two big comfortable chairs in front so that you could toast your toes on cold nights.

There was a set of glass doors that led to a huge dining room, I walked in and my mind's eye placed a beautiful table that sat twelve. There was another set of glass doors that led to the kitchen.

Oh y'all! The kitchen...

I forgot that I wasn't by myself when I walked through those doors...

The kitchen was amazing, it was the kind of kitchen every tea maker should have. But what I liked the most was the huge pantry...

"This is amazing!" I screeched when I walked inside. There was an island inside the pantry that was a perfect workstation. The shelves inside resembled the shelves in my shop...

What the world?!

I walked out of there so confused. Hitta was leaning against the big island in the kitchen waiting for me.

"What's going on?" I asked dumbfounded.

"Do you like your new home?"

"I-I love it, but—"

He shook his head as he stood coming towards me. "Don't always have to be a but, *Teacup*... Let's eat."

Chapter Five

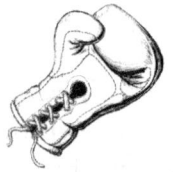

WHERE DO I BELONG...

> *I Crave So Much More Than Just a Physical Connection. I Crave Words and Depth. I Crave Who You are and Where You Came From, Your Desire and Your Fears. I Yearn To know Every Inch of You Beyond the Surface...*
>
> The Write Vibe Co.

Angel

"So... where do I sleep?"

We'd just finished cleaning up behind our meal. His men had left earlier, taking the U-Haul with them. It was just him and me now, facing the moment I've been very apprehensive about for the last hour. There were four huge bedrooms upstairs and neither of them had a stitch of furniture in them.

In fact, the only space that was fully furnished was the basement that had been turned into a state-of-the-art home gym. I asked him while we stood at the island in the kitchen eating our food—Well... while *he* stood at the island. He'd surprised me by lifting me and plopping me on top of it.

"Sit," was all he muttered.

So...I sat with my legs crossed Indian style on the big island facing him while we ate. It was kind of cool, I'd never done anything like that.

Anyway, I'd asked him why he hadn't bought a single chair. He chuckled as he rubbed his temple. That was the fourth time I'd seen him do that tonight and I wondered if he had a headache.

"That ain't my department, Teacup. Before I bought this place, I slept most nights on the couch in my office at the gym. I wouldn't know how to begin to shop for this joint. As a matter of fact, the thought of shopping for it is giving me a headache," he grumbled as he scraped the left-over food from my plate onto his.

"What?! How could you not be excited at the possibilities?" My mind had not stopped designing rooms since we got here.

"Sh*t, real easy." He reached into his pocket and pulled out a card, sliding it to me.

I looked down and was surprised to see that it was a Black American Express.

"Won't you handle that lil mama? Get whatever you want, don't worry about how much it cost."

The bottle of water I was drinking froze halfway to my mouth. "You want me to pick out the furniture for your house?!"

He chuckled before polishing off the last bite of food on his plate. "I want you to pick out the furniture for our house."

"But what if I get something you don't like?"

Why in the world did he just give me his credit card like that? I'm in this situation because I'd stolen ten-thousand dollars from him. Who turns around and gives the person who had just stolen that kind of money their credit card?

"I'm a simple man, baby. I don't give a sh*t what you buy. I'll be happy with whatever it is."

I grinned... "What if I buy cheetah print everything?"

He shook his head… "You like it…I love it. Go jungle crazy for all I care."

I sat there for a moment in a bit of a shock. I didn't know how to deal with this. My gaze went back to the card.

"Ummm, do you think it's wise of you to give me your credit card like that?"

He shrugged. "I ain't worried about it." And that was it, he didn't say anything else about it.

Okay, let me tell y'all something I discovered tonight about Hitta, he wasn't a big talker, but he was an ardent listener. Very ardent…

I've been doing this nervous rambling all night because I knew the time was getting closer to go to bed. Yeah…I'm one of the folks that talked to keep from freaking out and I'd talked his ear off tonight about everything, my shop, my teas, herbs, plants…

Most times, his only response was a grunt or a nod of his head. I thought to myself, he's so not listening to me, but then he would prove me wrong by making a comment about something I said earlier and connecting it with what I was talking about in the present.

Westly used to always tell me that the most dangerous man in the room was the quiet one because while everybody else was running their mouths, he was sitting back studying everything. That's how Hitta was. He was the man in the room that quietly took in everything like a sponge.

And you know…I think I liked that about him.

"What you mean, where you going to sleep? You going to sleep in *our* bedroom with me."

My heartbeat increased drastically. That's what I thought he was going to say.

Oh my God!

I was getting ready to have a panic attack. I opened my mouth getting ready to beg him to let me sleep in one of the other rooms, but the only thing that came out was a squeak.

As if he could sense my protest, he suddenly turned to face me before putting his big hands underneath my arms and lifting me until I was eye level with him. My toes dangled about twelve inches off the floor.

Goodness, he was strong!

"You listening to me?" he growled in my face.

With wide eyes, I nodded. How could I not be listening to him at this point?

"I f***ing hate repeating myself. I told you I was not going to force you to do nothing you don't want to do. When I make love to you, you're going to be hot and wet and begging me to soothe that hunger between your thighs. I ain't no f***ing rapist, baby. You got that?"

I was having a hard time getting past hot and wet, and hunger between my thighs. The power of suggestion was a monster because I'd be doggone if that hunger between my thighs did not stir at the thought of him soothing it.

Now, I could only guess at how he would go about doing it. Would he use his hand or his—

You know what? These were dangerous thoughts. Forcing my mind clean, I patted his big shoulder.

"Got it."

"Good." He set me back on my feet and still holding my hand, pulled me into the empty room after him.

Like the rest of the house, the master bedroom was amazing. I don't know what year the house was built; my guess would be some time in the forties or the fifties. The bedrooms all had an old-world French feel to them.

However, in the master bedroom, there were two pairs of glass doors that opened to a private balcony. I'd walked through them earlier and was pleased to see that the balcony overlooked the back-yard, although it was too dark to see what the yard looked like. I couldn't wait to explore when the sun came up.

This bedroom was the only one with its own bathroom and my goodness, what a bathroom it was! It was actually two rooms separated by beautiful white Victorian-style pillars. On one side of the pillars was a walk-in shower with glass doors that revealed three silver shower heads, warm grey stone, and cream marble floors and siding.

There was a beautiful marble bathtub that was so big it could easily fit two people comfortably and twin outer marble sinks located on the other side of the pillars as well as a bench with a base that was the same marble as the shower and the tub, but the top was a plush cushion that looked very comfortable to sit on.

I could see myself soaking in a nice, hot, and detoxing tea bath for hours. Mmmmm… That sounded so good I was almost tempted to do just that. However, all of my teas were packed away and it was really late. And although I knew he said he would not try and rape me or anything, I was still a little nervous around him.

It wasn't that I didn't believe him, I did, but it was because he was something different. The only man I'd been around so intimately since leaving my foster parents house was Westly. I was used to having him in my space.

Hitta was a whole other entity entirely. I've never slept in bed with a man. The one time Westly and I had fallen asleep on the couch watching a movie, he'd talked about me so badly the next day, because — Well…

I'm a wild sleeper…

There, I said it.

Outside of my snorting habit, it's the next most embarrassing thing about me. I think it's because I tossed and turned due to my nightmares. I don't know…But whatever is in the bed with me when I go to sleep…a book, my laptop, my covers, end up on the floor by morning.

"Damn, I should have at least got a bed," he grumbled drawing me out of my head.

"I have blankets, but they're all packed away. I have no idea which box they're in." *And I'm too tired to try and look for them.*

He shook his head as if he could hear my thoughts. "Forget it, I'll be your bed tonight."

And then he proceeded to arrange the few pillows that had come off my bed that didn't get packed against the floor and the wall before he kicked his boots off and reclined his powerful body on the floor.

"Come on, *Teacup*, I'll keep you warm," he said gesturing for me to climb on top.

I stood there with my hand on my hip looking down at him. "Ummm…I don't know about this. What if I get too heavy?"

One side of his mouth lifted in a grin. "Really?"

Okay, maybe that was a dumb reason. The man was a giant…I wanted to tell him that I'm a wild sleeper who suffered from nightmares but was just too embarrassed to do so. Instead, I stood there biting my lip.

His grin grew. "You know, I'm more comfortable than the floor."

I nodded…Yeah, I'm sure he is. Slowly, I slid out of my shoes and eased down to my knees next to him. It would have been easier if he'd just grabbed me and pulled me to him. Instead, he wanted me to come to him on my own.

"You don't trust me?" His words were barely over a whisper.

"It's not that. I—I've never done anything like this before." My words were just as quiet.

He chuckled. "It's a first time for everything, Teacup." He beckoned me with his hands. "Come on, you can do this."

Damn it! This shouldn't be so hard. Why can't I be normal? Any other woman would have no problem mounting this big gorgeous brother. He said he wouldn't hurt me, and I knew he spoke the truth, yet a part of me wanted to tell him that I was perfectly fine sleeping on the floor, there was no need for him to offer his body for my comfort.

But then again, there was a part of me that wanted to know what it would be like to lay my head against his strong chest and let the sound of his heartbeat lull me to sleep. I wanted to know what it would feel like to be held in those arms of his.

Would it still feel safe or was that feeling I'd gotten that day at the gym just a happenstance?

I inhaled. I can do this! I can do this! He was not Stan…He would not hurt me. It was time for me to take my life back from my stepfather. Because of him, I've never been able to have a successful relationship with a guy. Because of him, I've been too afraid to let anybody in. I was tired of being alone.

My gaze rose to Hitta's. He was not the man I'd imagined myself being with. He was dangerous and uncouth…yet there was something in his eyes that spoke to my soul. It was as if it was the answering call to my inner question, a question that I didn't know I had until I met him…

Where do I belong?

Slowly, I placed my shaking hands on the floor and began to crawl towards his big body. That must have been all the incentive he needed because he wrapped his hands around my waist and lifted me the rest of the way.

Goodness! I've always been short, but I wasn't skinny by any means. However, Hitta made me feel lightweight with the way he lifts and holds me.

At first, my body was stiff on top of his, but as soon as I lay my head on his warm chest, my senses were flooded with the delicious, masculine scent of his cologne and the sound of his strong heartbeat. And then he wrapped his arms around me.

Wow! It felt amazing!

I snuggled deeper into his embrace wrapping my arms around his waist, locking my hands together between his back and the pillow.

"Comfortable?"

I nodded. "Mmmmhhhmmm."

That was an understatement. I was past comfortable. For the second time in my life that I can remember, I felt safe.

So safe, I didn't remember falling asleep until the dream started.

I'm walking down Michigan Avenue, the famous Magnificent Mile. Only it's not the lights of the many stores that have it ablaze, but fire. Everything is on fire. There are so many who lay dead and dying in the street that I have to step over a body every so many feet.

My hands are shaking and although I'm crying, my body is in shock. I feel like I've just survived a nuclear blast. I can't understand why I'm still alive when it feels like my skin is on fire. A woman is lying up ahead with her legs missing, only bloody stumps exist where they used to be. She's trying to crawl to her little girl, whose body is still on fire, leaving a trail of blood as she goes.

I scream when the earth began to shake so violently that it throws me off my feet. A loud terrible sound fills my ears when the streets begin to crack open. The earth is splitting in half and I'm falling. I clutch at the ground trying to hold on, but I'm slipping. My nails bleed from where I'm clutching at the earth, I can feel the fire underneath me ready to consume me...

And then something happens...

Something that has never happened.

Hitta appears over the side and he grabs my hand, pulling me back to safety. I am so relieved to see him that I wrap my arms and body around his so tightly, clinging to him desperately. For the first time, I'm not alone. He is so strong and sure...he will keep me safe.

Now I can rest...because he can keep me safe.

———

Hitta

I'd felt the migraine coming on before I got to Angel's place. I didn't know if it would be a quick one that only lasted a day or two or a long drawn out one that lasted a week or two. I'd been seen by the best neurologists in the world and none of them could figure out why I got these damn headaches.

They began in my fifth year of professional boxing; I'd already held the heavyweight title in the WBC for three consecutive years and was working on my fourth. At first, we all thought it was a boxing injury, but the doctors could find nothing to indicate that. No scaring or bruising...in fact, each MRI I took came back as flawless as the first.

I'd tried to ignore the headaches and fight anyway. That didn't work, I began to lose my titles one after the other until I was forced into early retirement. The doctors had wanted to prescribe me narcotics because the regular over-the-counter pain meds did nothing for the migraines.

I took one pill from the prescription the first doctor had given me and although it dulled the pain for a short while, I never took them again. In my world, one had to be aware and always about their business. It was the same reason I never did drugs growing up...a high nigga gets caught slipping. And that can lead to his death or him being robbed of everything he had.

That was rule number one on my streets...don't get high on your own supply. Of course, these days...with this new breed of thug, this...softer breed, they get caught slipping all the time, because none of them can operate sober, they smoked more of their own product than they sold. The OG's of my day are a dying breed…being replaced by some damn jokes.

Anyway…the other reason I stopped taking the meds is because I didn't have time to get strung out on that sh*t. While I was fighting professionally, traveling in that circuit, I'd seen a lot of mutha f****s strung out on pills. Everybody was a damn zombie, popping pills like them sh*ts were candy.

Naw, I ain't about that life…So, I've learned to live with the pain. However, something happened tonight that has never happened before. As soon as I kicked in Angel's door and walked in her place, the pain began to ease.

And now that I'm holding her in my arms, I think I know why.

It's her smell…

Her apartment smelled like it. When I pressed her against the wall, that fragrance filled my senses…and yeah, it numbed the headache.

This is some wild sh*t!

At first, I thought I was just tripping… You know, just excited to finally have the object of my obsession within my grasp. I thought my mind was just playing tricks on me… but then she started looking around the house, taking her smell with her and the headache started to come back. When we started eating and I was standing by her, her smell filled my senses and once again dulled the pain.

Being careful not to wake her, I lifted a few of her braids and brought them to my nose…Even her hair smelled like it.

I don't know what that is…maybe some kind of flower with a sweet undertone.

Could it be possible this girl's smell was sending some kind of signal to my brain that worked like a pain pill?

Maybe I'll call Rome tomorrow and see if he'd ever heard of some sh*t like that happening to somebody else. Or maybe I won't…

Now that he was supposed to be dead, I had to be careful about contacting him. Of course, the little bastard was a f***ing genius and had set up a special line for me to use when I needed to get in touch with him that could not be traced.

But I still tried to use it only in an emergency. I'd had to stop myself from using it the other day when Angel's crack head a** brother fell for my bait and took the ten grand I left in the drawer in my office.

I knew from watching the cameras that when he cleaned in there, he sometimes peeped in my drawers…My sources told me the owner of the building where Angel's Tea Shop is, had started the eviction process for her because she hadn't been paid in two months going on three.

The rest was a breeze…she and her brother just fell into my hands after that. Yeah…Rome is a f***ing genius. I had been playing this cat-and-mouse game with Angel for a long time.

The thing is…she's too f***ing good for me, I knew that. She's clean where I am filthy. She has a good heart and soul. Rome sent me a file on her…the file was full of sh*t she did for other people.

She'd paid for her brother to go to rehab eleven times. She was paying the tuition for his child to go to a decent school. She sometimes paid the bills at his child's mother's place. She collected money for eight different charities at her Tea Shop. Twice a year she did a fundraiser for the soup kitchen around the corner from her shop. Three times a year she set up a bin inside of her shop and did a food drive where she asked folks to bring in canned goods for the soup kitchen. In the fall, she held a coat drive to give coats to needy children so they could be protected from the Chicago winter…

Keep in mind she's only twenty-one.

Hell yeah, she's too good for me. I'm a mean, selfish mutha f****. I take care of my own, everybody else can eat a d***. You cross me and I eliminate yo' a**. I don't give a f*** who you are, mama, daddy, sista, mutha f***en brotha…You cross me and I'm going to murk yo' a**… period. I don't play with mutha f****s. I got one friend and he lives all the way in f***ing Canada. I don't allow myself to get close to anybody else.

Now, I know what y'all saying, damn, Hitta, you f***ed up. And the thing is, I know it. I know that I'm f***ed up in the head. It's like I told Angel earlier, I'm a product of my environment. I had to be this way.

When I was a kid, my mom was a piece of sh*t junkie who would smoke the toilet if she could. There was never food in the house for me and my three younger siblings…if not for Rome's mom, who used to let me come and eat at their place and bring food back for my two little sisters and brother, we would have starved.

We never kept a crib. My mom lived with one John after another. The first mutha f***a I knocked out was a nigga who decided he wanted me instead of her. She didn't fight for me or try and stop him… I was eight years old and she brought me to him, said he and I were going to play a little game. He took off his clothes and I started crying for her, but she didn't answer me, she was in the next room smoking a rock while my siblings crawled on the nasty a** floor.

I knew that if I was going to make it out of there, I was going to have to make it happen myself. That mutha f***a went in to touch my d*** and I balled up my fist and swung with everything I had in me and laid that b**** out.

When he came to, he kicked us out. She was so mad that we had to go back to the shelter, she beat the sh*t out of me. My uncle G came and got me after he heard what happened and let me move in with him and Saw…

Sh*t, their place wasn't that much better, but at least I had a roof over my head. A month later, the state came and got my siblings. I begged G to take them, but he refused, said he didn't have time to deal with no babies. Two years later, my mom stole a lot of money from him…I guess she thought because he was her brother, he wasn't going to do sh*t to her.

He put a bullet in her head and we buried her a** few days later. That's my world…It's a cold and loveless cesspool of bottom feeders all struggling for their next breath. To survive that, you have to be mean and heartless.

Angel would never survive in my world. And yet, I couldn't stay away from her…I tried. Her light drew me like a moth. She was so innocent. Listening to her talk tonight was like a breath of fresh air. She talked about life and light…loving things and healing.

I realize that I'd grabbed a hold of her because I needed her to pull me out of the darkness. I'd always thought I was fine where I was…

But just maybe the reason I was so obsessed with her was because I was tired of living in this darkness…

"No!" she suddenly cried out, jerking violently in my arms...

I tightened my hold on her...She was having a nightmare.

"Please, somebody help me!" She was pushing against me trying to break away from my hold.

"Shhh...baby. I'm here, Shhh..."

She wrapped her arms around my neck tightly, clinging to me as if her life depended on it. I held her just as tightly.

"Hitta...don't let me fall!"

"It's okay, Teacup, I've got you...I'll never let you fall, baby. Not ever!"

She exhaled and settled back down into a calm sleep. I wondered what she was dreaming about that frightened her so. There was no demon I wouldn't slay to protect her. If I even thought something or someone was trying to hurt her, their a** was fried...period!

That was my last thought before sleep claimed me. I slept with no pain because Angel's sweet scent filled my senses even in my dreams. At some point right before dawn, I got up to use the bathroom. When I came back out, she was sleeping peacefully on the pillows. I didn't want to disturb her, so I settled down on my stomach next to her.

What happened next pleasantly surprised me. She turned over and climbed on my back as if I was a log, then she buried her head in the spot between my neck and shoulder before resuming her gentle snoring.

Damn! That sh*t was so f***ing cute...not only did my baby do that adorable snorting when she laughed, she was a f***ing wild sleeper. Imagine that.

I drifted back to sleep with a smile on my face...

Chapter Six

GETTING A TASTE OF HIM...

Angel

Okay, so…

The next morning, I got a taste of what it was going to be like living with Mr. Hard Hitta for the next six months.

And I do mean a taste…

After waking up extremely embarrassed because at some point in the night, I climbed on top of the man's back and fell asleep, only to be awakened by him doing pushups.

"Wake-up, Teacup."

His deep voice penetrated my dream that was surprisingly quite pleasant, so of course, instead of waking up fully, I wrapped my arms and legs around him, snuggling closer. The up and down motion was only lulling me back to sleep. It had been so long since I'd slept undisturbed and had a pleasant dream, I just wasn't ready to get up.

His deep chuckle rumbled through me… "Wake-up, baby."

I cracked an eye and frowned as the room dipped down, then back up.

My eyes flew open. "What the—" I cried when I realized I was on the man's back. "Eeekk!" I was falling.

Pushing himself and me up with one hand, he reached back with the other one and caught me before I hit the floor. I quickly wrapped my arms and legs back around him, clinging to him like a monkey.

"What's going on?!"

"You're helping me get my morning workout," he said calmly, like him doing pushups with me sleeping on his back was something he did every day.

"How did I get up here?" The man was so big, it felt like I was on the back of a horse or something.

He chuckled again. "You climbed on in your sleep."

My forehead hit his back. *Oh my goodness... He must think I'm a kook...clinging to him like Curious freaking George.*

I sat up so that I was straddling him. Would you guys believe I was so short that my feet did not touch the ground? I had to clutch his shirt to keep from falling again as he continued his pushups.

"Are you going to let me down?" I asked, secretly enjoying the ride.

"I'm almost finished with my last set."

If I was light-skinned, I would be bright red right now. "How many sets have you done?"

"Four," he grunted as he dipped down and then back up.

Wow! I couldn't believe I'd actually slept through that. He had to call me to wake me up. Goodness...I couldn't remember the last time I got longer than two hours of sleep. And I think I know why that happened.

Hitta was in my dream last night. Somehow, him holding me through the night had made me feel safe, which would explain why I ended up crawling on his back. I remember at some point feeling alone in my dream. I was very afraid, fearing that he had abandoned me. Then I remembered feeling his heat next to me and reaching out for it. Once I found it, I felt relief and relaxed back into a deep sleep.

And amazingly for the first time in a long time, I woke up feeling refreshed. With my legs still wrapped tightly around his waist so that I didn't fall off, I lifted my hands over my head and stretched. As I did, I noticed how stunning the bedroom looked with the sunlight shining in so bright and— I stiffened.

Sunlight!

"What time is it?" I asked although I knew whatever answer he gave was going to be the wrong one. I got to the shop every morning at six…my pastry boy was making his delivery by six-thirty.

"Ten forty-five."

"Shoot!" I cried scrambling off his back. "I'm late for work!" He turned over and tried to grab me, but I danced from his fingers.

"What's the rush?"

I chuckled… "I'm going to have a lot of folks angry at me because they couldn't start their day with their morning cup of tea."

He smoothly came to his feet displaying his strength. "What's the big deal about tea anyway? It's not like it's coffee."

I came to a halt and whipped around to glare at him. He couldn't have slapped me and insulted me more.

"How dare you insult tea that way?" I put my hand on my hip. "I'll have you know most people prefer tea to coffee three to one." Of course, I was totally making that up.

He stood with a little grin on his face that really showed just how cute his dimples were in the morning before he tilted his head to the side.

"Are you making that sh*t up, Teacup?"

I lifted my head…this man's ability to read me was frightening. "No, I'm not making it up. It's been scientifically proven." Sooooo making that up.

"Scientifically proven you say?" He had a look on his face that said he wasn't buying it.

I nodded. "Scientifically proven."

Chuckling, he headed into the bathroom. "Well, I guess if the scientists say it…it must be true."

His statement caused me to giggle as I continued to my boxes that had been labeled bedroom and stacked neatly in the corner. From here I could see him in the bathroom mirror taking care of his morning rituals.

I couldn't believe I'd slept till ten forty-five. How in the world? I have never slept that long. Because of my nightmares, I'm always awake by three am. Although most times, I'm exhausted from not getting nearly enough sleep. I generally have time to get my mind ready for the day, do some reading, soak in a nice bath, enjoy a nice cup of chamomile tea. And if I'm in the mood, a bowl of buttery chamomile oatmeal with a drizzle of honey on top.

Needless to say, I wasn't used to running late in the morning. I will need to contact Kelly from the bakery and ask if she could send my boxes of pastries over for my lunch crowd. Then I will have to call Jessie's house and make sure her mom feed her breakfast and toke her to school. And then—

Oh my God! He was stripping...

I looked away, blushing so hard the roots of my hair follicles were tingling. But then as if it had a will of its own, my head turned just a little bit so that I could take another peek... Just a quick one, I promise.

He wasn't paying attention to me and I didn't even know if he knew I could see him. Why isn't he closing the door?!

He stood in only his boxer briefs now, adjusting the water temperature of the shower. I felt like a Peeping Tom watching him. But I couldn't look away... my goodness! The man's body was gorgeous. He could easily be a model or something.

Now that his shirt was gone, I was able to see the tattoo that went across his chest better. What I had initially thought were two separate tattoos, one that was on his right peck that went up to the side of his neck and one that was on his left bicep, was really one tattoo that stretched from his bicep across his massive chest to end along the right side of his neck.

It was amazing! Although I still couldn't read the script, the picture was startlingly clear...and a bit frightening. It was a picture of a fierce lion ripping the heart out of a man with his sharp teeth. Whoever had done the work was a remarkable artist. Somehow, they'd managed to capture Hitta's personality perfectly in that picture. Now, I was very curious as to what the script said.

When he got the temperature to his liking he stepped back and his hands went to the waist of his boxers. I told myself to look away. I shouldn't be spying on him...*I really should look away!*

Yet...

My face heated to the boiling point as time slowed down. The more skin he revealed the more my eyes widened. By the time his drawers hit the ground, my mouth was hanging open in astonishment.

He was hu—

Right before he stepped in the shower, his sexy gaze came to mine and my thoughts instantly froze. He wore a little devious grin, letting me know that he had been aware that I was watching him and if that didn't confirm it, the little wink he gave me before stepping into the shower surely did. I collapsed back on the floor with my hands over my face in a heap of embarrassment.

Determined to be out of this room before he got out of the shower, I dug into the box with my clothes in it and began to pull out the first thing I laid my hands on which was my black baggy jumper... but something made me pause on that. He thought I dressed like a homeless person. That bothered me... I didn't want him to look at me like a hobo.

I wanted him to look at me and feel the way I just felt looking at him getting into that shower. I wanted him to think I was desirable. With my mind made up I stood, leaving the box I'd packed all the stuff from the front of my closet in. Those were the things that I wore every day.

Instead, I went to the box that I'd packed all the stuff from the back of my closet in. I really did have pretty things, it's just that my life is one big ball of stress and I'm the kind of person who dressed for the day, how I feel when I wake up.

Although beautiful things caught my eye, depression and grief kept me from reaching for them in my closet. But today... after waking up feeling refreshed for the first time in like...forever, I think I was ready to explore new possibilities.

My search didn't last long before I came across a burgundy Boho patch maxi dress that I fell in love with the first time I laid eyes on it. The dress was very expensive, but I had to have it...Very rarely do I get a chance to splurge on myself, this dress had been one of those times.

Although it was a maxi dress, it was only long in the back, the front of the dress came all the way up to center thigh. To go with this masterpiece, I'd splurged on a pair of burgundy suede thigh-length high-heeled boots with metal tips, another very expensive purchase...

However, I had the feeling that after today, the money I'd spent on this ensemble will have been well worth it. Quickly I gathered the other things I was going to need to pull myself together and headed to the bathroom at the end of the hall.

It had been so long since I'd actually taken the time to fix myself up, I wondered if I still knew what to do. It's amazing Hitta had taken a fancy to me at all. The fact that he had made me wonder what was it that he saw in me. What made him look past the fact that my brother and I had just stolen a lot of money from him?

He'd settled for me being his girlfriend for the next six months. He'd put me in this beautiful house, given me his credit card to furnish it however I saw fit, and wasn't even forcing me to have sex with him...

And just on a side note...that in itself was doing something to me. He's a brute, uncouth, and a goon...I expected him to be like Stan or even worse. I'd slept like a baby in his arms last night. Not once did I have to shove his hand away from being someplace it didn't belong.

In fact, I'd awakened to find that I was clinging to him in my sleep. It felt like he was playing hard to get, even though I knew he wasn't. And that just...I don't know, made me want to see what it would be like if he did touch me that way.

I had a strong feeling that his touch will not cause pain like Stan's. But first...

I wanted to show him how beautiful I was capable of being. I'd gotten used to downplaying myself, but not today...

Today, I wanted him to know who it was he'd made so many sacrifices for. Today, I was burying the girl Stan had terrified...and embracing the woman Hard Hitta the Brute through a few unselfish acts, had liberated.

Because it had been such a long time, I had to lay all of my supplies out on the sink in front of me and after brushing my teeth and taking my shower, I got started.

First, I moisturized my skin really well with a body butter that I'd made from passion fruit tea, then I slid into the burgundy panty and bra set that I'd bought the day I'd gotten this dress. The top of the dress had a deep V cut that would show my bra just a bit...so I thought, why not get a pretty lace bralette that would kind of give the appearance of having on a cami underneath? And of course, I had to get the matching panties since I was splurging on the bra anyway.

Once done, I slid on a pair of thigh-high burgundy stockings, that was topped with lace. I had a thing for thigh-high stockings...they made me feel sexy. Then, I put the loose-fitting dress over my head... I loved this style of dress because it went with my body type flawlessly. The dress itself was wool and the long sleeves were perfect for the Chicago winter.

After that, I moisturized my braids and piled them into a messy bun on top of my head, allowing a few key plaits to escape using a little hair gel to get my edge game on point. I was never a big makeup wearer, a few swipes of mascara, a little eyeliner, finishing off with my favorite cherry-lemonade lip-gloss...

Now, it was time for the accessories...

I added a few pieces of silver loc jewelry to my braids and then a slim three-layered silver necklace. The first link fit almost like a choker and had a little silver feather charm that rested against my throat. The next link was slightly longer and had a slightly bigger silver feather that rested against my chest...and the last link was really long and had a bigger silver feather that rested against my belly.

I slid about twenty-five silver bangles on both of my wrists with the friendship bracelets Jessie had made for me...then I added my rings.

Don't laugh at me, but I really liked rings. By the time I was finished, nearly every finger of mine had a silver ring on it. Some of them had two...That's just the way I rolled.

Heck, it had been so long, I'd forgotten I rolled this way. But by the time I slid my socking clad feet in the suede boots that zipped all the way up to the center of my thighs...I remembered.

I stood in the mirror for a moment taking it in. For the first time in a while, I felt pretty. I turned this way and that...

I looked good, y'all…

And now I was super nervous to leave the bathroom. What was he going to think? Would he still think I looked like a homeless person because I was still clearly rocking the Boho style? After I gathered all my stuff, I paused with my hand on the doorknob.

Hitta was brutally honest. It would devastate me if he looked at me and called me a hobo again.

Okay, …you can do this. Just go out there and pretend it's business as usual. Pretend you are just getting ready for work and don't really care what he thinks. Go find your box of teas and chew on a few chamomile heads…

Oh! Chamomile…Yes! I opened the door and walked out.

So, you guys may have already guessed it, but I have a serious chamomile addiction. I loved that flower. I ate them fresh, dried, in cake, teas…just because for a reason, when I was bored, while I was busy. My addiction was the main reason chamomile was one of the things I constantly had to order for the shop.

Jessie and Westly both thought that I was a weirdo because I was always munching on the flower that most people only liked in tea. I don't know, I wouldn't say I ate them because they tasted good per se…Instead, I would say that I ate them because I was addicted to the way they made my mouth feel if that makes any sense…

I chuckled, maybe I was a weirdo like my niece and brother always say.

Hitta wasn't in the bedroom. I put my things away and grabbed my bag and cell before making my way downstairs. I heard him talking on the phone in the living room. As soon as I reached the bottom, I saw him standing there dressed in a pair of black name brand sweatpants and a black t-shirt. On his feet were what looked like a brand-new pair of black and red Jordans.

He glanced my way before looking back out the window. A half a second later his head whipped back towards me. The look in his eyes as he slowly took me in was well worth the effort I had put into my look today.

"Sh********t!" he hissed, "Hey bo, let me holla at you later." He told whoever he was talking to on the phone, before he pushed the off button and slid it down in his pocket as he began to approach me.

"Damn, shawty! What you do to yourself?"

"Do you like it?" My question was barely over a whisper. I couldn't believe how much I needed him to like what he was seeing.

He didn't stop till he was standing in front of me, then he did the sweetest thing. Bending down just a bit he wrapped both of his arms around me and pulled me into the most perfect hug anyone has ever given me.

"I love it, Teacup. You so pretty you take my breath away, baby."

Awww! Shucks!

I closed my eyes as he tightened his arms around me. Goodness… he smelled so good.

"And you smell good too."

I giggled because I'd just thought the same thing about him. When he unwrapped his arms from me and stepped back, I felt the loss instantly…However, the look in his eyes as he once again let them roam up my body was making me feel something else entirely.

"What's the name of this style again? Hobo?"

I laughed before swatting his arm. "Boho, jerk!"

Chuckling, he pulled me into his arms again. "Naw, I'm just joking, shawty. You rocking the sh*t out of this look."

Man, y'all, I was cheesing so hard my cheeks hurt. But by the time he stepped back again, I had my face in order.

"Thank you," I told him as I turned to head towards the kitchen, however, I didn't get far before he reached for my hand and followed me. And I'm telling you, I got such a rush at having this big powerful man following me like he just wasn't ready to be away from me just yet.

"Sh*t, girl, you look too good to be going into work. You should play hooky with me so we can go shopping for this joint. Sleeping on the floor got my back hurting."

I looked back at him and laughed, he was so full of crap. "I thought you said you didn't want to go shopping. You said even the thought of it was giving you a headache."

"That was before you walked out here looking like every nigga's fantasy. I need to go with you to make sure nobody try to step to what's mine."

I wore a secret smile as I opened the box labeled herbs. He was jealous. This man who is a hood legend is jealous of other men looking at little old me. That should make me leery, but instead, it made me feel the exact opposite, it made me feel good, wanted, and yes...desired.

I pulled out my jar of chamomile flowers and after opening it, popped a few in my mouth. They worked their magic instantly against my tongue... As a matter of fact, I'm going to blame the zany way they made my mouth feel on the crazy and reckless words that came out of said mouth next.

"You know," I told him as I chewed, "You're only my boyfriend for the next six months...I don't think that qualifies you to be running off any future candidates."

"Future candidates?"

He looked away from me and chuckled, doing that thing with his hand where he brushed his nose as if wiping off dust. Now, I don't know how many of y'all out there has ever been around a thug, but for you who have and understand their mannerisms, you know the move I'm talking about. It's the gesture that lets you know they're getting ready to do something drastic.

I didn't have long to wait, he moved so suddenly he caught me entirely off guard. I squeaked when he suddenly lifted me plopping me down on the counter in front of him. The next thing I know he was spreading my legs with his big body as he came to stand directly in front of me...our faces were only inches apart.

I should be pushing him away. With my legs spread like this, it caused my dress to ride up my thighs exposing my burgundy panties. But instead of pushing him away, my heart was beating fast in excited fear. I knew I shouldn't have said that to him, I don't know why I baited him like that... Hitta didn't really look like the type that could take a joke.

You know what, scratch that, I do know why...It was to see what he was going to do.

"Future candidates you say?" He muttered these words in a way that should have intimidated me. But it didn't because I knew he wouldn't hurt me.

With wide eyes, now clutching my jar of chamomile to my chest, I nodded. Oh my God! Who knew I had this reckless streak in me? I was getting such an adrenaline rush I was practically pulsating with it.

He took the jar out of my hands and set it on the counter before his intense gaze came back to mine.

"I'm gon' let that sh*t slide 'cause you don't know yet." His gaze fell to my lips and I'm telling y'all the energy that was flowing between the two of us was electric.

I licked my shivering lips. "Know what yet?"

He lifted his hand and gently rubbed my cheek. I wasn't even aware of the fact that I was leaning into his touch. God, this man was spinning me in his web and I no longer knew if I wanted out or if I wanted to get wrapped in even deeper.

"You don't know what kind of mutha f**** you dealing with."

And then he was kissing me.

Hitta

Sh*t! She tasted so f***ing good!

Those little flowers she was eating on was the smell I was telling y'all about last night, the smell that was coming out of her skin that made my headache go away. And now I was kissing her and she tasted like them too.

God, she tasted good!

I had to tell myself to go slow. I could tell she was a little afraid, but she was turned on as well. I could smell her arousal. And I'll be damned if the two smells weren't working together to bring out the beast in me.

I wanted to rip this outfit off her and taste her deeper. I wanted to feel her heat surrounding me. She moaned wrapping her arms and legs around me, surrendering to me and I deepened the kiss.

When she'd come down those stairs dressed to kill in this little burgundy demo with these f*** me boots on, I'd had to hug her so that she wouldn't see the instant f***ing erection I got.

This girl was bad! For some reason, she dresses to play down her looks, but I saw her beauty the first time I laid eyes on her. I saw her through all that frumpy sh*t she likes to wear. I don't know what made her decide to go ahead and flex on a brotha, but I'm sure as hell glad she did.

Future f***ing candidates…

This girl don't know that I will crack a mutha f***a's vertebrae if I ever catch them even f***ing looking at her with the thought that they were going to try and step to her like that.

She was f***ing mine!

Now and mutha f***en forever…

I let her tell herself that six-month sh*t because I knew that made her feel comfortable. But the truth was, now that I had my elusive Angel in my grasp, I wasn't ever giving her up…No! Not mutha f***en ever!

———

Angel

When his hungry mouth latched on to my neck, I gasped as a pleasurable spasm shot from that spot to settle in my center that was pulsating with need. He held my waist in his big hands, moving it in a way that caused my soft heat to rub against his length. And it was driving me wild.

The fact that I'd somehow cracked his cool exterior to release a hungry beast was also working me over. It's like I knew he could be rougher with me; he was so big that he could easily rip me in two.

Yet… he was being so tender. How could something so big be so gentle?

His hand rose from my hip to settle on the spot just under my breasts and if it was at all possible, my heartbeat increased with my excitement. I couldn't believe this, but I wanted him to touch me so badly…I wanted to see if it would feel different than when Stan had roughly grabbed me there.

I looked down at his hand, his gaze followed. When our eyes met again mine was full of need.

"What do you want, Angel?"

I opened my mouth to tell him, but then closed it. Could I possibly tell him what I wanted?

He leaned in and kissed my lips again. Like before, it was a hungry kiss.

"Tell me, baby, tell me what you want," he whispered against my lips.

"I want you to touch me."

He closed his eyes and groaned. "Where?"

"My breasts…" My words were barely over a whisper, I couldn't believe I was being so bold.

"How would you like me to touch it?"

I looked up at him confused. Was there more than one way to touch a breast? "Is there more than one way?"

He grinned as he went down to one knee in front of me, bringing his face eye level with my breasts.

"Sure there is, Teacup."

In no rush at all, he lifted his finger and gently ran it over my nipple. I inhaled sharply at the sensation such a light touch caused.

"I can touch you with the tip of my finger." He did it again and again…

Each time he did it, it felt like he was striking a spark in me… However, what he did next caused me to gasp. He gently palmed my whole breast in his hand.

"Or I can use my whole hand to touch it…weigh it, marvel at how soft it is."

I was clutching the counter on both sides of me so hard my knuckles were turning white. He was moving my breast in his hand in a way that caused my bra covered flesh to spill out of the deep V of my dress.

"But the way that I want to touch it most is with my mouth."

My eyes widened as my breath became so heavy, I was almost panting. I licked my lips.

"Yo--your mouth?"

"Mmmmhhhhmmm." He nodded as he used the tip of his finger and slowly moved the cloth of my bra to the side until my nipple popped out.

When it did, I held my breath. No man has ever seen my breasts, not even Stan. Of course, he's tried, but I've always managed to fight him off before he got to that point.

"You're so beautiful, Angel...You make me so hungry." He whispered as his head got closer to my flesh.

When his hot mouth closed on the sensitive tip of breast my head fell back to rest against the cabinet as he feasted on me. My eyes drifted closed as strange unrecognizable sounds of pleasure came from between my lips. I didn't recognize the hands that reached up and grasped his head holding it to me as he fed on me.

At some point, he bared my other breast and feasted on that one too. When his hand lowered to my heat, I didn't have it in me to stop him. It felt like my body was on fire and only he could put out the flames.

He used his hands and mouth to work me over up there on that counter. At some point, I was begging him for something, but I didn't know what...

And then it hit me...

Like an explosion, my world shattered. I cried out his name as a feeling like I'd never felt before washed over me, consuming me, making my body feel drawn so tightly it was numb in places. He came to his feet holding me close, kissing me softly as I gently floated back to earth. And I clung to him, needing him just like in the dream...at that moment, he felt like my anchor, just like he had in my dream.

"I need you, Angel."

The pain in his whispered plea was very real, I put my hand on his chest, getting ready to give him whatever he needed, but my phone picked that moment to ring on the counter next to me. I would have ignored it, but it was Jessie's ring tone.

I picked up the phone. "I'm sorry, Hitta, I have to get this…it's my niece."

The muscle ticked in his strong jaw, but he nodded and helped me down off the counter.

"Hey, baby," I said into the receiver praying my voice was not still heavy with passion. I watched as Hitta took several steps away from me while grabbing his erection. I grinned because it looked like he was trying to tame it…or rather get it to behave.

"Where was you at? I was trying to call you at the shop."

I looked at the time on my phone, 12:30, she should still be in school. "Why aren't you in school?"

"My mama didn't never come home last night." I rolled my eyes.

Unfortunately, this news did not surprise me. Trina was legendary at pulling disappearing acts.

"Who's there with you?"

"Peaches…"

I rolled my eyes again. Peaches was Trina's little sister. Although she wasn't on hard drugs like Trina, she was well on her way. Every time I saw her, she was high on weed or drunk out of her mind. Plus, she had a horrible reputation with the fellas, her bedroom door was a revolving one and everybody knew it.

"Did you eat today?"

"Nah uh…and I'm hungry."

This sh*t really pissed me off! "Put Peaches on the phone!"

"Okay, hold on…" I could hear her beads bouncing around as she ran to take the phone to Peaches…

"Peaches…My Tee-Tee want to talk to you!" she yelled, banging on a door.

It's a damn shame, Peaches was her auntie too, but she didn't even see her that way. The phone was snatched from my baby.

"Angel, don't start this sh*t! Like I have told you a hundred times, this is not my kid! I got sh*t to do! And this lil mutha f***a finna be left here 'cause Trina dumb a** should have been back by now. That b**** told me she was going to the sto' yesterday! The ho' never came back! Like I said, this is not my mutha f***en child!"

Then she threw the phone on the ground, I had to take the receiver away from my ear when she did it.

"Tee-Tee..." Jessie said picking up the phone.

"Where did Peaches go?" I asked angry enough to shoot somebody.

How in the world could she sit her trifling butt up there and not feed a six-year-old child? Over the years, I have had to beg and even pay her to feed Jessie when Trina was too high to do it or was just not there. I have also had to beg and pay her to take Jessie to school as well.

"She went back in her room with her boyfriend."

Boyfriend my a**!

"Okay baby, what exactly do you have in your fridge—"

"F*** it...Let's go and scoop her up. We'll take her to get something to eat. She can help us shop for furniture," Hitta said grabbing his keys off the counter.

"Really?!" I asked him, breathing a sigh of relief.

I was just thinking about the bus and train ride to the southside and how I was going to do it to feed my baby but wasn't looking forward to the long trip.

He pulled me to him with one arm and leaned down and kissed my lips. When he lifted his head, the look in his eyes made me feel that everything was going to be okay.

"Yeah, Teacup. Tell lil mama we on our way to scoop her up."

"Jessie...do Tee-Tee a favor and get dressed. Make sure you have your hat, scarf, and gloves. I'm on my way to get you."

I had to take the phone away from my ear when she screamed, YESSSSS!!!

Chapter Seven

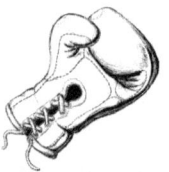

ALLOW ME TO INTRODUCE MYSELF...

> *I'm a Kind Person, I'm Kind to Everyone, but if You Are Unkind to Me, Then Kindness is Not What You'll Remember Me For...*

Al Capone

Angel

Jessie must have been watching for us because as soon as the truck came to a stop outside of her apartment, she came bustling through the door.

I smiled. My baby was so precious; I don't know why her parents couldn't see that. The little hat that I bought her sat lopsided on her head. It looked as if she'd tried to tie the matching scarf the way that I'd shown her but had only managed to tie it in a knot. She wore one glove and was trying to shove her hand in the second one as she hurried to the truck as if she feared we were going to leave her.

On her back was her overnight bag that I knew was horribly lacking. Every time she came to my house, I had to buy her new underwear and clothing items. I don't know what Trina was doing with all the stuff that I got her.

Two weeks ago, I'd gotten her new gym shoes, but I have yet to see them again. When I asked Jessie where they were, she said her mama put them up somewhere but now she thinks they're lost. Peaches told me Trina was selling the stuff for dope, but I refused to believe that. Even Trina wouldn't stoop that low.

Before Hitta could get the truck in park, my wild child had reached my door and was climbing up it. He made a surprised sound in his throat that made me giggle as I pushed the button to lower the window.

That was Jessie for you. She was my little tomboy. There wasn't a tree she couldn't climb or a fight she felt that she could walk away from. She was only six years old and I'd already been up to her school seven times because she'd beaten up one of the children for making fun of the way Trina sent her to school looking. The only reason the school had not suspended her any of the times is because each time had been a case of one of the other kids trying to bully Jess...

Big mistake...My little wild child doesn't take kindly to bullies. That's one of the things I love about her. She is fearless.

"Jessie, get down so—"

"Man, this a nice car!" she cried interrupting me. "This yo' car, Mr.?"

Hitta chuckled as he killed the engine. "Yep..."

I tried to tell her to get down again because it wasn't safe, this truck sat way up in the air, but I never got a chance.

"Hey, Tee-Tee!" she yelled in true Jessie fashion, just now remembering that she hadn't even spoken to me.

"Hey, baby..."

Leaning on her arms she hiked herself up even higher so that she could kiss my cheek, no doubt she was using her little feet to literally climb up the door.

"Damn!" Hitta hissed from beside me, clearly impressed with Jessie's strength. I shook my head. He would be impressed with her uncivilized behavior, something I have been trying to work on with this child.

"Jessie, get down so that I can open my door."

"Okay…but I got to tell you something real quick."

I already knew what she had to say. The fact that she came to the passenger door rather than trying to get in the back meant her mom was home and had sent her out here to ask me for money, which is why I had Hitta take me to the bank before we came.

"My mama said she need two-hundred and fifty dollars fo' the phone bill, two hundred dollars fo' the lights and a hundred dollars fo' some food."

I felt my face heating up in embarrassment. I really wish Trina wouldn't have sent her out here to ask me for money in front of Hitta.

"Dang it, Jessie, that's five hundred and fifty dollars," I muttered to her, trying to talk low enough so that Hitta couldn't hear me.

Jessie nodded before her excited gaze went back to Hitta. She didn't understand the value of money. She didn't know five-hundred and fifty dollars from fifty cents. She had no idea how outrageous her mama's request was.

"I remember you," she cried pointing to Hitta. I didn't even know how she was holding herself up on the truck with just one hand. The girl was strong.

"You the man that gave me them tickets at the carnival."

Hitta chuckled again before he nodded. "I am."

I turned to look at him just to see what he thought about all that was going on and exhaled when I saw that he was relaxed back in his seat looking fondly at my little wild child, which meant he was not upset that she was climbing his truck like a freaking monkey.

I quickly took the five hundred I'd gotten from the bank out of my purse and handed it to her.

"Tell your mother I only have five hundred. I'll bring the other fifty when I drop you back off Sunday."

Jessie nodded and then I kid y'all not, she turned, still holding on to the truck with one hand, used her feet to shove off the door and leap to the ground, where she quickly ran to the door. Hitta sat up in his seat to watch her go.

"Damn, we need to get her in the gym."

I chuckled as I sat back in my seat. "Please don't encourage her barbaric behavior. I've been trying to teach her to be more ladylike."

He grunted. "To hell with that...that kid's got natural talent. No need to wash it away with all that ladylike trash."

With my mouth opened in shock, I turned to face him in my seat. "What do you mean ladylike trash? I'm ladylike."

What the world? That didn't even make sense to me.

He chuckled as he took my hand and brought it to his lips where he gently kissed the back of it, instantly causing my inside to come alive, remembering the way he'd made my world shatter earlier.

"And baby, that ladylike sh*t looks good on you, but it ain't for everybody. Jessie got a different kind of energy that can only be worked out with physical activity. Trust me, I know the look well."

I exhaled, maybe he was right. She loved to run, climb, jump, climb, fight, climb...oh and did I mention climb?

"So...why do you give her mom money?"

Dang it! I'd hoped he would have done the gentlemanly thing and ignored that, but I should have known not to expect the gentlemanly thing from him.

I sat back in my seat. "Some time Trina need help with her bills. My brother is not able to do it all the time, so I step in and help out when I can."

That was the understatement of the year. My brother doesn't do it any of the time and neither does Trina. I do it so that Jessie will always have a phone to call me, lights to see, and food to eat. If I didn't, my baby would be in a really bad spot. I know what it's like to not have these things and I didn't want Jessie to have to go through that.

Blessedly, Hitta let it drop.

———

Hitta

Let it drop my a**! I know a con when I see one. Baby girl just told

Angel this morning that she was hungry, which meant her mammy wasn't using the money to buy food. And I doubt real seriously her f***ing phone bill is two-hundred and fifty f***ing dollars.

This b**** been running one on Angel. I wanted to ask how long it's been going on, but I can already guess it's been a while because she knew just how much to take out the bank.

Angel couldn't afford this sh*t! This is why her f***ing rent on her store and her apartment was late. This is why the f*** she had to steal money from me...because she had a group of vampires that had attached themselves to her and was draining her for all she was f***ing worth.

Lucky for her, I was in the vampire disposal business. Everybody doesn't have the heart to do what I do. I can assist a mutha f***a to their final rest without blinking an eye or losing a wink of sleep. In fact, I slept better knowing I've rid the world of another parasite, especially when one of them mutha f***as has attached themselves to one of mine.

I waited till baby girl came running out the building and got out to help her in.

"Go ahead and put your seatbelt on for me," I told her before walking to Angel's window. "I'll be right back. I know somebody that's looking for a secretary. I'm going to see if baby girl's mom is interested in the position."

The fact that I was lying to Angel to spare her feelings was foreign to me. I never did that. I said what needed to be said and I could give a f*** whose feelings got hurt, but the thing is...

She had a purity about her that I didn't want to dirty up with my reality. I could see in her face that she actually thought this trick was taking the money she was giving her and spending it on her child. She actually thought she was helping rather than hindering. Angel was one of those Care Bear kind of people that needed to help folks in order to feel whole.

I found myself not wanting to destroy that in her. I didn't want to dirty up the way she saw the world with reality. The reality was that she was feeding money to a mutha f***en lazy a** crackhead, who had no problem taking advantage of Angel's kindness.

Me on the other hand…

Well, I am the kind of mutha f***a that needed to extinguish. And I know that sounds cold, but it's the truth…I feel the most alive when I'm between a thick pair of thighs or when I'm beating a mutha f***a down in the ring.

It is what it is…

She grabbed my hand. "That is perfect! I'm sure Trina would love the job…but—" Her beautiful eyes glanced toward the backseat before she leaned closer to me.

"Be careful," she whispered so that baby girl couldn't hear, "Trina is a bit rough around the edges…and I don't want her to take advantage of your kindness."

I smiled at her naiveté. Bless her little heart. She thought she had to warn me about Trina instead of the other way around. You see what I mean?

She saw the world through a loving lens that I will protect at all costs. There weren't many people left on earth like her and I don't know why she's fallen into my hands of all people, but I know that it was now my job to protect her. I knew that sh*t like I knew how to knock a mutha f***a on his a**.

"What floor does she stay on, sweetheart?"

"The second," she answered, but she still wore that worried look. "You'll be careful, right?"

"Sure, Teacup, I'll be careful…" I assured her, doing my best to keep my expression even.

However, by the time I turned to face the building, my smile was gone…and the rage I felt at this moment had settled on my face.

No way in hell somebody like her should have to deal with the jackals…That's what God put me here to do. Angel didn't belong in this world. This was an evil place…a place too filthy for Angels. But now that she had me, I would do whatever it takes to make sure she keeps her wings…even if that meant burying every mutha f***a that had it in their hearts to hurt her.

In baby girl's excitement, she'd left her front door ajar. When I opened it to walk in, I was hit with a foul smell. The apartment was filthy. Stepping over old food containers and dirty clothes, I made my way down the hallway. The first bedroom I came to I was amazed to see the door wide open and some bustdown was on her knees giving a nigga brain right in the f***ing open.

Baby girl had just left, had she seen this sh*t?

Because neither of them noticed me standing there, I took the time to take in the room. Whereas the rest of the apartment was trashed, this room was surprisingly very clean. There was even a lingering scent of Pine-Sol in the air as if the floors had not too long ago been mopped.

The man's eyes fluttered open. When he saw me standing there frowning down at him, he nearly jumped out of his skin.

"Oh sh*t! That's a big mutha f***a!" he squeaked like a f***ing female.

The bustdown jumped to her feet wiping her mouth as her eyes took me in. Her greedy gaze went from my shoes to my watch, my chest, and then finally settled on my face with an inviting smile. She wasn't a bad looking girl, just looked like she was doing some hard living.

"Do I know you?" she asked as she strutted my way, licking her nasty lips.

I lifted an eyebrow. "You Trina?"

"For you baby, I can be…"

The poor buster on the couch held up his hands… "Peaches?! What the f***?! You can't blow us both at the same time."

I shook my head…This sh*t was pathetic.

She turned and rolled her eyes at him before turning back to me her smile back in place, but I was already headed the other way. I'd heard enough…She wasn't Trina.

My steps slowed in front of a closed door that had to be the one I was looking for. I could hear voices coming from the other side.

"Damn, she just give you cash like that?"

A female laughed. "Yep, her goofy a** drop that dough every week. She think she be feeding that lil mutha f***a. I told you, Jessie a** a goldmine. I ain't got to do sh*t but call Angel and tell her Jessie need this or Jessie need that…and her dumb a**get on the bus and come running every time. Sh*t, she even clean my damn house when she drop her off on Sundays!"

I balled up my fist and hit the door so hard that mutha f***a flew off the hinges. "All that sh*t done with!" I growled, squeezing my fists tighter so that I didn't knock the b**** out.

An older more broke down version of Peaches and an even more broke down nigga was laid out on the bed with a base kit between them. She jumped up but wisely didn't take a step toward me. She was smart because although I've never hit a woman, I would not see a problem in choking the sh*t out of this one.

"What the f*** is wrong with you, knocking down my mutha f***en door like that?!" She yelled pointing her crusty a** finger at me.

I looked around this room, not only was it filthy, it stank so badly it caused the frown to grow on my face.

"How the f*** you living like this with a six-year-old kid?"

"That ain't none of yo' mutha f***en business! You need to get the f*** out—" The guy grabbed her arm as his eyes widened in recognition.

"Yo, you Hard Hitta!"

"I know who the f*** I am, nigga," I growled at him, begging him to give me an excuse to knock him on his a**. I won't hit a woman, but I will mop the floor with this mutha f***a.

He held up his hands. "Naw, man, I don't want no trouble with you." He chuckled, "I ain't got a death wish. Plus, you my favorite boxer of all time. I won three hundred dollars on that fight between you and Panko. I bet that you would knock his a** out within the first twenty seconds of the first round. And that just what you di--"

"Shut yo' ho' a** up!" Trina snapped, glaring down at him before her gaze came back to mine. "I don't give a f*** who he is—"

I frowned. Her voice was giving me a headache. "Shut that b**** up."

My mans didn't hesitate. "Yeah...Shut up, b****!" And for good measure, he grabbed her arm and yanked her down on the bed next to him.

She went ham on him, screeching and swinging like crazy, but he muffed her up and kept her a** occupied as I headed for the purse I spotted on the dresser. I couldn't help but chuckle at the sight they made fighting each other on the bed.

F***ing crackheads…

I was relieved to see that Angel's money was right on top, who knows what all the hell could be found in this purse? I grabbed it out and counted it, all five hundred were there.

"Put my money down—" she began, but that pissed me the f*** off.

I whipped around. "This ain't yo f***ing money, ho'! Yo' days of leeching off Angel over."

She snatched away from ol' boy and came back to her feet. "And who the f*** are you? You must be trying to squeeze yo' way through that b**** stiff a** thighs. Good luck with that, she ain't f***ing. The b**** probably gay!"

She was on a roll now. She was so mad that I had this money in my hand that I think she might try and take it away from me. I wish she would come within my grasp so I could snap her f***ing neck.

"I got news for you," she continued as spittle formed around her mouth, "If anything happen to Jessie, yo' ho' gon' be broke the f*** up and good luck getting close to her then. So, I suggest you leave my money where you found it."

I clenched down on my teeth. "Is that a threat?"

Standing there I realized that like Angel, I viewed baby girl as one of my own. And if this b**** was standing here threatening to hurt her, her f***ing breaths were numbered.

"Nigga, that is a mutha f***ing promise! You got me f***ed up! I'll rob yo' b****! I'm gon' get mine one way or the other…even if I got to put that lil ho' Jessie on the stroll. You should have asked somebody about me…Trina gon' get hers!"

One of the things I've learned over my lifespan is that there are some people in this world that are cancers. They're evil and rotten down to the core and everybody that they touch, they start to slowly kill. You can't reason with a cancer; you can't ask it to kindly go away…

Naw…

You see a cancer has to be physically removed…It's the only way.

Angel had been saving baby girl by paying this trick. Trina wasn't lying, she would do whatever it is she needed to do to get her fix, including selling Jessie to the highest bidder. So, like any cancer, she needed to be removed.

I slowly approached her, wisely, she retreated and slid back across the bed with ol' boy.

I lifted one side of my mouth in a grin. "Naw, shorty…you should have asked somebody about me."

She put her hand on her skinny a** hip. "Is that a threat?!"

I shook my head. "Naw…that's a mutha f***en promise." And then I turned, stepped over the busted door and left out of the stinking a** room.

"B****, you dumb! Do you know who and the f*** that is?" I heard ol' boy say as I exited the apartment.

I took my phone out of my pocket and pressed nine.

"Aye, boss?" Maddox answered with his heavy Scottish accent.

Let me pause for a moment and tell y'all a little bit about Maddox. The night I won the WBC title, I'd been approached by this janky a** promoter who tried to pay me to throw the fight. I sent his a** packing out of that training room with a busted eye and a fat lip.

Not only did I not throw the fight that night, I became the holder of my first belt. Needless to say, that pissed a few people off, who lost a lot of money. After celebrating my victory at Exquisite, I and some random chick went back to my place to find Maddox there waiting for me.

When I turned on the light, he was sitting on my couch with his feet propped up on the table. I don't go anywhere without heat. I had my Ruger pulled and aimed at his head before he could even blink. He'd held up his hands and told me he'd not come to kill me.

"What the hell did you come for?" I growled, trying to sober up. I'd drank way too much and was now seeing two of the mutha f***as.

He chuckled. "Well technically, I did come to kill you, but I've decided not to."

Right off I could tell that he wasn't from around these parts, but at the time, I was too drunk to peg the accent.

"Yeah and I'm sure the barrel of my Ruger didn't help you come to that decision."

"Actually, the barrel of your Ruger did not help me come to that decision, especially when the barrel of my brother's Desert Eagle is pointed at your head even as we speak, since we've gotten into the gun naming business."

Right then, a shadow moved from my right, I turned my head and I'd be damn if there really weren't two of them. They were identical, so much so they could be the same man. They even dressed in similar suits. The only separation being was that the suit of the brother on the couch was a bluish grey and the suit of the brother pointing the gun at me was just grey.

"Allow me to introduce you to my twin brother, Lannox. Due to the actions of a very evil man that is no longer with us, Lan cannot talk."

As he said that, a scar going across Lannox's neck drew my attention. Someone had slit his throat.

"But he and I complement each other quite well. Where he is weak, I am strong and where I am weak, he is strong," Maddox continued.

As he spoke, his accent got thicker. I returned my gun to its back holster.

"I'm listening." What other choice did I have…?

"While your female companion is quite comely, I'm going to ask if she wouldn't mind coming back later. The information that I have to share with you is of a sensitive nature. You understand, right?"

As I gestured for said female to leave, I frowned at the guy on the couch. I don't know if it was because I was drunk off my a** or what, but hearing a black man speak the way that he did was tripping me the f*** out.

When she was gone, I sat down in a chair where I could keep an eye on both of the brothers. By that point, our mute friend, Lan had put his gun away and was just standing there watching me as closely as I was watching him.

"Who the f*** sent you here to kill me?" That was the first thing I wanted to know.

I wasn't surprised when he told me that it was the promoter who had come to see me earlier that day.

"Apparently, you lost our old boss and a few of his friends a lot of money and they weren't happy with that."

My frown grew at his words. "Why old boss?"

"Tell me…Do you believe in the supernatural, Mr. Taylor?"

I shrugged. At that point, my life had been so f***ed up… why the hell not?

"When we were two years old, our mum left us on the porch of the local rectory. They brought us in and took care of us for the next five years, but then kicked us out because the priest said that Lannox was possessed by the devil."

My gaze went to Lannox, he smiled at me and I'm not going to lie, the smile was a little creepy. There was something about his eyes…it's like they could see more than what eyes should be able to see.

"Father Eugene would hide food from us for punishment, but Lan would always know where to find it…no matter where he hid it."

As Maddox divulged this information to me, he watched me closely to see how I was taking it all in. If he was trying to shock me, he was sh*t out of luck. Growing up in the gutter created calluses over the shock effect.

"You see, Mr. Taylor, there is a voice inside of Lan's head that tells him things. Always has…Sometimes I can hear it too, but only because Lan and I share a special connection…well with being twins and all."

I nodded…I had heard of that, twins hearing each other's thoughts and whatnot.

"After the horrifically tragic death of Father Eugene, they kicked us out, and we became street urchins at the wee age of seven. A few years ago, the voice in Lan's head guided us here to America, where we've been ever since."

"Where y'all from originally?"

He chuckled. "As to our origins, like yirself, we dinnae know. Our best guess would be somewhere in northeast Africa. But as far as where we were born...Scotland."

I nodded...that made sense. It would explain their fondness for the European cut suits and the accent. In a way, Maddox had reminded me of Rome that evening, except whereas Rome didn't look as smart as he was...Maddox did.

"Alright, so, why have you decided not to kill me."

"Well, because Lan here says that working for you is our destiny."

One of my eyebrows lifted. "Excuse me?"

He chuckled. "The voice told Lan not to kill you because you are our master, we are to serve and obey you...as well as guard your back."

What-thee-hell?

I rubbed my hand down my face. This is why I didn't like getting drunk. It was always when I was drunk that wild sh*t like this happened. This man was talking about masters and serving and sh*t... What the hell...

"Look bo... I appreciate you not killing me and all, but that other sh*t you talking is f***ing nuts."

"I assure you, my words are anything but. If the voice in Lan's head said it is so...then it is so."

"Okay, ...let's just say I'm buying this sh*t. What the f*** do you and your brother do? Why the f*** would I need you to come and work for me?"

He smiled and for the first time, he came across as a little creepy too. "My brother and I are killers."

"What?! And why the f*** would I need killers working for me?"

He didn't speak at first. His gaze went to his brother and he just stared at him, every now and again nodding his head.

What the f***! At that point, they had started creepy me out really good.

"Lan says your destiny is still unknown to you. And that one day, you will need us to guard your back. We are very good at our jobs, Mr. Hitta...Lan and I were born to do this."

"Yeah...and why should I trust you?"

"What can we do to prove our loyalty to you...boss?"

"Ghost the mutha f***as that sent you here to kill me."

The next day, eight of the most powerful men in the boxing world were found with their throats slit in their beds...and Maddox and his twin brother, Lannox officially became members of my team.

That was ten years ago.

In that time, a few things have changed. The twins, which is what we called them around the gym, had been in the hood long enough to have changed the way they dressed. They no longer favor European cut suits and now wore American cut. And Maddox's prominent Scottish accent was now mixed with a healthy bit of hood slang.

However, a few things have not changed, their loyalty to me, the voice inside of Lannox's head, and their almost supernatural ability to make bodies disappear and become Jane and John Does.

"I just met a Jane Doe..." I told him as I headed for my truck.

Angel and Jessie both studied me as I approached to try and gage from my expression how my talk went with Trina. I smiled at them and Angel visibly relaxed.

"First name Trina, I don't know the last name...but I will send you an address."

"How soon?"

"Before Sunday."

"Consider it don."

I hung up the phone and slide it into my pocket as I opened the door and got in.

"How did it go?" Angel asked a look of apprehension in her beautiful eyes.

Damn, I hated to see that sh*t. Somebody with a heart like hers should never have to look that way. I put my hand behind her neck and pulled her to me for a kiss just because I needed to taste her again. And just like I figured, she'd been nibbling on those little flowers and her taste gave me instant relief.

"Ohhhh! Y'all kissing..." Jessie said propping her little face on the seat between us, bringing our kiss to an end. Both of us looked back at her and chuckled.

"Sit back and put your seatbelt on, lil mama," I told her, taking in the both of them. They were now mine... mine to take care of and protect.

My gaze went back to Angel...she was still waiting on an answer to her question.

"It went really good..." I handed her money back, and her startled eyes came up to mine. I shrugged nonchalantly. "Trina was so siked about the job, she told me to give that back to you, said she won't be needing it now."

Chapter Eight

THE ART OF SEDUCTION

> *The Smell of Her Hair, the Taste of Her Mouth, the feeling of Her Skin, Seemed to Have Got Inside Him, or into the Air All Around Him, She Had Become A Physical Necessity...*
>
> George Orwell

Angel

I clutched the sink as my shaking knees threatened to give out on me. Staring in the bathroom mirror, a brand-new woman looked back at me.

An awakened woman looked back at me...

Oh my God! Nobody ever told me it would be this way...

My flesh was still tender from his mouth and beard. I could still feel his strong hands on my body...

Still feel his hardness stretching me...

Still hear the sound of his deep voice when he whispered that I was a big girl and that I could take all of him…

Oh God!

What had Hitta done to me? I will never be the same… NEVER!

I turned the cold water on with shaking fingers and drenched my towel before wringing it out. As I lifted it and laid the cool cloth against my overheated skin, I realized that my whole body was still pulsating from his touch.

What we'd just done was not supposed to have happened…At least not yet.

Okay, so…

Do you guys remember when I said that I will last this whole six months without sleeping with Hitta because he was a brute and he wasn't my type and all that other nonsense I was spewing?

Well, let me tell you something…

There is a thin line between intention and reality. But for the record, nobody ever prepared me for this kind of man. Through my limited experience with the male species, I thought I had it all figured out. My brother, although I loved him dearly, has of late come across as kind of weak to me. For the last six years, he's depended on me to either find a way or make a way.

And I know that modern day society teaches me that that's a good thing. The fact is, it comes across as weak and if I'm being honest with myself, it's hard to respect that.

And then there is Stan…

He needed to prey on a small child in order to feel like a man… and yeah, to me, that is weakness. So, technically, I've only been around weak men.

How was I to know that all men were not made that way and that there were some men out here who were…

Heck…

Manly?!

And how was I supposed to know the effects a manly man can have on a woman's libido?

How was I supposed to know the way a manly man can make a

woman's body sing? He's this strong, fierce being that is capable of crushing, destroying, pulverizing, yet…

When he touches me, he's so gentle at times and aggressive at other times, creating a pleasurable orchestra and my whole body is his instruments… My lips, neck, breasts…

Mmmmmmm…my center.

And somehow, he managed to strum my instruments until he caused a little death to occur inside of me, only to then revive and re-stimulate to make me feel so… alive!

Now don't get me wrong, there is a part of me that knows Hitta is dangerous and a killer…because yeah, the streets talk. But there is a part of me that doesn't want to believe that because yeah, he can make my body sang!

Closing my eyes, I rubbed my hand up my neck as I remembered the feel of him holding my body close as he drove in and out of me…I begged him to stop and to keep going. I told him I felt like I was falling, only to cling to him and continue to ride the wave…

Oh God! I was lost…

I had seen a little bit of what he was capable of on the kitchen counter this morning, but it was only the tip of the iceberg of this man's ability to seduce. And let me tell you something else, I just learned a very important lesson…A brute in the bedroom was a very dangerous thing.

And now that I am looking back, I can see how he was never worried that I would be able to resist him. He knew that I'd judged him to be a brute and would not be expecting him to turn out to be a dirty talking, sensual touching, master of seduction.

Yeah…I hear what y'all thinking; dirty talking, sensual touching, Master of Seduction? Really…Angel? The man is a brute, he can't just turn that crap off and turn on Don Juan.

And I'm here to tell you….Yeeeesssss, he can! And he did…

It was because I'd prejudged him that I was completely unprepared for his seduction. Not only did he flawlessly take my virginity tonight…somehow, he'd managed to get me to beg him to do it.

Go ahead, shake your heads at me. I know I'd said I would hold out for six months only for my wanton self to turn right back around and give in the next day.

THE NEXT DAY!!!!

I should be ashamed of myself. I really should, but ya'll…

I just wasn't…

In fact, I felt the exact opposite, I felt…free. Hitta's lovemaking freed me from a prison I'd been in for years. A prison where I'd feared an act so beautiful because I'd been touched by a monster. A prison where I could only imagine what was possible but never consider experiencing it for myself.

Not anymore! Hitta's lovemaking was…

Well… it was good.

I mean….Reeeaaallly good!

Calm down, y'all…calm down. I'm not going to leave y'all in the dark. Of course, I'm going to tell you how it all went down…Just let me try and bring my body temperature back to normal with this here cool towel.

My goodness, that man unraveled me tonight. Apparently, the right brotha can bring the sex kitten out of the most uptight shrew. Just thinking about what we'd just done caused a shiver that took my breath to shoot through my body…

My goodness…

You see, his seduction didn't begin in the bedroom. It started this morning on the counter and continued throughout the day…

He was so very clever…so very clever indeed. Alright, y'all, let me tell ya'll how he trampled down my metal walls.

True to his word, he asked Jessie what she had a taste for. Of course, she wanted pizza, which is her favorite thing in the whole world to eat. He took us to this really nice Italian restaurant downtown. The owner came out to personally take our order because Hitta was his favorite boxer.

In fact, several customers approached us and asked for his autograph and if they could take a picture with him. I would soon find out that this was a norm for him because he was a big deal in Chicago.

Anyway, after all the fan fair had died down, Jessie wanted to know if she could have a cannoli.

"No Jess, you haven't even eaten yet. Maybe after you eat a few slices of pizza," I told her.

Now, do you guys remember me telling you that Jessie sometimes has a tendency to act out? Well, she was getting herself prepped for a monster performance.

"Why, Tee-Tee? I'm gon' still eat my pizza!" she whined.

Because I knew the signs and didn't want to be embarrassed in front of Hitta and the rest of the people that ate in that really nice establishment, I exhaled preparing myself to just give her what she wanted. Some battles just weren't worth fighting.

But before I could tell her yes, Hitta's deep voice cut across the table.

"Hey!"

Both Jessie's and my gaze flew to his. He snapped out that word like a drill sergeant.

"What did your tee-tee say?"

Her little eyes rounded in awareness as her hissy fit face evaporated like morning dew when touched by the sun.

"Answer me, Jessica."

"She said to get a cannoli after I eat my pizza."

He nodded. "So, when are you gon to get the cannoli?"

Her eyes still rounded in awareness, she swallowed. "After I eat my pizza?"

He smiled. "Good girl…"

And amazingly she returned his smile before she settled right on down and began to color the picture the chef had given her.

My stunned gaze rose to his… with the grin still on his handsome face, he winked at me…

Well…

Well…

I began to fan myself with my menu…I'll be doggone if that wasn't hot as heck.

Anyway, so that was the restaurant. Seeing him establish authority so quickly with Jessie, who was a wild child with everyone else did something to me. Now add that to the kitchen counter incident…

I want y'all to keep up with everything I'm telling you so that you too can see why my walls so easily crumbled. I'm not an easy girl, in fact, up until a few minutes ago, I was the oldest virgin I knew. But Hitta—

Mmm mmm mmm…Hitta!

Okay, Moving on…

After we left the restaurant, we headed to the furniture store. We had a lot of furniture to shop for; Hitta said we might as well take care of everything in one pop. I wasn't surprised that the sales rep who helped us turned out to be a big fan of Hitta's and neither was I surprised when a few more people came up to him and asked for autographs and that if he wouldn't mind posing for pics with them.

What did surprise me was when Jessie spotted a princess bed and asked him if he would get it for her and he said yes.

"You're probably going to need to get the whole bedroom set."

Jessie was jumping up and down with excitement, but my confused gaze connected with his over her head.

"She stays with you every weekend, right?"

I nodded…

"I figured she could have one of the bedrooms."

"I'm going to get my own room?!" Jessie screamed at the top of her lungs.

Embarrassed down to the tip of my hair follicles, I put my hand over her mouth and apologized to the other customers that were now staring at us as if we were some crazy folks.

"You're giving Jessie her own room?"

He chuckled. "Why not? We can't use them all."

"Yeaahhhhh!" Jessie muffled scream came from under my hand.

"Really?" I asked close to tears.

Jessie has never had her own room, she slept on that nasty couch in her mother's apartment that I did my best to clean when I dropped her off every Sunday. I always told her that as soon as I bought a house, she would have her room. Every time she came over, she asked me when I was going to get the house so that she could come and live with me.

He wrapped his hand around my waist and pulled me to him, then he leaned down and kissed me right there in the center of the furniture store. And y'all, I'm not talking about a little peck on the lips, the man kissed me in a way that made me feel as if he was going to consume me whole. And that wasn't the first time he did it either... My lips were deliciously sore from all the activity they'd experienced today.

Needless to say...those panty melting kisses served as another form of seduction, so please document that as well.

————

Hitta

I'd like to interject at this point and say...I'd become addicted to the taste of her mouth after she nibbled on one of those little flowers. She had a sandwich baggy full of them in her purse. She smelled and tasted so f***ing good that I felt like a feen that needed a fix every few minutes.

I had to stop myself from trying to eat her f***ing mouth. It wasn't time to introduce her to that side of me... She was still very new.

But it won't be long...It won't be long till she's used to my touch and can handle my aggressive appetite. Sh*t it won't be long till she comes to anticipate my touch.

Not long at all...

Okay, I'll give y'all back to Angel...

————

Angel

Now true to his word, Hitta was no help in the furniture store. Everything I pointed at he grumbled a nice or nodded his head, even when I pointed at the ugly stuff.

"Do you really not see a design in your mind for how you want your house to look?" I asked at some point getting frustrated.

He came behind me and after wrapping his arms around my waist began to nuzzle at my neck and ear, tickling me with his beard.

"Stop!" I laughed trying to escape him.

"Not till you say it's our house…" He grumbled in my ear continuing to nuzzle me, now using his teeth.

I laughed trying to get away from his ticklish beard until tears came to my eyes.

"Okay!" I cried… "Our house!"

He turned me in his arms to face him. "Man, shawty, I promise I don't have no designs in my head. When I look at this sh*t, all I see is chairs for sitting, couches for relaxing…beds for--"

His words stalled as his gaze shot down to Jessie, who ever since he'd told her that she could have her own room, has been looking at him like he'd hung the stars.

He leaned in and then whispered his nasty words in my ear. His words were so freaking nasty they caused my core to clench in response. In fact, by the time he finished telling me what he thought the bed was for, I found myself clutching the front of his t-shirt in my fist…

And it didn't help that as he whispered in my ear, his lips brushed against it, I even felt his tongue.

Goodness…

So, okay, I and Jessie picked out the furniture. The salesmen said he could get all the stuff delivered in about three days. Of course, Hitta told him that wasn't going to work because we needed the furniture tonight.

Can you guys guess when we got the furniture?

Yep, by the time we left that store, the salesman was calling in a team of workers to load our furniture on trucks that the store rented in order to fill our order. I'd told Hitta that for a minute I was worried that we'd have to sleep on the floor till Monday, then I'd asked him if he was worried.

At the time, he was responding to a text that he had gotten, so he didn't think about his answer before he spoke.

"Naw…we could have done it one of two ways, civilized or uncivilized…either way, they're going to deliver this sh*t today."

He said that so matter of fact that all I could do was stare at him for a moment. What did he mean uncivilized? Would he have threatened the poor man if he'd insisted on the fact that they couldn't deliver the furniture today?

I chuckled to myself to cover up the uncomfortable feeling that came over me…

Nah, he wouldn't do that. It's true, Hitta was a bit of a brute, but he wasn't that bad. I'd prejudged him before and he'd done nothing but show me how wrong I'd been. So, I wasn't going to go back and start looking at him that way again.

He probably just meant that he would complain to the manager.

And I was probably being the world's biggest fool for allowing how good the man made me to feel to blind me to his true self.

But hey, I was in a place I'd never been before, I was with a man that actually wowed me and caused me to want to be his fool.

On a side note though…I wouldn't have survived the things that I had without the warning voice that's always in my head. And although I was experiencing all of these firsts, that voice in my head was not quiet. In fact, it was ringing like an alarm.

You see, it told me to back out now before I got too far gone and would be willing to look past all his faults just to be with him. That voice warned that I didn't have enough experience to stay immune to a man with so much experience. It warned that he was a predator and I was his prey and that if I wasn't careful, he would consume me whole until there was nothing left to salvage.

But then my vanity kicked in and I thought, how bad could it get?

I was too smart to truly become a man's fool…it didn't matter how nice he was to me. Now granted I had that thought before the man actually made love to me and now…

Well…now I didn't know. Now I feared that I was truly lost and on my way down a road that will surely end with me broken and in tears.

However, I am getting far ahead of myself…Let me bring it back to how he trampled down my walls…

Where was I? Oh yes, we left the furniture store…

"Oh, my goodness…We're going to be busy all night trying to put this stuff together and situate it," I told him when we got in his truck.

"Bullsh*t, we're going to the movies and then to dinner."

And of course, Jessie was in the back seat celebrating that news with a little song and dance.

"What?" I asked him with a grin on my face. "Who's going to set up all that furniture?"

"My personal assistant will make sure it gets done."

"You have a personal assistant?"

He looked at me as if that was just the dumbest question in the world. "Of course, Teacup."

Well dang…

So that's how we ended up downtown at the movie theater that us Chicagoans called the Luxury cinema. It was called that because it cost about triple of what a normal theater cost, the seats were big, plush recliners…and they served alcoholic beverages.

But what I didn't know was that for those who could afford it, they had smaller theaters for private viewings. We were shown to a room that only had six of the plush recliners in it. The room was separated into two floors. On the main floor were three of the recliners and in something that resembled a theatre box at the opera were three more of the recliners. The raised box would allow a certain level of privacy for its occupants.

It was in this box that I would learn just how truly freaky Hitta was capable of being.

Oh y'all, I feel so scandalous. The things I let that man do to me in that movie were just…

Goodness, it was just too wanton!

I should have known something was up when he let Jessie pick the movie. Of course, she wanted to see the new cartoon with the black Mermaid. I think it was still called The Little Mermaid. He bought her a huge bucket of popcorn, a fountain drink that was bigger than the upper half of her body. A pack of M&M's… And then got her settled down in the seats on the first level.

In the box, a stand had been set up with a wine bucket that had a bottle of Dom Perignon chilling on a bed of ice. Next to it was two champagne flutes and a bowl of sugar frosted strawberries that looked simply delicious.

A waiter poured us both a glass of champagne and handed it to us when we sat.

"Will there be anything else, sir?" he asked Hitta, who was responding to another text.

"Naw...that's it." He reached in his pocket and pulled out two hundred-dollar bills and handed it to the man. "Make sure we're undisturbed."

The man perked up instantly. "Oh hell yea--" He caught himself and cleared his throat. "Yes sir! I will personally make sure of it."

Hitta chuckled. "Preciate that..." And then he went back to his text.

That man's phone never stopped dinging and ringing. Most of the time, he looked at the number and just ignored whoever it was. But then there were times when he'd excuse himself to speak with whoever it was. One thing was clear, he was a very busy man and although he'd played hooky with me today, his business had not.

I sipped my champagne to hide how impressed I was with this whole set up, Dom Perignon, frosted strawberries, Jessie downstairs and a good distance away...a private theater.

Hmmm, the possibilities.

As soon as the lights dimmed, Hitta turned off his phone and settled back into his seat.

"I love this movie," he whispered to me and that caused me to spit out a little of my champagne laughing at him, I put my hand over my mouth when an embarrassing snort escaped.

"The Little Mermaid? Really?" My voice was laced with disbelief.

He lifted an eyebrow at me. "Are you kidding me...this my joint."

I shook my head; he was so silly.

"How do you like the champagne?"

"It's really good," I told him before I took another sip. I don't know if it was due to nervousness or what, but I was almost finished with my first glass.

He reached over and poured me another. "I probably should have ordered two bottles; I didn't know I was dealing with an alcoholic."

My mouth opened in surprise, but a giggle escaped my throat when he grinned at me.

"I am not an alcoholic!" And right then as if cued, I hiccupped. "Uh oh…" I put my hand over my mouth but ended up erupting in another fit of giggles when he gave me that told-you-so look.

Good thing the movie was loud and Jessie couldn't hear us…Not that it would have mattered. Her seat was so big we couldn't even see the top of her head. The only thing I could see when I looked over the railing of the box was the big bucket of popcorn in her lap and her little hand going in and out of it.

"Thank you, Hitta. This is really nice," I muttered.

He pulled up the arm that separated us before scooting closer to me. My heart accelerated in both fear and excitement when he leaned over me, blocking out the rest of the theater with his big body, making it so that only he existed in my world at that moment.

"What did you say, Teacup? I couldn't hear you."

I bit down on my bottom lip as he slid between my legs on the seat, forcing me to open them in a way that brought him even closer and caused my dress to ride up my thighs in a way that exposed my red panties.

I know I should not allow this…but the rush that was going through me at being exposed to him this way was drugging. I drained my champagne glass and then licked its fruity taste from my lips. His gaze followed and the look of hunger that came into his eyes only stirred up what he'd started this morning.

"I said thank you for this. It's really nice and I'm sure Jessie is having a good time."

He grinned. "What about Jessie's aunt? Is she having a good time?"

"It all depends on if you're talking about the movie or…the company." The champagne had made my tongue a little loose.

He lifted an eyebrow. "I'm talking about the movie of course."

I chuckled and shook my head. "Then no, I'm not enjoying it at all. There is a big black man blocking the screen."

He frowned. "That's racist as hell."

My chuckle turned into a laugh. "How is that racist?"

"Everybody want to blame the black man for everything. It's not my fault you can't see the screen."

"Then whose fault is it?"

"It's yours…"

My mouth opened in feigned shock. "How is it my fault?" He took my empty glass from me and sat it on the stand next to his.

"You're the one sitting here looking good enough to eat and now you're trying to blame a hungry man for going after his food."

"Oh! I'm so sorry. I didn't mean to deny you…food." I frowned a bit, not really knowing what he meant, but tipsy enough to go along with it.

"What are those little flowers that you're always eating?"

Oh…did he mean he wanted some of my chamomile?

"It's chamomile. They don't really taste that good. I don't know why I like them so much…Jessie and Westly make fun of me all the time."

As I spoke, he reached behind me and lifted the arm to the third seat.

"Why do they make fun of you?" he asked as he put his hands around my waist and scooted me up to lie across all three seats. With the arms raised the chairs turned into a really plush sofa.

"Because the flowers are so nasty, but I use them for everything, chamomile oatmeal, tea, cookies…I've even made chamomile muffins," I chuckled. "I've even made chamomile soup."

I was doing this nervous rambling that I'm pretty sure I will be embarrassed as hell about tomorrow, but for right now, I couldn't stop.

"Do you like chamomile?" I asked, biting my lip to try and shut them.

"I like the taste of them on you."

I frowned, completely lost. "What do you mean?"

"When you eat them and I kiss you, the taste is addictive, I can't get enough. I have to tell myself to be easy with your soft mouth because I don't want your lips to be sore."

It was too late for that. He had kissed me so much today that yes, my lips were very sensitive, but in a good way, in a way that made me aware of the effect this man had on my body.

He gently pulled my hips until I was forced to lie back. My heart was beating so fast that I feared it would beat right out of my chest. But when he lifted my boot covered right leg to drape it over the back of the chair, exposing me completely to his hungry gaze, I thought that maybe I would faint.

Although I still wore my panties, no man had ever seen what he was now looking at.

"And now all I can think about is if you taste like those little flowers all over."

Oh my goodness!

His heated gaze came to mine. "Do you?"

"I—I don't know." My words were barely over a whisper. No way he could have heard me over the show.

He moved then and I nearly moaned in anticipation. I'm just going to blame that on the champagne. I wasn't a big drinker...in fact, I couldn't remember the last time I had a drink. And even I knew Dom P was the good stuff.

I've had two glasses of the good stuff, so when he easily positioned himself between my open thighs effortlessly supporting himself on his strong arms, the only thing I could think about was his question and where he could possibly be talking about and how excited that made me... in the words of Jamie Foxx...*Blame it on the alcohol.*

"Can I find out?" he whispered before he leaned down and gently kissed my lips.

You had better not say yes, Angel! Why not? Jessie is sitting in the same room. Yeah, but it's dark...and technically she's downstairs. She would have to walk upstairs and in the box to see us. Plus, it's not like she's going to do that...Jessie has tunnel vision when cartoons are on.

You little floozy!

Prude!

Again, the fact that I had that conversation with myself...Yep! The alcohol.

"What if Jessie comes up here?"

"She won't, she's all up in that movie. Plus, if she moves, I'll be able to see her and I'll stop before she even reach the stairs. Please, Teacup, I've been dying to taste you forever...I'm so hungry for you, shawty. You don't know how long I've waited to be here in this spot."

Oh crap! "Okay..." I squeaked.

And then...

And then...

Mmm mmm mmm....

He wasn't lying about being hungry for me. I felt like a sugary sweet in the hands of a starving barbarian.

When my world shattered, I screamed...He quickly put his big hand over my lips, but he continued to break me down with his mouth. He was relentless...I begged him to stop. I was so sensitive I couldn't take anymore...but he wouldn't. And my world violently shattered a second time...

At that point, there were tears coming out my eyes as I begged him to let my body rest.

"Please, Hitta..." I moaned. "Please, I can't take anymore."

His hungry caress gentled. "I'm sorry, baby...It's just that you taste so f***ing good. You taste just like those flowers... I'm f***ing addicted. I can do this sh*t all night."

His words and his caress that had gentled but had not stopped, had me moaning loudly for him within minutes...Until my world shattered a staggering third time.

"We finish this tonight," he whispered fiercely in my ear. "I need to be inside you so bad, shawty."

And so I found myself sitting at dinner...(no, I couldn't tell you what), counting down the seconds till it was time to finish it.

I was so fidgety in my seat I felt like a small child and Hitta wasn't helping. At one point, I looked up because he asked me if my food was good, but at the time he was licking his fingers in a way that reminded me of the movie theater. I zoned in on the action and completely forgot his question.

"Is it good, Teacup?" He repeated.

"Mmmmmhhhhhmmm," I told him.

It was Jessie's laugh that caused me to snap out of it. I blinked rapidly looking away from him. Dang it! The man had just cast a spell on me. I couldn't even eat dinner without sex on the brain.

By the time we made it back home, neither of us was doing well at hiding our anticipation. I was so relieved to see that all the furniture we had ordered was in fact set-up and placed in the rooms we'd gotten it for. Each room would need just a little tweaking, but not much...

And that's just because I'm a perfectionist and have to see my vision done to a tee.

After such a full day of activities, Jessie was out cold. Hitta carried her in and straight to her bed. I took off her coat and shoes and put the covers over her. Kissing her little head I smiled down at her, so pleased that Hitta was able to make this day happen for her. She'd had a ball and had not stopped talking about having the movie theater and a big bucket of popcorn all to herself.

I'd not stopped thinking about the movie theater either. And as I let myself out of her room pulling the door up, I ran into somebody else who still had the movie theater on his mind.

Hitta was walking out of our bedroom to meet me with nothing on but his sweatpants.

Have mercy on me! This man's body looked as if it had been personally molded by the hand of God.

He took my hand and pulled me into the bedroom. As I stood in front of him, I was finally able to read what the fancy script of his tattoo said.

> Blessed be יהוה my Rock, which teaches my hands to war,
> my fingers to fight: My goodness, and my fortress; my
> high tower, and my deliverer; my shield, and in whom
> I trust; who subdues my enemies under me.
>
> Psalms 144:1-2

A shiver went through me when my gaze went back down to the lion that was ripping his enemy's heart out with its sharp teeth. That's what Hitta put me in the mind of, a man who would tear his enemies' hearts out.

"I can't wait another minute, baby. I feel like I've waited forever to get you in my bed." His words were like a tender caress. And once again, I found myself wondering how could something so fierce be so gentle with me?

I held my hands up as he grabbed my dress from the bottom and pulled it over my head, leaving me standing there in only my red panties, bra, and thigh high boots as he took his time and looked his fill.

"Damn, shawty, you sexy than a mutha f****, way better than I'd imagined," he whispered as he fingered the birthmark on my shoulder. "Is that... Africa?"

I chuckled. "It looks like it, but it's a birthmark."

His bedroom gaze came up to mine and he grinned a bit. "Damn, Teacup, even that sh*t sexy as hell."

I reached up and pulled out the headbands and the clips that held my braids in a messy bun letting them drop to the floor as my hair fell down around my shoulders and back to my waist. All this Hitta watched as if I was putting on a show for him. Only I didn't know what to do next.

He took the decision out of my hands because right then, he wrapped his arms around my waist and pulled me into a kiss. The feel of his warm, hard body pressed against my soft one caused me to moan in his mouth.

In the blink of an eye, I was in his arms and he was carrying me the rest of the way to the bed. I couldn't believe it was happening. I was getting ready to lose my virginity.

I was getting ready to lose my virginity to Hard Hitta.

Gently he laid me on the bed and removed my boots one at a time. "These mutha f****'s been driving me nuts all day," he muttered before he ran his hand up my stocking clad leg.

And of course, I wore a secret smile because this came from the same man that had told me I dressed like a homeless person.

My bra was the kind that clipped in the front, so when he lowered himself over me, supporting his weight on his massive arms, I thought for sure he was going to have a problem opening it with his big hand.

My surprised gaze flew up to his when not only did he not have a problem, but had it unclipped and my breasts spilling out in record time.

He grinned, for the first time looking bashful. "Wasn't my first time."

I went to respond, but never got the chance because his head had lowered, and he was drawing the tip of my breast into his hungry mouth. I think it's safe to say that Hitta is a breast man. Just like my lips, my nipples have been deliciously sore all day. As a matter of fact, my whole body was still so very sensitive that it didn't take him any time to cause it to shatter.

However, when he finally took off his pants, real fear set in. I grabbed his hands letting him see my fear.

"I've never done this before," I squeaked sounding like an aroused mouse.

He gently stroked my cheek as he positioned himself over me. "I know, Teacup."

"I'm scared...wh—what if it doesn't fit? What if I can't take it all?"

Still rubbing my cheek looking lovingly in my eyes he smiled just a little. "Do you know how much I've dreamed of this? I used to sit in my truck and imagine what you'd look like open and ready for me."

He leaned down and kissed me under my ear as he continued to whisper to me. "You are a big girl Teacup, and you can take all of me, baby...I promise."

And then he was slowly filling me...

And yeah...although I thought it was impossible...

I took all of him...Even when just for a moment, it did feel as if he had split me in two. However, in that moment, there was such tenderness in his eyes.

He gently palmed my face. "I'm so sorry, baby...I promise, that's all the pain."

"I'm scared, Hitta, it hurts..." I whispered clutching his hands.

Holding very still, he kissed my lips as I got accustomed to him.

"I know, baby, but that's all the pain. Only pleasure from here..." Very slowly he began to move again. "Let me show you...Only pleasure from here."

And show me he did...

True to his word, there was no more pain, only pleasure...

Chapter Nine

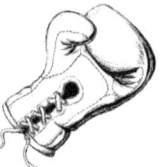

NOTHING LIKE THE TASTE OF CHAMOMILE IN THE MORNING...

Angel

I squatted down in the abandoned car where Hitta had told me to wait, but I wasn't alone. There was a small group of us waiting for him to give us the signal that it was safe to come out of the rust-eaten cars that the sun flare had shorted out and destroyed years ago along with every other thing on this planet that was electrical.

Hitta stood in the center of the street with several of his men. My gaze fell on one of them. He was a much younger version of Hitta, he had to be no more than fifteen or sixteen. However, he was a direct replica of him from the fierce scowl on his face to the huge hands. Amazingly he was nearly as wide and as tall as his father, but he had my eyes. I was so afraid for them both.

They were surrounded by the zombies. At least...what looked like zombies but was really blood feens. Blood, the synthetic drug that hit the streets shortly before the flare hit. They called it that because it came in little brown glass canisters that could only hold a few drops, but when poured out, resembled its namesake.

Before the flare hit, it was all the rage. Everybody was doing it...

kids, adults…movie stars, doctors…judges. It was popular because it was marketed as a safe, clean drug. Unlike other drugs, it didn't make one high. Instead, it sharpened the mind, made the dumb smart, the slow…fast, the weak…strong.

Because they said that it wasn't addictive, they sold the stuff everywhere…but I never trusted it and good thing too because now, something was happening to all of those people, who had come to rely on it. Because it had become very limited over the last ten years since the flare hit, the sore-riddled feens had started craving real blood in its place and they terrorized the streets for it.

They were the reason Hitta was now leading this group out of Chicago that had become a den for the zombie-like creatures. Just like me, this group had come to depend on him for not only their safety from the feens, but also to help find edible food and fresh water that had also become scarce over the years and unfortunately, the feens were not the only threat on these streets.

The people who were not feens and had survived the flare, were not all good people. Like us, most folks had formed groups or gangs… the fact was, there was safety in numbers. To be a lone traveler these days was a suicide mission.

But some of these gangs were worse than the feens. Something was happening to mankind as a whole. Most folks these days were just… evil. I don't know what other word to use. People were killing each other for no reason at all but for the sport of it. It was like everyone had gone mad.

Which is why Hitta was leading us east…everyday our numbers grew. The folks that were unfortunate enough to still have their scruples about them took one look at Hitta and his men and just knew that they would be safer traveling with us. Most times, they didn't even ask…in desperation, they just fell into line and understood that Hitta was the boss, no question. They'd do anything for his protection.

He said that we were going east because the voice in the mute warrior's head told him so. The mute warrior had a twin brother… both had a set of twin sons who were close to my son's age and like their fathers, also fought by Hitta's side. They said that we had a long journey ahead of us, neither of them knew how far east we were to go, only that we needed to start heading that way.

How had the world come to this? In one hour, life as we once knew it was gone...dead. The first few years, there were rumors that everything would get back to normal. They said that the United States Government was working with other world governments to get communications back up and running. There were rumors of governmental safety camps where one could find a hot meal and a safe place to sleep.

But there were also rumors that the people who have gone there disappeared, never to be seen again. Everyone has come to accept that life as we once knew it was over and was never coming back. A new world existed in its place. A new world that was run by monsters.

The first feen lunged at my son and I had to put my hand over my mouth to stop the scream that wanted to rip from my throat. But there was no need for me to be worried. He moved with amazing skill and precision and downed the feen that came at him. Hitta didn't even turn his way because he wasn't worried that his son wouldn't be able to handle himself.

After that, all hell broke loose...the feens no longer moved like humans, they walked as if their limbs were too heavy for their body. But it was their hunger for blood that caused them to be relentless in their pursuit. They swarmed the small group of men, but the warriors were so deadly with their hands and the few weapons they had that it wasn't long before they were surrounded by the sore invested bodies.

When there were no more to kill, Hitta looked at me... "Come on out, Teacup....It's safe, baby."

I reached for him, but the sound of his deep chuckle radiated through my body waking me. Frowning, I opened my eyes.

A dream... It had all been a dream.

I'd never had one in so much detail before. I wondered if I should write down what I saw...It was so terrible seeing the world that way. My heart still beat rapidly because it felt so real...The smell of the rotting flesh of the blood feens and the stagnant taste in the air...felt so real.

Hitta was there. I wrapped my arms tighter around his strong body, snuggling closer to him. I was so glad he was there for me. And…we had a son.

My bed moved waking me completely.

Oh God! I was on the man's back again. And to make matters worse, I was clinging to him butt naked.

"Oh my God…I am so sorry," I muttered as I eased back to my side of the bed wrapping the sheet around me.

He turned around and smiled at me. "Don't apologize…It don't bother me. I think it's kind of cool."

"Still… I pray it doesn't become a habit." Goodness…that was so embarrassing.

"And if it do?"

His question caught me off guard. I chuckled, "Ummm…then maybe I'll have to sleep in Jessie's room once she goes back home."

He got out of the bed and I bit my lip to keep from moaning at the sight of all that muscle flexing in his beautiful brown body. You would think I've had enough seeing as to how I and the man made love well into the night. I still had the soreness to prove it.

"Mmm mmm mmm," he said as he slid into his underwear grinning down at me.

"Mmm mmm mmm, what?"

"Mmm mmm mmm, I'd hate to see how Jessie's little bed is going to hold up under my weight…but if you insist on sleeping there, I guess I have no choice but to find out 'cause you for damn sho' won't be sleeping nowhere without me."

Still biting on my bottom lip, I grinned. "So, you really don't mind that I sleep so wild."

He shook his head before sliding his tank over it. "Nope…You climb on top of me 'cause you mine. It don't bother me at all." He leaned down and gave me a kiss before he headed into the bathroom.

I exhaled as I watched him go, although the dream was beginning to fade from my memory, I could still see the boy with Hitta's face and body, but my eyes…

I wondered what that meant. However, I had no more time to think about that because Jessie in true Jessie fashion, burst in my door yelling.

"Tee-Tee, come look at my room!"

She was so excited that she ran in and tried to come to a stop, but because the wooden floors were so polished and she was wearing socks, she ended up sliding on past the bed, hitting the floor. But her little excited face popped right back up causing me to laugh.

"Jessie, it's way too early for all that yelling."

She turned to look at the window where the sun was just beginning to lighten the sky.

"Well, what time can I start yelling?"

I grabbed her little smart mouth self, pulling her into my lap and then hugged her. I loved this little knucklehead child.

"There is never a good time to yell."

"Can you come see my room? It's so pretty," she asked with her little arm still wrapped around my neck.

"Okay, but then we need to get ready because I have to open the shop in a few."

After playing hooky yesterday, there was no way I could afford to do that today. Plus, it was Friday and Friday was one of my busiest days.

Greatie was a stickler about not working on the Sabbath. She used to tell me to always remember the Sabbath day and to keep it set-apart no matter what. So, because of it, I didn't open the Tea Shop on Saturdays. I didn't bother opening on Sundays either because that was the day I took Jessie home and most times, I spent the whole day cleaning Trina's apartment. You'd be amazed at how filthy it can get in one week's time.

After I pieced together Jessie an outfit from the few things she had in her bag and the things that were still packed in boxes that I'd had at my apartment for her, I got her started in the shower as I hurried to do the same. Hitta had disappeared in the basement. It was quite clear he was serious about working out every morning.

By the time he made his way to the kitchen showered and dressed for the day in another pair of brand-named sweatpants and a grey t-shirt, I'd unpacked a few of the boxes from my kitchen and had managed to get some chamomile tea and oatmeal on the table. Jessie was already eating her bowl of oatmeal.

Hitta walked to her and snatched her right out of her chair...Of course Jessie loved it and erupted in laughter as he held her way up in the air and tickled her. She was laughing so hard I was afraid she was going to pee on herself.

I shook my head as I spooned him up some oatmeal in a bowl. Jessie was so rough; I just didn't understand it.

"Are you hungry?" I asked when he sat her back down in her chair.

With a devious grin on his handsome face, he came towards me like he was going to snatch me up as well, but I backed up holding his bowl of chamomile oatmeal in front of me.

"Look at this...it's chamomile. You know how you love chamomile." For good measure, I picked up the little tube of organic honey and drizzled a little over the top of the oatmeal.

Just like I figured, once the scent of the chamomile and honey reached him, his eyes were drawn to the bowl in my hand. He didn't understand that he liked the smell of the chamomile because it was a natural stress reducer, which meant his headaches were tension headaches...

The absolute worst kind because there was no telling what the root of the problem was; Ninety-eight percent of the time it was something psychological.

He stopped stalking me and I exhaled. But then I squeaked when he suddenly lunged at me pulling me into his arms before taking my lips in one of those drugging kisses.

"You taste good as hell," he muttered as his hungry mouth went to my neck.

It took everything within me not to melt in his arms. If this man had his way, I'll be playing hooky again with him and we'd never leave the bedroom.

Although it was the last thing I wanted to do, I slid out of his arms.

"I bet you're going to love this oatmeal."

His hungry gaze went from my lips to the bowl of oatmeal. He frowned, "Naw, shawty, I don't really do breakfast."

He pulled me back to him. "I'd rather eat you instead," he whispered in my ear before taking my earlobe in his mouth.

I bit down on the moan that wanted to escape my lips. I could feel Jessie's laughing eyes on us. Once again, I slid out of his arms holding the bowl just underneath his nose, so the smell of chamomile could fill his senses. When it did, his gaze fell back to it, but this time, there was no frown.

"I think you're going to change your mind once you taste this."

He reached up and took it from me before bringing it to his nose sniffing it again.

"Smells like you. Yeah…okay."

I little while later, I had to press my lips together to keep from laughing as I spooned up a third bowl for Mr. Yeah…Okay. He loved the oatmeal and the tea.

When I first poured him a cup of chamomile tea in the little hand-painted teacup and set it in front of him, his fierce gaze went from it to me.

"What the hell am I supposed to do with that?"

I laughed. "You supposed to drink it. Like this…" I picked up the matching teacup and lifted it to my lips. But before I took a sip, I closed my eyes and let its healing fragrance into my lungs. Then I took a little sip and moaned.

"Mmmmm…nothing like that first sip of chamomile to start the day."

He watched me with one eyebrow raised, then lifted the little teacup that looked like a toy in his big hands. When he held it like I did, Jessie erupted in laughter. I'm not going to lie, he looked ridiculous holding the little dainty teacup with his big, rough, bruised fingers. The man had scars on top of scars.

He even put his big pinky in the air like mine. When he brought it to his lips, he closed his eyes and inhaled. I studied the area around his eyes and temple…when he exhaled, I saw the area visibly relax.

It came to me right then what needed to be done. Of course, it would only be a temporary fix until we found out what was causing the tension. But the ingredients for his daily blend became clear to me, I needed to get to the shop though, I didn't have all I needed here.

"Mmmmm…nothing like that first taste of chamomile to start the day," he said drawing my attention back to him. "But next time I prefer for mine to come from between your le—"

"Ooookay, time to go!" I said standing abruptly frowning at him. "We are going to have to do something about your habit of saying the first thing that comes to your mind."

The look he was giving me had me biting my lip to keep from laughing at him.

"I told you, Teacup, I don't sugar coat nothing." And then he lifted his teacup batting his eyelashes in a most ridiculous way before taking a sip. Of course, this caused Jessie to nearly fall out of her chair laughing at him.

Goodness, we had to get him a bigger cup.

————

"Damn, *Teacup*, this joint is *tight*!"

I was cheesing so hard my cheeks hurt as I flipped on the light for my tea display.

Hitta sat on the couch in the front of the store facing me with his muscled arms stretched out across the back of it. After I turned on the light for the tea display, he stood completely wowed.

"Wow!"

I nodded, very proud of myself. My tea display had that effect on everyone the first time they saw it.

"You did this all by yourself?" he asked, now looking at me as if I was some kind of wonder.

I grinned. "Yep!"

"What's up with that though?" He was pointing to the huge hole in my wall covered by the plastic. The wind was causing it to dip in and out.

I scrunched up my face. "There was a fire in the wall. I'm trying to get it fixed, buuuttt---ummm." I looked off to the side, too embarrassed to tell him that I couldn't afford it. I didn't want him to think my business was doing badly or anything.

"What caught fire?"

"The building has old electric wiring."

He grunted as he walked over to get a better look. He was so different from the kind of people who come in here. I don't think I've ever had anyone in here like him.

Today, he wore a gold chain around his neck with a charm that was a pair of diamond boxing gloves. One didn't have to guess that it cost a fortune. The gold watch around his wrist also had enough ice in it to catch the eye every time his hand moved.

Although he clearly liked to wear sweatpants…they weren't cheap sweats and neither was his t-shirt. Today, he had on another pair of brand-name gym shoes. I don't think I've ever seen him wear the same pair twice.

His assistant must have brought his clothes and shoes while we were gone yesterday too, because this morning when I went into the closet, his side was loaded with sweatpants hanging on hangers with plastic cleaner bags over them as well as jeans. Even his t-shirts were pressed and on hangers under plastic. The shoe rack had been built into the wall. My side was empty because I still had yet to unpack. But his side…

Goodness, the man had so many gym shoes that it was safe to say that he may have something of a fetish. And they all looked brand new…Of course, there were a few pairs of Timberland's sprinkled in there as well.

My gaze roamed up his powerful body. The way he dressed fit him. I really couldn't see him dressed any different. He looked good in his clothes too. His pants fit his muscled bowlegs very well, not too tight, but not too loose…just enough to show that he was an athlete.

And his shirts…

Shucks! Who was I kidding? It really wouldn't matter what he wore on the top half of him, his superbly sculpted arms and chest will always be the star of the show.

When my gaze made its way up his thick tattooed neck to his face, I jumped because he was staring at me…Too late I realized that he had asked me a question.

"Mmmm, what was that?" I asked tucking the braid that had fallen in my face behind my ear to cover up my embarrassment at getting caught staring at the man red-handed.

He chuckled… "I said, what is your landlord saying?"

I waved my hand… "Please, that old bat won't lift a finger."

The grin left his face and a frown replaced it. "I thought you said the fire happened because of old wiring?"

"Well, yeah…it did."

"So, shouldn't the landlord be the one repairing the damages?"

I nodded. "In a perfect world…but some battles are just not worth the fight. I asked her and she said she wasn't going to help, so now, I need to move on and just do it myself."

"Bullsh*t!" he growled.

Something crashed in the kitchen. At the same time, he pulled out his phone and started texting. I hurried to check on Jessie, but I gestured for him to wait. I didn't want him doing anything about this, I had it handl--

"Jessie! What are you doing!?"

Y'all, this child had climbed up on top of the freezer that was taller than Hitta and was trying to get into the cabinet I kept her treats in.

"Sorry, Tee-Tee, I was trying to get my fruit snacks."

I exhaled angrily as I took her down. "Dang it, Jessie, you're going to hurt yourself one of these days. You're always climbing and trying to do everything yourself!"

"I got to do everything myself at my house," she muttered back.

Her words made me stop. Closing my eyes, I got control over my anger. She was right, I pulled her into a hug.

"You're right, sweetheart. Tee-Tee sorry. Here, let me get your snacks for you."

I pulled my stepping-stool over and got the snacks out of the cabinet. After handing her a pack, I led her back to my office. There was a little couch and TV in here that I'd gotten just for her. Whenever Jessie came to the Tea Shop, I always had my hands full. Because she was incapable of sitting still, I had to keep a constant eye on her, which made my job extremely hard.

"Are you going to sit in here and watch your shows?" I asked, sitting down on the couch next to her. One of the best ways I found to deal with her is to just stop and have a little chat with her.

"How long we gon' be here?"

"Well…you know I don't close till seven."

She exhaled and her little head fell back on her shoulder. "I got to sit in here that long?"

I pulled her into my lap. Poor child was supposed to be in school. Of course, it was torture for her to be at the shop with me all day.

"You can come out front when the crowd dies down a bit, but only if you promise to sit at one of the tables and not bother any of the students on their computers."

Last time Jessie was here, she'd talked one of the students who was here studying for finals on her computer into turning on YouTube for her.

"Okay, I'm gon' be good," she lied. I kissed her on her chubby cheeks and turned on the TV tuning in to the PBS channel. Their morning line up would keep her busy till around lunchtime and then the chase was on.

When I made it back out front, Hitta had moved a piece of the plastic aside and was taking pictures of the hole.

"What's up?" I asked coming to stand next to him.

"I'm sending these pictures to my assistant so that he can get somebody in here today to fix this."

"Oh… no, Hitta, please… that's not necessary. I already have a guy coming out, it's already paid for—"

I squeaked when he grabbed a hold of my overalls and yanked me to him so close that my feet were barely touching the floor, our lips were only inches apart.

"What did I tell you about lying to me, Teacup?"

I stared at him with wide eyes, how in the world did he know I was lying? But then I remembered his threat to punish me for lying to him the other day outside of the gym and I swallowed. Because I couldn't take his intense gaze, mine lowered to the tattoo on the side of his neck that was thanking God for subduing his enemies under him.

"Ummmm…you said…ummm."

"Look at me, baby…" His words were low. My gaze came back to his. "I see you remembered what I told you."

I nodded…

"Then why are you lying to me?"

"You've already done so much for me. I just don't want you to have to pay for this too." It was true. Just this morning I'd tried to give him back the credit card he had given me, but he told me to keep it and use it for whatever I needed it for. I told him I didn't need it because I had my own.

"You have a black card?" He'd asked.

"Well…no, I don't have a black card. But I have a really nice blue one."

He chuckled. *"That's what I thought. Keep the card."*

I'd opened my mouth to argue with him, but the look he gave me shut it down. So, I put the card in my wallet, although I will never use it.

"Oh! You misunderstood…Yo' landlady gon' pay me back." He said bringing me back to the present.

I frowned… "She won't… I already tried to talk to her."

His head lowered to mine and he gently kissed my lips. "That's where you and me differ, baye. I'm not going to try and talk to her… I'm going to let Wayne talk to her, he really has an amazing ability to get folks to see things his way. And if he can't get through to her, which I really doubt, then I'm sure Kennedy will."

"Who's Wayne?"

"My assistant…"

"And Kennedy?"

The grin that came to his face gave me a bad feeling.

"My lawyer."

I clutched his arms… "Aww, Hitta…don't make no trouble for me. She already don't like me much and my lease is up for renewal in a couple of months. I can't lose the shop…it's the best thing I've ever don—" He leaned in and kissed me again.

But this kiss was different from the last…this was one of those drugging kisses that had my hands traveling up his strong arms to wrap around his neck. When he drew back, I'd forgotten what the hell I was saying.

"Do you trust me, baby?"

I didn't even think before I nodded…and I realized it was true.

Thanks to the dreams I'd been having of him, I trusted him very much.

"I know how much the shop mean to you. My word, I'll never let nothing or nobody take it from you. But I ain't got it in me to let no slumlord take advantage of you either. So just let me handle this and you go ahead and get the door."

Frowning, I looked over at the door and sure enough, my pastry boy was pulling his load out of the backseat of his car. My gaze went back to Hitta's. How in the world had he seen him? And how in the world did he know he was coming for me?

"How did you even see him?"

He chuckled just as his phone began to ring... "I see everything, shawty... Yo..." He said into the phone walking back toward the back of the shop.

After my pastry guy left, I took the receipt to my office, Hitta was sitting at my desk watching Sesame Street with Jessie. Of course, she had climbed up my desk and was now sitting on the front of it telling him about something Oscar the Grouch had just done.

"Excuse me," I told him as I pulled the drawer opened and tossed the receipt in it.

"Damn, Teacup...is this how you keep your records?" he asked pulling the drawer out farther to get a better look at the chaos inside.

"Of course not!" I told him before I pulled out the other drawers that were also full of crumpled up receipts. "I'm not a complete imbecile."

His stunned gaze came up to me to see if I was serious. I bit my cheek to keep a straight face.

He looked back down at the receipts in horror. "Where are your books?"

I blinked down at him. "Books? What do you mean, books?"

His gaze shot back to mine. "Teacup...tell me you keep books." Oh, my goodness! It was taking everything within me not to laugh at the look on his face.

I gave him a playful punch in the shoulder. "Okay, I keep books..."

He began to shake his head slowly at me, still looking at me with stunned eyes. And I couldn't hold it any longer. I erupted in laughter…

He exhaled… "Damn, baye, you scared me. I thought you was in this mutha f**** running a business without keeping books. I was getting ready to say, no wonder you was short on cash."

My laughter stopped as I looked at him. At first, I'd been joking about not knowing that I needed to do better with my books. But could he be right? Although the shop was doing quite well, was that why I always seemed to be short on cash?

"Do you think that's the reason?"

"Do you really not keep books?"

"I mean… I know I need to be. And I'm going to get to it, eventually…It's why I have all my receipts in the drawer. My tax guy helped me get them in order last year when he did my taxes—"

"Doing taxes is not keeping books, shawty. Plus, how the f*** do you know what he's doing if you don't keep yo' own records? Do you trust him?"

"Ummm…Kind of."

Damn it! I've been meaning to get these receipts in order. But it's true, I absolutely hate doing the books. I'd rather dance on a bed of glass… barefoot. I am a Tea Maker…one day I pray to be a Tea Master like my Greatie.

The only thing I want to do is be left alone to work with my teas! Why do I have to do painful things like keeping books and sorting receipts?

"Kind of?" he chuckled. "Do you even keep up with your inventory, so that you'll know if your income exceeds your expenditures?"

Okay…

So, let's pause right here in the story…

Did you guys hear the question the brute, thug, boxer just asked me? Now, by this point, I had figured out that Hitta was way smarter than I'd initially thought. But the question that he'd just asked told me something altogether different about his intelligence.

This man was not what he appeared to be at first sight. I couldn't believe I've been walking around for months turning my nose up at him as if he was in some way beneath me. I mean, I wasn't a jerk or anything...I would never do that to anyone.

It's just that I had it in my mind that he was this big, scary...bad guy that killed and beat up people. This is the danger of rumors. None of that is probably true about him. My former next-door neighbor was probably lying about all of that. And I'd gone and judged this poor man by all that crap that she fed me.

Well...That and the fact that he scared the heck out of me when we first met.

I exhaled... "Okay...You got me. I know I should be doing all of that. But the truth is, I'd rather eat gum from the bottom of a garbage can."

"Ewww!" Jessie said giving me the stinky face.

"I'm a Tea Maker!" I told him putting my hand to my chest. "Why can't I just be left alone to work with my teas?"

He sat back in his chair and pulled me into his lap. "You can, baye...why don't you hire a back of the house manager, whose job it is to do all that tedious boring stuff like keeping the books?"

"I would love to hire someone like that, I just can't afford it."

"Oh...you don't get a lot of business?"

"Quite the opposite. I have a steady flow of customers. I do really well actually. People love my teas."

"Well, if the business is doing so good, why can't you afford to hire on some help?"

I shrugged. "Beats me..."

He smiled before he leaned in and gently kissed my lips. "You know why you don't know?"

I folded my arms and pressed my lips together, already knowing what he was getting at.

"Come on, be a big girl and say it..."

"Because I don't keep my books..." I barely opened my mouth.

He laughed. "What did you say, Teacup? I couldn't hear you."

"I said... because I don't keep my books..." I still mumbled the last part.

"That's right because you don't keep yo' books. But you mine, so if you want to just focus on yo' teas, then you just focus on yo' teas…yo' man gon' handle the rest."

"Ummm…should I be afraid?" I muttered.

My question made him laugh… "Probably…"

Twenty minutes after I opened, Wayne showed up. Wayne was a multi-tasking, very handsome, smooth-talking, slender brotha, who was dressed to the nines in a three-piece suit. And I was quite convinced that he wasn't human. The things this man could make happen was simply amazing.

Apparently, he had been Hitta's personal assistant since his boxing days and after he retired, stayed with him.

"Nobody else will work with him, look at him…If I leave, he'll fall back into being a caveman." He shuttered. "God have mercy on the earth if that happens."

This he'd said while he was ordering my strongest cup of tea. My gaze went over to Hitta, who was sitting on the couch frowning down at his phone. And let me tell y'all, that frown of his was intimidating as heck.

It caused my customers to give him a wide path as they ordered their teas and pastries while stealing glances his way. However, little Jessie wasn't afraid of him. She sat right next to him with her arm on his leg as she talked his ear off about God knows what.

He was so patient with her and I was glad that he was here because he was keeping her behaving and not harassing my customers. He and Wayne had taken up shop over in that area. I think it was because of them that more customers decided to sit down and drink their teas rather than rush out to start their day like they normally did.

Wayne had two laptops set up in front of him on the table and a notepad. At some point, someone came in and took a few pictures of Hitta and the whole time he frowned. But at the same time, he looked like somebody famous and I'd seen more than one of my customers snap pictures of him on the low because nobody wanted to get on his bad side.

I loved to see Wayne and Hitta's interactions because Wayne spoke Hitta fluently. He understood every grunt, every hand gesture, every nod, and every rude look… Wayne was always one step ahead of his boss and could almost predict what he was going to want next.

And he wasn't afraid of him. They argued like women…

Wayne would say something like, "Smile, there's a camera pointed at you."

"I am smiling…" Hitta would mutter without changing his face at all.

Wayne would exhale. "You're not smiling."

"Mutha f****, what the f*** I look like, a clown?" Hitta would bark.

Not ruffled in the least, Wayne would calmly state, "No…at this very moment, you look like an angry ape, whose banana is stuck up his a**."

And of course, I was drinking something at the time and had to quickly put my hand over my mouth to prevent it from escaping with my laughter.

Hitta pointed his big finger at his assistant. "I know a lot of mutha f***as that want yo' job."

Wayne held out his arms. "Fire me then! What you waiting on? You been making the same threat for ten years! Fire me already! I'm sick and tired of your bullsh*t anyway! I have a degree from Morehouse I don't have to take this sh*t!"

Hitta gestured toward the door. "Go back to Morehouse then mutha f****, ain't nobody holding a gun to yo' head keeping yo' preppy a** here, you bastard! You killing me with this bullsh*t!"

"And you killing me by acting like I'm killing you for asking you to smile. It's not the world's fault you didn't get hugs when you were a kid, don't pass that negativity off on everybody else. You have a specific duty as a public figure to—"

But by this point in the conversation, Hitta would actually roll his eyes and exhale loudly and ignorantly before plastering a very frightening smile on his face.

"There, you happy, mutha f***a?" he would grumble from between his smiling lips.

Wayne would look at his smile and frown, before shaking his head.

"F*** it, go back to the frown. That sh*t on your face there is going to give small children nightmares."

And of course, I laughed the whole time. I would later find out that Wayne was so much more than a personal assistant. He played the role as Hitta's PR, agent, lawyer and all-around motivator. Heck, Wayne had a personal assistant...

Anyway, an hour later, there was a crew of three men who got busy fixing the hole in my wall. The whole time, I had a rush, so I couldn't be that involved with anything, but I didn't have to...Wayne was holding it down.

He made sure the work crew stayed out of the way of my customers. He even smiled and greeted a few of them. By noon, a camera crew showed up. I'd gotten a lull for a moment before the lunch rush and I took the time to make Hitta's blend.

When I came out the back with his mug and saw the camera crew, I froze like a deer in headlights.

"Hey, boss lady, what do you have there?" Wayne asked coming to rescue me.

"Who are these people?"

He turned to look as if it was no big deal. "Vice-World, have you heard of them."

My stunned gaze flew to him. "Have I heard of them? Are you kidding me? Of course, I've heard of them!"

I was getting ready to freak out. Vice-World was sitting in my Tea Shop!

Oh my God!!!!

VICE-WORLD WAS IN MY TEA SHOP!!!!

"Yeah, they've been following the boss around for the last month. Just pretend they're not here and go on with business as usual. However, you should prepare for an influx of customers after this episode airs."

"Oh my God! Wayne! That's great!" But then a thought hit me. I was already barely handling the customers I had.

"Wait, I don't know if I'll be able to handle more people—"

"I've already taken care of that. After your lunch rush, I have three very reliable people coming in to interview for a position." His words stalled for a minute and for the first time since I've met him, his dispo-sition changed to something that resembled hostility.

He slid his hand down the vest of his suit, straightening his already immaculate appearance.

"Unfortunately...Hitta's niece, Carmen is one of them. She's at The University of Chicago studying to get her B.A. in accounting. She is currently the bookkeeper at Hitta's Place and has agreed after her uncle offered her a very nice snippet of course, to also man the books here."

His disposition was frightening me. "You're scaring me, is there something about her that I should know?"

"You should be afraid. Carmen is a mini version of her uncle. She is a complete savage and should be put down."

My eyes widened..."Put down?"

"Put down...but come now, don't you worry about her. That's why I'm here. You just put a smile on your face and go on over there and give Hitta his cup of tea."

"Am I going to be on TV?" I squeaked.

My heartbeat picked up to the point that I felt like I was going to have a panic attack. He gestured to the guy who I assumed was the producer.

"Hey, this is Hitta's lady...we would like to plug the Tea Shop and the coat drive." He turned to look at me. "Isn't that the charity you have going on now?"

The only thing I could do was nod.

"She has a cup of tea for Hitta, I would like for you guys to get a shot of her handing him the tea and then we can cut the cameras a prep her to plug her charity. Got it?"

With his lips pressed tightly together, the producer nodded. It didn't look as if he was all that happy to be told how to produce his own show, but Wayne walked away obviously not caring in the least.

And so it went...Wayne instructed me on how to hand the cup to Hitta. Of course, the big grouch did not heed to any of Wayne's instructions and reached for me after I handed him the cup and pulled me down on the couch next to him.

Wayne had instructed me to sit in the chair that was next to the couch. Hitta took a sip of his tea and then plugged the heck out of the shop.

"This here…" holding up the cup. "Keep my headaches away." He leaned down and kissed my lips.

"I don't know what I would do without my shawty. She say she a Tea Maker…but to me, she a Tea *Master.*"

Chapter Ten

THE TEA MAKER

> *Men themselves have wondered, what they see in me. They try so much, but they can't touch*
> *My inner mystery.*
> *When I try to show them, they say they still can't see.*
> *I say,*
> *It's in the arch of my back, The sun of my smile, The ride of my breasts, The grace of my style.*
> *I'm a woman*
> *Phenomenally.*
> *Phenomenal woman,*
> *That's me.*
>
> Maya Angelou

Hitta

Because I'm the kind of mutha f**** that don't let people in my head, nobody knows how strange my life has been. For some reason, I've come in contact with a few extraordinary people and up until now, I've never thought to question why.

Many of you know my boy, Rome…I don't have to tell y'all about him and the things he's capable of or the fact that he believes he plays chess with an angel every Tuesday in the park. I don't know why I ended up with a best friend like him.

Neither he, Saw Buck, nor I graduated from eighth grade, but that didn't stop Rome from learning and that didn't stop him from bringing me along for the ride. Just for the fun of it, he and I took an IQ test at nineteen. Rome's score was so high there was not a level for it. The smartest man to be recorded tested in at a three hundred; Rome's score had blown past that.

But for anybody that knew him, there was no surprise in that area. However, if folks knew that I'd scored a one-thirty on mine, they would be very surprised. I'd been born with a speech impediment. Because of it, I used as few words as I could when talking. Also because of it, I came across as dumb.

Many folks would be bothered by that, but I wasn't. It's like chess; to underestimate your opponent is a great error that many commits when dealing with me… To my advantage of course.

It's how I was able to get Angel. She thought she had me figured out and the more she got to know me, the more she saw how wrong she was…and the more she felt guilty.

Did I take advantage of her guilt?

Hell yeah…

But I digress…I was telling you guys about my uncanny ability to bump into extraordinary people.

Take Maddox and Lannox for instance, not only are they extremely deadly…but we are all convinced that God speaks to Lannox and although he is a mute, he's become something of a priest to our crew. If he says we shouldn't do something or go somewhere… we don't. If he says we should be somewhere or should do something, we do. Nobody except Maddox understands the way his mind works, and the little Maddox is exposed to of his brother's mind, he cannot put into words.

He's tried, often…I don't know why those two ended up working for me of all people, but they have, and they are very loyal. Over the last ten years, we have become brothers.

Rome, Maddox, and Lannox you all know about. What many of y'all don't know is that back when I was a kid and G had decided he wanted to see me boxing professionally, he'd sent me to the Lyon's Den to learn how to do that. Lyon and G went way back. G said that it was Lyon who first put him on when he came into the dope game. He said Lyon used to run the streets with an iron fist and had niggas scared to even breathe without his permission.

But then he got locked up. G says when his boy got out, he was done with the dope game, but had opened up a gym where he trained certain people to fight. It was Lyon who taught me how to throw a proper punch and polish my natural ability of knocking mutha f****s out.

One of the amazing things about the Lyon's Den was that not everybody could come in.

I mean that literally…

There is some kind of force around the building that makes certain people sick to their stomach if they even touch the door. And if they manage to ignore that feeling and get inside the door, they never make it past the threshold before they hit their knees in unbearable pain.

I know…that sh*t sound wild, but that's what I'm telling you. For some reason, I've had some wild experiences in my life.

Lyon also had a real pet lion, I kid you not. The thing was huge, and it followed him everywhere. Not only that…to this day, Rome thinks I'm lying, but when I was a kid, I had gone up to Lyon's office to take my payment to him. He didn't see me and was talking to another guy in there. Whatever the guy told him made him so mad that he stood and hit his metal desk so hard he bent the b**** in two.

Needless to say, that sh*t ain't normal. However, it wasn't long till Lyon started working one on one with me. I was surprised as hell when he singled me out. He said although he knows G had sent me to him for him to teach me how to box, nothing happens that isn't the Heavenly Father's will and that I was meant to study under him.

I asked him why.

"I know you want to scrape your way out the hood, kid. But being a professional boxer is not your destiny."

Of course, back then, I thought I knew it all. Thought I had my whole life figured out.

"Can't nobody tell me what my destiny is. I make my own way."

He chuckled. "As long as you think that way, you're going to have a bumpy road ahead of you. Trust me, I know." He looked off to the side getting lost in his thoughts.

"The Most High have a way of getting your attention though. Sometimes, it's easy and sometimes," he shook his head, "It's the most painful thing you'll ever experience. Don't be like me, kid…Try and hear his voice before he strips you of everything you hold dear in order that you listen."

After that day, he started training me to be another kind of fighter, a fighter that fought spiritually as well as physically.

Because of him, I changed my diet. He said the things we put in our temple had a great effect on whether or not the Ancient of Days could use our bodies for vessels. He said the Rauch Ha Kodesh cannot dwell in anything unclean and some foods were unclean and polluted the body.

I changed my diet and started changing the way I viewed life, but G was not happy with the changes and pulled me out of the Lyon's Den before any of Lyon's teachings could take a real hold on me. Although I still kept the diet Lyon had shown me, I haven't been back to the Lyon's Den since.

Now you all are wondering why I've decided to reveal all of this information to you. Well…because I want you guys to see that I've come in contact with some things that can be described as nothing less than supernatural. So, it's safe to say that I now have certain qualifications to spot it when I see it.

That being said…Angel and what she does with her teas were some next-level kind of sh*t.

I've been sitting here watching her for hours, my phone been blowing up with calls and texts from the gym. I had two new fighters coming in today to start their training. One of the kids showed promise of going all the way…and yet here I still sat on this couch watching…

Hell…I don't know what I was watching.

First of all, for a tea shop, this mutha f**** stayed busy. At one point during the morning rush, there was a line out the f***ing door. Now, you ask me, why the hell would somebody wait in a line that long for tea? And well, let me tell you why.

She was more than a barista she was a healer. A healer that all of these people didn't mind waiting in line to see.

Some folks knew what they wanted. They stepped up to her register and asked for their blend by name. She sold bags of the sh*t… and no, it wasn't cheap. Everybody that bought a bag bought a cup as well.

Her hands moved across her tea display like a pianist on a piano. I was convinced that half the satisfaction for the customers was just watching her work. She'd grab a flower from here, a few granules of something from here…a scoop of this, a scoop of that…she'd drop what looked like a twig in one of the many wooden mortars that she had and grind it down before adding everything in a little mesh baggy.

Then she'd drop the baggy in a cup of hot water and then steam it. The loud sound of the steamer signaled to the customer that their order was almost finished. It also snapped them out of whatever satisfying trance they fell in watching her put together their order.

It was poetry in motion. No! Damn that… it was a symphony. Like her customers, I couldn't look away.

Now…what I've described to you was just the tip of the iceberg.

The true show came when someone asked for the manager's special. I've never in my life seen anything like it. She'd hand them a little herb; I couldn't see what. They'd pop it in their mouth and as they chewed and swallowed, she'd study their face or some sh*t… And then she'd nod in a way that reminded me of Maddox when he was listening to Lannox in only a way that he could.

When she turned around to her tea display, she moved with surety that what she was making was perfect for the customer at the register. She went into a zone, a pinch of this and a dash of that…no two recipes were the same. She'd grab stuff without even looking to make sure she grabbed the right thing.

When she handed the customer their cup, they wouldn't walk away before taking a sip. And each time…I kid you not…each time, the customer smiled at her and thanked her before walking away.

Damn…I know I wasn't doing what I saw any justice.

And get this, whenever she slowed down a bit, she would come around the counter and ask me how we were doing over here while holding some herb or another to my lips for me to eat.

As I chewed, she watched my eyes and the area around them.

What the hell?

I think in some way, she is reading me or some sh*t just like she did each customer that stepped to the register and asked her for the manager's special.

Now tell me that ain't some next-level kind of sh*t…

But just between you and me…It warmed my heart that she felt comfortable enough with me to bring the herbs to my lips and not hand it to me like she did her customers.

She was so good at what she did that I doubted if she even noticed the significance of it. She was putting me a tea recipe together in her head and that's all she thought about.

During my interview with Vice World, I'd started to get a headache. Because of my speech impediment, I really hated doing interviews. I thought that after my boxing days that crap would end, but it seems like it was only just the beginning. There seemed to always be some newspaper or magazine calling me for a quote.

The only reason I'd agreed to this was so that Jaheem, one of my fighters, who was almost ready to accept a major fight, could get the exposure he deserved. They did a whole episode on one of our training sessions. Since then, the kid had gotten several offers, but none of the offers is the one we're looking for…However, I had a feeling it was coming soon.

Anyway, I'd gotten a headache talking to these mutha f****s. They asked dumb questions about stupid sh*t. Angel came at the perfect time and handed me a cup of tea…

As soon as the aroma touched my nose, it felt as if all the muscles in my neck and back just relaxed. I could feel the pressure in my head easing. When I finally took a sip, its complex flavor exploded on my tongue and the only thing I could do was sigh as my headache magically disappeared.

And then I plugged the sh*t out of this joint.

"I don't know what I would do without my shawty. She say she a Tea Maker...but to me, she a Tea Master."

I meant every word.

———

Angel

"Here comes the devil, brace yourself," Wayne muttered as he came to stand next to me behind the counter.

I'd just interviewed the other two candidates he'd set up for me and was very happy with the both of them; they would begin their training Monday. But I shouldn't have been surprised that Wayne found the perfect people for me. I was beginning to see that everything the man did was perfect.

The bell on the shop's door dinged and I took Wayne's advice and braced myself. He said she was a mini Hitta. Hitta looked good on a man, so the same look on a woman could not be devastating. However, if she was good at her job, I will be happy, no matter how she looked.

Oh my...goodness! That daggone Wayne.

I braced myself to literally see the female version of Hitta. What I was not expecting was the petite young beauty, who could be no more than eighteen that walked through the door.

"Hey Unc..." she said as she went over to where he sat on the couch and leaned down kissing his cheek.

The only thing the two had in common was the fact that she was dressed in a pair of name-brand sweatpants and Jordans that looked adorable on her little feet, but that was where all the similarities ended.

She wore her hair in a chic asymmetric cut. The left side of it was shaved and lined up perfectly…the right side was in a bob that hung to her shoulder and it was fire engine red. It looked as if she was fresh from the beauty shop.

She had on a cute tank top that matched her sweatpants and molded to her perfect athletic body amazingly. As she and Hitta came my way, I was able to see that she wasn't that much taller than me.

My gaze went to Wayne's… "A mini version of Hitta…Really, Wayne? She's beautiful."

He chuckled. "Don't let her looks fool you. She-is-the-devil."

"Hey, Teacup, I want you to meet my niece, Carmen. Carmen, this my lady, An—"

"Angel…" she interrupted, reaching out her hand to shake mine. "Yes, Unc, I know who she is…you just obsessed about her for months. Everybody know who she is…" She smiled at me.

"Pleased to finally meet you. I am so glad you put my uncle out his misery and went out with him."

I chuckled. I liked her…

"It's nice to meet you too. And I am so grateful you came here to lend me a hand. I pray it's not an inconvenience."

She waved that away. "Not at all…I need a break from that smelly gym and being the back of the house manager here will look great on my portfolio." Her gaze rose to Wayne's and the smile left her face. With her hand on her hip, she covered the few steps separating them till she was standing right in his face.

Because she was so short…like yours truly, Wayne towered over her, but that didn't stop the feisty mama from facing off with him.

"Damn…I prayed last night for two things." She held up two fingers right under his nose, revealing the fact that her nails matched her hair.

"One," she put down her middle finger so that only her index finger was up. "World peace. And two," she put down her index finger and held up her middle finger…Hitta chuckled.

"That yo' homosexual a** got hit by a bus." Then she shrugged. "Neither of my prayers got answered…what am I doing wrong?"

Wayne didn't get ruffled in the least. He chuckled and ran his hand down his immaculate vest, his gaze roaming over her beautiful face in a way that made me feel as if he was taking in every detail.

"Perhaps, and I could be wrong, God is not in the business of answering the prayers of Satan."

Hitta chuckled again shaking his head. Carmen blew a huge pink bubble that matched her lipstick before she spoke.

"Aww...look. The homosexual has jokes. Tell me, Wayne, ...when are you coming out the closet. If you gay, you gay...stop lying about it."

"I know you're young and haven't traveled the world much, but here is a free lesson to start the ball rolling in your attempt at finding a little class. Every man that wears a suit is not gay." He leaned in and for a moment, it looked like he was going to kiss her. She must have thought so too because her eyes widened a bit and she stopped chewing her gum.

"In fact," his words were low as his eyes fell on her full pink lips. "If you weren't twelve, I'd show you just how much of a man I am...all night long."

And then he stepped away from her and after tilting his head at me, said, "If you will excuse me, I have to take this call."

My surprised gazed fell on Carmen, she watched Wayne go through narrowed eyes before her gaze rose to her uncle's.

"Ewww, Unc! Why don't you fire him?"

"Because you love him..." She opened her mouth to deny it, but he lifted his hand cutting her off. "Spit the gum out. You're on a job interview...remember?"

Her mouth snapped shut as she turned to me and smiled, remembering that she was in fact on a job interview.

"Heya, boss..."

That made me laugh, I realized at that moment that there wasn't going to be a dull moment around these parts with Carmen helping to manage the place. And I would soon find out that not only was she stunningly beautiful, she was also as smart as a whip for one so young. I showed her to my office and opened my receipt drawers.

She pulled out her laptop and told me not to worry about anything, the first thing she was going to do is inventory, so that she could put everything in her computer and personalize us a spreadsheet that will make taking inventory breezy.

She assured me that I wasn't making a mistake bringing her on board and that she was going to make me proud.

"No, I take that back...the first thing I'm going to do is update your filing system," she said laughing down at my receipt drawers.

I asked her if she was sure because I was now feeling guilty; I'd let this get so out of hand and now this poor eighteen-year-old girl, who should be out enjoying herself, was stuck in my little office trying to organize my chaos.

"Angel, this is what I do. I love crunching numbers and bringing order to chaos." She laughed at the horrified look that came on my face. "You should have seen what the gym looked like before I got there. I've been doing my uncle's books since I was sixteen."

"Well, okay...If you're sure, I'll leave you to it. I need to have a chat with your uncle before my after-work rush comes in. If you have any questions, please don't be afraid to ask."

So, after talking to Hitta about the animosity between Wayne and Carmen, I found out some juicy tidbits.

"They didn't always fight like that. My sista got locked up when Carmen was fourteen and she came to stay with me. At first, her and Wayne was cool. He helped me out with her a lot, but when she turned seventeen, something happened. They relationship got tense." He chuckled.

"Carmen was turning into a woman and neither of them knew what to do about their feelings for each other. It's their guilt for those feelings that causes them to fight each other...they're literally fighting their feelings."

"How much older than her is he?"

He wrapped his arm around my waist pulling me closer. "Not as much as I'm older than you."

"And you're okay with that?"

He chuckled... "Oh, I threatened to break both of Wayne's arms if he touched her before she was legal. Of course, he denied he even had feelings for her...but he got my message loud and clear."

"But now that she's legal...you don't mind if they start a relationship?"

He chuckled. "Wayne a good guy. And he strong enough to deal with Carmen. She'd run over a weak man. I know he'd love her and be good to her...you know?"

I nodded as I prepared my workstation for my after-work rush.

"I'm gon' get ready to head out. I need to take care of a few things at the gym. If you want, I can take Jessie with me. We'll meet you back here when you close and grab some dinner."

Oh, bless his heart! "Are you sure? Jessie is—"

He held up his hand cutting me off. "Have you met Carmen?" Chuckling, I nodded.

"I think I can handle Jessie."

He was onto something. That was exactly who Carmen reminded me of...Jessie.

"Okay...don't leave yet. I'm going to make you some tea to go."

It's the least I can do. This man had come in and in one day, made some things happen around here. The things that have frustrated me to no end, he'd handled. My wall was almost finished. The workers he'd hired had been professional and very knowledgeable. They'd worked quickly and quietly, not bothering my customers at all.

I had two new employees who will start their training on Monday and a manager that was hard at work right now. I felt so bad that he was paying them for me, but I think I found a way to pay him back. Tonight, over dinner, I was going to see what he thought about being an investor in the company. That way, the Tea Shop can pay him back all that he'd spent and more.

I went to the back and grabbed the stainless-steel thermos that I had. It was big enough to hold a full day's supply of tea. I also grabbed the mate to my favorite teacup here at the shop. I don't know why...It was even daintier than the one I had at the house. But thanks to Carmen and Wayne...and the fact that Hitta had taken care of most of my burdens here at the shop in one day, I was in a bit of a nutty mood and was anticipating the look on his face when I handed him the little flower painted teacup to take with him.

As I did that, I asked Jessie if she wanted to go to the gym with

Hitta. Of course, she was all for it, so I gave her a stern talking about behaving herself and not getting on the man's nerves.

"I'm gon' be real good." She lied before she ran off to tell Carmen that she was going to the gym.

If y'all needed further proof that Jessie and Carmen were alike… look at exhibit A. They've known each other for only a couple of hours and have taken to each other as if they were big and little sister.

While Carmen was working, Jessie had been in there talking her ear off and just like her uncle, she was not bothered at all by her. And I think I've got it figured out; Jessie was one of them…

And when I say one of them, I mean the tough people. They weren't afraid of anything. Somebody gets in their way they're going to run them over. They were so different from me. Somebody gets in my way I'm going to ask them to please step aside. And if they didn't, to avoid any drama, I'll just walk around them.

Sometimes I wish I'd been more like Jessie when I was younger. Maybe then, Stan wouldn't have been able to hurt me due to the fear that I'd slit his throat in his sleep.

When I walked out of the back, my steps came to a halt.

Dear God!

I'd spoken up the devil…

Stan was squatting down in front of the counter talking to Jessie. His hand reached up to touch her braid and I just reacted. I hurried around the corner and snatched her away from him.

"Don't touch her!"

When Hitta and Wayne heard the desperation in my voice they both stopped talking and hurried my way.

"Who the f*** is this?" Hitta growled coming to a stop right in back of Stan.

My foster father turned around to see who was standing so close to him and nearly jumped out of his socks.

"Christ!" he cried taking in the mountain of a man in front of him. He stumbled back clutching the counter for support.

"Angel, who are these people? And what are they doing here?" The fact that there was a quiver in his voice only testified to how big of a coward he was.

"I asked you a question," Hitta told him, taking another step towards him, causing Stan to stumble back even farther. "Who the f*** are you?"

Gaining control of himself, Stan stood a bit straighter. "My name is Dr. Stanly Baker and I'm Angel's father and Jessie's grandfather."

Both Hitta's and Wayne's stunned gaze came to me and my face heated. Now, I was regretting my actions. I wish I had not alerted their attention to Stan. The last thing I wanted them to know was how twisted my life had been.

"This yo' dad?" Hitta asked.

"My foster father," I muttered before pressing my lips together.

Calling Stan any kind of father to me was torturous, but I didn't want this thing to get bigger than it already was.

"And you are!?" Stan demanded, looking at Hitta as if he was a piece of trash. I balled my fists up...that angered me so much, I felt like screaming.

Hitta was more of a man that Stan will ever be. Stan didn't even deserve to be in the same room with such a man.

Hitta pulled me to stand in front of him before he wrapped his strong arms around my waist securing me against him. I nearly closed my eyes as the feeling of safety flooded my system. This was such a paradigm shift. I never thought I would ever feel this safe in the presence of someone that has caused me to feel such terror.

"I'm Angel's man...Hitta."

"Her what?!"

"You deaf, mutha f***a!" Hitta growled.

Stan began to sputter. He was so red in the face you would have thought someone had slapped him.

"Well..." He huffed as he walked a huge circle around Hitta. "I don't have to stand here and take this." His gaze fell on me.

"I just came by to tell you that Diana has taken a turn for the worst. I and her doctors don't expect her to last through the month. If you know where West is...you should probably tell him." He nodded toward Jessie.

"You may want to take her to see her grandmother before it's too late." When he was done speaking, he turned to go, but before he walked through the door, he turned back to look at me.

"Your new…friends are not welcomed in my house. So, don't bother bringing them."

Hitta's arms tightened around me. "That's too bad, bo. She don't go nowhere without me."

I didn't like the look that came in Stan's eyes then. Suddenly a feeling of dread washed over me. I'd seen that look before. Stan can be a vindictive, evil bastard when he wanted to. He may not be able to match Hitta when it came down to brute strength, but he was the type that would make trouble for him in other ways. He had a lot of powerful friends.

Heck! One of his best friends was a Cook County judge and I've seen Stan call in asking favors of him on more than one occasion.

Hitta turned me to face him as soon as he left. "What the f*** is up with that? Why are you afraid of yo' foster father?"

I shook my head, sliding out of his arms. "I'm not afraid of him… It's nothing."

Hitta

Once again, she was lying to me, but I could tell by the resolve in her eyes that I wasn't going to get any more out of her right now. I was learning that this girl could be stubborn as hell when she wanted to be.

I didn't have to say anything to Wayne. As soon as my gaze connected to his he nodded and walked to his computer. No doubt he will have a full bio on Stan's ho' a** for me by tomorrow. And just because I need to know all there is to know about the man that had just put that kind of fear in Angel's eyes, I was going to be calling Rome. Wayne was good, but Rome could find the sh*t folks go out of their way to bury.

I also put in a call to Maddox, I needed him and Lannox to keep an eye on her for me. I didn't trust her foster father and until I found out why she was afraid of him, she was going to have a little company at all times.

"So, you're not going to tell me what that was all about?" I asked her a little later as she handed me the thermos full of tea she'd made for me and another one of those girlie cups that she obviously got a kick out of seeing me use.

———

Angel

I smiled although my heart was racing out of control. I'd imagined all the ways Stan could ruin Hitta's life and I had to do what I could to make sure that didn't happen. Out of all the days he could have come in here, why the world did he have to pick today?

If I told Hitta what Stan had done to me, he would probably try and confront him. And Stan was such a coward, he and his judge friends would have Hitta thrown in jail or something. I couldn't allow that to happen.

"I told you…nothing is going on. Me and Stan just don't see eye-to-eye on some things. No big deal…"

I could tell in his gaze that he didn't believe me, but I didn't care. The less he knew about Stan the better.

He closed the gap between us, crowding my space in only the way that he could. The muscle ticked in his jaw as he stared down at me.

"You gon' be stubborn and stick to this lie, huh?"

I folded my arms. "I'm not lying."

He grinned and it was bone-chilling. I swallowed…

"Aight…you stubborn." He used his big finger to gently poke me in the chest. "But you might as well learn, I'm mo' stubborn."

My eyes narrowed. Was that a threat?

"I'd like you to meet two very good friends of mine."

Right then the door dinged. I turned around just as two well-dressed men walked through it, two well-dressed men that oozed danger.

They were twins...

Twins that were very familiar, I'd seen them from somewhere before, I just couldn't remember where.

One of them was dressed in all black, black turtleneck, black slacks, and a black blazer...He also wore black leather gloves on his hands.

The other was dressed in brown...brown button-up linen shirt, brown slacks, brown blazer...and brown leather gloves on his hands.

Everything about these men said bad news. The few customers that were sitting enjoying their drinks and pastries must have thought so too because their eyes were now glued to them.

"Until you tell me the truth about your foster father, one of my friends is going to be with you when I'm not able."

I turned back to face him, horrified. "What do you mean? Like following me?"

He looked up as they approached. "Maddox...Lannox, this is Angel. Angel, Maddox and Lannox." His gaze fell back to me.

"No, Teacup. They are going to be your bodyguards."

Chapter Eleven

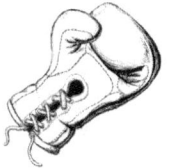

THE WARNING

Angel

I ran into Hitta's office, shutting and locking the door behind me. Seconds later the loud pounding came. The metal door was being hit so hard I was afraid it was going to burst in off the hinges. Fighting back tears, I backed up as I stared at it in horror.

No way was it going to be able to hold up under the pounding.

"Open this f***ing door, Angel! Or so help me God, I'm going to tear this mutha f**** down!" Hitta roared from the other side.

The tears began to flow. How did I get myself in this situation? How had I ignored all the signs…Including my Greatie's warning?

I'd allowed how he made my body feel to blind me to his true nature…A nature that I'd seen when I first met him and had sense enough back then to stay away from.

"Just leave me alone!" I cried. "I want to go home! I want to get away from you!"

"F*** that! Open the door!"

I jumped from the vibration his angry roar sent through the floor.

Dear God, help me!

Hitta was a complete savage…This gym was full of them. I just wanted to go home, back to my apartment, back to my life before I'd been stupid enough to let him in.

These weren't my kind of people…I needed to get away from here!

I know you guys feel lost right now and you're wondering what happened since last we talked…

Oh my goodness! So much has happened since last we talked that I don't know where to begin…

Trina is missing…It's going on two weeks now and Jessie is still with me. Hitta may or may not have a baby on the way by his ex, who he was still financially supporting, but I won't know for sure because she's been knocked out cold and her body was lying in the middle of the gym while these….people cheered it on like that was decent behavior.

Okay…

Wait… let me breathe and try to gain control of my emotions so that I can pick up my story from where last we left off.

I am so sorry about this; I know you guys are wondering what the heck is going on.

Okay…

Maddox and Lannox, the black twin Scottish bodyguards. I think that's where we last left off.

So, because I didn't tell Hitta why I'd responded to Stan the way that I did that day in the tea shop, which by the way, I still haven't told him, he brought in Maddax and Lannox to escort me everywhere I needed to go.

Now granted, for the most part, it's not horrible. The twins although clearly very dangerous men, were kind of cool. Maddox was a smooth talker and most of the time had very good conversation, and because they were so handsome, they were good for business. A lot of the college girls came around to chat with Maddox. They were taken with his good looks and thick Scottish accent.

However, I think he was smitten with my new barista, Summer, a single mom of two, who sometimes had such a haunted look in her beautiful eyes, but was a very dependable employee.

I've tried to talk to her and get in her head a bit to see what was troubling her, but she was really good at deflecting and covering up her pain with a smile. I know because I too was good at it. But I didn't pry too much because I liked Summer and didn't want to chase her away. She'd taken to blending the teas beautifully and my customers had accepted her quite well.

So, the last thing I wanted to do was mess that up…

And then there was Lannox… Lannox was a mysterious gem. I'd found out the day I met them that he couldn't talk. According to Maddox, a priest had tried to kill Lannox when he was a bairn, lol… Bairn is how Maddox says baby. He has so many funny sayings…Like the college girls, I could listen to him talk all day. Hitta gets all jealous when I come home and tell him some of the crazy stuff Maddox says.

"You know…just because he talks with a Scottish accent don't mean he talkin about sh*t…it just mean he ain't talkin about sh*t with a Scottish accent."

He is such a grouch…But up until today, I found his grouchiness adorable and now he was at the door scaring the hell out of me.

Anyway…So Maddox says the priest thought Lannox was possessed by the devil and tried to kill him. He'd locked Maddox inside his room and then took Lannox in the woods in the back of the monastery and slit his throat leaving him for dead. But knowing his brother was in danger, Maddox had managed to slip out the window and get help in time enough to save him…

Although Lannox survived, his voice box had been badly damaged, and he still had the terrible scar across his neck to remind him every day that he'd almost died at the hands of the Catholic priest.

It hurts my heart to think that somebody could hurt a small child like that. And Lannox was a real sweetheart in a hitman kind of scary kind of way… If that makes any sense.

The job of escorting Jessie back and forth to school had fallen on him and he was handling it like a champ. He even helped her with her homework. Because Jessie went to a school that also catered to the visually, hearing and speech impaired, all the children were taught sign language in kindergarten, so she could communicate quite well with Lannox. And if Maddox was not around, most times it was Jessie who told me what he was saying.

But now, get this...Maddox did not use sign language when talking to his brother. By some miracle, he was able to hear his brother's thoughts and they communicated most times without saying a word to each other...

Isn't that amazing?

Anyway, I've wandered off-topic. I was telling you guys how I got myself in my present situation.

Carmen...

So, because I was only about three years older than her, she and I had formed something of a friendship... She was my only friend if I was being honest. Well, ...she and Summer. Summer was coming around, opening up to Carmen and me a little at a time. Whatever was going on with her it was seriously affecting her and her children. Although sweethearts, I recognized that traumatized look in their eyes.

Okay, so back to Carmen...

Her bold in-your-face personality was how she approached her job here at the shop. She'd already gotten all of my books in order. She'd organized my office...created spreadsheets that made taking inventory much easier and was already working out a business plan so that we could buy the space next to us and expand.

I had several herb suppliers that I ordered my product from. Just because I loved the way one supplier grew their chamomile didn't mean I cared for the way they grew their lavender. I was very meticulous with where my material came from.

Thanks to Carmen's new system she'd set up, even ordering my supplies had become easier. And not only that, because she was back of the house manager, she did all the ordering herself, refusing to let me do it, stating that it was her job.

See what I mean? Bold take charge Carmen.

And she was also a wealth of information when it came down to learning a little bit more about my grouchy new lover. She told me so much about him, I feel like I've known him my whole life.

But the part that intrigued me the most was how much his mom and my mother had in common. Carmen said that Hitta's mom, who was also her mom's mom, was addicted to drugs so badly that she'd lost all four of her children, Hitta, who was the oldest to the streets, and the other three to the state, who separated them.

She said although they were separated, they all had very violent natures that landed her mom and her younger uncle in jail…and her youngest aunt in the grave. Her uncle was in jail on a life sentence for triple murder and her mom was there for thirty years for attempted murder. But Carmen was optimistic that she would be getting out in fifteen because of good behavior.

Although they were locked up, Hitta made sure they kept money on their books. She said that she and her uncle went to see them three times a year. Now, when she told me about her youngest aunt, I got a very bad feeling in the pit of my belly. She said that her aunt and her aunt's boyfriend had gotten into a fistfight and when her aunt threatened to tell Hitta on him, he shot and killed her.

Keep in mind, the whole time Carmen is telling me these violent stories about Hitta's upbringing, I'm trying not to cringe. I may have had it bad living with a pervert, but that was where my suffering ended.

I lived in a really good neighborhood, went to an amazing school…had fairly decent friends. I was born in the hood and lived there until I was seven years old, but that was my hood experience. I'd only just moved back to the hood because it was all I could afford at the time and believe it or not… don't laugh at me, I wanted to reconnect with my roots.

But after listening to some of Carmen's tales, I felt like a fish out of water. Hitta had come up rough, which would explain why he was so…. hmmm, what's the word I'm looking for? Ferocious…

Now get this…I asked Carmen what happened to her aunt's boyfriend.

She looked at me over her fire engine red glasses that matched her hair and nails and shook her head.

"Naw, Angel…You too soft for all that information. Just know that he's no longer with us."

I sat back floored. That night over dinner I studied Hitta and I couldn't help but wonder what kind of thoughts were going on in his head. How the world did he survive the things he'd been through? I didn't understand his violent nature...and no matter how hard I tried, I couldn't relate.

That's when the first wave of uncertainty washed over me. I wasn't made of the same stuff he was made of...I haven't experienced the same traumas. How long before he got tired of me or thought I was too boring or suburban?

However, as if he could sense something was off with me, that night he made loved to me so gently and as he did, he whispered to me about how much he loved each part of my body and why. Then he said something that chased away all my doubts.

"Everything about you calls to something deep down inside of me. I can't explain it...but it's like you quiet the roar inside of me. Only when you around do I feel grounded... You my calm, shawty...it's like you a gift from God."

Sooooo...Yeah...

Foolishly, I let down my guard again and started back fantasizing about all the things I and my big grouchy lover could be...

And then Carmen told me that after her mom got locked up, she moved in with Hitta. At the time, he'd had a place with Shantell. Now, remember that name because we're going to come back to her in a minute. It was because of her that I was in this mess now...

So, Hitta and Shantell had a place, but Carmen said they were having trouble, he'd used Carmen coming to live with him as an excuse to move out and get another place since Carmen and Shantell did not get along anyway.

Of course, I asked why they didn't get along.

*"The b**** was jealous of me and my uncle's relationship. And it's like I told the ho, me and him been tight since I was a baby."* She held up her little fists. *"It was him that taught me how to throw them thangs!"*

Carmen was a mess...

But she went on to say that for the most part, her uncle stayed at the gym or with whatever woman who was entertaining him for the night. But then she caught herself and said...

"I mean, with friends...You know...friends?"

I chuckled and told her that was alright. I'd have to be a fool to think Hitta didn't have women before me. He was handsome, rich, an alpha… Every woman's dream man.

"Yeah, but until you, I've never seen him in love. If he not at the gym, he home with you… He really like coming home to you. That mean something, you know."

I tried to play it off like her words didn't have me doing a little dance on the inside.

"Really? What about Shantell? He loved her, didn't he?"

"Hell no… my uncle used to cheat on her like crazy. He was never at home. That was another reason they was always fighting."

I shook my head.

"What?" she asked with a frown on her face.

"That's bad that he cheated on her. She didn't deserve that."

Carmen rolled her eyes… *"Girl, please, Shantell a** the biggest gold digger on the westside of Chicago. My uncle had this b**** ridin in a Benz. She was rocking Prada, Fendi, Versace… getting her hair and nails laid every week. And then went out and got that expensive a** apartment on the Lake Front just so she could bring her friends around and rub sh*t in they face."*

She shook her head. *"I told Unc to get rid of that thot when she first started coming around. But then all of sudden, she pregnant by him."*

"Oh my God! Hitta has kids?"

"Hell naw, she was lying. But she told him she lost the baby…and was feeling all depressed, so he kept her thot a** around. But he wasn't feeling her…he could see through all her shenanigans, which is why he barely came home to her. She used to call my phone every night like…You seen Hitta?" That she said in a whiny voice.

I was surprised by her words. It sounded like she was describing a different man. I'd come to look at him as something of a home body. Most of the time by the time I got home from the Tea Shop he and Jessie were there waiting for me with dinner.

He watched a lot of boxing on TV, but he mostly did that downstairs in the living room where he'd set up his gaming systems. Sometimes I watched with him, especially highlights of his fights, but most of the time when I wasn't with him, I was organizing my herb pantry or working in the rose garden.

Shucks, I guess I am a home body too…LOL

"But see, the thot didn't like me 'cause I used to tell her broke a** to get a job!" Carmen said drawing my attention back to her.

"Oh my goodness! You did not tell your uncle's girlfriend to get a job…" She put her hand on her hip and lifted an eyebrow.

"I used to tell her that sh*t every day without fail…sometimes twice. I don't like to see nobody trying to take advantage of my uncle." The only thing I could do was shake my head.

So yeah…That's Carmen for you… She was crazy, but the girl had a business head on her that was out of this world. Because Hitta was rarely at the apartment he'd gotten for them two and she basically had the place to herself, she decided to go live on campus when she started college because it was something she'd always wanted to do.

Now on a side note, I've also learned a bit more about Carmen and Wayne's situation, but I won't be sharing that with y'all. It seems as if Carmen is going to be sharing her own story with you guys, so my lips are sealed.

Moving on… Before I tell you guys about Shantell and Trina and all that drama… I want to first tell you about the warning because it plays a very important role in this whole thing. And had I listened to my Greatie, I would have never been in this situation to begin with.

With my shop being closed down for the Sabbath Day, on the first Saturday at my new home, I took time to unpack my things and do a little exploring because up until that point, I hadn't had time. After finding out that I didn't work on the Sabbath, Hitta decided to stay home with me.

So, he, Jessie and I ended up having a real chill day that will forever stay in my memory. It was just one of those perfect days. He helped me unpack and arrange things in the house to my liking. And no matter how many times I asked him to move the couch or the bed, he never lost patience with me…Just moved it three feet to the left and then an inch back to the right…and in some cases, all the way to the other side of the room because I'd thought it would look good in this spot, but the lighting just wasn't right.

After lunch, Jessie fell asleep in the den watching some crazy cartoon on TV. Hitta had gone down into the basement and started doing whatever he did down there...And I decided to explore the back yard... another thing I had been dying to do.

And that's when I found the true treasure of the place. Whoever owned this home before us was really into roses. I found a secret rose garden at the back of the property. Because it hadn't been taken care of, the roses were overgrown with weeds and quite wild but were still very beautiful.

Next to it was an old charming garden shed that still had a lot of tools in it...I grabbed a pair of shears and dived in trying to tame some of the bushes and vines and before I knew it, time had flown by. When Hitta found me, I was down on my knees trying to wrestle a stubborn weed out of the ground. I nearly jumped out of my skin when his vein-ridden muscled arm came down next to me, taking hold of the weed pulling it out effortlessly.

Somebody that big should make a sound when they walked. Anyhow, I'd discovered a new use for him, I put him on weed pulling duty immediately...Some of the weeds back here had been growing so long they'd become young trees.

Now, we didn't get far before his freaky tendencies got in the way. It was there in that secret rose garden that he taught me what a quickie was, only for us to go in and teach me what it was like to be made love to in the shower.

Needless to say, that day would go down in history as one of the best days of my life. Maybe it was because of that day and the fact that I felt So in Love (in my Al Green voice), Greatie showed up the next morning.

Sunday morning, like the previous mornings before, I woke up clinging to Hitta's back. I think I figured out why that was happening. It had something to do with him appearing in my dream every night. Not only did he make an appearance...but in every dream, he's leading me out of hell...

I think that was why I clung to his back like that...I don't know...

Anyway, so that morning...I woke up to the smell of elderberries. Only one person I knew could make a house smell of elderberries like that.

"Greatie's here!" Jessie cried as she hurried past my room and down the stairs.

With a smile on my face, I climbed off of Hitta's back and hurried into the bathroom to take care of my morning rituals.

"Where you going so early?" he grumbled from where he still lay in bed.

I grinned at him… "You'll see when you come down." Then I turned and followed Jessie down. I sure hope he wasn't the freaking out type because if he was, he was going to completely flip when he realizes that my Greatie can somehow come and go at will and don't always use doors…

When I got downstairs, Jessie was sitting at the table with a huge elderberry muffin that had been smothered in butter and honey in front of her. And Greatie was just taking another pan out of the oven. I ran to her and hugged her because I'd missed her so much and it had been nearly two years since I saw her last. I do believe the last time was when she'd given me the idea to go to Ms. Armstrong with the thought of renting the Tea Shop instead of buying it.

"How is my sweet girl?" she asked as she held me close.

Oh y'all…I loved hugging Greatie. She always smelled like elder-berries…because they were her absolute favorite. She made the best elderberry tea in the whole world.

"A lot has happened since the last time I saw you," I told her.

She smiled warmly at me. "I know, child…Sit down and have a cup of tea."

Eagerly I sat…A cup of Greatie's tea was a treat indeed. As she poured it, I fingered her beautiful multi-colored skirt, just like I did when I was a little girl. Every time I saw her, she wore the same thing. This skirt never got old or worn…or even dirty for that matter.

"Where was you at, Greatie?" Jessie asked around a mouth full of muffin. "I missed you."

The fact that Jessie was about four the last time she saw her goes to show you the effect Greatie's visits have on a person.

"Ow…I've been quite a few places, little one." She sounded tired, but not the kind of tired as in sleepy, but the kind of tired that goes way down to your bones…soul tired.

I took a sip of my tea and closed my eyes feeling the healing power of the herbs seeping into the soil that is my flesh...Only Greatie can make tea like this. I could only hope that one day I'll achieve her status, but I doubt that I ever will. Greatie's knowledge of herbs is too much to learn in one human lifespan.

Well...One normal human that is...

Greatie is human, she's just a human who was granted access to only die once...

At least...That's what she told me when I was a little girl. She said the righteous man is only promised death once and that she'd died, but that a great servant of the Master prayed that she would come back and well...She did.

She eased down into her chair studying me with her ancient gaze. "How have your dreams been of late?"

I grinned as I took another sip of my tea. "Different."

She nodded... "Which is why I've come."

"I figured that... I'm just wondering if you are bringing good news or bad."

"I come with neither good news nor bad, more like a warning."

I lifted an eyebrow. "A warning?"

She reached over and rubbed her hand down Jessie's braids. "The Master heard your prayers, little one. Things are going to get a bit easier for you." The smile left her face. "At least... for a little while."

Jessie nodded... "Okay."

I wondered if she really understood what Greatie was saying because I sure didn't. I opened my mouth to ask her to explain, but she looked at me and spoke instead.

"So, you've gone and fallen in love with one of the Preacher's boys, huh?"

I frowned...She was way off. There were no preachers in Hitta's family, not even close. Over lunch the other day, Carmen told me that Hitta's dad was killed by a rival gang when he was just a baby.

Wow! For the first time since I've known Greatie...She was wrong.

I shook my head. "No, Greatie, Hitta's father is not a preacher."

She inhaled before she gently hit the table in front of me. "Let me tell you a story."

Both Jessie and I grinned at each other. Greatie told the best stories in the whole world. You guys out there listening to my tale...settle in, you're getting ready to get a real treat.

"When the Master walked the earth in the flesh of a Man, he spoke of a parable. The reign of the heavens is like a man, a house-holder, who went out early in the morning to hire workers for his vine-yard. And when he had agreed with the workers for a denarius a day, he sent them into his vineyard." She lifted her teacup and took a sip of her healing brew.

"And then he went out about the third hour and saw others standing idle in the market-place and said to them, 'You too go into the vineyard and whatever is right I shall give you.' And they went. Having gone out again about the sixth and the ninth hour, he did like-wise. And about the eleventh hour, having gone out, he found others standing idle, and said to them, 'Why do you stand here idle all day?' They said to him, 'Because no one hired us.' He said to them, 'You too go into the vineyard, and whatever is right you shall receive.'"

The oven dinged and she got up and pulled another pan of muffins out of it before she reached up in the cabinet and took down Hitta's thermos.

"And when evening came, the Master of the vineyard said to his manager, 'Call the workers and pay them their wages." She turned her head and looked me in the eyes. "Beginning with the last to the first.'"

Turning back, she continued to fill Hitta's thermos with the tea she had been brewing for him.

"And when those came who were hired about the eleventh hour, they each received a denarius. And when the first came, they thought they would receive more."

After filling the thermos, she began to take the muffins out of the pan, stacking them neatly on a plate. I frowned at the number of muffins she made, wondering why there were so many.

"You'll see..." She told me before she continued her story. "But they too received each a silver piece. And when they received it, they grumbled against the householder, saying, 'These last have worked only one hour, and you made them equal to us who have borne the burden and the heat of the day.'"

She sat back down and lifted her tea. "Can you two guess what the Master said to them?"

Both Jessie and I shook our heads.

"He said, '*Friend*, I do you no wrong. Did you not agree with me for a denarius? Take yours and go. But I wish to give to this last man as also to you. Is it not right for me to do what I wish with my own? Or is your eye evil because I am good?' Thus the last shall be first, and the first last. For many are called, but few chosen."

When she was finished, she sat back in her chair and took another sip of her tea allowing us to digest her words.

And…Yeah. I had nothing.

I mean, I know the parable she spoke of, Mathew 20, verses 1-16, but I was completely lost as to what that had to do with Hitta's father, who was not a preacher.

Greatie chuckled, shaking her head at me. "Child, one of these days you're going to listen to yo' old Greatie and start studying yo' Word."

I took a sip of my tea to hide my guilt. My Greatie gave me a bible when I was eight years old. I still had it, I just never read it. I mean, don't get me wrong, I've read bits and pieces, like the MessiYah's parables…I really like those, but my Greatie wants me to pick it up and start from the beginning and read through to the end. And I am going to do it…I am…I just haven't gotten around to doing it just yet.

"That parable will mean different things to different people." As she spoke, she looked off to the side getting lost in her thoughts. "You see, like me, the Preacher has been out in the vineyard for a long time…in fact, he's been out there a lot longer than most, including me. But he doesn't grumble or moan. He just continues to work. It was he that explained that parable to me many years ago. He said, *Tabby girl*," she said that in a deep voice with a fond smile on her face, "*The Master was called good because he was able to see what we as men cannot. The workers that had worked since morning was not able to see past their own lives. They felt blessed when they were hired on by the Master because they knew at the end of the day, they will receive their reward. But they didn't think about their fellow brothers, who still waited to be hired, who too wished to be hired on to receive the reward. They also forgot the struggle in waiting and wondering if they'd ever be hired. They forgot that is the hardest part. While one waits outside of the vineyard, there are many things to battle, many things trying to convince you to fall out of line. The Master went out at different intervals throughout the day. Now, keep in mind, 99.9% of man never bothered showing up at all. Some got tired of waiting and left by the third hour, some showed up late, but they came. Others could not take the pressure of waiting and left by the sixth hour. Some showed up late, but they came. Other's legs gave out on them by the ninth hour. Some showed up late, but they came. And then there were those who could not endure to the end and got tired and left by the eleventh hour. And some who showed up late, but they finally made it. You see, the battle is not how long you've been in the field, the battle is getting to the field and enduring to the end. The fact that I know who I am and who I serve makes me have it easier than my brother who is still standing in line, although he has no idea who he serves, only that he heard the voice and is waiting to answer the call."*

She shook her head. "The Preacher's wisdom is something to behold, child. And Yah knows I've seen many fall by the wayside. But thanks to him, I now understand that those who make it in the vineyard and out to the end of the day, deserve their reward no matter how long they've bore the heat of the sun. Because the truth is, it was always easier to bear the heat inside the vineyard than standing there idle waiting for the Master where the heat feels much hotter."

"The Preacher carries a strength that many of us don't have. And it's that strength that exists in his bloodline. From him come children of battle. His seeds whether for the good or the bad, are people of war. Some of the most vicious crimes ever committed amongst our people were committed by his seed. In the same breath, some of the most valiant heroes are of his lineage." Her gaze fell to Jessie as she took her little hand.

"You, my sweet child, is one of his." Jessie nodded again as if she understood.

Greatie's eyes came back to me. "They are not like you, daughter of Sarah…They are not healers. They were created by the Ancient of Days to be a battle-ax of destruction, whether for the good or the bad."

"What does that have to do with Hitta?"

"He's a son of The Preacher, child. A man of war…and it's too soon yet to tell if it is for the good or the bad. But one thing is for certain, just like the others of his bloodline, he is a weapon and can cause grave destruction if he gets the mind to."

"I've come to you to warn you because although you are a Daughter of Sarah and like catnip to the Preacher's seed…You are also one of mine and I don't want you broken."

I bit my lip as I digested her words, like that parable, most of it I didn't understand. I was clueless as to what a Daughter of Sarah was… But I understood that her warning was about Hitta loud and clear. Although I did a stellar job at ignoring it these days and he was being on his very best behavior…There was a violent nature about him.

It was that violence in him that made people clear out of his way when he walked or caused some men's voices to quiver when they spoke to him and even some women for that matter. There was something in Hitta's eyes that I couldn't describe because it was foreign to me… But it was deadly. You knew and felt that he would not hesitate to use those big scarred hands of his to destroy if he in any way felt threatened.

But Greatie's warning came too late. I'd stolen from him…

Now thinking back, I remember the moment before I'd made up my mind to take the money, where there was a little voice in the back of my head that said very clearly…for every action, there is an equal or greater reaction.

And yet, I still moved forward, throwing caution to the wind. And now like he said, I belonged to him…

And not just because of the money…I'd become a slave to his touch. The man loved my body in a way that caused me to feel as if I was burning and only he could put the fire out. I knew that fact like I knew Greatie was not of this time or this place.

I'd only just learned pleasure and I've become addicted to it. I'd become addicted to the feel of his big warm body protecting me from my nightmares. I'd become addicted to the feel of his big strong hands, hands that are capable of causing great destruction, but when they touch me…they are so gentle, caressing parts of me as if it's his most precious treasure on the whole earth.

And his mouth…

The things he did with his mouth… He took his time with me, kissing me as if there is nothing else in the world he would rather be doing. When he fed from me, he did it like someone who had been starving and just found a delicacy and wanted to take his time and cherish it.

Mmmmm….

I had to stop my thoughts there, if I continued and spoke of the way other parts of him made me feel, how other mighty parts of him caused me to separate from myself as it drove me to the point of ravenous hunger before causing my world to combust…

Yeah…I had to stop there. But as you guys can see, I was hooked on his loving and I didn't know how not to crave his touch.

"What should I do?" I asked Greatie…If ever there was a time I needed her help, now was it.

She reached across the table and took my hand, giving it a reassuring squeeze. "You need to prepare yourself for a life different from what you're used to. You have been given as a gift to that slayer. He is a lot rougher than some of his kind. He's come up in a very hostile environment and I fear that he will not know how to protect your gentle heart."

"Protect my heart from what?"

She nodded toward the stairs. "Him."

Chapter Twelve

I'LL DO ANYTHING TO KEEP YOU...

> *Men Aren't Stupid, and You Don't Need A Complicated Set of Rules to Find One Who Loves You. Here's the Only Rule You Need; If A Man Loves You, He Will Do Anything He Can to Keep You Around...ANYTHING!*

Unknown

Angel

Frowning I turned to see who she was speaking of. Hitta came down the stairs and around the corner pulling a t-shirt over his head, his ripped brown stomach flexing as he did.

Shucks... I nearly licked my lips, remembering how I'd just ran my tongue over those same muscles only a few hours ago.

With heated cheeks, I turned back to face Greatie, but she was gone. Jessie pointed to the patio door that let out to the back yard.

"She went that way."

That sounds about right... She'd been coming and going like that for as long as I've known her. Apparently, she was not ready to let herself be known to Hitta… The only reason she used the door this time was because Jessie was watching her and she didn't want to freak her out by just disappearing.

"Baby, I need to go to the gym for a few hours, one of my fighters having some personal issues and taking his aggression out on my staff." He shook his head. "I swear I think that nigga doing steroids or some sh*t."

He wrapped his arms around my waist and pulled me up from the chair so that he could plant one of those kisses on me that was going to have me fantasizing about him for the rest of the day.

"When I get home, I'm gon' be hungry, shawty, so make sure there ain't nothing standing between me and my feast…" he whispered in my ear before he took my lobe into his mouth and sucked on it.

See what I'm talking about? I had to squeeze my knees together to soothe the need he caused in my center at his words… As he let me slide back in my chair, he studied my face as if he was trying to commit it to memory.

"I still can't believe I got you here with me…" he whispered. He leaned down and gave me one more quick peck on the lips before he stood and headed towards Jessie…

She watched him with a barely suppressed grin on her face…as if she was waiting for him too— She shrieked as he suddenly charged her, jumping out of her chair as if she had been expecting him to come after her.

"Where my money? You bet five dollas you was gon' beat my score in GTO…and you lost, so where my money?"

"I ain't got yo' money!" she screamed before she tried to dash past him to the steps, but he caught her and then held her upside down by one foot and started shaking her as if he was trying to shake change out of her pockets. She was now laughing so hard I could see the veins sticking out her neck.

I stood and gave him my no-nonsense look. When he and Jessie first hooked up his PlayStation in the living room and she asked him if they could play GTO, he and I talked about how that wasn't a good idea. But apparently, they went behind my back and played anyway… and bet on the game to boot!

"What?" he asked...Like he had no idea why I was looking at him this way. Jessie was already rough and she didn't need violent video games giving her any more ideas.

Although he'd stopped shaking her, he still held her upside down by one leg. Of course, Jessie's crazy butt loved it and was trying to swing at his legs with her little fists.

See what I mean? Violent...

I lifted an eyebrow and folded my arms.

Chuckling, he turned her around and eased her back on her feet. When she saw the look on my face her laughter died down.

"I thought we agreed that we would not let Jessie play GTO."

He shrugged like he was innocent. "I know...I was down here minding my own business, quietly playing a game when this one," he pointed at Jessie, who was barely holding on to her laughter, "Came down and was like, yo, I bet I can beat yo' score, sh*t...I got five on it."

I laughed. "She did not say sh*t."

He looked down at her and frowned... "I can't remember, did you say sh*t?"

Jessie could not hold on anymore and erupted in laughter... "Noooo!" she screamed before she leaped up and tried to punch his daylights out, but he caught her and started tickling her until she yelled that she had to pee.

I shook my head as I watched them. Jessie was so rough and Hitta was only condoning that behavior.

"Okay, Jess...You got yo' Tee-Tee giving me the mean eye... Plus, I got to ride."

She threw her arms around his waist. "Can I go with you?"

Chuckling he headed over to the counter where his thermos was with her still clinging to him.

"Not this time, lil mama." He picked up his thermos. "Is this for me?"

I nodded...wondering what kind of tea Greatie made for him. I also wondered if he will be able to tell the difference between our brews. He probably won't, only someone that knew tea would be able to. Tea was like wine, either you knew or you didn't.

He grabbed one of the muffins off the plate and took a huge bite as he headed for the door, but then his steps came to a complete halt as he whipped back around to look at the plate of muffins.

"Damn, shawty…these joints good as hell." He said as he walked back to the plate. "Did y'all eat already?"

Chuckling both Jessie and me nodded. He took down another plate and put two muffins on it.

"Just in case y'all want one later."

"How considerate…" I laughed. It was like twenty muffins on the plate and he only left us two.

He shrugged with fake humility… "It ain't nothing…"

I held my head back and laughed at that as he carried the full plate without covering it or anything out the door.

Note to self: Get the elderberry muffin recipe from Greatie.

For the life me I don't know how she always knows what to make, when to make, what to sew, what to say…but she does. I had no idea Hitta was getting ready to go into the gym or else, I would have made his tea. But somehow my Greatie did, she was always on time, it's one of the reasons I loved her so much.

However, the fact that she didn't let Hitta see her frightens me though.

Did she do that because she didn't like him?

Greatie was a good judge of character. Did her action mean that Hitta was bad for me?

Jessie exhaled loudly and miserably as she climbed up on the couch and watched his truck drive away… "I wish I could go with him."

I rubbed her back, poor baby looked as if she'd lost her dog…

Jessie thought Hitta was the best thing since sliced bread. Over the last couple of weeks, she's been going to the gym nearly every day after school. He bought her a little pair of pink boxing gloves and has been teaching her how to box. And believe it or not, she was a natural.

Hitta was so impressed with how well she was learning what he was showing her that he had Wayne start her a YouTube channel called Hitta's Little Princess… The daggone channel had over ten-thousand subscribers before that first week was out…

Because this was all so very new to me, I didn't know if he was a bad influence or a good one. All this time, I've been trying to teach Jessie how to be more ladylike and here he was teaching her how to throw them thangs…Hitta's words.

But at the same time, I've never seen her happier than when she was with him. And I guess I can admit that I was a little jealous that she didn't want to hang out with her Tee-Tee anymore. The other night, I was able to leave the shop early because Summer and Kayla, the other young lady I hired, assured me that they could handle the light evening rush and I didn't need to stay there hovering over them like a mother hen.

Hitta had called me earlier that day and said that he and Jessie were on their way to get some food and were headed to the house. So, I was super excited that they were home already because I wanted to do some curtain shopping and was looking forward to them going with me.

When Lannox dropped me off, I practically ran into the house I was so excited. That was when I discovered Hitta was still letting Jessie play GTO…I walked in on her and Wayne involved in an intense game. Hitta, Carmen, Maddox and two more guys I'd never seen before all sat in the living room eating chicken wings and fries.

I plopped down on the couch next to Hitta and after stealing one of his wings asked him if he wanted to go curtain shopping with me. You would have thought I asked that man to go get his colon checked with the way that he looked at me.

He shook his head… "Sh*t, naw… Yikes!"

"Why not!?"

He chuckled. "Shawty, I'd rather do anything else in the world than that…" He pointed at Wayne… "Ay, Bo…order some curtains, man! You see the lady want some curtains."

I slapped his arm. "You play too much."

This caused everybody to laugh at me. That was something else they always did…

Laugh at me…

I think to them I was a bit of a lame. Jessie came over and got a few fries. I stood and took her hand before turning to Hitta with my other hand on my hip.

"Forget you then…Jessie will go with me."

She made a startled sound in her throat and then just went limp. I turned to look down at her surprised because she'd just fainted.

"Jessie, are you alright?" I asked shaking her hand.

"Can't go shopping 'cause I'm dead," she muttered without opening her eyes.

Of course, this caused Hitta to roar with laughter. He laughed harder than I'd ever heard him laugh before. He laughed so hard he damn near choked on a fry…I kid y'all not, Wayne had to pound on his back.

I narrowed my eyes at him as I stood there still holding Jessie's limp hand while she lay on the floor next to me playing dead.

"Come on, boss lady, I'll go curtain shopping with you," Carmen told me, coming to my rescue.

I admitted to her while we shopped that my feelings were hurt that Jessie had abandoned me for Hitta.

"She never wants to spend time with me anymore."

"Don't let that get to you. My uncle may be a grouch, but he is really fun. When I was Jessie's age, he was my favorite person in the world."

"What about me? I'm fun!" I whined.

She rubbed my back. "Yeah…You are." I could tell in her voice that she was just telling me that and my eyes must have said as much.

"Well, look at it like this…at least my uncle thinks you're fun."

Both of us paused at her words… she cringed. "I didn't mean in that way." So yeah…we had a good laugh after that.

Hm?

Oh! Sorry about that…I got a little off topic again. I was telling you guys how I ended up in my most recent predicament.

That Sunday night when it was time to drop off Jessie, my heart was heavy just like it was every time I brought her back home. This was not a safe place for my baby…But because I was just her aunt and neither of her parents saw anything wrong with her environment, I was forced to do this every week.

I told Hitta that he may want to come back and get me because I would probably be a while cleaning up inside.

"Naw...I'll wait." He killed the engine and let his seat back pulling his baseball cap down over his closed eyes.

"You sure?"

He chuckled. "Yeah, I can catch up on my rest...making you scream all night got me tired."

My mouth fell open as I prayed Jessie didn't hear him. "Hitta!"

"Calm down, she ain't hear me," he muttered without opening his eyes.

Shaking my head, I headed into the building preparing myself for the task ahead. However, Peaches met us at the door.

"Uh-uh!" she said shaking her head, "You ain't dropping her off with me. Her mammy ain't been home since Thursday...I am not finna get stuck with her a**. I'll have Trina call when she get home." And then she slammed the door in our faces.

My stunned gaze went down to Jessie's. With a huge grin on her face, she shrugged.

"I guess I have to go back to yo' house then."

"I guess so..." And at my house she's been ever since...There has been no word from Trina and it's been two weeks. Hitta says not to worry about it and that Jessie is welcomed to stay here as long as she wants. But the crazy part about it was that Jessie didn't even ask after her mom. She didn't ask to call her or anything.

It was me who was calling Peaches from time to time to see if she'd heard from Trina...Well, at least I was. The last few times I called, I got a message saying that the phone had been disconnected. I called a few people who sometimes hung out with Westly to see if they'd heard from him or knew where he was with no luck...

Both of my babies' parents were M.I.A and I didn't know what was going on with that. So, yeah... that was one of the problems I'd been dealing with over the past two weeks. Now let me tell you guys about problem number two, Ms. Shantell, Hitta's ex-girlfriend.

Do y'all remember me telling you guys about the pretty lady who was working at the front desk of the gym that day, the one who I said was perfect for him because she looked like his type?

Well, that's Shantell...his ex, go figure.

Last Wednesday, Jessie wanted me to meet her at the gym so that I could watch her shoot her YouTube video…Her words.

After the afternoon rush at the Tea Shop, I told Summer I was going to take an hour lunch break and that I will be back before the evening rush. Carmen was working at the gym that day and Kayla was off, so I didn't want to leave Summer by herself for too long.

Don't get me wrong, she is a remarkable employee, and I was already thinking about making her front of the house manager. It's not that she can't handle being alone, I just didn't want to put that kind of pressure on her so soon.

Anyway, I got Maddox to run me by the gym and walked into several surprises.

First, I'd thought that Jessie's little YouTube videos were being filmed on Wayne's smartphone or something like that….

I was wrong!

There was a full camera crew there. Hitta was in the ring with Jessie holding some kind of pads on his hands and he was calling out punch combinations as she threw them in her little pink boxing gloves.

And…You know, I must say that although I wanted her to be more of a girlie girl like me, I was proud of her; it was clear that she wasn't and probably never will be.

He'd say something like…*Jab, jab, left hook, uppercut, jab,* and Jessie would follow through, throwing the proper punches…

My baby was good…I can't lie.

So, I'm standing there watching them practice when Ms. Thang walks up to me.

"Ummm, can I help you? If you not working out, you need to leave. We don't allow just anybody in here off the streets!"

I recognized her instantly. At the time I didn't know that she was Shantell, I just remembered her being angry with me the other day after I'd come in looking for Westly and Hitta shut her down and made her see to what I needed.

So, I smiled, trying to extend an olive branch as I gestured toward the ring.

"I'm Jessie's aunt…"

She rolled her eyes much like she'd did the other day… "Oh! Okay then, you need to go over there and take a seat like the other guests. We have dangerous equipment in here and don't need you falling trying to sue nobody." As she spoke, she rudely pointed at some chairs that were lined up against the far wall.

"Oookay…" I said as I turned and headed toward the chairs.

Although I didn't appreciate the way she was speaking to me, I did what she said. Maybe the gym had rules and she was just following the rules.

But as I sat and waited for Jessie and Hitta to finish, I watched Ms. Thang move around the gym like she was the queen. Dressed in black Nike yoga pants that hugged her perfectly shaped hips and a halter top that showed off the fact that she obviously worked out because unlike me, she didn't have a softly curved stomach with love handles. Her stomach was like a washboard. And she didn't have big full breasts like mine, she had perfect C cups that were playing peek-a-boo with that halter top in a scandalous way. Every time she held up her arms, I saw a few men visibly hold their breath at the off chance that top will raise just an inch more and they'll get that nipple shot that's been teasing them all day.

She joked, flirted with, and teased the guys… who all looked at her with desire in their eyes. She brought Hitta and Jessie a bottle of water and set it on the floor of the ring for when they were done shooting and said something to Wayne, who stood by the producer no doubt telling him how to do his job that caused him to laugh. The whole time, she made me feel like the outsider I was.

I looked down at my baggy jeans with the holes at the knees. I loved these jeans and I'd paired them with my cream cashmere sweater. That morning I thought I looked cute. Ever since Hitta has been in my life, I've felt good and had been dressing to reflect how I felt. But now, in the presence of Ms. Baywatch…tall, stacked and tempting, I felt frumpy again.

Carmen came out of a door that was close to where I sat. When she saw me, she frowned, "Why are you all the way over here by yourself?"

I pointed at Ms. Thang… "She told me to sit over here so that I didn't get hurt on the equipment."

Carmen put her hand on her hip as her face hardened. "Bullsh*t! Shantell a** just being messy!"

You couldn't have slapped me and surprised me more in that moment. "Wait! That's Hitta's ex?"

With her lips pressed together, she nodded. "Yeah, that's her trifling a**. Walking around here with that little bitty shirt on and no bra. Who the hell comes to a gym with no bra on? A hooker, that's who!"

I was floored. So, the woman who had walked around the gym for the last thirty minutes like she was the queen here was Hitta's ex?!

"I don't know why he won't fire her…Come on, you don't have to sit over here." Carmen took my hand and pulled me back toward the ring.

Oh, my goodness! My emotions were a mess…For the first time in my life, I was experiencing jealousy.

Why did Hitta have his ex working at his gym? What the heck?

All this time, I've been feeling like the outsider because I wasn't like Hitta and his crew, Shantell was here blending in well with everybody. Not once did I see anybody laugh at her like they laughed at me. She looked like she was a part of the crew…

Standing there I experienced a little bit of trauma and as I do whenever I experience trauma, I scrambled to obtain balance so that I didn't break.

I reminded myself that Hitta was never mine to begin with. My brother stole money from him. He and I had a six-month agreement. Yeah, I felt hurt because I'd foolishly let my feelings get involved. But it's okay, I was a virgin and he is very good at making me have amazing orgasms. It's quite natural for me to confuse that with something else.

But I was alright now. I will not make that mistake again. Two weeks had passed, I had five months and two weeks to go and then we will go our separate ways. Sex is just sex…

Okay, I'm alright…I can do this. This will not break me!

If my mom abandoning me didn't break me, then neither will this.

If me ending up in the foster home and living with a pervert didn't break me, then neither would this…

If I was able to put a smile on my face, although I was struggling to start my own business while supporting my brother in rehab and taking care of his daughter and her mom…then I can put a smile on my face right now…

And although it hurt like hell…When Hitta and Jessie finished their session, I smiled as if nothing in the world was wrong. He reached down over the ropes, wrapped one arm around my waist and lifted me all the way up to hug him.

"Hey, baby…I missed you," he whispered in my ear as he enveloped me in his embrace, causing everything else to cease to exist at that moment. As my eyes drifted shut, I knew I was doomed because here in his arms is where I felt the safest. Here in his arms is where it felt like I belonged…

Dear God, help me…I was so doomed.

———

So, okay…that was last week. I've been back to the gym a few times and managed to avoid Shantell…Although I wanted to, I didn't ask Hitta about her or why the hell he had her working at his gym with him.

So that brings us to today.

Believe it or not, the day started off beautiful. Because it was my day off and Jessie would be in school for the first half of it, Hitta and I decided to go downtown for lunch. The news said that we were going to get a break from the winter-like weather on this April day and that it was actually going to be pretty mild, mild meaning sixty degrees. And if you are from Chicago, you know that you take advantage of those days.

So, because I was feeling good, I decided to put on my favorite summer dress that I could get away with by wearing a shawl. I liked this dress because it was the same colors as my Greatie's skirt. But the thing is I'd had the dress since I was like fifteen. And I'd worn it so many times that one of the spaghetti straps refused to stay up on my shoulder, so I spent the whole time I wore it pulling it back up. But outside of that, it was a beautiful dress, light and breezy and fell on my body in a most flattering way.

Because there could be no bra straps, I wore my blue strapless bra underneath with the matching panties. After doing my hair and putting on my jewelry, I felt sexy. And when I left out the bathroom and Hitta tried to pull me into the bed, I knew I was sexy.

He couldn't keep his eyes or hands off me and as we walked around downtown, I had to constantly push him away or smack his hands from going where they didn't belong. My lips were kiss-swollen because he'd pulled me to the side and kissed me so many times it's a wonder we made it anywhere.

Several times folks stopped us for an autograph or to take a picture with Hitta. He took me to Oprah Winfrey's favorite restaurant and once again the chef came out to greet us and take our orders personally.

We were having such a good time that he got tickets to the Bulls game for me, him and Jessie because I said I'd never been, but he needed to stop by the gym for about an hour to have a quick meeting with one of his new fighters and the guy's manager.

I was alright with that; for the most part, I haven't been having any trouble at the gym and ever since Hitta's PDA, Shantell hasn't so much as looked my way. Plus, Carmen was there, and I had a few things to talk to her about the Tea Shop.

As soon as we walked through the front door, the smile that was on Shantell's face disappeared and I thought to myself that I had spoken too soon. The look she gave Hitta was a bit disturbing. It was a look that said I can't believe you brought her up in here. But of course, that didn't go well with him.

"What the f*** is your problem?" he grumbled. Mr. Grouch, never one to mince words, that he is.

Instead of her saying anything she slammed whatever papers she had in her hand down on the counter and stormed off.

Both Hitta and I just stood and stared after her for a minute.

"What was that about?" I asked when his irritated gaze came to mine.

"F*** if I know…"

"Angel!" Carmen called from her little office upstairs, "Come up here, I want to talk to you about the new developments for the merger."

Hitta lifted an eyebrow… "Merger?"

I chuckled… "Carmen's been going on about buying the store next door and opening a bookstore, merging it with the Tea Shop. Let me go and see what she has going on, I'll talk to you in a little while." I went to walk away.

"Yo…" He called after me.

I turned back to face him… Did I tell y'all how good he looked today? Mmmmm…please allow me to amend that.

Today he'd traded his sports appearance in for a more casual one and he was killing it in a pair of black designer jeans and a white button-up shirt that lay on his muscled frame perfectly. The first three buttons on it were unbuttoned and the top of his white tank top showed. He had replaced the big chains he normally wore with a smaller golden rope that was very casual. He had also traded his gym shoes out for a pair of tan Timberlands that looked as if he'd just taken them out of the box.

"Where my kiss?" he asked cutting into my thoughts.

I bit my lip trying to hide my grin. "You are not guaranteed a kiss every time I leave."

"The hell I'm not," he muttered before he suddenly reached out and grabbed the front of my dress pulling me to him so close that our heads were nearly touching. And of course, my strap slid down my arm exposing the top half of my right breast.

I reached up to grab it, but he took my hand stopping it and my dress fell a little more.

"Hitta!" I whined looking around to see who was looking, but no one could see me past his big body.

"You been driving me crazy all day with this dress. My word I been havin' to stop myself from pulling you somewhere and ripping it off."

I opened my mouth startled. "This is my favorite dress."

He brought his big hand up and ran his fingers along the top of it, causing it to fall a little more. And after groaning deep in his throat, lifted my strap back on my shoulder and then my shawl until it was covering both of my shoulders completely.

"Shawty, you can't wear this sh*t out no more. I almost killed seventeen mutha f****s today."

"You did not…" I didn't see him get upset not once…

He reached up and tapped his head with his finger. "You didn't know 'cause I was killing them mutha f****s in my head."

I reached up and palmed his face before bringing it down so that our lips could touch.

"Okay, I will only wear the dress in the privacy of our own home."

Whenever my shawl slipped, I did notice a lot of guys looking at me. Of course, they were trying to do it where Hitta couldn't see, but they were checking me out. And most of their eyes were glued to my double D's. It had been a while since I've worn the dress…over a year. The last time I'd worn it I had not filled it out like this.

"Thank you, Teacup. It's gon' kill me to watch you walk through this gym, knowing that all these nigga's finna be looking at what's mine," he grumbled.

Standing on my toes, I kissed his lips again. "There is only a handful of people here." It was true, the gym was practically empty and some of the folks that were here were women. "And the few guys that are here are not going to look."

"How do you know?"

I chuckled because he was acting like a little boy pouting about his favorite toy.

"Because, Hard Hitta, they're all afraid of you."

He grinned before he leaned down and took my lips in a kiss that damn near melted my dress off. By the time I made it upstairs to Carmen's little office, I had only one thing on the mind. I couldn't wait to get home, get Jessie to bed, and have some alone time with my big grouchy man.

After talking to Carmen for about fifteen minutes I excused myself to go to the washroom. When I opened the door and went in, I could hear someone talking, but it wasn't until I'd gone farther inside that I recognized Shantell's voice.

She was in one of the stalls talking on the telephone. Something told me to just turn around and leave, but she was crying and talking in a very frantic tone, and well…I'm nosy, so yeah, I listened.

"He told me Tuesday night that he wasn't going to bring her back here…" she paused for a minute as she listened to whoever she was talking to.

"Yeah, I know…but why he still paying my bills then? If that's his new woman, why he still coming to my house? Why he still f***ing me? He went to the doctor with me last week to hear our baby heartbeat for the first time. Why he still making plans with me to be a family?"

I felt like someone had hit me in the stomach with a bat. I couldn't listen to any more…I turned and ran out of that washroom desperately needing to get out of there and damn near crashed into Carmen.

"I was just coming to get you because I've figured out a way to solve our little problem with Ms. Armstrong's racis—" She stopped mid-sentence when she saw the look on my face.

"What's wrong, sis?"

I stood there breathing heavily, trying to get control over my emotions. I felt nauseous… as if I would be sick any minute. I was breaking…

I was breaking and I didn't know what to do…

She's lying! A voice screamed loudly in my head. Like someone drowning, I desperately clung to that like air. But I had to know. My gaze went to Carmen's.

"Does your uncle still pay Shantell's bills?"

The look that came over her face gave me my answer. I went to walk around her, I needed to get out of here.

"Wait, Angel…You don't understand!" she called after me. But I didn't need to understand any more.

Shantell wasn't lying. They had a baby on the way, why else would he be paying her bills?

I can't believe I was such a fool. I can't believe I bought all that crap he was telling me!

I had to get out!

I hurried through the gym, now running for the entrance.

"Wow, Angel, where you are going so fast?" Maddox asked, seeming to appear in my path out of nowhere.

"I have to go, Maddox!" I went to walk run around him, but he stepped in my way reaching out his hands to stop me.

"Where is the boss?"

"I don't care!" I screamed in his face as I once again tried to go around him.

"Calm down, lass."

"No!" I yelled, now trying to shove him out of my way, but it was like trying to shove a wall. "Move!"

"Angel!" Hitta's deep voice came from somewhere behind me, bringing my struggling to an end.

I turned around to see him standing in the ring with his new fighter and Carmen. She was telling him something frantically moving her hands. Whatever she was telling him was making him angrier. But I didn't care.

I turned back around to face Maddox.

"Can you please move out my way!?"

With a sad look in his eyes he shook his head... "Not going to happen, lass."

"Everybody out!" Hitta's voice boomed from the ring.

Maddox took my arm and pulled me to the side as the few people who had been working out inside the gym hurried to obey his orders including his new fighter and his new fighter's manager. I pulled at my arm wanting to go with them. I didn't know what was happening and I was getting a bad feeling.

When the last person left out Wayne shut the gym door and locked it. And that's when I started getting nervous because I knew that I was getting ready to meet the man my Greatie had warned me about.

Shantell was now back at the front desk and she wore a little smile on her face. She was happy I was suffering. Still holding my arm, Maddox pulled me back into the gym towards the ring, I tried to pull my arm from him, but again, he was too strong. The strap on my dress had lowered, I don't know where I'd lost my shawl, but at that point I was too angry to care.

Hitta stood there looking down at me like an angry bull. "Let her go."

Maddox let me go and I stood looking around, surprised that the only people left in the gym was his staff or who I liked to call his crew. And they had all gathered around us.

"Fix yo' dress, Angel..." Hitta muttered.

With hands that shook I lifted my strap back on my shoulder.

"Where you going, baby?" Although he asked his question calmly, anger poured out of his eyes like a faucet.

I held up my head, the pain I felt made me bolder. "I'm leaving."

"Without me?"

I didn't bother to answer his question.

"What happened?"

I still didn't answer.

"Shantell told her something, that's what happened. I saw her come out of the washroom shortly after Angel with a little grin on her f***ed up face," Carmen spat from where she stood next to her uncle.

"Shantell!" Hitta called and we all watched as she sashayed around the corner.

"Yes?"

Okay, I want to pause right here in my story and point out a few things. First of all, this was some strange stuff, right? I mean, y'all see that, don't you? It's not just me, is it?

Second, the way everybody was standing completely still, only speaking when asked a question, should have let me know a few things about Hitta.

It felt like I was standing in the middle of a mob movie and Hitta was the mob boss. Even Shantell was as meek as a mouse right now.

And I figured out why they were all like that...You see, up until that point, I had never seen Hitta in a rage, but they all had. So, they all knew what could happen if he got too angry, and they all were trying to be very still so that didn't happen.

The next few minutes were going to be what my Greatie had come to warn me about...but of course, I'd forgotten her warning and did not proceed with caution.

I was soon to learn the dangers of that... Let's continue.

"What did you tell Angel in the washroom?"

At that point, he was still very calm. In fact, I thought it strange that he was choosing to have this conversation in front of everybody instead of in his office somewhere.

Tears came to Shantell eyes. "I didn't tell her nothing, I swear. I didn't even know she was in the washroom with me. Once again, Carmen is lying on me so that you can look at me as if I'm some kind of witch set out to destroy you."

"You is a witch, bitc—" Carmen began, but Hitta lifted his hand quieting her as his gaze fell on me.

"Did she know you were in the washroom with her?"

I shook my head, still trying to control my emotions. I did not want to talk to him. I did not want to be here in whatever the hell this was. I just wanted to pick Jessie up from school and find me another place to stay.

He exhaled as if he was tired. "So why are you upset with me?"

"Are you paying her bills?" I did not want to ask that. It just slipped through my lips.

He frowned. "Why?"

Is he serious?!

"Why?" I asked, not believing he would even ask that.

The muscle flexed in his jaw. "Don't like to repeat myself?"

"So, when were you going to tell me about the baby? Or didn't you believe I should know?"

His frown grew… "What f***ing baby?"

"I told you that b**** been lying about being pregnant!" Carmen spat.

"No, I haven't! Both of them are lying on me. They just trying to get you to kick me out on the streets because she jealous of me, can't you see that, baby?"

My mouth dropped as I turned my head to look at Shantell. She said that crap so convincing that if I didn't know better, I would have believed her. She had these big huge tears coming out of her eyes, even her bottom lip quivered. And it dawned on me that she had set this up, all of it.

Hitta's gaze fell on me and for a moment, I thought that he was going to believe her.

"Did you hear her say she was pregnant by me?"

I nodded. "I did."

He looked down for a minute shaking his head, a humorless laugh escaped his lips. Then he reached into his pocket and came out with a wad of money before counting out five hundred-dollar bills... that he held up between his fingers.

Hitta had three women that were a part of his crew, four if you count Carmen. They were all boxers and they were all there in the gym working out that day. When he held up the money, all three of them stepped forward, but it was Carmen who snatched it out of his hands.

"Please allow me," she said before she ducked under the ropes and jumped out of the ring.

"You think I'm a joke, Shantell?" Hitta asked her as Carmen walked towards her.

I frowned, completely lost as to what was going on. Shantell began to step back.

"Carmen, don't even try to come at me with no bullsh*t! I will knock yo' little short a** out!"

Hitta laughed...When he did, his crew did as well.

"I don't know fellas, before Carmen went away to school, she was a beast. She done got all book-smart and I think she may have lost her hunger."

A few of the men nodded agreeing with him. Wayne shook his head as he reached into his pocket and came out with a hundred-dollar bill...

"I got a bill that say she still got it." Most of Hitta's crew came out their pockets with money to match his bet. Even Maddox got in on it, like this was something that they did...often.

Hitta still stood inside the ring with his hands on the robe...He was king here.

And I felt like a fool because I didn't know what the hell was going on. When Carmen finally reached Shantell, she held up her hand.

"Double, I knock this b**** out on the first shot!" she called.

"I'll take that bet…" Wayne said pulling another bill out of his pocket, the others soon followed.

Oh my God!

What was happening? My stunned gaze turned to Hitta's. He was looking at me with a grin on his face, but there was rage in his eyes. He was angry that I tried to leave him. I felt like him making this a spectacle was his way of punishing me or something.

"Carmen, I ain't playing, I will knock yo' little a** out!" Shantell told her again as she took a few more steps back, preparing to fight the younger woman…

And I don't know what happened after that.

One minute they were standing there facing each other, Shantell only let Carmen get but so close before she began to swing at her…

Carmen dipped left, displaying the fact that, yes, she was a trained fighter. Shantell swung at her again and she dipped right, but when she did, she followed with a right hook that caught the taller women square in the jaw. Carmen jerked back her hand waving it in pain as Shantell's eyes rolled to the back of her head.

The gym erupted in amazed hoots and hollers before the woman's body hit the ground.

"Oh! Sh*t! She did it!" Hitta laughed putting his fist to his mouth.

Reminding me of Jessie, Carmen ran back toward the ring and slid under the ropes jumping up in her uncle's arms as they celebrated as if she'd just won a heavyweight fight.

What-The- Hell!!!!!

I felt like I was having an out of body experience. What the hell was wrong with these people?

Shantell was knocked out cold!

This savage behavior was too much for me…

"What the hell is wrong with you people?!" I yelled getting everybody's attention.

"She had that sh*t coming," Hitta muttered as he turned to face me.

And I don't know what happened with me, but something snapped inside of me.

"No, somebody should have knocked you the hell out!" I yelled.

And when I tell you that you could hear a pin drop after that…I'm not lying. Even Carmen was looking at me with wide eyes as if she could not believe I was talking to her uncle that way.

But I was on a roll… "How about you stop being a big a** hypocrite?!"

"What the f*** you talkin' about?" he grumbled and I could see him getting angrier, but I didn't care.

"You are paying her bills…What the hell is she supposed to think is going on?" I pointed at Carmen. "A man is paying your bills, what would you think?"

Although she didn't say anything, she gave me the look that said… yeah, she would think the same thing.

I pointed to the fighter they called Cherry-Bomb; I didn't know her real name. "A man is paying your bills…What would you think?" She looked at her boss and although it looked as if it pained her, she nodded.

Hitta's nostrils flared…but as I said before, I didn't care! The only thing I could see was him looking at me as if I irritated him asking me why, when I'd asked him earlier if he paid her bills.

"You want to walk around here like Mr. Big Shot, taking care of all your women and buying them houses and cars…" Just saying that pissed me off, especially knowing that he bought me a house.

I DIDN'T NEED HIM TO BUY ME A DAMNED HOUSE! I yelled to myself…I felt cheap and for some reason, that brought out the ghetto in me.

"Well, you can keep yo' Martha Stewart house, 'cause I don't like her food anyway! And for the record, I don't need you to buy me a house!" I pointed at Shantell's a** lying on the ground, looking a hot mess.

"I ain't like her. I didn't wait around for no man to rescue me. I'm a success story! I have my own damn money and my own damn business! And guess what, Hard Hitta, I didn't need you to help me get it either. So, take yo' Martha Stewart house with her bland a**, unseasoned food and take your money and shove it up yo' a**!!! It's over!"

I turned to walk toward the door, but this time, Maddox didn't try to stop me.

"Who the f*** you think you talkin' to?" Hitta's deadly voice came from behind me...And right there, y'all, I should have stopped. That was the point that I should have just let it go, but no...for the first time in my life I was speaking up for myself and if felt AMAZING!

I turned around and nailed him with my gaze... "I'm talking to the piece of crap that would condone animal behavior. I'm talking to my ex-lover!" And I don't know what possessed me to say what came out of my mouth next, but it did...

"When she wakes up...tell her she can have you. I'm going to get me a real man!"

There was a collective gasp of breaths. Everybody now looked at me with their mouths hanging open, all except Hitta, whose knuckles were white from where he tightly grasped the ropes. His face distorted in rage before a growl came out of his throat and he leaped over the ropes displaying the power in his body.

But I never saw him land on the ground because that little bravery I'd found disappeared like twenty dollars in my mama's hand and I turned around and hauled a**.

The stairs were the closest thing to me, there was no way I would make it all the way to the door. Quickly I took the stairs two at a time. I could hear him behind me, and my heart felt like it was going to burst out of my chest.

"Stop f***ing running from me!" he growled way too close.

"Stop chasing me!" I yelled back pumping my legs and arms as if my life depended on it.

I ran into the first door which was Hitta's office shutting and locking it just in time.

His first blow to the metal door seemed to shake the whole office.

"You gon' go get you a real man?" he yelled from the other side and followed with a pound on the door. "I wish you would, baby, I'd f***en' snap his neck in two and stuff his head up his a**! You know why, Angel?! 'Cause you mine! You f***en mine! And I'll kill before I see you on the arms of another mutha f***a!"

Breathing heavily, I stood back against the far wall staring at the door in amazement. I couldn't believe I'd just said that stuff. I couldn't believe he was this angry. I looked at the phone and thought about calling the police, but even I knew better than that. These weren't the kind of folks that handled stuff like that well… and if I was being honest with myself…

Although he was angry as a raging bull, deep down inside, I knew he wouldn't hurt me. I can't tell y'all how I knew it…I just did.

"Earl, don't just stand there looking stupid! Bring me the goddamn keys up here!" I heard him call down to someone.

Oh crap! I forgot about the keys… Frantically I looked around the spacious office for somewhere to hide, there was nowhere to go but underneath the desk.

I didn't care how I looked, I quickly crawled underneath and sat there hugging my legs, wishing I could take back my reckless words.

Oh y'all, you talking about a praying sista… When I heard those keys in that door before it opened and then closed, I started praying.

My Greatie wanted me to start reading my bible and I swear, if God helps me through this, I will read my bible. If he just helps me out of this ditch I've dug for myself, I swear to never steal again.

If he just—

I screamed when the leather chair that was in no way small was violently snatched away from the desk so hard that it crashed into the wall way across the office.

My eyes widened when those two Timberlands came into view connected to a pair of bowlegs encased in black jeans…

Closing my eyes, I started praying harder…

Oh God, help me!

"Angel…" Hitta growled and I jumped, putting my hand over my mouth so that I didn't start crying. "Come from under there!" Each of his words was bitten out in a way that let me know that he was barely holding on to his rage.

I thought about just pretending I didn't hear him…but then figured there was no need to put off the inevitable. I sucked in a deep breath and crawled from under the desk.

He didn't move back for me, which gave me very little space to rise. The strap on my dress fell, but I was too nervous to make any extra movements. Biting my lip, I stared at his angry chest that moved in and out as he took deep breaths because I was not brave enough to look him in the eyes...

This was the same chest that I clung to every night in my sleep... the same chest I'd kissed. But now it may be the last thing I ever see.

The first tear touched my cheek and I didn't bother to wipe it away...It was his hand that reached up and did it, and then he surprised the crap out of me. He went down to his knees in front of me and after wrapping his arms around my waist, pulled me to him, burying his face in my stomach.

I stood there staring down at the top of his head in complete shook.

"Don't leave me, baby...I'm sorry!" His muffled plea came out of my stomach. "If you get another man that sh*t gon' kill me...I swear! That sh*t will kill me! I can't lose you, shawty! Please, baye...what do you want me to do? I'll do it! I swear! I can't lose you."

What the world?

And I'll be doggone if his pleas did not pull at my heartstrings...I wrapped my arms around his head holding him to me and his embrace tightened.

"It's alright, Hitta." My voice trembled with unshed tears... "It's going to be alright..."

Still on his knees, he looked up at me and I could see the pain in his eyes. "I'll fire Shantell if you want me to. I was still helping her with her bills and sh*t because I have this sense of loyalty to people that's loyal to me. She a gold-digger and was a horrible girlfriend and a bit of a slut, she done f***ed a lot of the men that come to the gym... But she mans the sh*t out of that front desk...So I let her work it." He shrugged. "But I will kick her a** out if it mean not losing you. Sh*t, I'll shut down this whole f***ing gym if it mean not losing you, shawty."

I smiled down at him through my tears...I'd never seen him this way. Big fierce Hitta...on his knees begging little old me to stay. I bet there was no one else on earth that has ever seen him like this. This was something that he'd only shown me. I knew that like I knew my name was Angel.

My Greatie didn't say anything about this. How in the world was I supposed to walk away from him when he's like this?

"I can't believe you're on your knees begging me to stay," I told him.

"Sh*t, girl, for you, a nigga will beg all night if I have to."

Smiling, I palmed his face staring down into his intense gaze.

Dang it! I think I loved him…

"Angel…on the real. I love you, shawty. I'll do anything to keep you…anything."

Wow! He'd just spoken my thoughts to me. He loved me… Dear God, this man had my heart. I was so gone I don't think I'll ever be able to find my way back.

"Anything?" I asked…

He nodded. "Anything, baby…just say the word."

I bit my lip as I worked up the courage to say the word.

"Make love to me…"

"Sh*t…I thought you'd never ask," he hissed before his big hand came up to the top of my dress pulling it down, causing my breasts that were still swollen from his kisses this morning to spill out.

My breath sucked in sharply when his hungry mouth closed over the tender peak and he began to feed on me.

And I don't know if it was the fact that we'd just fought or what, but damn!

The sex was hot!

He raked his hand over his desk clearing a way for my body and I could tell that it was taking everything within him not to rip my dress open… but rather than tackle the buttons while he still feasted on my breasts, he pulled it up to my waist.

And as his hungry mouth lowered and I gave in to this man that I loved, my last coherent thought before I got swept away in the storm that was Hard Hitta, was that I prayed with everything in me that I wasn't being a fool.

Chapter Thirteen

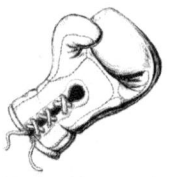

THE WEAVER'S TAPESTRY

" *When I was little girl, my mama told me that God is a Master Weaver and that life is His tapestry. She said no one knows what in the end the picture will unfold, but that we are all threads intertwined in His divine masterpiece. Some threads are dark, and some are bright, but one can't exist without the other because then the picture wouldn't be precise. She says balance is needed in order to bring God's plan into sight, but that in the end, everything will be alright. For it is written that Yah spoke into the darkness and said, let there be Light.*

Edwina Fort

Angel

"That feels so good, Angel," Hitta moaned as I used both of my hands to gently massage his head with the shampoo I made especially for him.

The relaxing fragrance of the herbal blend filled the bathroom, combining smoothly with the soothing melodic sound of Jill Scott that came from the speaker in the bedroom. Cupping my hands, I filled it with the warm water from the tea bath I made from the same blend as the shampoo and rinsed his hair.

Once done, he shamelessly rested his head against my breasts soaking the front of my tank top. I smiled down at the top of his head. Y'all, when my big strong man is in pain like this, he can be such a baby. But of course, I didn't mind at all.

Lifting the towel, I began to bath him with soap that I'd made from the same blend.

Instead of turning on the overhead lights, I'd lit candles; the synthetic lights only made his head feel worse. However, in another thirty or so minutes, he will not be feeling anything because the blend I'd used for his tea bath, shampoo and soap was going to knock him out...He just didn't know it yet.

"How do you do it, shawty? I swear you a real-life healer. I've gone to the best specialists in the world and they'd not been able to do what you did with just a bath."

My smile grew as I continued to run the towel over him making sure to saturate his skin so that the healing brew seeped way down into his pores.

"We've been programmed to view modern medicine as the best thing since sliced bread, but there was a time when all man needed to heal was the herbs that grew from the very earth we came from... It's kind of like milk from mama's breast."

I spoke softly, using the sound of my voice to give him comfort and to help relax his big body further, lulling him into the sleep that will heal him...

At least this time...

"When I was a little girl, my Greatie said that after the great flood, God sent an angel to teach Noah how to use the herbs of the earth to heal his children. She said that every sickness that plague man is an unclean spirit, and that the right combination of herbs can chase those spirits away."

Once I'd finished washing as much of his big body as I could reach, I used a bowl and scooping more of the healing water up, gently poured it over his head as I continued to speak. He now looked at me through lids that were getting lower and lower.

"Why do you think I get these headaches?" he muttered... fingering one of my braids that fell into his tea bath.

I shook my head as I gently continued to pour the water over his thick neck and shoulders...

"I don't know, but I believe it's psychological as well as spiritual."

He frowned a bit. "Spiritual?"

I nodded... "Yeah, have you ever heard the tale of King Saul?"

He shook his head his eyes growing heavier.

"Many years ago, there was a great king named Saul. You see, what made him great is that he had been appointed his seat directly from The Ancient of Days. But like many men who receive such power, it went straight to his head and he forgot all about The Ancient of Days and started believing that by his own might was he great. He even got a statue erected of himself in the Set-Apart Land, something the Heavenly Father hates with a vengeance. So, God sent his prophet to anoint a new king, Dawid... Or who you may know as King David."

I stood and retrieved the big fluffy towel, holding it open for him as he stepped out. I didn't want him falling asleep in the tub. Once his eyes closed, he needed to be able to get a few hours of undisturbed rest.

"Once Saul got wind of this, he became jealous of the young handsome Dawid and in his heart, decided to kill him."

As he stood before me, so powerful and strong...I could imagine that King Dawid was very much like him. I had to go up on my toes to dry off his mighty shoulders. Biting my bottom lip as my hands lowered to his chest drying the water off of his well-defined pecks.

This man's body is gorgeous...

Mmmm…

I quickly continued with my story before my mind went elsewhere.

"The Ancient of Days rejected Saul and an evil spirit began to plague him, causing all kinds of havoc in his life. His servants begged him to call Dawid to come play his musical instrument for him because it was a well-known fact that when he played it, it chased away sickness."

Once I'd dried all the water from his beautiful body, I took his hand and led him to the bed. He was so relaxed he looked drugged. He didn't put up any argument as I held the covers back and gestured for him to lie down. I'd already closed the curtains blocking out the midday sunlight.

Crawling into bed next to him I propped my back up on the pillow a bit, smiling when my big baby turned over wrapping his muscled arm around me, once again resting his head on my breasts.

As I continued my tale, I gently rubbed his head massaging his tense areas.

Hitta grunted. "I thought he wanted to kill Dawid." His words were heavy, he didn't have long.

"He did…" I told him as I continued to rub his head and neck. "That great king, who had begun to believe he'd gotten that way by his own might, had to humble himself because the very man he wanted to kill, was the only one that could cause his sickness to go away, but God had rejected Saul, so whenever Dawid stopped playing, the evil spirit would come right back."

"Do you think that's what's happening to me? Do you think I get these headaches because God has rejected me?"

"No, I don't think he's rejected you, but I think he is trying to get your attention. My Greatie says he speaks to us through the unexplained. Nobody knows why you get these headaches. You've gone to the best specialist in the land and they can't tell you anything."

I gently kissed his head… "My Greatie would ask you at which point do it cross your mind to go to God?"

He grunted again… "Maybe yo' Greatie is right. But I don't think

God want to have nothing to do with me. I'm not really the type of person he mess with, you know? I'm not like King Dawid…"

"How do you know that?"

"Because shawty…It's a lot of blood on my hands." I could barely understand his words at this point. I was positive he was half asleep.

"There was a lot of blood on King Dawid's hands as well. He was feared in the land amongst all people, you know why?"

"Hmmm?"

"Because he was a goon."

He chuckled. "What you know about goons, Teacup?"

"I know that I love one."

He stiffened before he lifted his head and looked at me through lowered lids. "You love me?"

I bit my bottom lip to tame my grin. "How do you know you're the goon I'm talking about?"

"Sh*t…I better be the goon you talking about."

I gently kissed his lips… "Yeah, you the goon I'm talking about."

He studied my gaze for a moment before he spoke. "I love you too, shawty…"

This was his first time telling me that again since that day in his office a month ago and my first time telling him period.

I've been too afraid although I don't know why…

You know what? Scratch that, I do know why…

Although Hitta and I have grown so much closer after what happened at the gym last month, there has still been something inside of me that has held me back from giving my heart completely to him. Maybe it was my Greatie's warning that she feared he would break it, or maybe it was the fact that for a moment he had broken it…

Well… until I found out the truth, I'd gone off halfcocked and believed Shantell's lies like a fool.

That night after we had wild, passionate makeup sex in his office… so passionate that I was extremely embarrassed when we finally walked out of the office two hours later. Everybody pretty much did their best to ignore us, pretending like they didn't know what we'd just done…

Although one didn't have to be a genius to figure it out, he'd chased me into the office shouting and cussing and we'd come out of the office holding hands with that satisfied look on our faces that one gets after good loving.

Yeah, everybody was pretty cool about it… helping me not to feel so embarrassed.

Well…all but two people. Carmen grinned from ear to ear and gave me two thumbs up and Shantell, who was back at her spot behind the cash register, gave me the evil eye, but because there was a huge bruise forming on her cheek, it kind of took away from the effect she was shooting for.

Anyway, Hitta had kept his word and took Jessie and me to the Bulls game and then out to dinner. That night after we put Jessie to bed, he and I stayed up late and talked about everything. You guys might have guessed that after the truth came out, I felt so very foolish for believing her crap.

"Yeah, I paid a few bills for her, but only because she came to me in tears, talking about how she was struggling to cover all her bills with what I'm paying her at the gym. And sh*t… I wasn't giving her a** a raise so I gave her a loan…and took the sh*t back out of her check over the next couple of weeks."

I put my hand over my face shaking my head. *"Wow!"*

A loan… Unbelievable. But then I asked him about her working for him.

"But why do you have your ex-girlfriend working at your gym anyway. I'm not going to lie, that threw me."

He chuckled… *"Why didn't you say something, shawty? I would have kicked her a** to the curb a long time ago. For real… After she and I broke up, she came to me crying, asking me how she supposed to keep up with all the bills she acquired while we were together. Sh*t, I told her a** it ain't my problem. But then she got to going on about how I was heartless and what not…and that I should help her 'cause if not for me, these are bills she wouldn't have had on her own. And I thought about it…She was right. If not for me, she wouldn't have gotten that nice a** whip…"*

For those of you out there who don't speak Hitta, whip means car… LOL, over the last month, I've learned how to speak Hitta fluently like Wayne, something I'm very proud of…Anyway, back to the story.

"If not for me, she wouldn't have that nice a** apartment on the lake…so, I took pity on her and gave her a** a job."

At that point in the story, I was crying laughing because I thought he was going to say he paid off her car note or rent. Goodness, Hitta is a mess…

"Little did I know, she was going to come in there trying to make me jealous by dressing all provocative and flirting with all my customers. But then I started seeing an influx in the numbers and realized…damn, she good fo' business."

"How so?"

He chuckled. *"Let's just say she keep all the fellas very happy and that keeps them coming back, which mean more money in my pocket."*

My mouth opened in shock. *"Hitta! That is so wrong. That makes you a pimp!"*

Of course, he took that as a compliment.

He shrugged with fake humility. *"Well, you know…somebody got to do it."*

He'd asked me if it would make me more comfortable if he fired her. And I'm telling y'all, it took everything I had in me to be the bigger woman and say no.

The sad part about it was that she probably really did need that job. Like she told Hitta, she had to pay for all the stuff she acquired while they were together. Now many of you, like me, may ask…What kind of gold digger doesn't get suspicious when the man that is supposed to be supporting you, sets up everything so that it's all in her name so that when he leaves, you're left holding the torch?

I know that I'm not the swiftest lady in the game…hell, I'd just lost my virginity a month ago. But to me, it doesn't sound like she was that good of a gold digger…but I'm going to leave that alone. However, that brings me to the other reason that helped me be able to be the bigger woman and tell him I didn't want him to fire her.

And really, all it took was my emotions stabilizing enough for me to be able to look at Hitta's own actions to see how he felt about me and her.

She walked around that gym half-naked and he didn't blink an eye. That day, I had worn a whole dress with a strap that fell occasionally and a shawl and he'd acted like a little boy who didn't want to share his toy. That spoke volumes.

However, after I told him all what she'd said on the phone in the washroom, he got really angry and fired her anyway.

And you know, although I was being the bigger woman and all...

I was alright with his decision.

The sound of his gentle snoring pulled me out of my thoughts. Poor baby could not fight that sleep any longer. I eased from under him, replacing my breasts with my pillow for his head.

I looked down at him sleeping peacefully... He and I had been together going on two months and in that time, it felt like we've bonded together. I couldn't imagine sleeping in a bed without him at night.

Do you guys know that every morning I still wake up on top of his back clinging to him? Do y'all know that every night since coming to live with him, I've gotten a full night's rest? My insomnia is gone... And it's all because of him.

Leaning down I gently kissed his head that smelled like my knockout herbal blend...Yeah, I loved my goon. I loved him very much...

When he'd come into the shop today after my morning rush with his face distorted in pain, something shifted in me.

You see, I'd studied his headaches and from what I could see, they came in three levels of intensity:

Painful, which he said the tea I made him every morning to take to the gym normally took care of.

Throbbing, which he said the tea did nothing for...Now, don't laugh at my sweetheart when I tell y'all this, but remember I told y'all he can become a bit of a baby when he's in pain. When his headache is throbbing, he comes and finds me, no matter where I am and press his face in some part of my body because he swears my scent make his headache go away.

I don't know if that's true or not, but he seems to think so. The other day, I was at the shop and he walked in and pulled a chair to where I stood at the counter thumbing through the latest herb catalog from one of my favorite suppliers. He sat down behind me and wrapped his arm around my waist burying his face in my lower back.

And I kid you not, he sat there till I feared he'd fallen asleep.

Carmen laughed at him and told me that I had a giant baby attached to my hip...but he didn't care, he didn't move. And if we're home, he would curl up and put his head in my lap.

The other night while Jessie and I were watching The Gilmore Girls, Hitta lifted her and put her on the other side of me, then stretched out on the couch burying his face in my lap, seconds later he was asleep. So, I had to sit there and pretend that his deep breathing so close to my center was not driving me crazy.

The third pain level was how he'd come in the shop today complaining that his head felt like it was going to explode. In the two months we'd been together, it had only happened once before, and the only thing I could think about doing was relaxing him in an herbal bath with my knockout blend.

It had put him to sleep and he'd awakened pain-free. He'd been so grateful to me that he'd gotten Carmen to babysit and took me out for a night on the town, just him and I...which was a treat indeed.

I prayed this time the same thing would happen and he wakes without the headache...but I feared his headaches were getting worse. I wish Greatie would come back so that I could ask her about them. The first month we were together, he could last the whole day on the tea I made him in the morning.

Now, he came into the shop sometime after the afternoon rush for a refill. He'd become an official believer of my teas. He said everybody at the gym was talking about him behind his back because he was always walking around with the little flower teacup I'd given him in his hand, but he didn't care. The only thing he cared about was living pain-free.

I'd tried to give him another more masculine cup, but he wouldn't take it.

Anyway, I'd told him that story about king Saul for a reason. Not that I felt that God had rejected him like he did the old king...but to show him how God can allow evil spirits to plague us if we are not doing what pleases him. And somehow my tea is serving as a temporary fix, like King David's musical instrument. But when he's not drinking it, his pain comes right back.

I don't know if that's the case...but I have a feeling that it's something like that. Like I said, I wish Greatie would come back because that's something that she would know.

Carefully I eased out of the bed before texting Maddox and telling him that I was ready for him to pick me up and take me back to the shop.

When Hitta had come in earlier complaining that his head felt like it was going to explode, I'd asked Summer if she would hold it down for me for a couple of hours while I drove him to the house and took care of him. She agreed but I knew she was a little leery because Hitta had handed me his truck keys to drive, which meant Maddox was going to be left there with her.

Okay, so really quick, let me fill you guys in on a few more details about Summer. She wasn't big on dealing with the men that hung around the shop. She understood that it was Hitta paying her check and although she was cordial with him, she didn't' speak to him much, but she spoke to him more than to the others because technically he was her boss.

However, Wayne, Lannox, Maddox and the other fellas didn't get so much as a hi or bye. Now, for the most part, they all were pretty cool about it, understanding that she'd obviously gone through something that had scarred her. Most of them didn't push it.

But Maddox...

Maddox did not know what no meant...

She takes the bus back and forth to work. Since most times he's taking me home anyway, he'd offer to take her as well. She says no...

Somehow, she ends up in the car with us anyway.

Sometimes I'll have lunch with Hitta, leaving her there alone and Maddox would ask her if she'd like for him to get her something to eat. She says no...

Somehow, he ends up feeding her anyway.

He asks her why she's crying, swearing that he will take care of whatever it is so that she doesn't have to cry anymore. She just rolls her eyes and pretends like he hasn't said anything at all...

Hmmm... I don't know this for sure, but something is telling me he's going to follow through on that promise whether she wants him to or not. And just between you and me, I don't think she's as immune to his charm as she puts on.

I think that smooth-talking Scottish man is breaking down her walls and she doesn't know what to do about it.

Over the last month, I've learned a lot about the twins, who are the head of Hitta's security team. They may not be outward brutes like their boss... But they definitely had that killer instinct and it was clear Maddox was determined to get Summer...

If he's anything like his boss...It's only a matter of time.

However, that's about all I can say on the matter. Outside of the fact that Summer, Carmen and I have grown really close...and that Summer Washington definitely has a story to tell...

But she's going to be the one to tell y'all, so be looking for that.

———

"Checkmat---"

"No!" I screeched practically throwing myself over the chess table to grab Hitta's hand before he could knock down my king with his queen. "No, you're cheating!"

He chuckled. "Yeah, cuz I'm the one holding my hand trying to stop me from making my move."

"But I helped you! Because of me, you don't have a headache anymore," I whined like a little girl.

He'd shown up shortly after my last customer in a great mood because he'd awakened with no headache. And just like he'd done the last time I helped him get rid of a splitting migraine, he'd gotten Carmen to come over and babysit Jessie so that he could take me out to dinner.

I don't know how he and I had ended up sitting in the two chairs before a roaring fire involved in an intense chess game.

I pointed at him. "Don't you say it!"

He chuckled and put his queen down anyway, knocking my king to the side

"Checkmate…"

Still clutching his hand, I narrowed my eyes Clint Eastwood style and muttered, "Didn't I tell you not to say that?"

The cocky grin that came to his face was too much. "Baby, I can't help it that I'm a better chess player than you. You supposed to say Checkmate…" He leaned closer and drawled the next words out in the most irritating way.

"When you win the game…it's the rules, I didn't make it up." His grin grew. "Hate the game, not the player, Teacup." And then he winked.

That was it! That was the icing on the cake. Before I knew what I was doing, I had his arm between my teeth and I was biting him hard.

"Arghhh! Sh*t Angel!" he half yelled half laughed as he tried to pry his arm out of my mouth.

I just bit down harder. I don't know what had come over me. The only thing I knew is that I'd not been prepared to lose to him. I'd had this chessboard in the Tea Shop for nearly a year and a half, and in that time, I'd been challenged to thirty-six games…not once had I lost!

Not once!

And in one day, Hitta had broken my perfect record. I bit his arm harder.

"Damn it, you savage a** girl!" he said before he curled his arm bringing my whole body crashing into his lap.

Using his other hand, he tickled me until I released his arm due to my laughter.

"You trying to hurt me?" he muttered in my ear continuing to tickle me until I was laughing so hard I couldn't control the embarrassing snorting.

"Stop, Hitta!" I cried trying to escape from his lap, but he only wrapped his arm around me keeping my back pinned to his front.

I was so short that my legs were drawn up and I was able to rest my feet on his knees. Good thing I kicked off my shoes after I got the fire started.

"How did you get so good?" I sulked sounding like a spoiled little girl.

"Rome…"

Ahh! His best friend who Hitta and his crew swear is a real-life genius.

"That guy has been spanking me in chess for years. When we first started playing as kids, I used to win sometimes, but after he started playing with his angel, I couldn't beat him again. But because I'm competitive as hell, I never gave up."

Resting my head on his big shoulder I looked up at him as he talked. Hitta loved Rome. When he spoke of him you could hear it in his tone. I wish I'd gotten a chance to meet him. Whenever I asked Hitta where he is, he simply says…

"He's not with us anymore."

"Oh, I'm sorry to hear that! How did he die?"

And that's the question he never answers, he just changes the subject. I've come to the conclusion that Rome wasn't dead, but that maybe he and Hitta had some kind of falling out.

The bell dinged on the shop door reminding me that I'd forgotten to lock it back after Hitta had come in earlier.

I looked up and my stomach clenched in anguish at the sight of Stan walking through the door. His angry gaze went to Hitta's arms that were wrapped around me and I went to try and stand, but Hitta only tightened his hold.

"Don't f***ing think about it," he growled in my ear.

Stan came to a stop looking down at us, waiting for me to get out of Hitta's lap. When he saw that it was not going to happen, he cleared his throat in a way that let us know that he thought we were being rude.

"Diana died earlier today," he muttered, still eyeballing Hitta's arms around me.

"What?! Oh my God!" I put my hand over my mouth startled by the pain his words brought.

It was true that Diana had been jealous of me because Stan couldn't keep his eyes or his hands to himself, but there were times that things were alright between us. There were times where it almost felt as if we had a mother-daughter relationship.

I relaxed back into Hitta's arms resting my head in the crevice of his neck, no longer wanting to look at Stan anymore. Because of him, poor Diana had died miserable. She had spent her whole life trying to live up to the image he'd set forth.

She became obsessed with keeping up with the Joneses. We were the only black family in our neighborhood, and she wanted everybody to know that we deserved to be there. If someone down the way got a new pool, Diana would upgrade ours. If somebody hired a new lawn care service…she would hire a better one.

Stan would show up at the house and tell her to prepare for guests within the hour.

"Stan, why didn't you call me sooner?" she would cry in panic.

He'd just shrug and say, *"Must have slipped my mind."*

Then he'd go into his study and kick up his feet as she and I ripped and raced around the house trying to put together a small dinner party in only an hour.

"You need to find Westly and let him know that his mother is gone and then the both of you need to come to the house and lend me a hand in planning her funeral."

His disgusted gaze fell back on Hitta's hand that was now rubbing my back in a soothing matter.

"Come alone—"

"Man, you can kill that because it ain't happening! How about you worry about getting yo' wife buried rather than worrying about sh*t you can't change?"

Still without looking up at Stan I clutched Hitta's shirt, so glad he was with me.

Stan shuffled on his feet, taking a step back toward the door. The coward probably did it subconsciously.

"I've already told you; you're not welcomed in my home. You step one foot on my property and I will have you arrested so fast your head will spin."

"And I've already told you…Where Angel go, I go. If I'm not welcomed, then she ain't coming either."

"I understand that you might be a big deal on the streets, but my reach goes higher than your little ghetto…You don't want me as an enemy."

I closed my eyes at Stan's threat. What I'd feared was happening.

Hitta grunted, not in the least ruffled by Stan's words. "I ain't worried about it."

"Oh! But you should be!" Stan's voice shook with his anger.

"And you should think about leaving before I get up from this chair."

"Angel, do you have anything to say about this-this savage behavior?" Stan bit out.

My grip tightened on Hitta's shirt. "You heard him. You should think about leaving…now," I muttered, still without looking up at him.

Stan drew himself up. "I see…" He turned to head for the door. "I guess I will see you at the funeral then, don't worry about helping out your family, we'll manage." And then he was gone.

"Are you going to tell me about Stan?" Hitta asked quietly after he left.

"Please…can you just hold me? I don't feel like talking about it."

"Yeah, shawty…I'll let it go for now. But I'll give you till after the funeral, and then you and me is sitting down and having a little talk… period."

I exhaled, relieved to hear that he'll be letting the topic drop…At least for now.

That night when I broke the news to Jessie about her grandmother, I tried to prepare myself for her grief, but surprisingly there was none.

"My mama probably dead too," she said matter-of-factly.

I was so shocked by her words it took me a moment to answer her. "Don't say that, sweetheart."

She shrugged. "I don't want her to be alive."

"Jessie! No! You can't speak that way about your mom."

"Why come?"

"Because, baby, no matter what she's done, that's still your mother." She frowned as she thought about my words.

"Why do you want your mother dead?"

Her eyes welled up with tears. "Because if she comes back, then I'll have to leave, and I want to stay with you."

I pulled her to me and hugged her close... "It's okay, honey. It's okay..."

Although I said those words, I didn't know if they were true. I hadn't heard from either of Jessie's parents for two months. Both of them had always played disappearing acts, but they'd never stayed away for so long.

After Stan left, Hitta drove me around to look for Westly. We went to all of his known hangouts, but nobody had seen him. I asked some of his close associates if they knew what friend he was working with in California, and they all claimed they didn't know anybody from California and never even heard Westly talking about anybody from there.

By the time of Diana's funeral and I still hadn't heard from West, I got a bad feeling in the pit of my stomach. I'd awakened that morning with a heavy heart. I told Hitta about it and he said that it was natural for me to feel that way with that being the day of the funeral and all.

I don't know what I would have done without him. That morning I felt weird all the way around. I don't know if it was due to the anxiety of knowing I was going to be around Stan again for a good length of time, or just the stress of looking for Westly to tell him about his mother's death, but after I got out of the shower I fell to my knees in front of the toilet when a sudden bout of queasiness came over me.

Because I didn't have anything in my stomach, I ended up dry heaving. Hitta heard me and came into the bathroom helping me to my feet. But I felt another bout of nausea and had to hurry back to the toilet.

After it was safe for me to walk away, he carried me to the bed and put a cold towel on my head.

"Just lay here and rest for a minute, Teacup. I'll help Jessie get ready for the funeral, don't worry about nothing, I'll take care of everything."

"Thank you...I think all the stress is getting to me."

He nodded. "Yeah, it's a lot going on. But try and rest, baby...I got this."

True to his word he took care of everything else while I focused on pulling myself up out of the bed and putting on my black dress.

When I finally made it downstairs, I took one look at Jessie and my whole day brightened as laughter bubbled up in me.

She was wearing a ballerina skirt with a pair of jeans underneath, the little Chicago Bears jersey Hitta had gotten her, and a pair of cowboy boots. Her braids had been divided into two ponytails, one that sat on top of her head and the other that was cocked off to the side. There were two pink ribbons tied around the base of each one.

My gaze went to Hitta, who looked very handsome in blue jeans, a black button-up shirt, and a pair of tan Timberlands.

"What?" he asked looking at Jessie, not seeing anything wrong with the way she was dressed.

"What happened?" I asked around my laughter.

He shrugged. "I told her to get dressed and after, I helped her with her hair."

Jessie looked down at herself, holding out her arms. "You like it, Tee-Tee?"

I grabbed her jacket off the coat rack. "You look lovely, baby."

Heck! Why not…?

Diana's funeral was miserable. All of her and Stan's snobby friends used the occasion to peacock and try and show off their wealth in front of the other. The only one there who I felt sorry for was Barbara, Diana's mom. She was the only one there that seemed to be genuinely hurt.

When Jessie and I hugged her, she clung to us and cried, so happy to see us.

"Where is Westly?" she asked through her tears.

It broke my heart to tell her that I couldn't find him. Barbara has always been kind to me. She treated me like I was her real grand-daughter and not like a foster kid. She was also the only one in her family that had accepted Jessie.

Everybody else including Diana had taken one look at Trina and instantly deduced that Jessie was not Westly's child. So, although they didn't outright deny her…they didn't go out of their way to try and have a relationship with her either, all except Barbara, who loved her like she'd loved me.

When Barbara had gotten too old to take care of herself, Stan made Diana put her in a nursing home. Diana had wanted to bring her to live with us and hire a nurse to help take care of her... But Stan would not have it.

"And who is this handsome fella here?" Barbara asked looking up at Hitta.

"This is William..." I gave Hitta an apologetic look for using his real name over her head. "William, this is Grandmother Barbara."

He went down to one knee next to her wheelchair so that she didn't have to strain her neck looking up at him.

"It's very nice to meet you, ma'am," he said taking her hand.

I chuckled because right there before my eyes, Grandmother Barbara blushed.

"Ohh! It's nice meeting you too, shugga. My, my, my, you sure are a big fella, aren't you?" she told him actually rubbing her hand up his muscled arm. I shook my head...Goodness.

Barbara wanted us to sit with her. She said that she didn't want to be next to all of these snobby folks who couldn't care less for Diana... Including Stan, who for the most part, stayed away from us because of Hitta.

True to his word, Hitta did not leave my side. He stood there and held my hand as Diana's guests expressed their condolences for our loss to Jessie, Barbara and me. When Jessie and I had to go to the bathroom, he stood outside the door and waited for us. When I started feeling a little too hot, he went and got me a cup of water, but then the water made my stomach feel queasy, so he took it away.

He was my fierce protector and I was so grateful to have him there.

"Are you coming back to the house for the repast?" Barbara asked me as we all headed back to our vehicles at the cemetery. One of the workers from her nursing home was wheeling her back to the transport vehicle.

I went to shake my head, but she grabbed my hand. "Please, Angel. You and Jessie are the only real family I have here. It's bad enough my baby Westly couldn't make it. Please don't abandon me and leave me with all these strange people."

The desperation in her voice was real. I wanted to tell her no. The last thing I wanted to do was to go back to that house. Plus, Stan had threatened to call the police on Hitta if he stepped one foot on his property.

Barbara squeezed my hand… "Don't abandon me…"

"Of course, I won't abandon you, sweetheart. Jessie and I will meet you there." My concerned gaze went to Hitta who frowned when he saw the look in my eyes.

"Hell no, Angel. I am not letting you and Jessie go in there alone!" he told me twenty minutes later as we pulled up to my old house. The driveway and the street were full of the cars of the well-wishers. Barbara's nurse and handler were helping her out of the van right in front.

"Please, it will only be for an hour. I just want to make an appearance and then we can leave. Grandmother Barbara was the only one in this family who was kind to Jessie and me, I can't abandon her. One hour and then we can go… and never have to step foot in this place again."

His nostrils flared angrily as he exhaled. "I don't like this!"

I rubbed his arm soothing him. "I know, but there are a lot of people here. Stan will be on his best behavior."

He pointed at me. "When you come out, you tell me what's up with this dude."

I bit my bottom lip…and he shook his head. "Well then, no deal…I'm going in there with you."

If he went in there Stan will keep his word and call the police, I know him. I didn't want Hitta arrested. But it seemed that no matter what decision I made, it was bound to happen. If I told Hitta what Stan had done to me, then he was going to confront him…I know him. He was going to hit Stan or something. And then by the time Stan's judge friends got done with Hitta, he would be going to jail for a long time.

But if I didn't agree and he went in here, he will be going to jail a lot sooner. I exhaled…I was damned if I didn't and damned if I did.

"Fine…I'll tell you everything." My words were barely over a whisper.

"You got one hour. If you're not out in that time, I'm coming in there…I don't give a f*** what stiff a** have to say about it."

———

When I was a little girl, my Greatie told me that faith is having belief in that which is not seen. The hand of God is an invisible thing that has a tangible effect. One never knows what way that hand will lead you, but the question is…

Had I known that my life was getting ready to change so drastically in one hour, would I have still gotten out of Hitta's truck and gone into that house? Or was it always The Ancient of Days will for my world to implode, throwing me into utter darkness?

Can we as humans really control our destinies or are we just walking out a path that has already been paved? These are all questions that I will find myself asking…

And now looking back, I can't say that I would change a thing… because I now know that everything that happened that day…had to happen exactly like it did.

When Jessie and I walked through the door, I once again found myself feeling queasy and it didn't take a rocket scientist to figure out why. Not only was I back in a place that was full of negative memories, I felt Stan's hungry gaze zone in on me instantly.

I did my best to ignore him as I stayed by Barbara's side speaking with the guests. Jessie had wanted to go to the back yard and play with a few of the other children and I let her, making sure to keep an eye on her.

Barbara was speaking with a few of Diana's old classmates and I was only half listening. So, when she spilled a little bit of her drink on her dress, I volunteered to go get her a napkin out of the kitchen.

As I was walking down the hall, I cried out when Stan came up behind me, roughly grabbing my arm and shoving me inside of his office locking the door behind him.

"That thug of yours should have listened to me and not set foot on

215

my property. Sit!" he spat as he shoved me down into one of the chairs on the other side of his desk before he turned his computer monitor around so that I could see it.

I started to jump back up out of the seat and run, but what I saw on the computer monitor made me pause.

It was footage of Hitta leaning against a police car being hand-cuffed. He was surrounded by six or seven cops, who all had their guns pointed at him. The veins protruded from his neck as he barked something at them, but they weren't listening to him at all.

I ran to the window needing to see with my own eyes instead of through the lens of a camera and sure enough, several of the officers were putting him in the back of a squad car while the others still pointed their guns at him.

With tears in my eyes, I whipped around. "You can't do this!"

"Sure I can," he said from where he was now sitting in his office chair watching me.

I headed for the door. "That's okay! I'll just go down there and tell them they've made a mistake…"

"Before you go, you should know that I'm soon to be Jessie's guardian."

That brought my march to a screeching halt. "What are you talking about?"

He reached into his desk and pulled out some pictures throwing them on top. "A week ago, a Jane Doe was brought into the hospital."

I picked up one of the pictures off the desk and my hand began to shake as I looked down at it.

"It's Trina… Her throat was slit, her teeth, and her hands removed. Had I not known what she looked like, she would have slipped through the system. My attorney has already begun the guardianship paperwork."

It felt like someone had snatched the rug from under my feet. I sat down in the chair before I fell down as my mind raced to comprehend the information that had just been stuffed into it.

Trina was dead!

I looked back at the picture in my hand…It was her. She lay on a metal table with her throat slit. There was a look of horror in her eyes, like the last thing she'd seen had terrified her.

I put my shaking hand over my lips. "Oh my God!"

Jessie's mom was dead!

My gaze flew up to Stan's. "Wait! Did you say you're trying to get guardianship of Jessie?"

He grinned reminding me of the rat he was. "Not trying, my sweet Angel…It's as good as done."

I shot out of my chair. "The hell it is! I'm going to fight you!"

He laughed. "Come now, do you think any judge in America is going to give an unmarried, twenty-one-year-old young lady guardianship over someone like me? Please…use your brain."

"What about her father? Westly will have guardianship!"

He sat up in his chair, his greedy eyes widening in his zeal. "I'll challenge it! He's unfit…I'll demand the judge give him a drug test."

I hurt my brain trying to think of a way around that. There is no way in hell I could let Jessie end up in the hands of this pervert.

No way in hell!

"You might as well give up, Angel and just ask me what I want." The satisfied smile he wore on his face made me want to kill him.

I eased back in my chair, feeling like dying myself…All of my worst fears were happening, Hitta was being put in jail, Trina was dead…and my baby was going to end up in the hands of this pervert, forced to live the life I did.

"What do you want?" At this point, I would be willing to do anything to make sure that doesn't happen.

He sat back in his chair content with the knowledge that he had me right where he wanted me.

"Regardless of what you may think, I'm not a monster. Unlike that-that thug that you've let put his hands on you…you've let taste your sweetness, that same sweetness you've always denied me." For a moment it looked as if he was going to cry.

"I would have given you everything…"

I looked away from him, not wanting to hear any of his B.S…

"But at last…I can't have what I want." My gaze went back to him. His mouth turned into a sneer. "But neither can he…"

I frowned confused… "What are you talking about?" I wanted to say crazy a**…But decided against riling him up.

"It's simple. If you want me to withdraw my paperwork for Jessie's guardianship, you agree that you will never see your thug again. If you so much as walk into a room where he is, I will know, and I will take Jessie from you. Maybe she'll be kinder to me than you were."

At the moment I would have given anything to have only half of Hitta's skill. I wanted to pound this man's face into the ground. I balled up my fist as I struggled to stay in my chair and not try and do just that.

"You are a sick bastard!"

He chuckled. "Maybe I am… But I'll be a sick bastard with a beautiful young girl to play with if you don't agree to my terms."

"And what about Hitta?"

"What about him!?" he spat.

"Drop the charges and get the police to release him."

He stared out the window for a moment before his gaze came back to mine.

"So, it's true then?"

"What's true?"

"You love him."

I exhaled before shaking my head. "No, I don't love him. I just don't want him going to jail because of me."

I could tell by the way his eyes lit up that it was the right answer. Had I told this maniac how I really felt about Hitta he would have no doubt done his best to make sure he stayed in jail for as long as he possibly could.

"Fine, I'll drop the charges. But you take Jessie and leave town. So help me God, if that bastard so much as looks at you one more time… You will never see your niece again. I will have eyes on him constantly."

"What about my business, Stan? How am I just going to pack up and walk away from that?"

He grinned as he shrugged. "I don't know, my sweet. I guess you're going to have to ask yourself what's more important, your precious Tea Shop or Jessie."

"Why are you doing this?" I hated the fact that my voice quivered on the verge of tears that had turned into a knot in my throat.

The grin left his face as pure evil replaced it. "I want to deny you pleasure, just like you did me. I want you to know what it feels like to have to go without what you've come to crave. Maybe next time I see you, you'll be kinder to me." He sat back in his chair.

"What do you say? Do we have a deal or not?"

So, I guess my Greatie had been right because the next words that came out of my mouth broke me in half.

"We have a deal…"

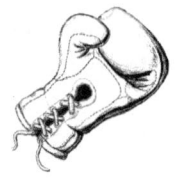

Chapter 14

IT'S TOO LATE

> *Time, Time is Ticking By, And I Can Feel an Explosion Inside, And Time, Time is Ticking By, And I Can Feel An Explosion Inside...*
>
> *As in The Days of Noah, There Will Be Drinking, Marrying, Laughing,*
>
> *As in The Days of Noah...*
>
> *What a Fool They Say, To Build a Boat on Sand, What a Fool They Say...*
>
> *And Many, Many Scoffers Will Come and Say... "It's Never Rained Before..."*
>
> *But When the Rain Starts Falling, It's Too Late,*
> *It's Too Late...*

Misty Edwards

Angel

. . .

By the time I'd gathered Jessie and said my goodbyes to Barbara, the police had taken Hitta away and there was a tow truck towing the Hummer.

"Tee-Tee, what's the matter? Why are we leaving without Unc?" Jessie asked as I nearly dragged her down the street toward the bus stop. My heart raced as the only thing I could focus on was getting her as far from Stan as I could.

I couldn't believe Trina was dead! Dear God, how was I going to break this news to Jessie?

"Tee-Tee!" she cried when I still didn't answer her or slow my steps. My longing gaze went back to Hitta's truck that the driver had gotten hitched up and tears filled my eyes.

I needed him right now. I needed to feel his strong arms wrapped around me as his deep voice assured me that everything would be okay.

But everything would not be okay…

Trina was dead and Stan had threatened to take Jessie away. I looked back at that tow truck one more time but nearly crashed into my mom who was hurrying around the corner.

"Mom! What are you doing here?!"

She gasped as her gaze flew up to mine. "Angel?"

"Hey, Cheryll…" Jessie said waving, excited to see her.

"Hey, baby…" She reached for Jessie's hand, but I snatched my niece back before their hands could touch, there was just no telling where my mother's hands had been.

"What are you doing here?" I repeated, past shocked to see her here of all places.

She looked towards the ground reminding me so much of myself when I was trying to avoid answering a question.

"Mom!?"

"I- I can't tell you."

"What do you mean you can't tell me?" This was just too much. The last thing in the world I needed right now was my mother throwing her kind of drama into the mix of all the other disasters happening in my life at this moment.

She went to walk around me, but I stepped in her path.

"He told me not to tell you," she hissed trying to step around me again.

I didn't allow it. "Who told you not to tell me?"

She exhaled. "Westly, okay?!"

And then she tried to walk around me yet again as if she didn't just rock my world. On the verge of a nervous breakdown, I let go of Jessie's hand and grasped my mother's shoulders so I could get her complete attention.

"You- talked- to- Westly?"

My system was being attacked by too many known unknowns. Trina was dead, Hitta was in jail, Stan was threatening to take Jessie…

My mother had talked to Westly!

"Damn it! Angel, you hurting me, sh*t!" she said slapping at my hands, but I didn't let her go. In fact, I shook her, needing her to know how important this was.

"Mom! Focus! Where is Westly? It's important that I find him!"

She shook her head. "Naw, baby girl, he told me not to tell you."

"What?! Why?"

"He said something about yo' boyfriend wanting to kill him."

When my fingers flexed to dig into her thin arms, I snatched them away not wanting to hurt her. Instead, I raked them through my braids trying to get control of my emotions so I could think. Although it felt like my head would explode from being crammed with so much, the one thing I knew without any doubt was that I needed to find Westly.

As Jessie's only remaining parent, he held power to fight Stan that I didn't. Maybe if I could find him and tell him that his stepfather was threatening to take Jessie, it would be the one thing that would finally convince him to clean up his act. Maybe now, he would stay in rehab and see it through till the end, knowing that if he doesn't, his baby could end up in the hands of a pedophile.

I whipped back around to stare at my mom causing her to jump, startled at my sudden movement.

"For once in your life, can you not be selfish and be there for me?!" For a moment, it looked as if I'd hurt her feelings, but then she swallowed and nodded.

"Yeah, what you want to know?"

"Where is Westly?"

Her gaze went to Hitta's truck. "Where yo' boyfriend?"

"Gone!" I snapped, trying hard not to lose my patience.

"He stole the keys to his parents' beach house in California, he been staying there for the last two months."

My mouth dropped…

Why the hell hadn't I thought about that? The beach house had been one of Westly's favorite places to go when we were kids, but after Diana had found out he'd been going there to do drugs, she'd forbidden him to return. And I'd assumed he'd honored her wishes because I hadn't heard him mention the beach house for years.

"Look, Angel, you can't tell yo' boyfriend. Westly is scared to death of him. Fo' some reason he believe he want to kill him."

I frowned. "But why did he tell you all of that?"

As far as I knew, Westly and my mother's contact was over. Every now and again they ran into each other and got high together, but as far as them being close enough for him to call her instead of me…

Yeah, that was just crazy.

She shrugged. "I was just as surprised as you. One of our old friends found me and said that Westly had been calling around looking for me. He gave me a number to return his call. You know, I thought he was trying to contact me and tell me something had happened to you. It had been a minute since you and I talked."

Yeah, it had. I hadn't seen her since the day she borrowed twenty dollars from me. But I knew it was only because I had moved and she didn't know where. Although, I'm surprised that she hadn't shown up to the Tea Shop by now.

"Anyway, when I got him on the phone, he said that his ma had died and he needed me to come to the house and give Stan a message."

"Why does he need you to do it? Why not just call himself?"

She shrugged, getting irritated with me. "Look, Angel, I don't know all the details. Only that he's too afraid to come back 'cause yo' boyfriend want to kill him and he need Stan to wire him some money."

If I wasn't so distraught, several things about her story would have stood out as suspicious to me, the main one being my mother did nothing without there being something in it for her. So the fact that she came all this way to tell Stan that Westly needed him to wire him money out the kindness of her heart was off. But because my mind was all a mess, I took her words at face value.

"Okay look, do me a favor and hold off on telling Stan what Westly said."

She frowned. "You sure? 'Cause it sounded like he really needed the money."

I grabbed Jessie's hand, knowing what I needed to do. Although it grieved my heart to walk away from Hitta, I needed to get Jessie secured. He was a big strong man, capable of protecting himself. If Stan got a hold of Jessie, after they threw me in jail for trying to kill him, there would be nobody to protect her.

I needed to get to Westly!

"Yes, I'm sure!" I told my mom as I headed for the bus stop.

"Where you going?" she called after us.

"To the airport!"

———

"Thank you for calling the Tea Shop, this is Summer speaking, how can I help you?"

"Hey, Sum, it's me."

"Angel… How are you, sweetheart? I'm so sorry to hear about your loss."

I exhaled, wishing I could tell her just how I was. Summer was the exact opposite of Carmen. She was a gentle steady strength whereas Carmen was an in-your-face-take-charge strength. Between the three of us, Summer was the most experienced and level headed. And more than anything, I wish I could tell her what was going on and get her advice.

But now just wasn't the time. "Honestly, I've been better. However, now isn't the time to go into that. Can you do me a favor?"

She didn't answer right away. And I knew it was because she was trying to process my words. "Sure… anything."

I gazed around the crowded airport from where I sat in my seat, waiting on my flight. Jessie was asleep with her head in my lap, but I couldn't shake the feeling that I was being observed.

Stan said that he would have someone watching us. I just prayed that if he does, they will relay the message to him that I was in fact leaving town so that he can leave Hitta alone.

"I have to go out of town for a few days. Can you and Carmen look after the shop for me?"

"Of course... you don't even have to ask. What's going on? You don't sound so good... Have you talked to Carmen?"

"I can't call her right now."

Summer's gasp came through the phone. "Angel, what's going on? Now, you have me worried!"

I wiped away tears as I tried to get myself together. The last thing in the world I wanted to do was worry Summer, she was already going through so much. I should have never called her...

It's just that she was the only one I could call that wasn't loyal to Hitta, and I knew she would keep my secret. Carmen would not... She loved me, but make no mistake, her loyalty went to her uncle first.

"Don't worry, Summer." I tried to keep my voice even so she couldn't hear that I was crying, but I knew I was failing miserably.

"Where are you going? Do you need me?"

"I can't tell you where I'm going, but I need you to call Carmen for me and tell her that her uncle is in jail and that she and Wayne need to make sure he gets out okay."

"Oh my God, Angel! What happened? Maddox just left to get dinner for us, do you need me to call hi—"

"No! Please... Don't call him! Hitta can't find out where I'm going."

"Why not?! I don't like this!"

"I know, but I need a few days and then I'll be back, I promise. Tell Carmen I just need a few days. I will fix everything. Thank you, Summer... I love you!"

And then I hung up before I gave into my tears. I felt like my heart was being ripped out of my chest. Being forced to walk away from

Hitta was the worst feeling I'd ever felt, but I knew I needed to see this through.

Once I told Westly what Stan was up to, he would take it from there. My brother was not the father of the year, but I knew he loved Jessie and would do anything he could to keep her from falling into his stepfather's hands.

He'd had to battle him to protect me, his sister. There was no way he would let his daughter go through what I did.

Please God, let Westly do the right thing!

My phone rang in my hands startling me. I dried my eyes so I could see the number. However, when I saw that it was Carmen, my tears only increased as I turned it off and removed the battery with hands that shook so badly that I nearly woke up Jessie.

More than anything, I wanted to answer that, but Carmen was almost as boguardish as Hitta. She would insist on coming with me and telling Hitta so he could bring the goons to bust up Stan's house and kneecaps no doubt.

I loved my people, but they didn't understand that not all battles could be fought with their fists. And Stan was one of those battles that needed to be fought with the pen. We needed to get Westly here and get him cleaned up, that way when Stan comes with his bullsh*t, we'll be ready for him…

There was no way I would be able to stay away from Hitta. They had only separated us for a few hours and already my soul felt like it was being split in half. When he got out, he will be pissed that I'd left to do this without him, but once he finds out that I'd gone to find Westly, he'll be all right.

At least I prayed…

Dear God, please make this all right…

———

The park was alive with activity today…

There was a happiness in the air that was contagious. I exhaled as I strolled through it, taking in all the beautiful sights.

To the left of me, a small wedding was taking place in the community garden connected to the park. The couple must have chosen red and purple for their colors because all of their guests were dressed in the most brilliant shades of scarlet and magenta. I smiled at the love I saw in their eyes for each other as they held hands and spoke their vows.

Across the park, small children stood and cheered as several white horses pranced through the street. One little girl cried out when she made a mistake and dropped her strawberry ice cream, her mother went down to her knees to soothe her.

On the same street, booths were set up where different artists displayed their works to sell from paintings to statues and everything in between. The brilliant colors of their creations contrasted beautifully against the lush green of the trees and the grass.

I don't know why, but everything seemed to be in multi-color today. Or maybe I saw things that way because I was deliriously happy.

I settled down in my favorite spot underneath the huge maple tree and pulled out the new book I'd just bought on the Tibetan tea culture. I've always dreamed of eventually traveling there to visit their famous herb bazaar. For as far as the eye could see, there are stalls and stalls of herbs... Every plant known to mankind could be found there, so at least I've read.

"Look, mommy, that cloud looks like an hourglass," a little boy said pointing up at the sky from where his mother pushed him on the swing.

I cupped my hand over my eyes to block out the intense glare from the sun to see what he was pointing at and sure enough, there was a giant cloud shaped like an hourglass.

All the people who were at the wedding and the art fair began to look up and take pictures of the phenomenon with their phones. I placed the book I was reading on my chest as I took it in amazed at the sight. I'd never seen anything like it... It looked so real. There were even small specks of clouds that looked like falling sand.

The festivities seemed to pick up as the people looked away forget-ting about it. I watched as the sand continued to rapidly fall, frowning when it got down to the last few granules. Sitting up the book fell from my chest as a strong urge to warn the people to stop celebrating and pay attention to the hourglass came over me.

I came to my feet as the last grain fell.

"Hey—hey, guys!" I muttered just as the sun without warning got so bright it burned away the cloud.

I bundled the bottom of my maxi skirt in my hand and took off in a run.

"Hey! Look! Time is up!" I screamed as the sun got closer.

"Time's up!"

But no one was paying attention to me. They continued in their celebrating. The wedding went on and the white horses continued to prance in the street, it seemed as if the little children cheered louder. The many colors from the art fair began to fade in the sun's brightness.

"Can you guys see what's happening?!"

I was now screaming at the top of my lungs. The heat from the sun was becoming unbearable. I looked around horrified that the people didn't seem to notice. Their clothes were smoking on their bodies…

Some of them began to… Oh my God!

They began to melt.

I put my hand over my mouth as I gagged. The sight of their skin bubbling up and melting like hot wax to mingle in with their blood was too much.

"Hey! Wake up! Can you feel the heat from the sun?!" My voice was now hoarse as I choked trying to hold down the contents of my stomach.

Still nothing. They continued to laugh and play…

I looked up just as something broke away from the sun. I opened my mouth to scream one more warning, but I never got the chance—

BOOM!

Jerking up in the bed, I cried out from the intense heat, my stomach revolting violently. I clutched it, taking deep breaths so I didn't vomit.

A dream…

It had all been a dream… I wasn't really in the park. And the people were not really melting.

With hands that shook, I wiped tears from my eyes, looking

around my old bedroom at the beach house feeling lost; the only light was the soft glow from the television.

Dear God, that dream felt so real... The flare hit and I was burning. The memory of the people melting caused a shiver to race down my spine. I was trying to warn them, but they couldn't hear me. They didn't even notice that their bodies were burning. The heat from the flame was so intense that the thought of it caused me to whimper.

I put my hand on my mouth when Jessie stirred in the bed next to me. This was my first time having a nightmare that scared me awake in a long time and it didn't take a rocket scientist to figure out why either.

For the first time in months, I was sleeping without Hitta's big body next to me. It's like my subconscious could feel the loss or something.

"This is not an act of God! Day 14 and the Amazon rainforest is still burning."

I picked up the discarded remote to turn down the volume on the TV so it wouldn't disturb Jessie, but my hand paused as I took in the sight of the rainforest burning on live news.

I blinked, wondering if I was still dreaming. The coolness of my bed sheets felt real enough.

"The rainforest makes up 20% of the world's oxygen and helps regulate the temperature of the whole planet. What does it mean that it's now burning like this?" the female news anchor asked the guy on the panel who I assumed was the *specialist*.

He gave his spiel about global warming as the camera panned out to encompass just how much of the Amazon was burning. I turned to look at the clock on the bedside table, three-thirty in the morning.

This was a huge deal; the TV has been on since Jessie and I got here a little after midnight. The only thing that had been trending on damn near every channel including the news was some ongoing chicken sandwich war between several popular restaurants.

Why in the world weren't more news circuits reporting on the fact that the daggone rainforest was on fire?

"The Amazon is not the only thing burning at a record pace," the specialist continued, but the female newscaster tried to cut him off.

"Okay, thank you, Mr—"

"No, don't cut me off! Why is there a blackout on this? The people should know that there are two even bigger blazes in Africa. The Congo is on fir—" The screen cut to two famous black football players sitting down at a table in front of three chicken sandwiches.

"We have Tyrone Johnson and Antwon Richmond here with us today, and they're going to take the chicken sandwich challenge. Okay, guys, which piece of chicken do you like the best?"

I turned from the channel searching for more reports about the fires. I don't know if I was paranoid because of my dream or if it was because there was something to these blazes. However, I gave up my search after turning to several more news channels and only managing to find out that the world liked Pluto's chicken sandwich over Bird-Fil-Up's.

Exhaling, I tossed the remote on the bed in front of me…

"It was just a dream…"

Careful not to wake Jess, I eased out of the bed and made my way to the bathroom to splash cold water on my face, praying that regulating my body temperature would help settle my stomach. One night away from Hitta and I was back to the no-sleep routine.

After drying my face, I made my way out of my bedroom to check and see if Westly had made it back. When the cab had dropped Jessie and me off a little after midnight, my heart had leaped with joy when I saw a few lights on in the house. However, after standing on the porch knocking on the door for five minutes, I realized that he wasn't here.

Diana used to keep a key under the decorative rock in front of the porch, but thanks to Westly, she'd removed it. So I had to go around back and break into the back door. Luckily, it was after midnight and there wasn't anybody out on the beach.

The house was a mess. One thing was clear, Westly had certainly been here. I had gotten Jessie some food at the airport when we landed, so she was good and sleepy. Once I got her settled in the bed in my old room, I straightened up a bit and tried to wait for West to return but ended up falling asleep.

I exhaled; he'd still not made it back. I just prayed he'd not gone some place and would be away for days. Sitting on the couch, I balled my legs up underneath me before picking up the remote to turn on the television.

I must admit to being a little surprised that all the beach house appliances were still here and had not been sold. When my mother told me that Westly was trying to hit Stan up for money, I'd just assumed it was because he'd pawned all this stuff and had run out of ways of supplying his next hit, but surprisingly he hadn't.

Okay, so I know you guys are wondering what the world I'm doing. And some of you may even be out there calling me stupid for walking away from Hitta to take care of this little issue on my own…

I don't know, maybe I am. But the thing is, I'm used to fixing these kinds of things by myself. And I really am trying to do what's best for everybody, although I know I can't stay away from Hitta…. I mean, I'm physically incapable of it. I need to still try to keep him and Stan away from each other as much as possible.

Stan is the kind of bastard that made you want to lay hands on him. And Hitta is the kind of man that didn't mind laying hands on someone that rubbed him the wrong way. However, Stan is also the kind of bastard that after forcing you to punch him, holds his wound while crying assault.

And come on, guys. Who do you think the judge will believe? Hitta or Stan?

Exactly…

So, although Hitta will more than likely be pissed with me, I have to do this without him. And I may not be a master criminal or anything, but I've been paying for everything with cash. I don't know what connections Hitta has, but I know that they could easily track me through my credit card purchases.

You know what's crazy though? I may be doing all that for nothing. Hitta may get out of jail and realize I was more trouble than he'd thought. Because of me, he'd gotten thrown in jail and there was a maniac threatening to destroy his life. Maybe he'll find out that I'm gone and say good riddance.

And then what am I supposed to do?

I'd only just gotten up enough nerve to tell him I love him. I'm not the begging type, but if I get back and find out that he doesn't want to have anything to do with me, I'd feel like I might beg him to stay with me.

Can any of you guys out there reading my tale explain to me what has happened to me?

If I get back after clearing up all this mess and find out he's moved on, it will break my heart into a million pieces. I've never experienced anything like that. How does one survive that?

As I flipped through the channels looking for more reports on the fire burning in the Amazon and Africa apparently, I forced myself to think about something else. I just needed to clear this all up and everything will be all right.

Instead, I thought back to the conversation Jessie and I had on the flight from Chicago to California. I didn't want to tell her about her mom on the plane so she could grieve her loss in peace, but I didn't know when I would get another chance to do it, there was no telling what we would walk into here at the beach house either.

So, since it was silent because most of the passengers on the Red Eye were asleep, I told her.

However...

Jessie didn't shed a tear.

No, not one...

"Hey, Jess, can I talk to you for a minute?" I'd asked after she'd finished her peanuts.

She nodded, although she didn't look away from the little TV show she was watching. I reached up and turned it off. That got her attention.

"What's the matter, Tee-Tee? And why isn't Unc coming to California with us?" She'd taken to calling Hitta that, mimicking Carmen.

"It's just us, sweetheart. We're going to go on a little girl's trip, okay?"

She nodded and I picked up her little hand pulling her into my lap.

"Baby, I've got terrible news for you." My voice broke as I spoke. It was taking everything within me to fight back the tears that wanted to fall. I hurt for Jessie. Her mama was dead. Her father was missing, and only God knows what Stan would do.

It wasn't fair that one little soul should have to carry so much.

"*What news?*"

"*It's about your mama.*"

She turned in my lap so that she was looking up at me. "*She dead, ain't she?*"

I opened my mouth but then shut it back. I'd gone over a thousand ways to say those words and here Jessie had cut right to the point. With my lips pressed together, I nodded. "*Yes, sweetheart, she is.*"

Her gaze went down to her little hand where she was fingering the material of my black dress. When her head shot back up, I expected to see pain in her face, but there was none.

"*Does that mean you can be my mama now?*"

Once again, Jessie had stumped me with her bluntness. I wanted to admonish her, but something stopped me. What could I say to her?

Hey baby, I know Trina was the world's worst mother and she didn't love you at all, but you should at least pretend you're broken up about her dying. At least that's what we adults do…

Could I really admonish her for being honest?

Chewing my bottom lip, I thought about how to respond to that… But then decided just to take a page out of Jessie's book and just be open and honest about everything.

"*Would you like me to be your mama now?*"

A huge smile came to her face and she nodded before she threw her arms around my neck.

"*Yeah, Tee-Tee! I always pretended you was my mama anyway!*"

I was so surprised by her response that it took me a moment to gather myself. Jessie has always been a blunt child. I think it's the reason she and Hitta got along so well, but I had no idea she felt this way about her mom.

The whole time I'd been trying to keep the truth about her parents from her or at the very least soften the blow of their reality. But I couldn't help but wonder how much of all the things I'd tried to protect her from she understood.

"*It's okay to hurt, baby girl.*" I'd told her turning her around in my lap so I could see her eyes.

She shrugged. "*But I ain't hurt.*"

I scratched my head trying to dissect this. I know my niece wasn't cold-hearted. She's always told me how much she loved me and had started telling Carmen, Hitta, and Lannox the same thing. But she was declaring that she didn't have any love for her mom in such a matter-of-fact way.

"Did you love your mama, sweetheart?"

She shook her head.

"Why not?" I was trying to keep my voice nice and calm so she didn't think she'd done anything wrong.

She scratched her nose. *"'Cause she don't give me baths like you do. And she don't buy my favorite cereal like you."* Her little face frowned up as she thought about it. I could see that she was getting impatient and was ready to go back to watching her little show.

"She don't never hug me and kiss me on my cheek like you do. She get mad at me all the time and call me names... And she hit me. I don't like Peaches either. I don't like the men she bring to our house. I don't like the way my mama smell... or that white gooky stuff that always be around her lips when she talk. I hate when she come to my school, 'cause she be falling asleep while the teacher talkin' to her, and the other kids make fun of me." She shrugged.

"I just don't like her... or Peaches. I'm glad you my mommy now."

I wanted to ask her how she felt about West but was not quite ready for Baby Hitta's here blunt force truths. So, I just hugged her and told her everything would be all right.

At least, I prayed.

Chapter 15

THE PERFECT PLAN

THE NARRATOR

Shivering from the freezing rain, the thin body slid into the front seat of Stan's rental. The smell of her unwashed flesh assaulted his senses. Placing his finger on the button he lowered the driver side window just a bit, preferring the early morning Chicago chill to the ungodly smell that clung to the crack head.

Hard to believe that his beautiful Angel came from this creature.

"How did it go?"

Still shivering she blew on her hands trying to warm them, filling the small space with her rancid breath.

"Just like you said. He was mad as hell. I thought his big ass was gonna snap my neck, but he bought it. By the time I was done, he looked ready to kill Angel." She shook her head.

"I sho' pray my baby girl never falls into his hands."

Stan snorted, that was the furthest thing from the truth. Cheryll had never given a damn about anybody other than herself. However, he couldn't knock her for it, he was the same way.

"Yeah right, if you're praying at all, it's for your next hit."

Not insulted in the least she smiled at him. "Speaking of my next hit, you got the stuff?"

Nodding, he started the car. "I do, but I can't give it to you here. I know a motel where I can give you the injection and you can ride out your high in peace."

She pointed a dirty finger at him. "If you trying to f*ck it's going to be extra."

Stan nearly laughed in her face as he pulled the car away from the curb. The fact that this piece of garbage thought he would waste his time with her when her sweet succulent daughter awaited him at the beach house was beyond belief.

Don't get him wrong, she was Angel's mother and underneath the grime, stench, and blisters was a face that resembled his dear girl's. However, years of hard living had taken away anything that would ever come close to alluring him. But this he didn't tell her, realizing that her believing he was taking her to a motel to f*ck only meant that she would make this last step to his plan coming together perfectly that much easier.

"Why don't we cross that path when we get there. For now, tell me exactly how things went with William."

"Who?" she asked, scratching at an open sore on the corner of her mouth.

Stan exhaled, he was surrounded by idiots. "Hitta... How did things go with Hitta?"

"Ohhh!" She nodded as recognition washed over her face. "Sh*t... Just like you said it would, one of his guys found me over there on Pulaski. Real fine brotha with a fancy accent. He asked me if I was Angel's mother. I told him yeah, and he said his boss wanted to talk to me. Of course, I told him I didn't do nothing for free, so then he slipped me a hundred bucks and I was like, *I'm all yours, fancy accent*."

Rolling his eyes, he couldn't hide the disgust he felt for her. The only reason he didn't fear that she'd betrayed him was because he offered her a high that she couldn't find anywhere on the streets. Although it was Fentanyl, it was a form that only certain doctors can get a hold of and can only be taken through injection.

Several times he'd given her a little taste for doing his will, including seducing his imbecile of a stepson all those years ago and getting him hooked on heroin. For that, Stan had rewarded her greatly. It was the least he could do for taking care of the little sh*t who thought it was his job to protect Angel from him.

Of course he could have hired someone to take Westly out quickly, but that wasn't the way Stan worked. He liked to see his enemies suffer. A quick death was too easy. He wanted them to hate themselves before they succumbed, which brings him back to the most recent bastard who thought to stand between him and Angel.

"What happened next?" He didn't want her to leave out any details wishing that he could have been there to see Hitta's face the moment he realized that Angel had begged Stan to help her get away from him.

"The guy drove me to the gym to talk to his boss." She shivered. "You owe me big time! That giant mutha f*cka scared the sh*t out of me. I didn't want to lie to him. It felt like he woulda killed me if he even suspected I was bullsh*tting him. I can't believe my little girl was able to take on a man like that. Gon, girl!"

Stan clutched the steering wheel tighter to keep from punching her in the face. He hated her for those words. Hitta was no man! He was an animal! An animal that deserved to die for putting his uncouth paws on his beautiful girl.

But leave it to this filthy whore, who was used to sleeping with alley rats to think it was a good thing that something so precious had fallen into the hands of a savage. He nearly smiled when he thought of what he had in store for this slut.

"Not to worry, sweetheart, I'm going to take good care of you."

She grinned at him showing off the places where she used to have teeth, but nothing was left but black rotting flesh.

"What happened next?"

"He asked me if I had seen you, West or Angel. I told him that I had seen Angel a week ago and that she told me that she went to her foster father for help getting away from her abusive boyfriend. And then I paused like I just realized that he was the abusive boyfriend and acted like I didn't want to say nothing else." She cackled, the sound grated on Stan's nerves, causing him to bite down on his teeth to keep from yelling for her to shut the f*ck up!

"But then another fine brotha in a really nice suit handed me five hundred dollars and bebe, I started singing like a canary! I told them that she asked you to help her find West. I told them that it was her idea to get him thrown into jail in order to buy y'all some time. That's when I thought he was going to snap my goddamn neck. He was pissed! I told him if I knew where y'all was I would tell him because it was wrong how y'all did him. He bought all that sh*t so I got the hell on out of there before he changed his mind."

She held up her hands. "And here I am, mission accomplished."

If you've ever heard the screech of a cat in the middle of the night, you've heard Cheryll's voice. Although it pained him to do so, Stan smiled because she'd done well. If not for her, getting to this point would have been twice as hard. It was a shame he now had to kill her. However, he couldn't risk even the smallest thing going wrong with his carefully thought out plan.

After years of waiting, Angel was his...

And he owed it all to the letter he'd received in the mail a month ago from a writer, who preferred to remain anonymous. They explained the trickery Hitta used to trap Angel. How he'd planted the money for Westly to conveniently stumble across, only to then come back and confront Angel for the missing loot. She'd fallen into his dirty hands hook, line and sinker.

Well, not anymore. Stan had set his beautiful butterfly free. It didn't take much for him to make the beach house look as if Westly was staying there.

What was that?

You guys are wondering why he chose the beach house?

Well... this was the most brilliant part of his plan. He'd won it in a poker game about eight years ago from a good friend, who had purchased it for his ex-mistress. In order to hide the purchase from his ever-seeking wife, he'd disguised it as a timeshare acquired by his company for employees. The only thing his friend asked was that he keep the house registered as it was, as to not draw the attention of said wife and the IRS.

At the time, Stan didn't think it was a big deal, so he agreed. Now, he was glad he had. The house could not be traced to him or his family. So if anybody was looking for Angel, they would never think to look there. In order to get Angel there, he'd fed her that bull about him getting custody of Jessie, knowing that it would make her want to seek Westly, which brought Cheryll into play.

It took him nearly two weeks to coach her through what to say. He'd had to balance giving her just enough of the Fentanyl to keep her satisfied, focused…yet willing to come back because she was thirsty for more, while at the same time taking care of his b*tch of a wife.

She was the only thing that kept Angel from loving him back. Knowing years ago, that he was going to have to find a way to get rid of her without divorce so that the twat couldn't take any of his money, he started adding an untraceable toxin to her daily medication that encouraged the growth of her cancer.

Thanks to the whistleblower that exposed Hitta's treachery, Diana's time had run out, he had all the information he needed to trap Angel, which meant he had to speed up his wife's death by adding another toxin that although traceable, caused her to have a massive heart attack. It took a lot of maneuvering, but he'd managed to get his little additive deleted from the toxicology report.

He chuckled. Damn, he loved it when a plan came together. All that was left was separating Angel from the beast that had all but consumed her. That was the only glitch in his plan. Jail was full of niggas like him. Stan had paid a lot of money for him to get thrown in there and lost in the system. But apparently, the thug had more connections than Stan had originally thought.

He had a member of the black elite on his team, the only son of Wayne Steward, a mogul and owner of a very influential investment firm. Imagine that, this animal had a man working for him, whose family held more power in this city than Stan ever had and ever would. He had Hitta free and walking the streets in no time.

Of course, that little set back rocked Stan and it took him a minute to think his way around it. But thanks to his little crack head, it was a town soon conquered.

"Sh*t! How far outside of the city are we going?" Cheryll grumbled realizing they'd been driving for a while.

"Just a little longer," he assured her.

After he took care of this last obstacle, he would drive to St. Louis and catch a flight to California. He'd taken a leave of absence under the guise of not quite being able to cope with his wife's death. Of course all of his colleagues understood because they'd all seen how devoted he was to her as they battled her illness together as a loving couple.

He nearly choked on his mourning act but was willing to do whatever it took to give him the time he needed to convince Angel to be his. He wanted her to love him back. He'd tried everything, buying her beautiful clothes, making sure that she was one of the sharpest dressers in her school, even signing for her to get her Tea Shop. Would have bought it for her if he'd thought she would have accepted it.

But now that there was nothing standing in their way, she will see him for the catch that he really is. Handsome, rich…a doctor, how could she not see it? He didn't care how long it took, by the time they left that beach house, she was going to be in love with him.

After his anonymous informant told him all about what Hitta had done and was doing to woo Angel, he had to grudgingly admit it was a damn good idea while kicking himself for letting an uneducated savage outthink him.

"We're here," he grumbled as he turned off the main road and onto the side one that led to the rundown motel he'd thoroughly researched.

It was heavily used by prostitutes and their johns, so the owner didn't waste his time or money to make sure things like the security cameras stayed working. His clientele that generally rented rooms by the hour wasn't big on those anyway.

This place was perfect to implement the last detail of his plan because there was no way that he could be traced back here.

"Here's two hundred dollars, go and rent a room for the whole night. I'm in a good mood."

She smiled seductively at him as she took the money. "Okay, baby, I'll be right back."

Killing the engine, he watched her disappear inside the smudged glass door that he was sure was decorated with a bullet hole or two.

Angel, I'm on my way, my sweet!

He couldn't wait to taste her nectar fully. The little sips he'd managed to steal when she lived with them had been torture, like little whiffs of honey to a starving drone bee.

You see, he was well aware that many of you thought he was a pedophile because his desire for her had begun when he'd first laid eyes on her at the tender age of twelve. But he'd like to make one thing perfectly clear.

There was something about Angel...She'd been a beautiful girl, but she was a stunningly alluring woman. She'd been the only woman he'd ever loved. When he made love to his b*tch of a wife, it was Angel's face he saw as he drove inside of her.

Always Angel's face...

"Ready?" Cheryll asked throwing the door open.

Stan slid his hands into a pair of leather gloves. "More than you'll ever know," he told her before he followed her into room 118.

An hour later, he emerged in the night and slid back behind the wheel of his rental. It was done, after giving her a lethal dose of the Fentanyl, Cheryll was dead. And now he can--

"Well now, ah wasnae expecting for things to go quite so well. Ye made me job mair easier. Thanks, mate."

The Scottish accent coming from Stan's back seat caused his eyes to widen as his gaze connected with a strange man's through the review mirror right before a sharp pain filled his head and everything went dark.

———

"Aye, Bo! Wake yo' b*tch ass up!"

Stanly Aiden Baker was very aware that he was a bad man. He knew he preyed on the weak and robbed the needy. There weren't many doctors who could milk some poor sap who's afraid of dying, insurance like him.

In fact, he'd just received the Allen Rayne Award for Modern Medicine because of said gift of draining one's medical insurance for all it was worth, but of course in his field, it's called Medical Achievement.

That being said, every bad man knows that eventually, he will have to answer for all the wrong that he's done in life. However, Stanly will argue to his last breath that the way in which the One who holds all accountable for their actions chose to punish him was too extreme to say the least.

When he opened his eyes and saw the raged-filled ones standing over him, he nearly sharted himself. He knew that by some twisted stroke of fate, he'd fallen into the hands of a complete and utter barbarian.

"Damn, Bo, you look like you finna sh*t yo'self." A wicked smile spread across Hitta's face and Stan's spirit tried to leave his body. He would rather be looking down the barrel of a shotgun than to face this monster of a man.

Hitta shook his head. "Tsk, tsk, tsk, you been a bad boy, Stanly."

He stood up straight and turned to address the others in the room. Only then was Stan able to see what was happening around him.

He was sitting in a chair in an abandoned mechanic garage. There were several pieces of old rusted equipment scattered around. The big door at the front of the shop was pulled back and Hitta's truck sat in front of it. Loud rap music blasted through the open window causing the walls and the floor to vibrate.

There were three men standing with Hitta looking down at him. Stan was able to spot the mogul instantly. The elite carried themselves differently from common folk, and if that wasn't enough to set him apart, then his style of dress definitely would. Stan, like anyone else who's had dreams of one day being allowed in that club, had an eye for spotting out men like this in the crowd.

The other two very intimidating men that stood looking down at him were clearly twins. The only thing separating them was the different colors of their linen suits and gloves.

"What should we do with Stanly boy?" The goon and leader of this bunch asked as he slowly circled his chair.

"You can't do this to—"

"Shut up, b*tch!" Hitta growled in his face causing a feminine squeal to escape Stan's lips before he could catch it. As if mystically cued, the song coming out the Hummer speakers changed. An obnoxious rapper's voice filled the garage.

"I'm the man right here!"

Stan blinked, wondering if somehow Hitta had a theme song. At this point, he was shaking so badly that the metal chair he sat in tapped out a tune against the cement floor that could be heard over the music.

"Let me tell you how this sh*t gon' go. I'm gon' ask you a question. If I don't like yo' answer, I'm going to break yo' jaw…"

Stan cried out again when the angry man jabbed his finger painfully in his cheek. It took him a moment to realize that he hadn't been punched. That had just been his finger, and it hurt like hell!

Hitta bent down so that his face was only inches from his.

I'm the man right here! Once again filled the garage as if cued.

"Where- the- f*ck- is Angel?!"

"She asked me to do it!" Stan blurted out losing his nerve completely. "She was afraid of you and didn't know how else to get away from you!"

Through his peripheral, he saw the Scotsman who'd been sitting in his backseat when he'd gotten into his car at the motel chuckle before shaking his head. Something about the gesture made a cold feeling crawl up the back of Stan's neck. Well, that and the fact that his words only seemed to anger the monster in front of him more.

When Hitta's nostrils flared, Stan panicked and kept speaking even though everything in his soul told him to remain quiet and play dead like a wise person would do in the face of an angry bear or lion. But dread had a way of making one do foolish things.

"She came to me for help, and I did what I thought was—"

Those were the last words Stan remembered uttering before his face exploded in more pain than he'd ever felt in his entire life. Before he succumbed to the blessed darkness, he wondered how his perfect plan had gone so terribly wrong.

———

Hitta

. . .

Watching this weak neck b*tch crumble to the ground at my feet only angered me more. The rage I felt inside of me was nowhere near assuaged. Not only had this nigga taken Angel and Jessie away from me, he had me locked up in a mutha f**ken cage and paid to get my paperwork lost so that I'm just sitting in that mutha f**ka like a ghost.

It's been damn near a week since I laid eyes on my Teacup and I felt like I was f**king suffocating. Not knowing if she and Jessie were safe or not was driving me insane. Not to mention I've had a week-long migraine that feels as if my f**king head is going to explode. The only relief I get is when I bury my nose in her pillow.

F**k!!!!

I began to pace back and forth in the garage feeling myself about to lose my sh*t! I needed my f**king girl back! We've looked everywhere for her. Wayne's been using all of his resources in searching for possible places Stan could have stashed her.

I'd question Summer's ass to death, but she couldn't tell me anything other than what she had. She insisted that the only thing that Angel told her was that she was leaving town but would not say where she was going.

Because I knew that Rome could find out sh*t that Wayne couldn't, I've been blowing his phone up. But of course, the one time I needed him to help me continue to f**king breathe, he was nowhere to be found.

Every cell in my body was commanding me to rip this mutha f**ka lying on the ground apart! Taking deep breaths, I tried to fight my fury.

"She was afraid of you and didn't know how else to get away from you!"

I clutched my head trying to drown out his whiny ass voice! It was causing my sh*t to pound worse than it ever had.

"She came to me for help…"

A sharp pain filled my chest that actually drowned out the pain in my head. It was the same pain that had filled it earlier when her mother told me the same thing.

God! Could this be true? Did Angel want to leave me?

Thinking, back to the day of the funeral, I couldn't understand why she was so dead set on going to that house if she hated him so much. I'd tried to talk her out of it. Plus, Summer said that Angel willingly left town.

"She came to me for help…"

A hand on my shoulder caused me to look up. "Hitta, he's lying! Angel wouldn't do that."

Maddox and Lannox nodded agreeing with Wayne. I wanted to believe them, but they weren't in my truck on the day of the funeral. They didn't see how she insisted on going into that f**king house.

A fresh wave of anger filled my veins drowning the pain in my heart, anger I knew and understood.

"Wake this b*tch up!"

Lannox and Maddox picked Stan up off the floor and repositioned him in his chair before reviving him with a smoking match.

As soon as he came through, he yelled out in pain like the ho' he was. "You shattered my jaw!"

Well… at least I *think* that's what he said. It was really a garble of words that spilled through his swollen lips that was getting bigger by the second.

"Shut the f*ck up!" I'd lost all patience. "Where is Angel?!"

"I toth you-" he began, but I cut his ass right off.

"Wrong answer, pu**y nigga!" I channeled all my rage into the blow I sent into his other jaw, feeling the satisfying crunch underneath my knuckles. His head banged back so hard on his weak ass neck it sent his unconscious body slamming to the ground.

I stepped back. "Wake him up!"

This time he came through screaming with blood and saliva dripping from his mouth. Both of his jaws were shattered and he could barely move them. Po' unfortunate bastard just learned why they call me Hard Hitta.

I leaned down so that my head was level with his. "Stanly, I suggest you start talking. I can do this sh*t all day, bruh."

Now crying like a baby, he told me what I wanted to hear. "Sheth's at the beath house! I swear! Pease don't hit me again! Pease!"

"What f**king beach house?!"

He rattled off the address through his damaged mouth. As soon as he was finished my gaze went to Wayne, who had been typing it on his laptop.

"Got it!" he told me holding up his thumb.

With a satisfied smile on my face, I turned back to this dead man, but as I looked down at him, my smile disappeared.

"Do you know what it took for me not to snap yo' neck as soon as my boy brought yo' b*tch ass in here?"

"Pease! I'm sorry! I've got money!"

I tilted my head to the side. "Do I look like I need yo' money, nigga?"

He shook his head. "Justh let me go and I won't tell anybody! I pomise!"

That made me chuckle. "I'm sorry, Bo, I ain't got it in me to let you walk away from this sh*t with yo' life."

"Pease, don't kill me!" he cried reaching for my hand bowing over it. I looked down at his head as he begged for his life. I don't know what disgusted me more about him, the fact that he'd dared to take what's mine or the fact that he wasn't man enough to stand on his action.

I rested my other hand on the top of his head leaning down so that only he heard my words.

"I understand why you did it, Stanly. It's something about Angel, right? Something about her calls out to the primal side of you. I know, Bo... Yo' mistake was not realizing that I too had fallen under her spell. As a matter of fact, I've become obsessed with her. She in my bloodstream, man, and I can't f**king focus without her. Between me and you, I'm the terror you should have prepared better fo'. You should have known I will never stop until I have her back. You always had a problem on yo' hands, Bo. You- would- have- never- known- peace."

When I stood his gaze rose to mine and for a minute, I let him see my need for her in my eyes. He should have known better. He should have known that I didn't have it in me to let her go. It was the fact that he didn't and that he'd tried to take her away from me that had the rage settling back in my gaze.

This time when I hit him and his body crashed to the floor, I followed and continued to punch him. I let all the pain, fury, fear, and yes, uncertainty I've felt over the last week come through each blow.

I could hear my men trying to stop me, telling me that it was enough, Stanly was dead, but I couldn't stop. At some point, Wayne, Maddox and Lannox tried to pull me off him, but I was unmovable. I could not stop pounding his f**king face.

Not because he'd taken Angel away from me. Not because I'd been more afraid than I've ever been in my life this past week. Not because I've dealt with the constant pain of a raging migraine.

No...

None of those reasons were why I couldn't stop hitting him.

It was the idea of her coming to him to help her get away from me. It was knowing that there was a good possibility that his and her mother's words were true and Angel had willingly walked away from me, leaving me alone.

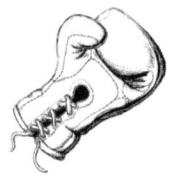

Chapter 16

A WOMAN SCORNED

> *Heaven Has No Rage Like Love to Hatred, Nor Hell No Fury Like A Woman Scorned...*
>
> William Congreve

Hitta

"Hitta! That's enough, man! Come back to us, bro! Damn!" Wayne grabbed my arm, but I snatched away from him to deliver another blow to the face that no longer looked human.

Maddox and Lannox joined him in trying to pull me off this mutha f**ka. Their attempts only enraged me more. They were trying to get between me and the bastard who took Angel's love away from me.

I've never in my life had a love so pure. I didn't even think it was possible for a hood nigga like me. But there she was, filling my senses with her sweet scent, calming the beast inside me, making me feel like a king, looking at me with eyes that said I was worthy of her.

And this son-of-a-b*tch took it away!

"Get the f**k off me!" I yelled shaking all three of them away from me like rag dolls.

"F**k it, stand to the side, I'm going to knock his big ass off!" Wayne told the twins before he charged me.

I grunted when his body slammed into mine, but it did not move me, neither did it penetrate through the red haze that clouded my vision as I continued to pound this smug bastard's face. I felt like he was laughing at me. Even though he was dead, I wanted to destroy all possibilities that this mug will ever wear a smirk again.

Yeah! I'd f**king gone insane!

The sound of Wayne's expensive shoes slapping against the floor as he continued to try and push me over only testified to how much effort he was putting into his action.

"Got damn it, don't just stand there! Help me!" he yelled at the twins.

They gave each other one last look before they too charged me. Their combined effort sent me slamming back to the ground. Growling in my throat, my energy was now focused on getting them the f**k off me.

Maddox was the first to go flying. Wayne soon joined him. I balled up my fist to take out Lannox, but Maddox threw himself in front of the blow nearly wrapping his whole body around my arm.

"Whoo, boss! Clamy doony! Donna poond Lannox. He says your wee lass luvs you, mon!"

It was those words that sliced through the red haze clouding my vision. My fist stilled as my gaze shot to Lannox. Desperately he nodded confirming Maddox's words. I relaxed and all three of my men collapsed in an exhausted heap around me.

Slowly the rage that was pumping like a piston through my veins began to evaporate along with the temporary insanity that settled over me. After getting to my feet, I looked at what was left of Angel's foster father, his blood dripped from my fists.

I brought my shaking hands to my head that was pounding fiercely now that my fury was abating. The pain was so intense it nearly took me back down.

Still on his knees, Wayne struggled to catch his breath as he loosened his tie. "Goddamn! Felt like I was wrestling with a silverback f**king gorilla."

Bent over with his hands on his knees, Maddox held up his hand, he too struggled to catch his breath.

"She luvs you, mon! This minger was lying!"

I shook my head, I wanted to believe them, but for the life of me, I couldn't let go of Stan's words. As I looked down at his dead body, I realized that this bastard had won, because he truly had the last laugh.

I grunted. "Yeah well, she's going to have to prove it to me."

Stepping over Lannox where he still lay on the floor trying to catch his breath, I headed towards my truck.

"Before our plane touch the ground in California, I want to know what hold this mutha f**ka had on her."

———

The Narrator

With a smirk on her face, Shantell stopped her phone from recording after Hitta declared Angel was going to have to prove her love to him. Using the skills she'd picked up from her father, who had been one of the best PI's in the Chicagoland area before he was murdered, she held very still where she squatted down between the two garbage cans so that he wouldn't see her as he got into his truck and pulled off. Minutes later, Wayne emerged from the garage talking on his phone as he headed for his car parked farther down the alley.

They'd brought their victim to a side of town that was abandoned by most. Inhabited only by fiends and prostitutes, nobody will ever think to look for evidence of the missing doctor here. She continued to hold very still as Maddox and Lannox removed the body and cleaned up all signs of them being there.

No doubt, the twins will do what they did best and the good

doctor here will become another John Doe. It was a shame... She'd had such high hopes for him. If she had known he was such an imbecile, she wouldn't have wasted her time and energy sending him the information he needed to go after what he craved.

She had all but given him that nappy-headed, geeky black b*tch on a platter. And what did he do? Put all his cards in the hands of a crackhead. The twins had f**king followed her from the gym. She led them right to him.

Not wanting to take the chance with Lannox's creepy ass, Shantell didn't move from her hiding spot until they were long gone. It would be just her luck she stands up to find him farther down the alley watching her.

She'd been surveilling Hitta ever since he'd called it off with her and she couldn't shake the feeling that Lannox was on to her.

A few weeks before she'd gotten fired, she carried a stack of papers into Hitta's office to file away like she always did. While in the drawer, she quickly changed out the battery in the little recording device she kept in there. When finished, she left, pulling the door closed behind her. Since it was no big deal to see her come in or go out of his office, nobody paid attention to her. Maybe it was paranoia that made her casually glance around the gym to make sure, but when she did, she nearly tripped over her feet when her gaze connected with his where he leaned against the wall across the open space watching her with a knowing look.

It took everything she had to keep a straight face and not run back into the office and remove the bug. If Hitta found out she was spying on him, she was dead. There would be no questions asked; she would become the next Jane Doe to wash up from Lake Michigan. That whole week, she was paranoid waiting for the ax to fall on her operation.

The fact is, she'd invested too much in Hitta to let a mute or an ugly tea-drinking b*tch ruin her chance of securing a ring from him. And Shantell will get that ring, even if she had to kill for it. Let there be no doubt that he was not someone she was willing to let slip through her fingers.

She'd began hunting him well before they actually met. Her father and his partner ran a very successful private investigation firm, one that made them both extremely wealthy. After her dad died, it came to light that he'd squandered his half of the company and it was his partner keeping it afloat.

When it was all said and done, her family found themselves in debt. They lost their nice house and all of their nice things, she couldn't show her face around her friends because she'd become poor.

It was then her mother pulled her to the side and told her how she'd used her looks to trap her father into marriage. She explained that her grandmother had trained her in the art of snagging a rich man and that it was time for her to teach Shantell so that she could help pull her family out of the muck they were in.

Shantell has always been a very sexual being. But her mama told her that rich men weren't always the best at sex and that she was going to have to learn how to please herself until after she'd gotten her benefactor to marry her and become pregnant with the child that would secure all of their future. She said only then would it be safe to acquire a lover that could take care of her sexual needs.

Not surprisingly, they realized that Shantell was a natural at being a gold digger. At first, she put her focus into snagging a professional basketball player. But then, she and a few of her girlfriends had gone to Vegas for a weekend and ended up at one of Hitta's fights. She'd taken one look at him and knew that he was the one for her.

In spite of what her mother said, she didn't *just* want a rich man. Shantell wanted a rich man who could f*** her the right way. And she had enough sexual experience to size Hitta up and see that he carried all the signs of a man who knew how to handle a woman's body.

She and her friends followed his prefight media tour for weeks trying to get past his security team long enough to get his attention. The problem was there were fifty other women with the same idea, who too seemed to be following the tour. She had to do something that set her apart from the other groupies.

Soooo…

She cornered one of his security guards in the washroom at a nightclub and struck a deal with him. She'd pleasure him and in return, he'd help her slip past the crowd of women and behind the red divider rope that separated the untouchables from the have-nots.

Shantell could remember the rush she'd gotten when she'd finally entered into Hitta's space. He was way more powerful up close than he had been from afar. Strength oozed from him, dwarfing every other man in the club.

She'd pulled every trick in her arsenal to end up at his hotel room that night. And just like she'd figured, he was an amazing lover. In fact, he was the best she'd ever had. He was the first and only man to put her to bed.

Yes, he wore her completely out...

However, thinking that they had made a connection that night, she was disappointed when he woke her up thirty minutes later and kicked her out of his hotel room, saying that he needed to get some rest for his training the next day.

That was a setback she hadn't counted on, but Shantell wasn't the giving up type. She'd already picked out their wedding colors. It took several more attempts, several more sexual favors for her little security guard friend, and several more hotel rendezvous with her big strong fighter till she had finally gained a more permanent spot in his schedule.

He'd gotten her the apartment of her dreams, the car of her dreams, and a wardrobe that made all of her friends green with envy. She was on top of the world.

The challenge came in becoming pregnant. No matter what she did, she couldn't get him to go into her without a condom. It didn't matter how drunk he was or how tired, he always managed to get a damn condom on his very impressive man flesh.

Most times he flushed it afterward, but there was one time he slipped up and tossed it in the wastebasket by the bed. She waited till he went to sleep and used a turkey baster to draw his seed from the rubber. The next few weeks, she and her mother were some praying sistas, praying that Hitta's seed would take.

When she got her period, they both cried. Hitta gave Shantell enough money to help her mom pay her rent, but it wasn't enough to keep her mother from having to go back to work. She had two little brothers who now had to attend public school. She needed to get Hitta to marry her so that she could have access to his bank accounts.

Shantell began dropping hints, showing him beautiful star couples in the magazine and telling him that she would make a gorgeous bride worthy of him. Like him, she was serious about her work out and had the body to reflect it. She told him that they could do something like a fit couple's wedding.

It seemed like the more she hinted that she was ready for marriage, the more he stayed away from the home she had created for him. She'd followed him a few times and saw that he was messing around with random hood rats, nothing that she should be worried about and never one more than once.

She wanted to yell at him and demand he stop cheating on her, but she knew that would only push him to stay away more than he was already doing, so she held her tongue and pretended like she didn't know. Her mother told her she should start flirting with Wayne, saying that he would make a very nice plan B.

Shantell would have agreed if she wasn't so f**king sprung on Hitta. Her mama didn't understand what it was like to be loved by a thug nigga like that. He is a complete beast in the bedroom and made her turn into putty in his hands. That sh*t was important to her. She will never find another man that put it down like that.

No!

She wanted *him*! Nobody else will do!

But then something happened. He brought home that little bratty b*tch Carmen after her mother got arrested. She'd taken one look at Shantell and decided that she didn't like her, and no matter what she did, the little b*tch still didn't like her.

It wasn't long before she started telling her uncle to leave Shantell and that was when she began to notice him pulling away from her. Because she and Carmen could not stop arguing in those days, the little brat spent most of her time at Wayne's place.

That was just fine with her until Hitta started staying away sometimes for weeks at a time. She became desperate at the thought of losing him and in a panic, told him she was pregnant.

Shantell will never forget the look on his face. It was a mix of disgust, disbelief, and amusement. It was then she realized getting a ring from him was going to take strategy. As far as she was concerned, he'd just declared war on her.

She loved him. She was perfect for him. All she needed to do was to get him to see it too. After putting on a performance worthy of an Academy Award, she managed to convince him; that bought her a little time. He'd even began to come home more often than he had been, although he was still cheating on her and still using a goddamn condom when they had sex.

Her mom was pressuring her to do whatever it took to get pregnant by him, even if it meant drugging him. Shantell didn't give that suggestion the time of day. Her mother didn't know Hitta, although not from the lack of her trying to integrate him into her family. She'd invited him to every event that they had, but he was always too busy or just flat out didn't want to go. Her mom had offered to make him dinner many times. Again, he would always turn it down or say he had something very important to do.

Because of this, her mother had no idea of how rough he was. She didn't know that her baby girl had gone out there and fallen hard for a goon that would snap her neck if he even thought she was trying to drug him.

Anyway, when it looked as if she would not be able to get away with her pregnancy lie a day longer, she faked a miscarriage. Once again putting on a stellar performance, she convinced him that she was so broken up about losing the baby she was thinking about killing herself; that bought her some more time.

But after that, he began to stay away for several weeks at a time. And then the day came when the ax fell and he came home and told her he was moving out. Of course, he used Carmen as an excuse. Shantell begged him to stay, assuring him that she and Carmen could get along, she would make sure of it, but his mind was made up.

It was while his men were moving his stuff out of their place that he broke up with her, completely cutting her off. She'd tried everything to get him to change his mind, but no matter what she did, he wouldn't take her back. Her mom told her to forget about him and to focus her energy on Wayne. Shantell refused. She loved Hitta and was a good woman to him! He'd ruined her for other men. She wanted him and was determined to get him back.

Although it was humiliating as hell, she went to him and begged him for a job at his gym, knowing that if she could just be around him, she could convince him of what he'd lost and make him want it back. She even seduced other men in attempts to make him jealous.

It was working, he was noticing her. He'd even began to flirt with her. And then *she* showed up…

Angel!

That f*cking black, fat b*tch! That f*cking tea-drinking, man-stealing whore!

She saw the look in his eyes when he looked at Angel; it was like he was hypnotized. He'd never looked at Shantell like that. He'd never looked at her with such need…

Balling up her fists, she stood from where she had been hiding between the garbage cans. She'd rather die than let Angel have him. She'd seen him first! He was hers! And goddammit, if she couldn't have him then nobody will!

Now that her plan A had failed, it was time for her to implement plan B. Once she succeeded and Angel left Hitta for good, she will be there waiting for him with open arms. Then she was going to handle that little b*tch, Carmen. Hitta's twin assassins weren't the only ones who could make a body disappear.

———

Angel

"What do you mean she can't have the blue one?!" I yelled at the Indian man who owned the beach's cotton candy stand.

This stand has been here ever since we first started coming here when I was fifteen and so has its ill-tempered owner. For the life of me, I couldn't understand why someone who obviously hated kids would open a damn cotton candy stand.

I've never heard him speak kindly to anyone. *It's always you buy and go! Don't touch! Don't stare at! You stare you buy!*

Well today, I wasn't in the mood for his crap. It had been a week since last I slept. Westly was still a no-show and I missed my man!

"She touched the pink one already, that is the one you buy!"

"What the hell is wrong with you, man?! The candy is in plastic! She just touched it to move it out the way to reach for the one she wants!"

"I don't care! You buy or you go!"

I put my hand on my hip ready to go to war with this creep. He'd done something very similar to me five years ago. Because I'm short and had to get on my toes and reach for the one I wanted, I made a mistake and grabbed the wrong bag. When I told him I didn't want that one and that I wanted the bag next to it, he went berserk on me, accusing me of trying to steal. In order to calm him down, I'd let him bully me into buying something I didn't want.

Well, not today!

I moved Jessie to the side and took a step closer to him. "Now you listen to me—" I began, but his eyes suddenly grew wide and all the color drained from his face.

He was so spooked the blue cotton candy he'd snatched away from Jessie shook in his hand.

"I- I'm very sorry... here, you take!" he shoved the candy into my niece's hand.

For a moment, I was dumbfounded. *Oh my God! Did I just frighten this man?*

Wow! I guess I did...

"That's more like it," I told him straightening my tank top. I don't know why, but all of a sudden, I had more bass in my voice.

"How much do I owe you?"

He shook his head. "For you, no charge!"

Well, will you look at that? I guess I showed him...

Shucks, I think Hitta must have rubbed off on me or something. I just scared the hell out of this guy. Feeling kind of good to finally be the one doing the bullying, I wiped the smile from my face.

"Yeah! It should be free!" Y'all, I had so much bass in my voice that Jessie, who now had a mouth full of blue candy looked up at me and laughed.

"You should really work on your customer service skills!" I spoke a little louder so that all the poor folks that had been bullied by this terror could see how I was handling this.

"I am very sorry, ma'am." I squared my shoulders now, trying to make myself appear taller, completely high on power.

"You should be sorry! Don't let it happen again! Come on, Jessie…" I grabbed my niece's hand and after giving him a final threatening stare, turned around and ran smack dab into a wall.

I squeaked as I felt myself falling back, my eyes widened when at the same time, I saw who the wall was. Hitta's arm shot out and wrapped around my waist catching me and bringing me back up against his body.

I stood in his grasp with my free hand resting on his big chest staring up into his face in complete and utter shock.

"Hitta…"

Chapter 17

CONQUERING HER FEAR...

> *And One Day She Discovered That She Was Fierce And Strong, And Full Of Fire, And That Not Even She Could Hold Herself Back Because Her Passion Burned Brighter Than Her Fears...*

Mark Anthony

Angel

"Oh my God! How did you find me?"

The look of pain that flashed in his eyes when the startled question escaped my lips was unmistakable. Before he got it under control, his moment of vulnerability shot through me and straight to my heart. I felt his pain as if it was my own.

Too late, I realized that my question came across as if I wasn't thrilled to see him, when I really was. Needing to explain my response

I opened my mouth, but before I could say anything, Jessie's squeal of excitement pierced the air.

"Unc! I missed you!" Her little body flew past me as she threw herself into his waiting arms.

A smile came to his face as he caught her. "Hey, lil mama...I missed you too!"

Watching them embrace caused a feeling of loss to grow inside of me that nearly took my breath. He had yet to say a word to me. I knew there was a risk that he would be angry because I'd left without telling him and had been gone for a week now, but the pain I saw in his gaze puzzled me.

Why was he hurting?

From where we stood at the cotton candy kiosk, we could see the back deck of the beach house. I didn't want to risk traveling too far just in case West showed up. Standing on the patio waving at us was Carmen, her flaming red hair looking like a burst of autumn on a bright summer day.

"Carmen!" Jessie yelled and as soon as Hitta put her back on her feet, she took off toward the house.

"Jessie, wait!" I called after her, the beach was crowded and I didn't want her to get lost. I went to follow her but before I did, my gaze went back to Hitta's and again, I caught the look of pain in his eyes as he stared at me before he covered it with his anger.

There was so much I needed to tell him about Stan, my upbringing, and why it was so important for me to make this trip to help Jessie, yet my tongue was tied, like the very first day we met at his gym.

"Hitta..." I began but didn't have time to say more before I had to hurry after Jessie, she was good and entangled in the crowd of bodies.

By the time I caught up to her, she was in Wayne's arms offering him some of her cotton candy as she told him all about our *girl's trip*. Both Carmen and Wayne looked at me with sympathetic eyes, only confirming that I was in hot water with Hitta.

"How you doing, boss lady?" The immaculately dressed mogul said flashing me with that million-dollar smile of his.

"I've been better." There was no need of me lying about it.

Carmen hurried down the patio steps throwing her arms around me and I clung to her needing the comfort of a friend. It felt so good tears burned the back of my eyes.

"Angel, we was worried about you, girl. Why did you call Summer and not me? My feelings are so hurt."

"I know, sis, I was just—" Hitta grabbed my arm pulling me away from her. He wasn't rough about it, but he wasn't all that gentle either.

"I need to holla at her. You two take Jessie to town and get her a burger or something." As he mumbled off his instructions, he never stopped walking and was now pulling me up the deck stairs and into the house.

"Dang, Unc, you could have let us say hi to each other!" Carmen called after us, but he never stopped or acknowledged the fact that he'd heard her at all.

My gaze went back to hers and Wayne's one last time, the three of them still stood at the bottom of the stairs watching us go in. Even Jessie had paused in her excited chattering for the first time, sensing that something was wrong. Carmen gave me a little encouraging smile, but it didn't reach her eyes.

"Where yo' room?" Hitta's question was so low I barely heard him. I pointed to the third door on the left.

After walking in he shut the door and locked it behind us. I stood there in the center of the room waiting on his next move. However, when he walked around me and took a seat in the oversized lounge chair in front of my window, I was left confused.

I continued standing, waiting on him to say *something*, but he only exhaled before sitting forward resting his elbows on his knees using his fingers to massage his temples.

Okay, so he had a headache, that explained the pain in his eyes.

"Hitta, I can explain everything—" I began, but he held up his hand cutting me off.

"Naw, shawty, I can't deal with yo' explanations right now...my head is f***ing killing me." This he mumbled without looking up at me.

Alrighty then...

Biting my lip, I eased down on my bed at a loss as to what to do now. The healer in me beat at my chest wanting to be set free so that she could help him and the woman in me needed to embrace him. It had been far too long since the last time I felt his strong arms wrapped around me holding me close. That little encounter on the beach had been just a tease.

But I was afraid.

There was no doubt in my mind that he was angry with me, it poured from him like his strength. But was he so angry that he didn't want me to touch him? Had he decided that he didn't want me anymore? Maybe that was why he didn't want to hear my explanations…

That's stupid, Angel! Do you think this man would have traveled all this way if he didn't want you? Damn, girl, use your brain and get your butt off that bed and go to yo' man!

Hmmm… my inner voice had gone gangsta on me, but she had a point. I don't know how Hitta found me. I've been using cash since I've been here and I hadn't told anybody back home where I was, yet he still managed to find me. And the fact that he had come after me had to mean something, right? If he didn't want me anymore, he could have just stayed home, right?

Plus, this was Hitta we were talking about, he was still the same man that turned into a big baby when he was in pain. He's always talking about what he doesn't have in him to do, but I knew for a fact he didn't have it in him to turn away a soothing hand when he's hurting.

Okay, I can do this! I can get off this bed and help him… I-can-do-this!

Taking a deep breath I stood and because I am a big coward, I didn't look his way, although I felt his gaze on me. Instead, I walked to my purse and retrieved the little bottle of oil I made for him with the left-over tea blend from his soap a few weeks ago. I threw it in my purse just in case he got a headache while we were out and about. Now, I'm really glad I did.

I also took my iPod out and connected it to the speakers turning on the soothing sound of *Alina Baraz*. Her gentle voice combined with therapeutic properties of the tea blend and my fingers should help relax him quite a bit. I just prayed he didn't have one of those headaches that required me to put him completely out.

At this point, y'all, my heart was beating so fast I literally had to take deep, calming breaths to regulate it. This was a first for me. Yes, Hitta and I had grown quite close over the last few months and had experienced a wide range of situations together, but this was the first time I was the one to cause the rift between us, which meant I needed to be the one to fix it.

My gaze went back to his powerful form where he sat on my lounge chair watching me move around the room. He reminded me of a lion at rest. Although regally sitting, you knew that one wrong move would cause him to become a deadly foe. And damn, nobody wore that look like him. I'm just going to be honest; being around his masculinity again was doing something strange to my femininity...if y'all know what I mean.

I don't know what is going on with me; in this moment, sex should be the last thing on my mind. I should be worried about Stan and what he was going to do now that Hitta had found me. I should be worried about West and why the hell he never came home. Hell! I should be worried about the very angry giant sitting in that chair watching me as if he wanted to throttle me.

But I wasn't thinking about any of that, in fact, over the last few days, my hormones have been raging out of control. I've found myself thinking about the way Hitta makes love to my body, imagining his big hands and warm mouth moving across my skin, touching me in all my secret places. I've longed for the sensation of his strength filling me until I cried out begging him to give me the relief that I so desperately craved.

Don't get me wrong, I know that he is angry with me and that he has a headache, but my goodness, it's been a week since he's caused my world to shatter in that very special way that he does and a girl has needs too.

Because it was so hot here in California, I was sporting a simple tank top and a pair of jean shorts, but the way Hitta's gaze was raking over my breasts and bare legs made me feel as if I was dressed in the sexiest lingerie.

And you know what, y'all? That's the day I learned something new about him. However, not wanting to jump to conclusions, I decided to test my theory. You see, he *was* livid with me. But then this happened...

I turned around till my back was facing him and bent down to untie my shoes. Not obviously poking my butt out, but come on, I got some serious junk in my trunk, so it doesn't take much. My jean shorts weren't Daisy Dukes or anything, but they surely weren't the longest pair in the world either. In fact, they came to just below my upper thigh. However, when I'm bent over like this—

"Sh*****t..." I heard him hiss from the chair behind me, or at least I thought that's what he said, it really was incoherent.

The power that shot through me almost made me high. To think, little old me can still make this big, strong man go all tongue-tied.

Hmmm... Let's explore further, shall we?

I turned around pretending I was completely clueless of the scandalous thing I'd just done. But when I saw the way he looked at me from under his lowered lids, I nearly gave up on my experiment, remembering that Hitta is a master lover and I really was no match against him.

He drew his bottom lip between his teeth in that way that he does when he's ready to fight or make love. No, scrap that. He doesn't make love when he draws that lip in like that. I'll give you guys a hint, the last time he did it, we were in his office after I ran from him.

Yeah! You got it, he draws that lip in when he wants to, hmmm... what's a tasteful word for it? Well, you guys get my meaning.

Goodness gracious!

Give me the strength. Whew!

Okay get it together Angel, you can do this. You are a scientist testing out your theory. Stick to it!

"I made you some oil that may help with your head. But—" I purred my words, intentionally letting my sentence drop as I lowered my eyes to the bottle in my hand.

Don't ask me where this sex kitten came from, because I couldn't tell you. Maybe every woman turns into one when they get to a certain level of horniness.

He sat up again, resting his elbows on his knees. I knew his anger was completely gone like I knew my name was Angel.

"But... I'm going to have to climb on your lap and massage it into your temples. However, if you can't stand my touch, then—" Again, I let my voice trail off as I used my finger to play with the button on my shorts.

His gaze followed my action. I had to bite my lip to keep from smiling when I saw his Adam's apple move up and down in his throat as he swallowed.

"You sit on my lap, Teacup, we f**king."

I put my head in my hand and chuckled. Dang it! Leave it to him to skip past the cute little word game and get right to the point.

"Make sure that's what you really want to do before you do it," he continued, watching me in that way he does, making me feel as if he's controlling me.

Slowly, I began to walk toward him, swaying my hips in that way we as women do to let our man know we want them. In that moment, y'all, I had no cares and no worries. There was no Stan and no Westly. There was nothing but me and Hitta, and the knowledge that we hadn't made love in a week.

"Ohhh, I think I'll be alright," I told him as I grabbed a hold of his big shoulders pulling myself up so that I stood on the chair with my feet planted on both sides of his legs. Because he was still sitting up, this position brought his face really close to my center.

I brought my hand back to the snap on my shorts. "I hope you don't mind, but I'm going to have to unbutton these. They are a little tighter than I remembered."

Without moving back an inch, I unbuttoned my shorts before slowly unzipping them a bit. I hadn't lied about them being tighter than I remembered...but I guessed that's to be expected since it's has been five years since I wore them.

As he watched my hand lower the zipper exposing just a peek of my panties underneath, he licked his lips before a dangerous little grin came to his face. I nearly lost my bravery right then because I knew what he could do with those lips, but I was determined to play the game, so I took my time coming down to straddle his lap, moving my hips back and forward until I found the most comfortable position.

The whole time he watched me through narrowed eyes, again reminding me of that lion that lazily watched his prey, giving them a false sense of comfort before they pounced. When I positioned my warmth just right over his hardness, I smiled.

"Now, let's see what we can do about that headache." I held up the little vial of oil, but he lifted his hand and nonchalantly swatted it out of mine, sending it skidding quietly across the carpeted floor.

"Do I look like the kind of mutha f**ka you can play games with?"

Instead of frightening me, his growled statement only excited me further. See what I mean? My hormones are going crazy!

I opened my mouth in feigned shock. "Why, Hard Hitta, whatever do you me—"

His mouth suddenly captured mine cutting off my words. I sank my nails into his shoulders pulling him to me as his hungry lips ravaged mine. He brought his hand up fisting my braids angling my head just where he wanted it.

Oh God! He was so insatiable…

Or maybe it was me, I couldn't tell. We both tore at each other's mouths seeming to share the feeling of desperation. I moaned when he deepened the kiss as I wrapped my arms around his neck clinging to him.

He stood holding me in his arms and I could feel his hardness pressed against my soft curves. So gone was I in our kiss I didn't feel him cross the floor to my bed, all I know is one minute I had my arms and legs wrapped around him trying to climb him like a tree and the next I was lying sprawled out in my bed with his powerful body standing between my spread thighs.

Mmmm…there was such need in his eyes and I was thrilled to see it.

My tank top had ridden up a bit in all the frenzy and he brought his rough hand to rest gently on my soft stomach that was exposed. And for a moment, neither of us spoke, we just stared down at his scarred hand as it made lazy circles around my belly button.

"I missed you so much, shawty." His words were so low that if I wasn't in tune with him, I may not have heard them.

"I missed you too…" My breath caught in my throat when his head slowly lowered to my stomach where he lapped at my belly button with his tongue.

But a squeak left my lips when he nipped me.

"So, you decided to tease me with something I've been starving for over the last week, huh?" As he spoke, he continued to plant kisses on my stomach raising my shirt up farther with each one.

Biting my lip, I nodded.

"Didn't nobody ever tell you that little girls shouldn't tempt wolves?"

I held up my arms so that he could pull my tank over my head. "No, nobody told me. Am I in danger?"

Chuckling, he unsnapped my bra. However, when my breasts sprang free the smile left his face and a groan escaped his lips. Gently he palmed both of them in his hands.

"Damn, I missed these." He muttered to himself taking his time to massage my soft flesh. He rubbed from the base to the sensitive tip, pinching them gently between his fingers. I wanted to press my thighs together to relieve some of the pressure that was building in my core.

His gaze came to mine. "Every time I make love to you, I tell myself to be gentle. I tell myself you ain't ready to meet the real me, but after not having you next to me for a week, I can't be gentle, shawty. Let me just apologize now."

My eyes grew wide in excitement. "Apologize for what?"

An evil grin settled on his face. "You awakened a wolf."

And then his hungry mouth closed over my tender nipple drawing it strongly between his teeth. The pleasure of that caress caused my back to arch up off the bed. I clutched his head as he fed from me.

True to his word, he was not gentle. I'd never seen this side of him. And let me tell you, if I thought that I was sprung from the way he'd made love to me before, I was now completely ruined. He didn't make love as much as devour.

But first, he gave me a lesson in teasing, causing my world to shatter twice before ever entering me. And when he did, he lifted me in his arms growling for me to wrap my quivering legs around his waist. Then he proceeded to take me in such a way that I thought for sure would tear me asunder.

When my world shattered that time, the scream that came from my throat was unrecognizable. The only thing I could do was pray that Wayne, Carmen, and Jessie were still out and about, because if they weren't, there was no way they wouldn't know what was going on in this room.

I had no way of knowing how much time passed, the only thing I knew was that I had awakened a beast and he was hungry for me. When finally he growled his release and his warm seed filled me, I thought that he was done, but he was nowhere near done.

He picked up my shattered body and carried me to the chair and took me again in the same ravenous fashion, relentlessly driving into me until I screamed as another staggering release washed over me. After that, he helped me to the shower, at that point I was a quivering mess. But Hitta wasn't done, he took me again in the shower.

When at last he let me rest, I collapsed on his chest well satisfied. The last thing I remember thinking before I succumbed to the sweet darkness of sleep was that now I could rest, because Hitta was here to keep me safe.

Hitta

Her little short ass passed out as soon as her head touched my chest. And now I felt bad for the way I took her. I'd been holding myself back when I made love to her. She was so small and soft; I've always been afraid of hurting her.

But she'd showed me tonight that my fears were in vain. Not only did she take all of me, she gave as good as she got, meeting each of my strokes brazenly, purring and responding beautifully to each of my caresses. She was so damn sexy when she came apart for me. The thought of it was giving me another f**king erection.

Not to mention her taste.

Poor Stanly… if he'd ever gotten even a sample of it on the tip of his tongue, he was hooked. I chuckled. Sh*t, it had been the death of his goofy ass.

Her taste was enough to drive a sane man crazy with want. I'd never in my life had anything like it. She ate so many of those little flowers they were coming through her pores. When I licked her stomach it tasted like it, when I sipped from her lips the taste was even stronger… but if I began to think of the place where it was the strongest I would be waking her up, so I forced myself to think of something else.

It was bad enough she was clinging to me like she feared I would leave her in her sleep, pressing all her soft lush curves against my body. The love we'd just made was nowhere near enough to soothe the appetite I had for her. And to think, she'd tried to tease me.

Can y'all believe that sh*t?! After the f**king week of hell I've been through.

While she's been here living it up on the f**king beach, I'd been back in Chicago tearing up the streets looking for her. And then after all that, she'd gotten in her head to f**king tease me. She had no idea how much I needed her. Hell yeah, I let go on her.

But now I felt like sh*t for doing it, especially after the information I'd found out during the plane ride here. Maddox and Lannox had gone to explore Stanly's house and the sh*t they found shocked the hell out of me. That mutha f**ka was sick.

The twins had found thousands of pictures of Angel that were taken without her knowledge, some while she was asleep and some while she was in the f**king bath. He'd hidden a camera in her bathroom and recorded her as she showered. They'd found several boxes of tapes.

They'd even found a few pairs of her panties in the boxes. I balled up my fists wishing I could bring his punk ass back and kill him again. My movement must have disturbed her because she wrapped her arms tighter around me burying her head deeper in my neck.

"Hold me tighter…" she muttered without waking.

Smiling, I did as she told me, pulling her closer inhaling her scent.

Damn, I missed this. I haven't f**king been able to sleep because I didn't have her little ass draped over my back.

"Where have you been, Hitta? You left me alone," she continued.

I frowned down at her and although I knew she was talking in her sleep, I felt a need to respond to her.

"I was looking for you, Teacup."

She snuggled deeper in my arms, digging her nails in my back. "You better not leave me again."

Her bossiness made me chuckle. "I won't, baby. That's my word. I will never leave you again."

She was clearly stuck in one of her nightmares. She told me before I came along that she didn't get much sleep because of them. I wonder if that's why she was sleeping so hard right now.

Could this last week have been as rough for her as it was for me?

It didn't matter. This sh*t was never happening again. By nightfall tomorrow, she was going to be my wife, and I'd like to see her short ass try to walk away from me then. I wasn't lying to her, I ain't never letting this sh*t happen again. My heart can't take it. I'll be the youngest nigga in the hood to have a massive f**king heart attack and drop dead on the sidewalk.

If y'all wondering how the hell I'm going to get her to agree to marry me, then wonder no more. I'm going to do whatever the f**k it takes, even if that means lying to her.

Yeah, you heard me. I got a little trick up my sleeve.

You see, the twins found out what Stan's b*tch ass was using to control her. Apparently, that mutha f**ka found out about Trina and was threatening to take custody of Jess if Angel didn't agree to leave me.

He somehow got her mother in on the sh*t too, convincing her to come to the gym and feed me that bullsh*t ass story about Angel going to him to help her leave me, which would explain why he had to ghost her in the motel room.

Everybody knew a crackhead was only as loyal as their last high. However, the only thing his stupid ass accomplished was giving me the perfect leverage to convince Angel to agree to a speedy marriage.

Rome had finally gotten back to me just in time to assist me with my little plan. He was able to find some camera feed that put Stanly boy at the scene of the crime. And thanks to an anonymous tip to the CPD, the good doctor was now wanted for murder. Rome also cleared out all of his bank accounts so that it looked like he made a run for it. Maddox and Lannox will make sure his body never sees the light of day.

Wayne and Kennedy, my attorney, were already working on custody papers for Jess; I just needed to convince Angel that the courts would be more comfortable granting her custody if she was married.

Now, before y'all shake yo' head at me and sh*t and start talking about all that I need to be honest bullsh*t, let me remind y'all of the sh*t that had just went down.

Angel need a nigga like me for a husband. You see how easy Stan was able to manipulate her? And what about her b*tch ass brotha? I swear, if that mutha f**ka show his face again, we gon' introduce him to some hood justice. Ima beat his ass so bad, he gon' disappear and never f**king come back again, which is just how the f**k I want it!

Period!

My phoned dinged on the nightstand next to the bed. Careful not to wake my girl, I grabbed it.

Rome: After doing a little more digging, found out yo' boy been very busy. He purchased 8 milligrams of Digoxin three weeks ago from a very questionable source. So, I decided to check out the toxicology report from his wife's autopsy. Came back squeaky clean. Too clean for someone with stage 4 bone cancer. I also found it very strange that it came back so fast. Did a little more digging and after poring over hours of hospital footage, got yo' boy Stan bribing the hell out of a technician in the medical examiner's office. Didn't take long for me to find the original report and guess what it shows!!!! (Dramatic pause)

I exhaled shaking my head. Rome had a brilliant mind, but his brilliance came with a lot of unnecessary theatrics. When we were kids, he used to drive me nuts because the nigga had a playlist for every situation. He used to blast classical music while he kicked my ass in chess. Often, I wanted to strangle him and his f**ked up music.

Me: What, nigga???!!!

Rome: Tsk, tsk tsk… Nigga, is a word that minimizes all my possibilities. You've place me in a box, to do so is dismissive--- Yada yada yada.

Not it the mood for his crap, I put my phone back on the stand until he got down off his soapbox. He'd given me the nigga speech a million times and I didn't need to hear it again. Hell, I think he was the reason I didn't use the word as often as most of the folks around me.

The phone dinged after another two minutes, shaking my head again at his nonsense, I picked it up.

Rome: You put the phone down, didn't you?

Me: What the f**k you think?

Rome: (sighhhhh) Fine, continue to be a barbarian.

Me: What the report show, bastard!?

Rome: Lol, it showed that Mrs. Diana Baker died from a staggering amount of Digoxin. Yo' boy killed his wife. I went on and forwarded the information I found to the detective on his case. Stanly is now wanted for the murder of his wife and Angel's mom. You're welcome!

I smiled; This sh*t shouldn't be this easy.

Me: Thanks, Bo

Rome: This message will self-destruct in 3, 2, 1

The reel on which he and I were texting went black before a bunch of laughing skeleton faces appeared, followed by a dancing naked lady with a bangin' body that held a sign saying, *Brought to You by Rome*. And then it went completely blank. When I turned my phone back on, it showed no evidence whatsoever of his and my texts.

See what I mean with this one? Unnecessary theatrics…

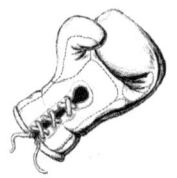

Chapter 18

THE MARRIAGE

Angel

We've been walking along Interstate 57 for many days now. Because it was too dangerous to travel at night, Hitta always found somewhere not too far from the road to make camp. As far as I know, we were still in Illinois, but it felt as if we've been walking for months.

Our number has grown tremendously; we were now over fifty

strong and seemed to be growing by the day. Hitta and his men, including our oldest son were securing the area he'd chosen for us to camp tonight, making sure there were no blood fiends or stray travelers looking for trouble nearby. This they did while everybody else pitched tents and built fires so that each group could start preparing their dinner.

The tents were truly a gift from on high and one of the many blessings the Ancient of Days has bestowed upon us. A few days ago, we came across a fallout bunker that was well-stocked with supplies, tents, food, water, weapons, ammo, medical supplies. Amazingly, that had been the second Apocalypse bunker we've come across since setting out on foot leaving Chicago. But sadly, like the first one, we found the owners' dead bodies closed in with their stash.

What is the irony? They'd managed to store enough food and water to hold them over for a while, enabling them to survive the flare, blood fiends, and the looters should they happen to cross their path only to then succumb to that strange flu that was going around. It had killed a mother and daughter who had been traveling with us last week.

We crossed some travelers who were heading west, and they told us that they'd just buried their parents who had both succumbed to the sickness. Many of the folks in our group had wanted to stay at the bunkers we'd found, but Hitta refused, saying we will only take what we can carry but that we had to keep moving east.

"If these walls can protect you from what's going on out there, then why are these people dead?" he'd asked, gesturing to the owners of the bunkers. "Anybody that want to stay is more than welcome, but me and my family is continuing east."

I looked down at the dead bodies with a heavy heart. These poor folks were called *preppers* before the flare hit. I used to see TV shows and movies about them. They'd spent most of their lives prepping for the Apocalypse but had no way of preventing the plague from seeping through the cracks of their doors.

That night as Hitta and I lay in our tent with our two youngest children asleep on either side of us, I asked him to explain further to me why he didn't want to stay there at least until the supplies ran out.

"Many were misled and gathered food and water to prepare for this day when the only preparedness that was required was obedience. The time has come, and all will be held accountable for their ways. There is nowhere to run..." He kissed the top of my head. "And there is nowhere to hide. We need to continue east, Teacup." And continuing east we have.

Every day I have to battle the fear that my three children will starve or get that strange flu that's going around, but my husband doesn't seem to be worried at all. He says the Heavenly Father will not let us be without and that Yah had not brought us this far to leave us now. Hitta's assurance gives me the strength to be brave when all I want to do is curl up into a ball and weep.

Miraculously, we came across the first bunker after the few supplies we'd taken from Chicago ran out. Hitta never lets us take more than we can carry, although some of the folks with us tried to be greedy and take more anyway. Of course, their actions incurred his wrath and I don't think they will do that again. It's funny because I don't know who they fear more, Hitta or the blood fiends.

We came upon the second bunker when the supplies we'd taken from the first ran out. Do you guys think that is a coincidence?

I don't, I think my husband was right and that we're being guided by the Heavenly Father. So remember, if you find yourself making this journey, have faith. He didn't bring you that far to leave you.

Rubbing my hand gently over my daughter's head that was resting on my lap, I watched as the little old Italian man who was traveling with us, stirred a pot of spaghetti over the fire he and I had built for our little area. Before the flare hit, Alessandro and his wife owned a restaurant in downtown Chicago, so he'd taken to cooking for us.

I assured him that he didn't have to, but he insisted, saying it was the least he could do since he was too old to fight with the warriors. Hitta had not only been kind enough to put him under his protection, but he'd also let him break bread with our family so he wouldn't be lonely.

Although we traveled as one big group, when we camped down for the evening, everybody still split up into smaller groups. Most wanted to be with their families and friends, struggling to hold on to the last bit of life as they remembered it.

Unfortunately, we had a few like Alessandro, who was all alone. His wife had not survived the flare, she'd been out in their yard when it hit. We'd crossed his path on our way out of Chicago. He'd been sitting all alone in what was left of his restaurant; Hitta and Wayne had gone in to search for food to take with us. Alessandro said when he looked up and saw Hitta, he knew that the Heavenly Father had answered his prayer. Not only did he have tons of food for us, but he'd also pledged himself to be Hitta's personal chef for saving his life.

So many had died because they'd been outside or in their cars when the blast happened. For some reason, it had a worse effect on some structures than it had on others. It was only a blessing that when it hit, we'd been having something of a get-together at the gym and its walls had withstood the impact.

However, the streets were full of charred vehicles and bodies that were burned past recognition. When we finally made it back to our home, it was to find it in ruins along with a few other houses on our block. But then there were some we passed that withstood the impact perfectly. It was quite confusing and none of us could figure it out. It was almost as if when the blast hit, there was some kind of shield over certain structures, protecting them.

I don't know, maybe I was being fanciful, but that's what I think happened to the gym. How else can you explain why so many were dead and we were still alive?

I'm sure the government, if there was still a government, had figured out what happened, but since the blast had killed everything electronic, they had no way of communicating with the people, not even by radio. The only information we have about anything is what we get from other travelers. And who knows what could be trusted on a grapevine so large?

The sound of the gentle humming coming from a sewing machine drew me out of my thoughts. I would recognize that tune anywhere, having heard it aplenty from Greatie. It was a sound that always caused my heart to swell with joy.

I looked around to see if anybody else was hearing it. When no one looked away from what they were doing, the joy I felt grew. I eased out from under my sleeping daughter, carefully placing my sweater underneath her head to serve as a pillow.

"I'm going to go for a little stroll, I'll be right back." I told a very pregnant Carmen and Mr. Alessandro, who were sitting in front of the fire not too far from our tent.

Carmen just nodded, not looking away from the fire. No doubt she was worried about the safety of her unborn child, whose due date was drawing near. Mr. Alessandro, bless his heart, managed to make her feel better by always seeming to have a little treat for her to snack on to keep her pregnant hunger tamed.

"Don't travel too far, bella," the little Italian chef muttered giving me a warm smile. "Dinner will be ready soon and I don't want your husband to be angry when he and his men get back and find you gone."

Quite used to everyone going out of their way to stay in Hitta's good graces, I just nodded and assured him that I'd make it back before the fellas.

The place Hitta had found for us to pitch our tents was surrounded by a small group of trees that would serve to hide us from anyone who may be passing on the highway. I followed the sound of the sewing machine until I reached a little clearing.

Sitting at the foot of the hill was a very tiny one-room house, but the warm candlelight that came from it beckoned me. With a smile on my face, I hurried to the door already knowing who was behind it. I lifted my hand to knock, but Greatie's voice came to me before my fingers touched the wood.

"Come in, chile."

Twisting the knob, I opened the door, but I was taken aback. Inside the house was huge! Frowning, I stepped back out unto the little porch and leaned over the rail to look around back to make sure my eyes had not played tricks on me. Yep, on the outside, it was still a one-room shack.

What the world?!

Oooookaayyy...

I walked back inside closing the door behind me. The sound of the sewing machine came floating down a long hallway.

"We're back here, chile!" Greatie's voice came from that direction.

I walked past a massive kitchen and started down the hall. To the right and left of me were many doors, but I knew the one that I was supposed to go in because it was the only open door and the golden light that spilled from it was beckoning.

"There you are," Greatie greeted me as soon as I reached the opening. She was not alone.

The golden light came from the most magnificent sewing machine I'd ever seen. It was so mesmerizing it didn't look as if it was made by the hands of man. It was the color of pure copper, but on it had been carved beautiful swirls that looked a lot like vines. So spellbound was I by it that it took me a while to notice the lovely woman operating it. The same golden light that shined from within the sewing machine spilled from her eyes.

Greatie gestured for me to come closer. "Come on in, daughter."

As I slowly walked in, my eyes were drawn back to the woman operating the machine. She looked like she could be related to Greatie and me, but where our skin was dark, hers was the color of amber.

"This here is your cousin, Brooklyn. She's one of my daughters like you."

I could definitely see that, but I wondered if Brooklyn was real. Not only was she amazingly beautiful and her eyes shined the golden light, the garment she was sewing went into the machine a tattered rag but came out a masterpiece made of pure gold.

"What is she making?"

"Armor," Greatie said leaning over Brooklyn's shoulder to check her work. She pointed at something for the woman to correct, speaking quietly to her.

"Armor for what?" I asked stepping closer to get a better look at it.

I've never seen anything like it. Gently I lifted one of the sleeves and the golden material wrapped itself around my fingers; I inhaled when a sudden burst of strength shot up my arm. Startled, I dropped it stepping away from it.

Brooklyn lifted her head then and her bright gaze fell on me, at least I think she was looking at me, it was hard to tell because where her eyes should be, there was just light. One side of her mouth lifted in a grin before she went back to her task.

Greatie picked up the garment Brooklyn completed and after inspecting it one last time, put it on a hanger. She opened a door that led to a closet that was longer than the hall I'd just walked down and amazingly, hanging on two racks on both sides of the closet were many more suits of armor just like the one she held in her hand.

"This armor is for the coming battle," she told me after hanging it on one of the racks and closing the door.

"What battle?"

She smiled as she headed to a little table that had a tea set on it. I nearly drooled when I saw it. It had been so long since I had a cup of tea. Greatie gestured for me to take a seat and she didn't have to tell me twice.

"The battle between good and evil. The Ancient of Days warriors will be arrayed in clean gold," she continued as she poured me a cup of steaming hot elderberry tea.

I lifted the beautiful cup to my nose and just inhaled.

"Do you know why I called you here?" she asked as she took the seat across from me before pouring herself a cup of tea.

I shook my head as I took my first sip, closing my eyes for a moment to just cherish the taste. I was aware that I was dreaming, but this tea tasted amazingly real.

"When you awaken, the Slayer is going to ask you to marry him."

I frowned. "But we're already married."

She nodded. "Yes, in the spiritual world you and he are already one, but it needs to take place on the physical plain as well. I know that you love him, child, and that you will agree to marry him in a heartbeat. It's just that..." Her words died off as she frowned down into her cup, thinking on how best to tell me what was on her mind.

"It's just that he's not the man we pray he will eventually become, and if I could, I would have prolonged your meeting each other until then." She stirred her tea. "However, that was not the Heavenly Father's will, and here we are. Very soon, he's going to break your heart beloved. Do you remember when I warned you in your kitchen?"

A knowing look came over my face as I waved away her concern. "Yes, but no worries, we got over that little hiccup. It was just a misunderstanding."

She shook her head. "It wasn't that little hiccup that I came to warn you about that day. It is the storm that's heading your way. The enemy has set his sights on you two, and it will stop at nothing in trying to destroy the seed before it grows."

Holding up her hand, she gestured toward the closet. "Your man and the son you carry in your womb have been called by the Ancient of Days to wear this armor. The enemy's job is to make sure many of those suits remain empty, as many as he possibly can. For it is written, many are called but only a few chosen."

"If you can't learn to forgive your man for the pain he is soon to cause you, it will destroy him. He will give up and not even try to fight. He will never become the man you see out there." She gestured toward the front of the house. "He will never become the man your son need him to be."

Her voice became very faint as I recognized the signs of me waking up.

"Wait, Greatie! Forgive him for what? Tell me!" She just smiled as she, my cousin, the sewing machine, and the room began to fade.

Brooklyn looked up from her work. "It's okay, cuz." Her voice sounded so far away I could barely hear her. "I will help you. You just come and see me, and I will help you." And then they were gone.

I cried out as my safety left taking the heat with it, plunging me into the cold darkness. Clutching desperately for it, I came awake to see Hitta getting up from the bed.

"Where are you going?" I clutched at the sheet reaching for him... needing him.

It took me a moment to grasp what was real and what was the dream. The more I took in my environment the more the dream faded from my memory.

Hitta slid on his underwear and tank top before stepping into his jeans. Without buttoning them, he sat back down facing me. My bed that was just full-sized, dipped under his massive frame, causing me to slide toward him a bit.

"We need to talk."

I could tell by the tone in his voice the time had come for me to tell him everything. Sitting up I rested my back against the headboard and after wrapping the sheet around my naked body, drew up my legs tucking my toes under his thigh.

It looked like the sun was just now beginning to set, which meant I'd been asleep for a few hours. Goodness, I'd been so tired I don't even remember falling asleep. The sound of Jessie's laughter came through my closed door from the living room. *Wonder how long they've been back.*

My dream had faded completely from my mind as I tried to think of the best way to explain to Hitta that my stepfather was a creep.

"I'm sorry you got thrown in jail," I muttered, rubbing my finger idly over his rough knuckles.

He shrugged. "It ain't the first time."

My startled gaze came up to his. "You've been in jail before?"

"Don't try to change the subject."

Ooookaayy…

"I'm sorry I didn't tell you I was coming to California."

"Yeah, let's explore that for a second." His anger was back big time. "I was worried to death about you, shawty! You had a nigga tearing them streets up looking for you. And where do I find you? Chilling on the f**king beach!"

I was now rubbing his arm. "Okay, I know that looks bad. But there is a reason why I left."

He shook his head. "There ain't no reason that can justify that sh*t! You my lady, you don't just bounce without telling me! That sh*t was irresponsible!"

Let me tell y'all something. If I didn't know for a fact that he would never hurt me, the way his nostrils flared and his teeth bared would be intimidating as hell. I'd seen some of his old fights where he wore a very similar look while the ref told them the rules before each fight.

No way I would stand and fight him with that look in his eye. The look he was giving me right now wasn't that bad, but still very daunting.

"I know it was, but I had to do it to protect Jessie."

The frown grew on his face. "Protect her from what?"

"More like from *who*." I chewed on my bottom lip, praying he didn't look at me differently after I told him this. "My foster dad...Stan."

"Why did you need to protect her from him?"

Oh boy! Oh boy! Here we go!

After taking a deep breath, I dove in and told him everything, all about how Stan used to touch me inappropriately and about the times I'd come awake to find him trying to get in the bed with me.

"I learned how to sleep with one eye open, which wasn't that hard to do thanks to my nightmares." Chuckling, I pulled his big hand into my lap, just needing to have his strength close.

"Until you came along, sleep was my enemy."

I don't know how he knew, but right then he reached out, putting one arm underneath my legs and the other around my back lifting me in his arms. He then took the spot I'd been sitting in, resting his back against the headboard while holding me in the safety of his arms.

Dear God, thank you so much for the safety of his arms...

"What else?"

I continued to tell him how Westly used to protect me from Stan while he was there and about the huge fights they used to have.

"Several times, the police had to come to the house. Of course, that was all bad publicity for Doctor Stanly. It wasn't quite the look he and Diana were shooting for. So, in order to keep West calm, he tapered off on some of the assaults. He stopped coming in my bedroom and outright touching me inappropriately, but he would do things like walk past me and rub against me or sit too close to me."

I shivered. "I hated his touch, I hated everything about him. The day I left that house wasn't soon enough."

Hitta tightened his arms around me, pulling me closer. I rested my head on his chest.

"I know that I'm luckier than most kids that end up in the system. Outside of dealing with Stan, I had everything I wanted, lived in a really nice home, went to a great school, had awesome friends. I know there are children that are abused worse than me. I know that having

Westly there was a blessing from God. But I still can't—" My voice broke as tears burned the back of my eyes.

"Naw, shawty, nobody deserve to have to fight off a pervert. To have to sleep with one eye open. You can't get used to that sh*t!"

The rage in his voice made me turn in his arms to face him. "Hitta, you have to promise me you won't get tangled up with Stan. He doesn't play fair and he has a lot of powerful friends that can make your life hectic."

He didn't look at all worried. Goodness, men and their stupid pride! I just wanted to shake him.

"He threatened to take Jessie from me."

He exhaled nodding his head. "Yeah, I know. We heard about Trina."

"You have? Oh my God! Was it on the news?"

He shook his head. "Naw, word came to Wayne."

I frowned, confused. "It did?"

"Man, sh*t. Don't even ask me how he find out the sh*t he find out…he got his ways, I guess."

I nodded. That made sense. Wayne did have a way of being in the know in Chicago.

"He also found out Stanly had looked into trying to get custody of Jessie."

"Oh my God!" I was now digging my nails in his arms. "He said, if I didn't stay away from you, he was going to file. Oh my God, Hitta! I can't let that happen! If he—"

"Calm down, shawty! No way that sh*t happening! I told you… you mine. I take care of mine. Wayne and my lawyer already got the ball rolling in the other direction."

His words knocked the wind clean out of my sails. "What?! Really?! How?!"

"They've filed for you so that you can get custody of lil mama."

Joy exploded in my heart. I was so excited that I came to my knees and was now sitting on them between his spread legs facing him.

"That is wonderful!"

But then a horrible thought crossed my mind. "But what about Stan? He's going to try and fight it! No judge will grant custody to a twenty-two-year-old woman over a seasoned, well-established doctor."

Hitta grinned then, reminding me of the cat that had just discovered a piece of meat. "He will if that twenty-two-year-old was married to a retired professional boxer, who now runs a very successful gym and who's assistant is the only son of the wealthiest black man in Chicago."

My mouth dropped open.

Oh!!!

My!!!

God!!!!

Did Hitta just ask me to marry him?

I pulled my braids back behind my ear. "What did you say?" My words were barely over a whisper.

One side of his mouth was still lifted in a grin. "You heard me."

I shook my head. "No, I swear I didn't… say it again."

He reached into his pants pocket and came out with a little black satin bag. It was so small that his big hands looked strange opening the little strings. My mouth dropped again when he pulled a diamond ring out of it.

Little Bag…

Huge Diamond…

He picked up my hand that was now shaking like crazy and slid the beautiful ring on it.

"Will you be my wife?"

Speechless, I lifted my hand so that I could make sure what I was seeing was really happening. Hitta must have taken my shock as hesitation because he started speaking really fast.

"This way, the judge will more than likely grant you custody. It will look good that you're married and—"

I brought my other hand to his lips cutting off his words. I couldn't hear them anyway. I hadn't gotten past—

"You want me to be your wife?"

A look of longing came into his eyes as he searched mine. "More than anything in the world, Teacup."

A squeal escaped my lips as I threw myself into his arms. Over the last week, I'd worried myself sick with the possibilities that he may not want me anymore or that after he found out about Stan, he would think I was some kind of freak.

And here he was asking to marry me!

Me!

Little shy, hobo dressing me!

"Yes!" I cried.

He clutched my shoulders pulling me back so that he could look at me, the smile on his face matched mine. "Yeah?"

I nodded. "Yeah!"

He grabbed me underneath my arms and lifted me so that he could plant one of those drugging kisses on my already well-kissed lips.

I let the sheet drop offering him my breasts that I knew were his favorite things to play with (his words) as I wrapped my arms around his neck, deepening the kiss.

He tore his lips away. However, when his gaze fell to my swollen peaks, a moan escaped his throat.

"Damn, shawty, as much as I want to take those beauties in my mouth, we ain't got time, you need to get dressed so that we can go."

I frowned. "Go where?"

"Go to get married, where else?" He stood, causing me to rock back and forward as my little bed shifted under his weight.

Clutching my sheet, I struggled to sit upright. "What?! You mean, now!?"

"Yeah…now," he muttered, placing his phone and wallet that he'd sat on my nightstand earlier back into his pocket.

Still sitting on the bed clutching the sheet to me, I stared up at him like he'd lost his mind.

"Where in the world are we going to find somewhere to get married so late in the day?"

He chuckled… "Just come on and get dressed, I know a place."

Chapter 19

GOD SENT ME AN ANGEL

Angel

"It's beautiful!" I gasped, staring at myself encased in the cream and yellow frothy bohemian creation. It was too beautiful to compartmentalize it as a wedding dress.

"It's Vera Wang, darling!" Dame Marjorie gushed before instructing one of the three women who were working on my dress to pinch the corset tighter around my bust before pinning it.

This had to be Wayne's doing, it had his signature of excellency all over it. I'd thought when Hitta said that he knew a place to get married that he meant a little hole-in-the-wall that sported a neon sign that said *Get Married Now by Elvis* or something like that.

I never expected to end up on a private jet to Beverly Hills and taken to a place that can safely be classified as paradise. Sitting on twenty-plus acres of rolling hills, lush lawns, and palm trees was the human-sized version of the Barbie Malibu Mansion. Apparently, it was where all of the stars came to elope. For the right price, one could have a glamorous wedding whenever the notion hit... And I do mean glamorous.

As soon as we walked through the door of this mind-boggling manor, I was whisked away from Hitta by Dame Marjorie, who was part owner of this wonderland along with her husband, who will be the one marrying us.

"I'll need three hours to prepare the lovely bride for a wedding night she'll never forget!" she called over her shoulder as she pulled me up a pair of golden stairs. Another woman came for Carmen and Jessie, but led them to a separate part of the house away from where I was being guided.

Flabbergasted, I looked back at Hitta, he and Wayne stood at the foot of the stairs with Dame Marjorie's husband. With a grin on his handsome face, my soon-to-be husband waved at me. Feeling slightly nervous, I asked the Dame why Carmen and Jessie couldn't get ready for the wedding with me.

"Because, darling, becoming a bride here at Château de Fontainebleau is an experience. And when the curtain is pulled back on my creation, I want all to remember the magnifique. There will be no peeking, dear."

As she spoke, she made sweeping gestures with her hands reminding me of one of the actors in the operas that Diana used to drag me to in her never-ending endeavor to keep up with the Joneses. I don't know if you guys have picked up on it yet, but Dame Marjorie was a bit eccentric, to say the least.

I don't think she was French, although she clearly had a keenness for all things French, from the name they chose for their estate to the few French words she sprinkled throughout her sentences. If I wasn't so nervous, I would have found it funny.

However, I didn't have time after that to worry about much. She took me to a pair of golden doors that sat at the end of a huge hall and when she threw them open, I was floored by all the activity that was taking place behind it.

There had to be at least eight women bustling around the room, however, several of them were sitting on stools surrounding a—

Dear God!

In the center of the room hanging on a mannequin that sat on a pedestal was a yellow and cream frothy creation of my dreams. For just a moment everything in the room faded to black and a light seemed to shine down from heaven encasing the dress.

It was a bohemian masterpiece. That's the only word I could use to describe it. The top half of it was a strapless cream corset that was laced down the back with a yellow ribbon; its overlapping ends had been made into a big beautiful flower that sat on the side of the dress.

However, it was the gown's petticoat that was the true art of this creation. I'm going to try and describe it to you guys, but I can tell you now, simple words cannot do it justice. It appeared as if the frothy cream tulle materiel that made up the majority of the petticoat, fell to the floor in tattered layers. Somehow the designer successfully pulled this risky move off, calling out to the boho girl inside of me. The material was so soft it looked like a cloud. On top of it was a layer of yellow tulle that flowed into a train that had to be at least 10 feet long.

It was simply amazing…

My stunned gazed went to the Dame. "How did you know?"

I don't know if I was asking her how she knew that I was into the Boho look or how she knew that I would love this particular dress, seeing as to how there were no others here in the room.

She got so much satisfaction from my response her eyes sparkled. "Because I'm good at what I do, bunny." Turning, she clapped her hands together getting her workers' attention.

"Ladies, this is our bride-to-be… Let's give her the Château de Fontainebleau experience!"

And then it began, the whirlwind of me preparing for my wedding. I was plucked, tucked, waxed, perfumed, powdered, plucked some more…tucked a bit more, but the end result nearly brought tears to my eyes, which would have been catastrophic because it had taken the young lady nearly an hour to apply my makeup.

I loved everything about my look, including my hair that had been flat-ironed and styled. You see, I generally didn't like to straighten my hair, but the beautician showed up to show out. Once she took my braids down, she went to work, and I ain't gon' lie, that girl laid my hair. It tumbled down my shoulders and back to rest just above my waist.

According to the Dame, she was the personal beautician of a very famous singer, but for privacy purposes, she couldn't tell me her name, she just made the buzzing sound of a bee before winking at me.

My mouth dropped… "Oh my God! Did Beyoncé's beautician just do my hair?!" I screeched.

The Dame just chuckled before shrugging one of her shoulders as she carefully positioned the gorgeous yellow veil on my head.

"As you are walking down the aisle my beauty, there will be a gentle breeze just overhead and it will cause your veil to float around you in a most alluring way. It will make you appear to be the Angel you were named after. Your groom will take one look at you and see you for the gift that you are."

Dang it! Now her words were going to bring me to tears.

I chuckled trying to play it off a bit. "I don't know about that. Hitta is not really the sentimental type if you know what I mean." My voice quivered a bit.

Goodness, I was losing the battle.

"Trust me, bunny, I've been doing this for over forty years. Something happens to certain men when their eyes land on their new brides for the first time. Forty years and I've been able to call which marriages will last forever and which were doomed before they even began. I've never been wrong about it"

She tapped my hand with her finger. "You have found your soulmate. Many are not as lucky. Mark my words, you and your handsome man will grow old together."

Yep, I didn't make it, that tear I was fighting broke the surface, but Dame Marjorie was ready and seemed to produce a tissue from thin air to dab at my eye before it could fall.

"I've never been so beautiful," I admitted to the older woman as she and I stood looking at the finished results in the mirror.

"And that, my dear, is the Château de Fontainebleau experience." She came and air-hugged me in fear that we would mess something up if we actually touched.

"Come, let's get you married, shall we?"

Y'all, I was a nervous wreck. When she positioned me behind the door that led to the little hall where the wedding was taking place, my teeth were chattering. A few of the ladies who worked on my dress situated my long train. Dame Marjorie gave me parting instructions on how to walk to keep it straight and then she and her staff disappeared, leaving me standing alone before those doors that will lead me to my fate.

Please God, don't let me do something like trip over this dress and fall to my face.

"So, you're the tea maker that got my boy wanting to be a better man, huh?"

Startled, I whipped around and nearly toppled over in the many layers of my dress. However, when the handsome man with the light brown eyes saw that, he hurried to catch me before I hit the floor.

"I'm sorry, shawty, I didn't mean to frighten you. Rome..." he said holding his hand out once the threat of my going down and disappearing into a pile of tulle fabric had passed.

"But my wife and mother insist on calling me Romeo."

As I shook his hand, my mouth fell open for what seemed like the hundredth time in a matter of hours. So, this was the famous Rome, thug genius extraordinaire.

"Wow!" was all I could say.

That made him chuckle again. "I see the big guy has been talking about me."

"All the time," I admitted. "But mostly about how you were always beating him in chess."

He nodded his head. "Well, you know, I am pretty great!"

That made me laugh, causing me to forget all about my nervousness. "And very humble too, I see."

He shrugged. "That I am..."

"Not," I finished for him causing us both to laugh.

"I would be honored if you will allow me to escort you down the aisle, lovely lady," he said when our laughter died down. He accompanied his request with a little bow.

"That would be a great relief. Before you scared me, I was praying that I didn't fall on my face."

He held out his arm for me to take. "Well, we can't have that now, can we?"

No sooner had I wrapped my shaking hand around his arm, the door was thrown open and the beautiful sound of a harp greeted us.

"You ready?" he whispered, smiling down at me encouragingly.

I nodded... "Yeah, let's do this."

As soon as I took my first step into the hall, I could feel the gentle breeze the Dame spoke of; it wasn't overly aggressive. In fact, one would probably pay no attention to it if they didn't know about it. It was just enough to cause the soft veil resting on my head to gently blow behind me.

I was amazed to see that there were quite a few people inside.

"Who are all of these people?" I asked Rome without moving my lips.

He chuckled. "You ain't marrying no scrub, baby girl. Didn't you know? Yo' man famous."

His silliness was just enough to knock off the initial panic I felt at seeing so many new faces. Nervously, I scanned the crowd searching for someone I recognized. Carmen, Wayne, and Jessie waved at me from where they sat in the front. All three of them looked very nice in their dressy clothes; I smiled at them, so glad they were here.

But then my gaze landed on my husband-to-be and everybody else disappeared. He stood looking like a great African king, more handsome than I'd ever seen him in a cream suit that had a yellow flower sticking out of the top pocket, but it was his eyes as he took me in that I will never forget. He looked at me as if I was the most beautiful sight he'd ever seen.

And when he lifted his hand and placed it over his heart, I feared that those makeup destroying tears were going to come back with a vengeance.

———

Hitta

I'm not a very spiritual man. I mean, don't get me wrong, I know there is a God, but until today, I thought that maybe he had forgotten about me. I feel like I've been fighting my whole life, it was the first thing I remember ever doing. I know it will probably be the last thing I ever do.

Until this moment, I ain't never felt like my life was worth sh*t. Yeah, I made a name for myself, but without money, nobody would even have known it. It's hard to feel accomplished when the only thing you got to show for it is a little bit of dough.

I ain't like my boy Rome, who masterminded bringing value back to the hood. His name will always be remembered because he left behind a legacy. The only thing I can do good is destroy.

Yeah... Didn't think God paid attention to nothing ass niggas like me. That's what my mama always called me when I was a shawty, a nothing ass nigga.

But that was before He sent me an Angel. I put my hand on my chest to try and stop my heart from racing. Maybe God had made a mistake and meant to give her to another man who was worthy of her. Maybe He got his wires crossed and thought I was something I wasn't.

As I watched her come down the aisle toward me, I knew without a shadow of a doubt that I'd somehow been gifted something very rare and I couldn't figure out why. I tried to think about something I'd done to deserve her but could come up with nothing, which meant God had made a mistake and gifted me with one of His jewels.

It's the reason why as soon as she said yes, I had to see the deed done. I couldn't let daybreak come before making her legitimately mine. That way when God realized His mistake, it would be too late. Although I wasn't that learned in the Scriptures, even I knew that He is a just and righteous Power that honored contracts. And today, Angel and I were entering a binding contract.

I blinked trying to see if my eyes were playing tricks on me. She was so beautiful; she didn't look real. It looked like she was floating down the aisle toward me. I took a deep breath trying to calm my racing heart, but it didn't help.

Sh*t! I was getting ready to lose my cool. Never have I ever felt so unworthy of somebody. When she came to a stop in front of me, I lifted her veil from her face with hands that shook. I couldn't look away from her beautiful eyes. Her smell wrapped around me bringing my rapidly beating heart back to its regular pace and I was able to breathe again.

I know it wasn't time to kiss her, but I couldn't help myself, I needed the calming effect of her taste. The hall erupted in cheers as I wrapped one arm around her waist and lifted her so that I could devour her mouth, her taste calming down the unsteady beast that's always there inside of me.

When I placed her back on her feet, she bit her bottom lip as she bashfully looked at the cheering crowd. Like me, she probably wondered who all these mutha f**kas were. Leave it to Wayne to be able to plan a wedding to make the Princess of Wales green with envy in only a day's time. I told him my plan to get Angel to marry me last night; he'd been on the phone ever since and had managed to get all of this done.

He was even behind this beautiful dress my baby was wearing, telling the crazy broad that run this joint what color and style to get. Sh*t! This the first time I can honestly say I appreciate his controlling ways.

The minister or whatever he was started his wedding spiel. And after about fifteen minutes of the sh*t, I wanted to snatch his ass and tell him to hurry the f**k up before Angel changed her mind and realized she was marrying a f**kan gutta rat. I felt like I couldn't breathe easy until it was done.

As if she could sense the turmoil going on inside of me, my baby reached up and placed her little hand in the center of my chest. And y'all gon' think I'm bullsh*tting you, but I felt an instant calm. I smiled; this girl got me wrapped around her baby finger and I was loving every bit of it.

When finally it was time for me to kiss the bride, I wrapped both arms around her lifting her for my kiss. The crowd erupted as Rome and Wayne patted me on the back. Having eyes only for Angel, I placed her back on her feet, although I kept my arms around her holding her close.

She looked up at me and smiled with tears of joy in her eyes, and I knew that I was the luckiest man in the whole world...

You know what? Scratch that. What was happening to me didn't have nothing to do with luck. I was *blessed*, only God can give a man a woman like Angel.

"Hey you," I told her, drowning out everyone around us.

Biting her bottom lip, she hit me with that sexy ass smile. "Hey."

"You're mine now, Teacup. Now and forever, baby..."

———

Angel

"See, the trick is making sure to keep your layer of strawberry cream cheese very thin as you spread it across the chicken sandwich meat. Then you place your pickle slices in the center and roll it all up like a cigar." Rome's lovely wife held up her finger indicating for me, Carmen and Jessie to pay close attention.

"Last but not least, you come back with a gentle sprinkle from a fresh lemon." Her gaze was so serious. "If the lemon isn't fresh, it's not going to taste the same, trust me." I nodded from where I leaned against the sterling silver island. My elbow was on the cold metal and my head was resting in my raised hand. I was barely standing thanks to the four glasses of champagne I'd had and the fact that it was like three in the morning. I'd danced like a crazy woman at my wedding reception for the last two hours.

My gaze went to Jessie, who was sitting on the island watching Nak roll up our snack with a look of disgust on her face. I couldn't believe she was still bright-eyed and bushy-tailed.

"That look nasty," she told her.

"Yeah well, what do you know? You're just a kid," Nak muttered before lifting one of the treats and handing it to me. She tried to hand one to Carmen, but she shook her head.

"Naw, playa, I'm good."

Nak shrugged. "Suit yourself, you missin' out on some good eating." And then she took a healthy bite of whatever the hell this was she'd just made.

I'm not going to lie, the way she was chewing made it look really good, so I took a bite. And would y'all believe it tasted AMAZING?!

"Mmmmm, this so good!" I told her before taking another bite. She gave Carmen and Jessie an I-told-you-so look before she handed me another.

Let me tell y'all something about Nak: first of all... I looooooovvvveedddd her!!!!

She had this really innocent face. When Rome had first introduced us, I thought to myself, "Wow, he has a sweet wife." I think I may have expressed my sentiments to Hitta who couldn't stop touching my hair as we posed for a few pictures, because it was his first time seeing me without my braids.

"Don't let her face fool you. She's deadly," he said, speaking loud enough for only me to hear.

"What do you mean deadly?"

"I mean, she will beat the sh*t out of everybody in this room while eating a f**king sandwich and still make it home in time enough to catch the nightly news."

I laughed at his silliness, but when he didn't laugh back, the smile left my face. "Are you serious?"

"As a heart attack. She damn near beat my ass."

My mouth dropped... "Nooooo!!!"

He nodded. "Thought I was gonna have to turn on these guns." He held up those monster paws he called fists.

Then I overheard him and Rome talking about some kind of mission or something he and Nak had gone on a few weeks ago to help rescue somebody's wife, who'd been sold into a sex slave ring in Argentina. Ever since then, I tried not to be too obvious, but I couldn't help but stare at her, trying to figure out how something that looked so delicate, could be so dangerous. She and her husband were like real-life secret agents.

However, I was not the only one drawn to her, Carmen and Jessie were as well. But you didn't need Rome's mind to figure out why. The three of them shared a similar personality. They were all troublemakers and Nak was the biggest one. She was the reason we'd snuck into one of the Château's kitchens that wasn't open to the public. It wasn't even in use tonight, but we'd gone on a hunt for strawberry cream cheese that she claimed was simply imperative for the tasty treat she was going to make the four of us, so here we are.

"Ladies, here y'all are. Damn, we were about to send out them boys to look for y'all," Rome's deep voice came from behind us.

I turned to see him, Hitta, and Wayne walking across the empty dining room that was connected to this kitchen. I couldn't help but smile…those are some good-looking men. They all had ditched their ties and bowties somewhere. Each of them carried a glass with Hennessy in it. I knew that because Rome had gifted Hitta with a bottle of *Hennessy Paradis Imperial* for our wedding and my husband decided to drink it with them. However, when he told me it was a three-thousand-dollar bottle of cognac, I nearly spat my drink out.

"We decided to ditch the party to find some real food," I told them around a mouth full of… heck, I don't know what I was eating, but it was good.

It was a hundred percent better than what Nak and Jessie called that Hollywood food downstairs. That crap was horrible. I nearly threw up when I walked past the oyster bar.

"Oh yeah? I can dig that! I don't like that food either," Rome said coming to a stop next to his wife. He reached over and snagged one of her snacks popping it into his mouth, seconds later, he began choking and gagging as he desperately searched for a garbage can.

Taking a sip of his cocktail, Hitta chuckled from where he stood next to me, he put his other hand on my hip and pulled me in front of him so that my back rested against his front. I was grateful for his strength because I was tired.

"Damn, Nak!" Rome cried after he spat the offensive food out. "What the hell is with you lately? Eating all that nasty sh*t!"

Jessie nearly fell off the island laughing, Hitta had to reach over and catch her. "I told you it was nasty!"

"Yeah well, what does he know?" Nak grumbled as she scooped up another spoonful of cream cheese and put it on the bit she had left in her hand. "His idea of a tasty treat is chicken fried zucchini, without the chicken."

That made me chuckle as I reached over and grabbed another off the plate.

"Baye, don't eat that sh*t!" Hitta cried as he watched in horror as I brought it to my mouth.

"I know it looks gross, but it's really good."

"Is that strawberry cream cheese with pickles?" Wayne asked from where he stood awfully close to Carmen, who surprisingly has been very chill during this trip. She and Wayne had been forced to spend a lot of time together and amazingly, they'd done it without biting each other's head off.

Nak nodded as she took the second to the last treat before offering me the last.

"If I didn't know no better, I would think you heffas was pregnant!" Carmen said as she watched us eat the last of the snack with a frown of disgust on her face.

That caused us all to laugh.

That was just too funny.

Me…pregnant.

That was just too fu—

Hmmm…

As if the possibility hit us all at once, everybody stopped laughing but Carmen, Wayne, and Jessie. Rome's and Nak's faces reflected Hitta's and mine.

I don't know what they were thinking, but my mind was racing as I tried to remember when I had my last period. And then another thought came to me, Hitta and I have never used a condom. We've never even *discussed* using condoms, I just assumed…

You know what!? I don't know what the hell I assumed!

WHAT THE HELL, ANGEL?!

I looked up just as Rome and Hitta looked at each other before they both turned to look at Nak and I. There was a slight grin on Hitta's face as his eyes lowered to my stomach.

"No, I can't," I heard Nak whisper from the other side of the island, however, she didn't sound too sure. "Ca-can I?"

Wayne exhaled before he turned his glass up to drain the last of his drink. When he was done, he turned to leave the kitchen.

"Get two of them!" Rome called after him.

———

"I can't believe you beat me in that f**king obstacle course pregnant!" Rome growled from where he paced back and forward in the kitchen of me and Hitta's suite

Wayne had been back for ten minutes now and we all sat here eagerly awaiting the results. Jessie had finally crashed and was knocked out cold in our bed. Still in my wedding dress, I sat in one of the kitchen chairs gripping the edge of it so tightly my knuckles were white.

Hitta sat in the chair next to me, I wondered what he was thinking. He didn't seem to be freaking out or anything. In fact, the little grin had not left his face. Could he be happy about this?

Dear God, had he tried to get me pregnant?

"Just wait till that chump Jo hear about this. He ain't gon' never let me live it down," Rome continued to grumble to himself.

Nak, who had not stopped nervously eating since she peed on the stick, shook her head at him. "You're always worrying about what the hell Jo thinks. Technically, I beat him too. He was there."

He looked at her as if she'd grown a frog out of her head. "That's not going to matter. He gon' say some sh*t like, "At least my wife ain't a better athlete than me." I just know he is." He began his angry pacing again.

"I been trying to get Journey to work out. Damn girl lazy!" he muttered under his breath.

"Oh, leave her alone. Everybody is not competitive like you," Nak told him before she filled her mouth with some microwave popcorn. How she'd spotted that bag as nervous as she was, I'll never know.

I couldn't think of anything but the results. Oh my God! I was probably getting ready to be a mom.

Hitta reached for my hand. "Are you okay?"

I nodded. "You?"

The grin grew on his face. "Fan-f*ckin-tastic!"

"Really?"

"Yeah! I'm ready to be a dad."

I squeezed his hand; his certainty was having a calming effect on me. "But what if I'm a bad mom?"

He looked at me as if I'd lost my mind. "Don't believe that negative voice that's trying to convince you of that sh*t. Believe yo' own actions." He gestured toward the bedroom.

"You the only real mama she ever knew. If not for you, she wouldn't be so amazing. It was when I saw you with her that I knew I wanted you to be the mother of my children."

I was up and out of my chair and into his arms in a flash, needing to feel his strength in this moment. *He wanted to have children with me from the very beginning.*

Dear God! Please let it come back positive...

"They're ready!" Carmen screeched from where she had been standing in front of the counter staring down at the sticks. I don't know who was more excited about this, she or Hitta.

Nak eased her popcorn bag on the table before slowly coming to her feet. For the first time, I could see how much of a big deal this was to her. Rome didn't speak, he just walked to her and pulled her into his arms.

I didn't move off of Hitta's lap. If the test was positive, I would need his support, and if it was negative, I would need his support.

"What do they say?" Wayne asked looking over her shoulder.

Carmen could barely contain her excitement. "They're both positive! Congratulations, guys! Y'all are both pregnant!"

Nak began to weep and Rome lifted her in his arms and carried her into one of the spare bedrooms, shutting the door behind them.

My gaze came to Hitta's to find the grin back on his face. He lifted his hand and gently rubbed his finger along my cheek.

"Thank you, Teacup! This was the best wedding present you could have given me."

I returned his smile before I threw my arms around his neck. The thought of becoming a mom is terrifying and magnificent all at once. But knowing that he wanted this so much was even more amazing. Dame Marjorie was right; this is a wedding night I will never forget.

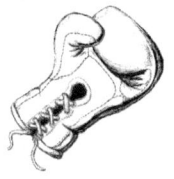

Chapter 20

THE HONEYMOON...

Angel

"If you could go anywhere on earth, where would you go?"

As I thought about my husband's question, I stared into the small lagoon hidden deep inside the intimate garden Hitta and I had disappeared into about thirty minutes ago. It was beyond extraordinary here. There were lights at the bottom of the sparkling blue water that cast the whole area in its gentle glow, making it so very romantic. The moon sat high and full in the sky only serving to intensify the feeling in the air.

I don't know how Dame Marjorie and her husband did it, but they'd managed to create a couple's paradise here on their forty-plus acres of land. This little area where we are is one of many private, themed, rendezvous spots spattered around the grounds. This one was called the Blue Lagoon and Dame Marjorie assured us it's the most sensually stimulating out of all the hidden little nooks. She also assured us we will have our privacy for the rest of the evening.

"Hmmmm, if I could go anywhere?"

He nodded from where he sat on the plush grass behind me. I

leaned against his strong body more satisfied than I'd ever been in my life, even though I was sitting on this grass in my wedding dress.

"Yeah, anywhere."

"There is a little village tucked securely between a group of mountains in Tibet called Minling Gangri in the Himalayans. They have an herbal bazaar there where they sell some of the rarest herbs and plants in the world, things that can only be grown in the Himalayans. My Greatie says she found some of her best tea ingredients there."

"Damn, yo' great grandmother been to Tibet?"

"Oh yeah, quite a few times."

"When am I going to meet her? You always have these wild stories about her."

I shrugged; this wasn't his first time asking me that. I didn't know how to explain her to him outside of the fact that she's my great grandmother. I could say she gets around really well for her age, she was a bit mysterious, and came and went as she pleased. Of course, he thought I meant that she was just another kooky old lady who liked to travel. *But if only he knew.*

"She'll come around one day."

He moved my hair to the side and placed a gentle kiss on my neck. "With yo hair like this, it make you look completely different."

"Different in a good way I hope."

"Shawty, I don't care how yo' hair look, I'm hooked. So, all yo' difference is good to me."

I chuckled. "The beautician spent nearly an hour flat ironing it, but all it would take is one second in that water and it would draw up like this." I snapped my finger.

"You know what? That sound like a good idea." He stood and began undressing.

"What are you doing?" I asked laughing at his silliness.

"Going swimming. Come on."

"Are you nuts?! I'm still in my wedding dress."

He pulled me to my feet. "I know, here, let me help you out of it."

"Oh my God, Hitta! What if someone sees us?" I screeched as he quickly untied the big bow at my waist before unzipping it.

"I been waiting to peel you out this boy all night. For real! Sh*t!"

I held my head back and laughed when he suddenly lifted me straight out of all the layers of the dress. When he placed me back on my feet, I stood in a pair of cream thigh highs and panties with the matching strapless bustier.

"Damn," he hissed as his gaze took its time raking over my body.

The way Hitta always looked at me made me feel so sexy. He looked at me as if I was something rare, as if he'd never seen anything like me. Slowly he went down to one knee in front of me.

"Sh*t, I *did* want to go swimming," he muttered before he palmed my soft behind in his massive hands bringing my body towards him.

I bit my lip to try and stop the huge grin that was trying to take over my face. "Oh yeah, and what do you want to do now?"

I grabbed on to his shoulders when his warm mouth touched my belly button. I was so distracted with his talented tongue that I didn't notice he'd hooked his fingers in my panties and was pulling them down my legs until he was urging me to step out of them.

"Now, all I can think about is making love to my wife."

I chuckled nervously. "We can't do it here. There's nothing but the ground."

When he lifted his handsome face to look at me, there was a devious grin on it. That grin unnerved me. With horror I watched his gaze lower to the puffy cloud that was my wedding dress. Before I could open my mouth to protest, his hands came to my waist and he was lifting me, turning me and then laying me on top of my beautiful gown.

"Absolutely not, brotha! Have you lost your mi—" The last of my sentence ended on a moan, because that talented mouth of his was once again at work. He had this way of ravishing me that scrambled my brain, causing me to only think about pleasure.

Yes, I was very aware that my husband was getting ready to make love to me on my Vera Wang wedding dress, but the only thing I could think at the moment was: *What the hell? I can just take it to the cleaners when we get back to Chicago.*

"Let's go to Tibet."

Now good and sleepy, I grinned at him. We were still in the secluded garden lying facing each other on top of my puffy wedding dress. My husband had made love to me twice and now as the sun rose slowly in the sky, I was ready to drift off into a deep sleep.

"When?"

"Today…now."

I chuckled. "You're so silly." As I spoke my eyes got heavier. I was literally fighting to keep them open. I was so tired I didn't care that somebody may come along and find me and Hitta lying here in our birthday suits.

"I'm serious, Teacup. Let's go to Tibet for our honeymoon."

I reached up and gently rubbed my fingers through his beard. "That would be awesome, but I don't think it's a good idea to leave Jessie until we get the custody issue squared away. Who knows what tricks Stan will pull out of his sleeve while we're gone?"

The look that came into his eyes caused me to frown a bit. He exhaled before he sat up resting on his elbow. For a moment he didn't speak, he just stared at his hand as if he was contemplating how best to tell me something horrible.

"What's the matter?" I was getting a bad feeling in my stomach.

"I ummm…" He paused again really thinking hard about his words. "I wasn't going to tell you this until after we got back to Chicago."

Oh goodness! Now he really had my attention. I too sat up on my elbow. "Tell me what?"

"I don't think you have to worry about Stan no mo'."

"Why not?"

When Hitta didn't answer immediately, I put my hand on his chest, encouraging him to continue.

"He killed his wife, bae."

My mouth opened as a gasp escaped my lips. "Whaaat?! How do you know that?!"

"The sh*t was in the paper. He poisoned her to make it look like she died from her disease. And I guess he must have known that the police was going to be looking for him, 'cause he cleaned out all his bank accounts and got little. The last known traces of him was like in Russia or some sh*t."

I brought my shaking hand to my lips. "Are you serious?"

He nodded. "I wish I was joking, Teacup."

Oh my God! Poor Diana!

What the hell is wrong with Stan?! Why would he do that to a woman that worked herself into exhaustion trying to be the perfect wife to him? This news was going to kill Westly. He was already going to hate himself for not being there when she died, and now this.

Dear God, give us the strength to overcome this.

"That's ain't all," Hitta continued, drawing me back out of my head. "They say evidence show that he may have killed another woman, whose identity have yet to be released."

"Stan killed somebody else?! Is there any clue to who it could have been?"

He shook his head. "Naw, but I'm sure it's nobody for you to worry about." He reached up and dried tears from my cheek. I hadn't even been aware I was crying.

"Don't cry over these people who didn't give a f**k about you. The only reason I told you is because I want you to enjoy our honeymoon without worrying that dude was going to try and f**k with Jessie. Trust me, where he at right now, he ain't thinking about you or Jessie."

I didn't know how to take this information. Stan was on the run. He'd killed two people. I mean, I knew he was sick, but *murder*?

"We'll only be gone for two weeks," Hitta continued. "Carmen gon' come to the house and babysit. And you know I got the twins on watch. Ain't nobody getting past them. Come on, Teacup, this is supposed to be our time."

His hand came down to my stomach. "We getting ready to have a shawty. What we gon' tell him or her about our wedding and honeymoon? That we let the fear of some f**k boy destroy it?!"

His words made me laugh a bit. You would think that after being with him for a little while now I'd grown used to his frankness.

"Tibet, huh?"

He nodded. "To the mountains with all them plants and herbs you dreamed of checking out."

I *have* always wanted to go. And I guess technically, I didn't have Stan to worry about. However, I did want to wait for Westly. I wanted to be there for him when he found out all this information. He was not going to take it well.

But who knows when he was going to come back around? And this was my honeymoon, I didn't want the memory of it smeared with thoughts of Stan. Last night we'd found out that we were going to be parents. I didn't want to be the reason we fell off of this high. Leaning forward I gently kissed my husband's lips.

"Yeah, let's do it! I'm ready…"

———

Hitta

I know a lot of y'all is out there wondering if I felt guilty about the lies I'd told Angel. My answer is no, but before you jump on me, allow me to explain. I want her to always remember our wedding lovingly. I want the thought of it to bring a smile to her face, no matter where she is or what she going through. That way, when she realized who and what she'd truly married, she could remember that, although I'm f**ked up. I'm the man that took her to a place she always wanted to go and made sure she lived out her dreams.

I was telling the truth about waiting till we got back to Chicago to tell her about Stan, but when I saw that she was going to buck against going away for our honeymoon, I had to say something to put her heart at ease.

Now, as for her mammy…

Sh*t, I didn't feel no need to break that news to her. As far as I'm concerned, she don't never have to bear that burden. It ain't like her mom was worth sh*t. She was doing Angel a favor by f**king dying anyway.

Of course, my Teacup being super-sensitive, wouldn't have seen it that way. She would have started crying and getting all depressed and sh*t. Hell naw, I'm not trying to have her feeling that way during our honeymoon. Maybe I'll tell her when we get back to Chicago, but then again, maybe I won't.

Rome had always teased me about not being smooth like him with the ladies. But as we checked out of the Château, Angel and I was all smiles because of my little lie. Meanwhile, Mr. Smooth and Nak was arguing like crazy.

Apparently, they'd stopped by to celebrate our wedding with us on the way to another mission their boss had sent them on. But after Rome found out his girl was pregnant, had called Judah and told him he had to send somebody else 'cause he didn't want to risk her getting hurt. Of course, Nak wasn't feeling that sh*t and was letting him know just how much.

I chuckled, shaking my head. She was wasting her time; once Rome got his mind set on something, it was a wrap. I'm sure they were going to have a very interesting trip back to Canada. But see, me, I didn't have them kind of problems. My lady was happy.

———

Our trip to China was a very pleasant one. In fact, Angel slept most of the way. She admitted that she hadn't gotten much rest during the week we'd been apart.

I'll let y'all in on a little secret; I will never admit this sh*t to nobody else though. It makes me feel good that she need me in order to have a peaceful night's sleep. I know that's f**ked up, but it does. It lets me know that I'm not alone and that she feels this crazy pull between the two of us as well.

I don't mean to randomly switch topics on y'all like this, but it's some sh*t y'all need to know about Angel that I'm about to find out during our honeymoon. You remember way back when I told y'all what it was like to watch her make her teas? I told y'all that it was something supernatural about it.

Well, this trip will confirm my thoughts on that. My baby was a damn superhero. Let me tell you how I found this sh*t out.

So, we touched down in Shanghai, where our guide met us at the airport with a small security detail; they would be with us for the next two weeks. Of course, everything was planned to a T; Wayne would have it no other way. As soon as I told him me and Angel was coming here for our honeymoon, he got on his phone. No doubt he's still on it making sure everything goes according to his plan.

You know, over the last few years I've threatened to fire him many times because he's a f**king control freak, but I'll never do it. Wayne was a godsend; my life had gotten substantially easier when he came into it. I don't know if it's because of my speech impediment or my size, but people seemed to respond better to him than me.

Our guide knew what food I ate and what I didn't, so he took us to eat at a very nice restaurant that also served American food. Of course, my baby wanted to try something she'd never tried before while I just stuck with a burger and fries, can't go wrong with that. We were in route to another airport where we were going to be chartering a plane to Tibet.

Once we touched down in Tibet, I learned why the security detail was needed. Apparently, in this part of the world, they didn't see too many black people, especially none with my height and build. Folks wanted to touch Angel and me and take pictures with us, but our security didn't allow it, making sure everyone gave us our space.

We drove for about two hours until we reached our… Hell, I don't know what to call it. It wasn't quite a hotel, it was more of a small apartment that had been built into the side of a mountain. The low tables and round open windows facing the snow-capped mountains wasn't quite my thing, but Angel loved it.

She literally ran all over the apartment gushing over everything, pulling me to see this and that. I was worried that I was going to end up breaking some of this little ass furniture. This sh*t wasn't made for brothas my size.

Angel didn't want to rest, she wanted to head right out to the herb bazaar. She was so excited she was literally jumping up and down.

"You remind me of Jessie," I teased her as we got dressed. Wayne had set it up for the guide to bring clothes for us. He told me in his broken English how hard it was to find clothes for a man my size and then I think he called me a giant in Tibetan, but I can't prove it.

"I'm so excited I can barely keep still! Here, help me put on my coat," Angel said handing me the beautiful white woolen coat that I was sure cost me a small fortune.

The guide had brought us some traditional Tibetan garb. I opted out of what he brought for me; imagine a player walking around looking goofy. However, I did decide to wear the big ugly brown coat with the matching hat, because I didn't think the leather I brought from the Chi was gon' stand up against the weather higher up in the mountains.

Angel on the other hand, was all for wearing the traditional clothes, and I ain't gon' lie, she looked good in the sh*t. She had on a pair of white woolen pants and a matching long white tunic that fit her as if it had been made just for her. The outfit was brought together with a pair of white leather boots. The guide told us that Angel's clothes had all been made by the best seamstress in all of Tibet. Again, Wayne at his finest.

We found out that the only way to reach the village of this mysterious herb market, was by hot air balloon, helicopter, or by foot, which would be a three days journey. Can y'all guess which one Angel chose?

If you guessed the hot air balloon, you would be right. But the thing is, she got all the way up there and found out that she was afraid of heights. She spent most of the journey up the mountain hiding inside of my coat, shaking and screeching like a little ass girl.

When we finally made it to the little village, I swear I felt like I'd stepped into some other realm or some sh*t. The clay houses were all multi-colored and looked like they belonged on a movie set. Even the people wore colorful clothes.

The guide explained to us that this place was very rich. The farmers here worked their land during the spring and summer months and then traveled to Shanghai and Beijing for the fall and winter to trade and sell their goods. Just like Angel said, the herbs and plants they grew here were wanted all over the world.

"I think the earth is so rich here because the air is pure in these mountains, plus, what wouldn't grow well if its water came from the Himalayans?" Angel asked me as she excitedly stared ahead of her at the many booths of herbs and plants spread out before us.

I just nodded my head like I knew what the hell she was talking about, and I would continue to do so as she proceeded to pull me all over that joint, pointing out this plant, showing me this herb, slipping something between my lips asking me how I liked it. Luckily, after being with her for four months, I'd grown used to her doing that. Now, I just chewed and swallowed whatever she slipped in my mouth and just nodded while saying, '*Mmmm*'.

She was so enthralled in what she was seeing that she didn't notice the people who was now following us, watching her actions.

"Why they following us?" I asked the guide, wondering if I was going to have to hurt one of these little people.

Our security detail had stayed at the base of the mountain because the guide said this place was inhabited by peaceful people that never warred, *whatever the f**k that mean.*

"The Tea Master lives in this village. The people believe another Tea Master may be in their presence," he said gesturing to Angel.

And sure enough, although Angel didn't speak their language and they didn't speak hers, they were somehow communicating with her. Now, this is where the story finna get a little strange.

She's going up to these different booths picking up herbs, sniffing them and tasting them. Whoever's manning the booth is studying her selections. They can tell by her choices that she ain't no rookie. They'll pick up something and offer it to her, she'll either take it and taste it, or shake her finger at them and pick up another plant or seed and hand it to them. They in return would digest her combination and then look at her as if she was some kind of mystique.

I don't know what kind of f**king exchange was taking place, but I was tripping out a little bit at that point, 'cause Angel went into a zone or some sh*t. And I think I was like her test dummy. Without speaking she would lift something to my lips and as I chewed, she'd watch me, studying me in a way that made me feel as if she could see my deepest, darkest thoughts. But her head would gently move from side to side like she was listening to music that only she could hear.

Now keep in mind, the whole time she doing this, the little people is studying her. At first, I thought these folks was watching her and following her because my baby looked ethereal in this environment. I don't know if it was something different about the air up here or if we'd flown into another dimension or some sh*t, but her coffee-colored skin radiated as if it was a light within her shining out... I kid y'all not. It contrasted beautifully against the white garments she wore and the snowcapped mountains. She didn't look real.

After about forty-five minutes of this, a small girl no bigger than Jessie walked up to Angel and took her hand. As she spoke, our guide translated.

"My great mother would like for you to join her for tea." Angel smiled down at the child and nodded.

Confused I looked at the guide, "What's up?"

"It is a great honor to be invited to the Tea Master's home," he said as he gestured for me to follow Angel and the little girl. I was going to pass, but it looked as if my wife really wanted to do this because she didn't hesitate to follow the little stranger.

She led us away from the common area onto a tiny pathway that crossed over a few hills and down a lane or two. Sh*t, the deeper we got into the mountains, the more uncertain I felt. We walked so long I was about to say f**k this and take Angel back to the plant market so that she could buy what she wanted and then we could get the f**k back to normal.

I ain't gon' lie, the feeling up here had a brotha tripping. I felt like I was in *Lord of the Rings* in the land of the Hobbits or some sh*t.

But just as I was reaching for Angel's arm to stop her, the little girl pointed to a small hut up ahead. This house was different from the ones in the village; it was not made of the colorful clay the other homes had been made of. There were no fancy designs or uniquely shaped windows. It was just a little stone house with a few windows.

Strangely enough, it felt homier than the ones in town. Maybe it was because there was a gentle puff of smoke coming from the chimney, or the small herb garden next to it that was surrounded by a patched together wooden fence. All the plants had turned brown and withered from the cold, but it still somehow gave off healing vibes, if y'all know what I mean.

I know this all sounding crazy as hell but imagine how I felt being the one witnessing this sh*t. Angel, on the other hand, seemed to be right in her element. The whole way here, the little girl pointed to patches of ground, telling Angel what grew there in the summer while our guide translated her words to English for us. I could tell that all that talk about plants and herbs was exciting my wife.

Again, not my thing. But the fact that it was thrilling the cowboy sh*t out of her, was enough for me. It was making me happy to make her happy…

Hmmm…

That's how I know this girl was meant to be mine. I ain't lying to y'all, I can't remember ever feeling that way for another woman. Hell, I can't remember ever having one that I wanted to be around like this. Look at playa, up in the f**king Himalayans mountains about to have tea with the hobbit queen, but because I was doing this sh*t with Angel, I was satisfied as a mutha f**ka.

I shook my head; this girl done came and changed the game on a nigga. But I ain't gon' get into that right now. I wanted to finish telling y'all how wild this trip up this mountain got. And trust me when I tell y'all this next sh*t I'm getting ready to tell y'all finna blow yo' minds, because it damn sho' blew mine.

So, as we were walking up to the house, a small Asian woman with sun-kissed brown skin that was withered with age and long white hair stepped out on the porch. She looked up at us and smiled before she continued on to the little garden. As she opened the wooden gate, she gestured for us to follow her inside.

Although a lot of the things in her garden had died back from the frost, surprisingly, there still were a few signs of life with a peek of green, a flash of red, or a streak of orange that would catch the eye here and there. The wall that separated her little house from her garden was covered in vines that were a healthy green. Kinda felt like her little house was giving them what they needed to be sustained against the winter winds. This somehow made the garden feel cozier.

She eased down on a little stool and gestured for Angel to sit on the ground next to her leg. My wife didn't hesitate to join her, sitting right against her leg as if they knew each other.

By this time, I'm really trippin'. I turned to look at the guide, but he too is taking it all in amazed. I nodded my head in a way to ask him what was up with his look.

"The Tea Master is a very powerful soul. But rarely does she interact with anyone that is not her relative. She was an old woman when my grandfather was only a child," he said so that only I could hear him. "There is not one from the village who can say they've ever spoken to her. Her children and their children, yes, even the little one who led us here, but never her."

The Tea Master spoke to Angel, palming her face and holding it up so that she could see her better. But since she spoke in a language neither Angel nor I understood, our guide translated for us.

"Come, sister, let me see you better." She turned Angel's head to the left and then to the right. "My Great Mother told me you would come one day."

Now it was Angel's turn to frown. "Greatie?" she asked.

The guide translated for the Tea Master, who gently shook her head. "I don't know her by that name. My grandmother before me and her grandmother before her always called her Tabitha."

Excitedly Angel nodded her head, now clutching the woman's hands. "Yes, that's my Greatie. She's my grandmother too!"

The Tea Master nodded. "Yes, I can tell. You are the spitting image of her."

"Wait… did you just say y'all have the same grandmother?" For the first time, the Tea Master's eyes lifted to me. I didn't mean for my question to come across as indignantly as it did, but I was f**king buggin' out.

My girl had gotten up here in this strange mountain air and lost her damn mind. The people up here did have darker skin than some of the folks in the mainland, but they were clearly Asian. There was no mistaking that.

The older woman spoke and the guide translated. "Why does the slayer find this hard to believe?"

I lifted an eyebrow. "Say what?"

"She wants to know why you find it hard to believe that she and your woman share an ancestor." The guide said.

I threw up my hands. "Let's just say, I can get over the fact that she's Asian and Angel is African-American. How the hell do either of them know what their great, great…" I can't even

313

remember how many greats the Tea Master said, "grandmother looks like?"

Angel grinned at me then and it freaked me out a little more. "Because I've seen her and talked to her." The guide translated Angel's words for the Tea Master.

"And so have I," she responded.

I chuckled, shaking my head a bit. "Yeah…okay! Baby, won't you go ahead and finish up your meeting with your long-lost cousin here so that we can get back to reality."

Wow! If I didn't know no better, I would think I was being punked. This was some next-level kind of sh*t.

The little girl disappeared in the house and came back with a tray that had several clay cups on them. She handed one to each of us and I was surprised to see that there was steaming liquid inside of them. The warm clay felt good in my hands that were all but frozen because I didn't have on any gloves.

Following both the guide and Angel's lead, I lifted the cup and took a sip and was amazed by the flavors that exploded against my tongue.

What the hell?!

Lifting the cup, I peered into it to see if I could see what was in it. Angel closed her eyes and moaned as she savored the taste. The guide did the same. The woman studied us all as we drank her brew before she began to speak.

"When I was a little girl, Tabitha would come to see me right out here in this very garden. She used to tell me amazing stories about the world before the Watchers cut down the great trees." She looked off into the distance and my gaze followed hers.

"The trees stood so tall that they seemed to touch the top of the expanse."

My mouth opened as right before my eyes a vision of a huge tree grew past the mountain and continued up through the clouds.

"In that day, all of men spoke one language and understood well the gift the Ancient of Days had blessed us with."

Everything began to change around us… but not change. I know that sh*t sound crazy but that's what was happening. Although the plants and the herbs were still dried out from the frost, a vision of how the world used to be formed on top of everything. I reached out my hand to touch a vine that was coming to life in front of me, but there was no substance because it was just a vision.

That was good tea! She'd make a killing selling that sh*t in the hood.

"The soil was so rich that as far as the eye could see, there were fields and fields of every flower and plant that was good for the nourishment of our bodies."

As she spoke, we became surrounded by flowers that grew on strong, healthy green vines. I wasn't a big plant person like Rome's little sister Journey or nothing, but I'd never seen anything like this. Even I knew that flowers this healthy and vivacious no longer existed. The vision was so vivid, I could smell the sweet fragrance coming from them.

"Wow…" I muttered, taking another peep into my teacup.

Good and caught up into the vision the old woman was weaving around us, Angel stood, overcome by the beauty, holding her hands out and turning as if she was trying to take all the flowers with her.

For a minute, the woman didn't speak. She just sat on her stool watching Angel, who looked as if she belonged in this mystical garden. I've never seen my wife more beautiful than she was right now. She held her head back as she continued to turn, completely taken by the vision.

The little girl came to stand next to the woman as she too watched Angel. A feeling of sadness came over me. I was sad because I know I can never make this happen for her. No amount of money or might can bring back such beauty.

"In that day, man understood that our health was reflected in our planet. During the time of the great trees, to die at a hundred was to die young." She reached up and took Angel's hand pulling her back to her.

"But then, something happened. The giants came." With tears in her eyes, she suddenly looked out across the sky just as a terrible yell ripped through the air. Walking towards the mountain was a monstrous man… No! It was no man, although its grotesque face could be that of a man, it was no man.

I knew it was just a vision and not real, but I stepped in front of Angel, ready to fight it if I had to. The old woman watched me, nodding with a knowing look in her eyes.

"The giants came and they began to consume this gift of ours from the Ancient of Days. They began to kill it…"

As her voice trailed off, visions of people screaming as they ran away from the giants could be seen in the clouds. The grotesque monsters would just lean down and pick up a bunch of them in their mighty six-fingered hands as if they were peanuts and chug them into their mouths.

"They were the beginning of the end and the more they consumed, the weaker our planet became until it could no longer sustain the great trees." The vision changed and the giant trees began to fall.

"Hitta!" Angel cried, coming to wrap her arms around my waist as she watched the trees fall in horror through tear-filled eyes. I held her shaking body close, not believing what I was seeing. That sadness in me grew.

"Something was happening to mankind. We took on the nature of the giants and began to consume our earth. We began to destroy this gift from the Almighty Power."

The hauntingly beautiful notes of a violin swept across the sky. The Tea Master stopped talking as she listened. Closing her eyes, she began to gently sway to the tune. The little girl that stood next to her eyes closed and she too began to sway.

My arm fell away from Angel when her body suddenly went stiff before her eyes closed and she too began to sway to the tune. I stepped back away from her astonished. The sound of the violin was real. It was not a part of the vision.

Puzzled, I turned to look at the guide for an explanation, but he only shrugged, shaking his head just as bewildered as I was.

"The earth is crying out," the Tea Master spoke without opening her eyes. She shook her head saddened. "How could we allow this to happen to our gift? How could we be so careless with our gift?"

I continued to watch the vision of the giants and men destroying the earth. And the more I saw, the more the sadness in me faded to be replaced by rage. I'd always been an angry mutha f**ka, but never as much as I was in this moment.

I wanted to kill the giants. I wanted to destroy them for what they were doing to the earth!

"Slayer," the Tea Master's voice came to me, stronger than I'd heard it this whole time. I turned my head to look at her but ended up hitting my knees. The light that came from her eyes tore through me like a laser, paralyzing me. I felt so unclean in its presence I couldn't lift my head.

Angel and the little girl still stood with their eyes closed, swaying to the tune of the violin. The guide still stared off at the vision of the giants. He didn't see what was happening to me.

"You think you are so mighty that you will slay a giant all on your own?"

The voice that came from the woman was not human. I couldn't look up at her, nor could I respond. The light that was coming from her eyes was traveling through my body, dissecting me down to my very cells. And I couldn't shake the feeling that I was being found wanting.

"Are you so mighty that you will bring down Liwiathan all by yourself?"

I bit down on my teeth, fighting tears. I didn't feel mighty right now. For the first time in a long time, I felt helpless and didn't like it.

"How will you do it? Will you use a hook or snare his tongue with a line which you lower? Would you put a cord through his nose or pierce his jaw with your hook? Tell me, slayer. Will he keep pleading with you? Will he speak softly to you? Would he make a covenant with you to be taken as a servant forever? Would you play with him as with a bird or leash him for your daughter to play with? I tell you, if you put your hand on him, you'll never live to do anything else. No one is so foolish to even wake him. Who then is able to stand against Me?"

"Tell me, slayer!"

I jumped at the raised voice. My tears felt like hot wax rolling down my cheek. I could not stand underneath this reprimand. "Who has given to Me first, that I should repay him under all the heavens that are mine? Tell me!"

I cried out as paralyzing fear shot through me.

"I would not keep silent concerning his limbs or his mighty power if it were so." The woman stood and the light came closer to me. The closer it came, the lower I got to the ground until I was lying face down in the dirt.

"At last, your time has come and you must choose. Your brothers need you. Stand and fight with them!"

I felt the light dimming; gentle hands that smelt like chamomile touched my shoulder.

"Hitta! What happened? What's wrong?" I turned over to my back to look up at Angel, but when I saw that light circling her irises, I gasped flinching away from her.

It was the chuckling of the old woman that drew my attention. She still sat on her little stool shaking her head at me. When she spoke, it was in her language again.

"It takes more than a strong body to be a host for the spirit of the Ancient of Days," the guide translated for her. "Look at you; you cower in the dirt like a scared girl child."

And then she held her head back and had a good laugh at my expense.

Chapter 21

THE HONEYMOON'S OVER

Not Everything That Is Faced Can Be Changed, But Nothing Can Be Changed Until It Is Faced.

James Baldwin

Angel

I think that I may have made the biggest mistake of my life by marrying Hitta. And y'all, I know that's a hell of a way to begin this chapter of my life. I wish with all my heart I didn't have to, but it's true; I've made a terrible mistake.

Hold on, let me get myself together because as I write this, I'm in tears. I can barely see the words on the screen in front of me because of it. Heartbreak is a bastard that I wouldn't wish on my worst enemy. I feel like my whole life is over. What have I done? And now I have this baby growing in my womb that I may have to raise by myself.

You know, that old saying is true, what he did her, he'll probably do to you. How many times had Carmen told me about Hitta's cheating on Shantell and about how he used to stay away for days and not come home?

I guess I should feel lucky because he's not staying away for days; he still comes home every night, but it's always after Jessie and I go to bed. Okay, I know you guys are like, wait…what? Let me go back a few weeks and bring y'all up to speed.

Hitta came back from our honeymoon a different man. In fact, I take that back, he came down from that mountain a different man. That's when I first noticed the change in him. It was like he was there, but he wasn't. He was withdrawn… you know. Although he still talked to me and even joked with me from time to time, he didn't feel like the guy that lay with me in the Blue Lagoon Garden and made love to me under the stars.

I tried to talk to him to see what was going on in his head, but he would always tell me that he was cool and that I was tripping. I started getting this bad feeling like maybe he was regretting marrying me or that he was beginning to feel trapped or something, especially now that we'd found out we were having a baby. Remember I told you guys when this first began that some men were just attracted to the chase, but once they secured the prize, they lost interest? I think that may be what's going on.

But then, I didn't know if it was just my hormones making me feel this way because he still made love to me every night without fail. And each time, he made me feel as if he was so hungry for me and only me. Every night he held me close and still didn't seem to mind that by morning, I somehow found my way onto his back.

It was like this weird energy fell over him when he came to bed at night, where he felt that he had to prove to himself and me that it was he who caused my body to go up into a million fires. Sometimes his lovemaking felt cruel and sadistic, not because it hurt or anything, but because of the way he would skillfully cause my body to go up in flames. Then he would wait till I was on the verge of an explosion to slow down his strokes, holding me right there on the edge.

"Why are you doing this to me?" I'd moan, sometimes on the verge of tears. He would get this look in his eye, studying me in a way that was frightening before growling, "Who do you belong to?"

"You!" I had to bite down on my bottom lip to keep from screaming at him as his proficient touch continued to hold me on that ledge.

He'd have this little wicked grin on his face, very aware of the torture he was putting me through.

"What's my name, Angel?"

"Mmmm, Hitta..." would come from between my lips on a moan.

He'd close his eyes as my breathy words washed over him and when he opened them again, the possessiveness in them only served to heighten my pleasure as he gave me what I needed to achieve the ultimate release. And as I floated back to earth, he'd gently kiss my neck right under my ear.

"I'll never let you go, Teacup..." he'd whisper before masterfully restoking the flames...

Ugggh! And the bad part was that I wanted to deny him for hurting me, but I just couldn't because my own lust served as a weapon against me. Why the hell can't I resist him? He is such an asshole!

He doesn't even come to the shop to get his daily tea from me anymore; he sends one of his lackeys. He claims he's gotten busy with clients, but I know it's a lie. He has to know that he's hurting me by staying away like he does. I refuse to believe that he can't see that he's tearing me apart by withdrawing from me like this. I just don't understand what is going on with him. The mixed signals he's sending out is driving me crazy.

When I scheduled my first doctor's appointment, he was right there next to me. And when the doctor told us we were almost four months pregnant, he had genuine amazement in his eyes just like I did.

Oh y'all, that one threw me for a loop, it completely sucker-punched me. I did notice I had picked up a little weight in my hips and butt, but I've always been bottom-heavy and never really had a flat stomach anyway, so I didn't think much of it. And according to the doc, I was one of those people that carried my weight in my hips anyway, so she wasn't surprised that I didn't notice.

Another reason I didn't notice was because I'm pretty sure this last month was the first month I'd missed my period. I remember Hitta pouting at least twice since I've lived with him because I told him that he and I couldn't have any fun for a few days. This was another thing the doctor says is not uncommon. She told us many women get their periods during the first trimester of their pregnancy and that we had nothing to worry about.

Then she handed us the first ultrasound of our baby and told us that we were having a boy. We both gushed over the picture amazed that we could produce a little being so perfect.

As we drove home from the hospital, we laughed at how silly we were for not realizing we were pregnant earlier and how beautiful our baby was. We laughed, we joked, and then he didn't come home for dinner. He didn't call or anything.

I lay in bed that night and cried because I knew that this was the beginning of the end. I wasn't like Shantell, I couldn't stay with him knowing that he was with other women. Now don't get me wrong, I can't say that this is a fact. I just know that the things he used to do, he doesn't do anymore, like be home to have dinner with Jess and me.

When he finally came in sometime after midnight, I pretended to be asleep. I didn't want to talk to him, and I sure didn't want him touching me anymore.

Well…

That wasn't really true and that was the damn problem! I *did* want him touching me because I was horny. I was freaking horny all the time and he was taking advantage of that. But I was fed up, and I wasn't going to put up with his sh*t anymore! At least that's what I told myself.

But then…

He eased in the bed and wrapped his strong arm around me, pulling my stiff body against his.

"Mmmm, I missed you, shawty," he said in my ear just before taking my lobe between his teeth and sucking on it.

I pressed my thighs together as my traitorous body began its journey of betraying me. Goodness! I don't know if it was his scent or how good his hard muscles felt pressed against my soft skin, but I felt my defenses weakening quickly.

Angry with myself and him, I threw the covers back and his arm with it before getting out of the bed and hurried into the bathroom without looking back. I tried to slam the door, but he was right behind me.

A startled sound escaped my throat; I had not heard him get up from the bed. But I guess the three weeks' worth of pent up frustration I was feeling because of the horrible way he's been treating me must have bubbled up and out. That startled sound turned into a growl and I tried to beat the hell out of him with that door.

"What's wrong, Teacup?" he asked with that evil ass grin on his face as he caught the door before I could do any real damage, only frustrating me more.

"Won't you leave me alone?!" I screeched at him, trying my best not to scream at the top of my lungs so I didn't wake up Jessie. I was so angry with him.

He chuckled, shoving the door open. "Naw, bae. Why would I do that? I've been hungry for you all day."

In a huff I leaned against the sink with my arms folded, looking straight ahead at the tub. I didn't want to talk to him, look at him, nothing. And I felt angry tears burning the back of my eyes, which only pissed me off more because I didn't want this asshole to think I was crying over him.

"Come on, don't be mad at me," he whispered, crowding my space trying to pull me into his arms.

Y'all see what I mean? That crazy energy has come over him. He's doing this on purpose! He's hurting my feelings on purpose!

"Let me go!" I screamed trying to shove his big self off of me.

It didn't help that he wasn't wearing anything but a pair of black boxer briefs and so now, I was trying not to appreciate his body while trying to hold on to my rage.

Goodness!!!

There was a chaotic blend of emotions warring inside of me and I just wanted to yell at the top of my lungs and probably would have if I didn't think it would wake up Jessie.

"I'm sorry, Angel..." he whispered wrapping his arms around me pulling me close although I struggled with him.

Well…

At least I told myself to struggle with him, but when his hungry mouth touched my ear and then my neck…

"I'm sorry baby, don't push me away. I need you…" His hands fell to the ribbon on my nightgown untying it, looking down at my body in that way that he does, the way that makes me feel like he sees only me. He gently palmed my breasts, letting my gown slide to my feet.

In my mind, I was still pushing him away, but in reality, my nails were digging into his biceps. If I was being absolutely honest with myself, it could be said that I was holding him to me at this point.

Dammit!

Underneath his lustful gaze was that smirk. He knew I couldn't resist him. The bastard!

"You still mad at me?" he asked as he continued to gently knead my breasts.

I swallowed my response, not wanting to risk him stopping. His head lowered and when his hungry mouth latched on to the tip of my tender flesh, the moan that left my lips should have been answer enough for him. But because he was an asshole, he just had to rub it in.

"I can't hear you, Teacup. You still mad at me?" And then he was lifting me in his strong arms.

I wrapped my legs around his waist, so glad I hadn't bothered to put on any panties. Still grinning at me, he opened his mouth to say something else, but I slapped him.

"Shut up and do it already…"

This caused him to chuckle, but I didn't care because a half a second later, he was filling me and at that moment, my world was complete.

Damn! I am so screwed…

———

Now, I don't want you guys to think that everything has been going wrong in the few weeks since our honeymoon, because it hasn't. As a matter of fact, three amazing things have happened to me in that time outside of finding out I was having a boy.

My first day back at the Teashop, I walked in to find Carmen and Summer already there, and they were both grinning at me in a way that told me they had something up their sleeve.

"Okay, what are you guys up to? And should I be worried?"

"No, silly," Carmen said taking my coat from me and hanging it on the rack by the door. Summer linked hands with mine and pulled me toward the office.

"We have a surprise for you," she gushed.

"What is it?"

"Duh, what part of surprise don't you understand?" Carmen cried putting her hands over my eyes.

I chuckled. "Did y'all redo the kitchen?"

"Nope!" they both chimed.

When Carmen removed her hands from my eyes, I stood looking around my office. Everything looked the same to me. Summer gestured toward my desk. I walked toward it and saw that there was an envelope laying on top with my name on it.

"What is this?" I asked picking it up.

Carmen could barely contain her excitement. "Open it!"

With a grin on my face, I did as she said removing the neatly folded piece of paper. However, I didn't get it all the way unfolded before I saw what it was. My hand flew to my mouth as tears came to my eyes.

It was the deed for the Teashop!

My gaze flew back up to Carmen's. "How?" was all I could say.

She shook her head. "Don't worry about that. It's our wedding gift to you."

There was no way in hell that was going to fly. This property was too expensive and Ms. Armstrong too difficult for it to be that simple.

"Carmen... What did you do?"

With a cheeky grin on her face, she shrugged in that sassy way that she does. "Nothing outside of being the best business manager you've ever hired."

"You're the *only* business manager I've ever hired."

"Exactly," she said before turning and leaving the office.

My gaze went to Summer, she wore a secret smile on her face, letting me know she knew what happened.

"Summer?"

Giggling, she zipped her lips. "My lips are sealed."

"Summer!" I cried stomping my feet.

She laughed. "Angel! I promised." And then she too turned and left the office.

No way was I going to let this topic drop just like that. I can't see Ms. Armstrong selling this property to Carmen for a dime less than the price she quoted me and neither I nor Carmen could afford that. So, where the hell did she get the money? And what the hell did she do to Ms. Armstrong to pry this deed from her little old-timey hands?

I had my answer by noon that day. I waited till Carmen left to go to the gym around lunchtime and then I dug into Summer.

"Okay, Angel, damn!" she cried giving up after the seventh time I asked her how the hell Carmen got this deed.

"Now I don't know all the details. All I can tell you is shortly after you did your little disappearing act, Carmen ran out of the office in something of a panic. That whole week, she was acting strange, barely leaving the office, on and off the phone. Had her eyes glued to her laptop all the time."

"When I asked her what was going on with her, she'd say nothing, but I could tell that something was freaking her out big time. Fast forward a few days, I see her and Mr. Wayne talking in his car outside the shop. Whatever the conversation was about seemed to be upsetting her. When she got out of the car and came in, she was so lost in thought I had to call her name twice before she looked up and acknowledged I was in the room."

"All of sudden, I'm seeing a lot more of Mr. Wayne, and Carmen who as far as I know used to hate his guts, is all sweet to him."

I tapped the counter. "Yeah, I've noticed that too. They've been spending a lot of time together. And you right…they're not fighting anymore."

She nodded. "Mmmm hmmm… So, here is my theory. You know she's been looking into getting the property next door to expand the

Teashop, but she knew before going forward with that, y'all was going to have to square up with old Armstrong's racist ass. Knowing Carmen, she probably went to talk with the woman and ended up cursing her out or something like that. No doubt, Ms. Armstrong got upset and threatened to terminate your lease, seeing as to how your review was coming up anyway. And Carmen in a panic, tried to fix it before you got back from your honeymoon and couldn't. Sooooo…"

She wiggled her eyebrows at me, causing me to laugh. "She had to go to Mr. Wayne for help. Who else could afford to bail her out besides her uncle? And you know she couldn't go to him, because he would tell you, and you would kill her for going behind your back dealing with Armstrong."

She leaned in closer as if she was about to tell me a secret. "And if she had to go to Wayne groveling to save her, that could explain why she so nice to him all of a sudden and also why they've been spending so much time together. She could be paying him back the old-fashioned way, if you know what I mean."

My mouth dropped. "Nooooo!"

She nodded, "Yes, girl…" And then she flawlessly lifted her teacup and took a sip while cutting eyes at me. I nearly fell out of my chair laughing at her silly self.

However, her theory got me to digging. Of course, Carmen was no help, but thanks to the guy that does my taxes, I found out a few things. Ms. Armstrong had suddenly fallen into some financial troubles, something to do with the bank she and her family had been banking with.

He could not find out the intimate details, only that she'd been forced to liquidate her assets or face some jail time. It took me a moment to get over that shock. Old Ms. Nasty was knocked off her mighty horse.

After finding out that information, I cornered Carmen and tried to force her to talk again, but because she's stubborn as a mule, she refused to give me the information I sought.

"Why can't you just accept my wedding gift to you?"

"Because this is an expensive gift and your little narrow butt can't afford it."

She rolled her eyes before flicking the long side of her red hair over her shoulder. "You don't know what I can afford."

"I know you can't afford this," I told her holding up the deed.

"Maybe I did it because I'm interested in being partners."

"And are you?"

She grinned at me. "Yeah, what do you think?"

"I think it's a great idea! I would love to have you as a partner."

She clapped her hands together. "Great, you handle all the front of the house stuff and I will handle all the back of the house stuff." She held her hand up in the air.

"I can see it now... We'll have a Teashop in every city."

I chuckled, shaking my head at her. "Chile, let's just try not to lose this one."

She laughed. "You know what? That's a great idea."

I would eventually find out what happened, but it's not my story to tell. However, I can tell you guys this, Ms. Armstrong and her son, who has taken over handling their family's business, garnered the wrath of Wayne and it was not a pretty sight. Apparently, he knew the man who owned the bank that she and her family did most of their business with.

And get this... it's a black man.

Can you believe that? I sure couldn't. Who knew a black man held her family's financial security in the palm of his hand? Needless to say, Wayne called in a favor from his friend and well... One thing led to another.

By the time they were done, all of the financial skeletons in the Armstrong family closet had been exposed and everybody was making a mad dash to re-cover them. In the end, Ms. Armstrong learned that her son and lawyer had their finances tangled up in some unsavory things and in order to avoid certain ruin, they had to liquidate everything.

Carmen cheerfully told me that Wayne had ended up paying next to nothing for the Teashop. It's funny how un-picky one gets when desperate. However, I found myself feeling sorry for Ms. Armstrong. I could only imagine how surprised she must have been once she learned of all the nefarious things her son had involved them in.

Anyway, I told you guys that three amazing things happened to me since coming back from my honeymoon. Well, that was the first. The second was that I officially became Jessie's guardian.

Hitta's lawyer came to the house to talk to me a few days after we came back from Tibet. And let me tell y'all something about Ms. Kennedy, she was not a sista I would want to find myself standing across the aisle from in a courtroom.

When she first walked through our front door, I found myself feeling under…

Under what, you ask?

Underdressed, under-educated, under-sophisticated, etc. This sista was drop-dead gorgeous, sharp as a knife and tough as nails. She had a no-nonsense attitude that intimidated everybody but Hitta and Wayne, and I think that was only because Hitta was her boss and Wayne's father was the wealthiest black man in Chicago.

I thought Carmen was a force to be reckoned with, but she was a baby compared to Ms. Kennedy.

"Just think, if you and my uncle ever get a divorce, that's who your lawyer is going to be going up against," Carmen jokingly said when she and I had lunch later on that day after I'd mentioned Hitta's attorney.

"Are you trying to scare me to death? Is that your goal?" I asked, failing to see the humor in the situation. But of course, my crazy friend found that even funnier.

"Naw, I'm trying to scare you away from ever leaving my uncle."

Hmmm… You know what? I'm not going to go there at this point in my story, but I'm going to warn y'all now, we will be revisiting that topic. I was telling you guys about the great things that happened to me.

Anyway, so after talking to Kennedy, she assured me I had nothing to worry about and that she should have the matter with Jessie cleared up in no time. And y'all, she was a woman of her word. A few days later, she informed Hitta and me that all that was left to do was for me to go to the Daley Center and sign on the dotted line.

I was surprised because I expected it to be a long drawn out process. However, I should have known better. Wayne has so many connections in this city it wasn't funny. Between him and Kennedy, Stan never had a chance. I feel stupid now for worrying about it in the first place.

The day I became Jessie's guardian was a good day for more than one reason. After we left the Daley Center, Hitta took us to Dave & Buster's to celebrate. We actually had a lot of fun. At least that day, we felt like a real family.

However, there was something plaguing the back of my mind that kept me from being too happy about becoming Jessie's guardian. I was worried about what my brother was going to say. As her father, he should have played a role in this decision, which brings me to the third awesome thing that happened to me...

Two days ago, Westly showed up at the Teashop....

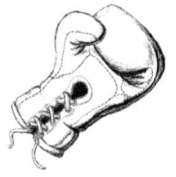

Chapter 22

WEST IS BACK

Angel

"Here sis, let me cut the rest of this up while you take out the trash," Summer said, taking the little knife I was using to cut orange peels to restock the fresh bar for the afternoon rush.

I frowned as she hip-butted me to the side. "What, the garbage?"

I mean, I know that we'd all grown close and everything, but I was still the boss and I didn't take out the trash.

She looked toward the chairs where Maddox sat playing chess with one of my regulars before cutting her eyes back to me, jerking her head toward the back door.

"Yeah, can you run the trash out for me?" "*You need to go out back...*" she mouthed.

I nodded. "Okay, sure, I'll be right back." Taking off my apron I picked up the garbage bag and slipped out the back door to the alley.

Leaning against the wall on the other side of the big blue garbage cans was Westly. My heart leaped in my chest as I dropped the bag and ran to him.

"Westly!" I cried, throwing myself into his arms.

He chuckled as he stumbled a little under my weight. "Hey, baby girl." He sounded tired.

"Where have you been? So much has happened."

"Yeah, I heard."

I reached up and palmed his face as I studied him. He didn't look good at all. There were black bags under his eyes and open sores on his face. When he left, he had a few sores, but now he had more.

"How are you doing?"

Tears came to his eyes, but he held his head down so that I wouldn't see them, shaking it slightly.

"Not good, Angel. I feel like a piece of sh*t. Right when you, Jessie, and my mom needed me most, I was too high to even know it."

"Hey," I said rubbing his arm with a bright smile on my face. "Why don't we grab something to eat and go have lunch at Millennium Park like we used to do when we first moved into our apartment?"

I needed to get him away from here before Maddox came looking for me. Granted these days, I don't know if he still hung around the shop for me or Summer, but I didn't want to take a chance. Hitta didn't bite his tongue about what he felt for my brother. Getting them two together was going to take a little finesse.

"So, that is his hitman sitting in there, huh?"

"I don't know if I would call Maddox a hitman, but yeah, he is a part of Hitta's security team."

Westly chuckled, shaking his head. "How are you going to get away without him noticing?"

"Leave it to me. You just wait here; I'll be right back."

I slipped back through the door and put my apron on. As soon as I walked into the dining room, Maddox lifted his head to look at me.

"Everything a'right?"

I nodded. "Oh yeah, I was just taking out the trash."

He smiled and it seemed as if it took him a minute to look away from me, or maybe I was just paranoid. My heart was racing so fast I feared he could see it. Trying to act normal, I made my way back to the fresh bar where Summer still stood cutting up pieces of fruit.

With my eyes, I told her I needed to go. She nodded and put the knife down, drying her hands on a towel and then she inhaled and walked over to Maddox, saying something in his ear. I tried to pretend like I was not invested in their conversation as I restocked my lavender jar.

Maddox stood and I held my breath, but he didn't come my way, instead, he grabbed his coat from the coat rack putting it on. However, as he did, his eyes came to me.

"A'm aff tae git Summer some fairn, dae yi'll waant anything?"

I shook my head. "No, thank you!"

Maybe I was being paranoid, but it seemed as if he was studying me as he slipped his hands into his gloves.

"A'richt, ah will be back then."

I didn't exhale till he left out the door. "I owe you one," I told Summer as I headed to the coat rack for my coat.

"Yeah, you do. You forced me to talk to that worrisome man."

I leaned in and kissed her on the cheek as I slipped on my jacket. "Mmmhhhmmm, you know you love him."

"Ha! Like a mouse loves a cat. Where should I tell him you went when he gets back?"

I thought for a minute. "Tell him I made a supply run."

"But he normally takes you for those," she called after me.

I stopped at the back door thinking about that. It was true. Poor Maddox had become our errand boy.

"Tell him it couldn't wait."

———

"You got to know that I would have never knowingly put your life in danger. Had I known he was going to trace me taking that money back to you, I would have never done it. I just—" He scratched at his head, digging into his scalp in a way that told me he was in need of his next hit, but trying not to break down.

Millennium Park was bustling with people coming and going on their lunch break, but we managed to find a little secluded area not too far from Michigan Avenue. We'd taken the train down here like we used to do, stopping at the deli to grab a couple of sandwiches on the way. Of course, I bought them and paid our bus fare, because Westly said he'd spent his last two dollars making his way to the Teashop.

"I just felt the pressure. I couldn't let you lose the Teashop because of me and my family. You always doing for us and was about to lose something you been wanting since you was a little girl. I had to do something!" He held out his hands in front of him.

"And the money was just sitting there!"

I reached over and hugged him. It was breaking my heart to see him this way. He looked as if he hadn't slept in days and his clothes were filthy. My brother, although addicted to drugs, has always kept up on his hygiene. His clothes may not be new, but were always clean. The fact that they were so dirty now was testament that he'd hit rock bottom.

"It's alright, everything worked out. He didn't hurt me or anything like that."

"Yeah, but he forced you into a relationship with him. Did he force you to…you know?"

I vehemently shook my head. "No, I swear! He was a perfect gentleman."

A look of doubt crossed West's face. "Hitta? A gentle-man?"

I laughed. "Believe it or not, he is very gentle with me."

He smiled, pleased he'd made me laugh. "Oh, I believe it. If there's anybody that can bring a man like that to his knees, it's my sweet little sister." He took one of my braids in his hand, studying it.

"I just wish it wasn't because of me that you had to be forced to do something…you know."

"Hey," I said, drawing his eyes back to mine. "By no means am I condoning what you did, but if you hadn't done it, I would have lost my shop. So, in a crazy, dangerous way, everything worked out. Well… almost everything." He and I were both quiet for a minute, lost in our thoughts.

"I better not ever see that mutha f**ka Stan again. I swear, I'm going to kill him for what he did to my mother!"

I rubbed his hand. "Just let the police deal with it. They're looking for him."

Westly shook his head. "I should have killed him a long time ago. When he first put his hands on you, I should have took his ass out."

"Yeah, and you would have broken your mother's heart."

His angry gaze came to mine. "I should have did it anyway! Maybe then, she'd still be with us today! I'm always f**king up, Angel! And my mother had to pay with her life."

"You can't blame yourself for this! Diana chose Stan. She loved that bastard! We tried to tell her, she wouldn't lis—"

He snatched his hand from me shaking his head. "Naw, Angel! That doesn't matter! I still should have—"

I snatched his hand back. "It *does* matter, West! You can't save nobody who don't want to be saved!"

Too late I realized how bad a choice of words that was. Westly got this bittersweet look on his face before he lowered his eyes back to his hands.

"Like me, right?"

I shook my head. "No, not like you! Like our mother… Not you. I know that you love dearly and deeply. I know that you don't like the darkness that's got a hold of you. You want to fight it."

His gaze came up to mine, that bittersweet smile still on his face. "You've always thought so much of me, Angel."

"It's because you were my very first hero. You saved me from the bad guy."

"And then *I* became the bad guy," he whispered.

I shook my head again as tears came to my eyes, but I dried them determinedly. "No! I don't see you that way. In my eyes, you're still my hero."

He chuckled with no real humor. "Yeah, well, you always did have a way of seeing only the good in folks and turning a blind eye to their bad."

"That's not true… I saw Stan's bad."

He pushed the braid that had fallen in my face behind my ear. "Yeah, you did."

And so it went. Westly and I talked for over an hour, mostly about Diana and Stan, a little about me and Hitta, and our marriage. But then the conversation turned to Trina and the time had come for me to tell him that I was Jessie's guardian.

"I can't believe they found her dead. Damn! I leave for a couple of months and everything goes to hell."

"There is something else," I told him, now it was me playing with my braid, avoiding his eyes. "Because we didn't know where you were and with Trina being dead and all, there was a matter of what would happen with Jessie…"

My gaze came back to his. "I'm her guardian now."

He smiled and I exhaled a breath that I wasn't aware I was holding. "Come on, baby girl. You wasn't worried I'd be upset about that, were you?"

I nodded. "Very."

He shook his head. "Why? Let's just tell the truth, you've always been Jessie's guardian. She loves her Tee-Tee. I'm so glad you were there for her, 'cause only God knows where she would be if she depended solely on me." As he spoke, tears came to his eyes.

"Thank you so much, Angel. I don't deserve to have you in my life, but I thank God for you every day."

I hugged him again, but then I told him I had to go. I didn't want to risk being gone longer and Maddox contacting Hitta.

"Where are you staying?" I asked him as we walked back towards the train.

He held up his hands. "I have no idea. There's a shelter—"

I shook my head cutting him off. "I will get you a room at the hotel around the corner from the Teashop."

I knew better than to give him money. I loved my brother dearly, but I could not buy his drugs for him. I will get him food, a place to stay, and clothes to wear. I just can't bring myself to give him money, knowing he will buy drugs with it.

After we got back to Oak Park, I showed him where we lived and then we walked the short distance to the hotel and got him checked in.

"Hitta doesn't come home till really late. So after you get some rest, why don't you come by the house and have dinner with Jess and me?"

He got an uncomfortable look on his face. "Are you sure he's not going to be there?"

I nodded. "Positive, he's barely there these days really; he just comes home to sleep. He'll never know you've been there."

He pushed my braid back behind my ear. "Are you okay?"

I forced a smile on my face and nodded. "Absolutely." And then I changed the subject. "You can stay here for a couple of nights. That will give me time to talk to Hitta. There is a spare room in the basement that we can turn into—"

He shook his head. "There is no way he's going to go for that."

"You don't know that. Just let me talk to him."

"Angel, he ain't the kind of man you can steal from and just walk away without any consequences."

"I paid the consequences, now the slate is wiped clean. Plus, you're my brother and I'm his wife, that got to count for something."

He laughed at that. "Again, I reiterate, these ain't those kind of people. Men like him will take out their own mother if they crossed them."

"You don't know Hitta. He's not like that at all."

With the smile still on his face, he leaned in and kissed my forehead in the way that he always has.

"There you go again, only seeing the good in people and completely turning a blind eye to their bad. I'll see you guys tonight, baby girl," he said before stepping on the elevator.

The whole way back to the shop, I was a nervous wreck and I didn't know why. What I said to Westly was true. I'd paid the price for him stealing the money, so there should be no hard feelings. Only... my gut was telling me that it would not be that easy.

West thought I only saw the good in people and that may very well be true, but even I knew that Hitta is a hard man and probably wasn't going to be quick to forgive. However, I had to find a way to get him to see that my brother was a really good guy at heart.

I couldn't wait until Jessie saw her dad tonight. Now, I didn't feel so bad about Hitta not coming home for dinner. At least some good would come out of it.

However, when I walked into the house after work, it was not to find the neighbor's fourteen-year-old daughter, who we paid to babysit Jessie after she got out of school until I got home. It was Hitta sitting in the living room helping her with her homework and I almost had a freaking heart attack.

"Hey, where's Kayla?" I asked as I hung my coat on the rack by the front door.

He sat back on the couch resting his massive arms on the back of it as he studied me.

"Hello, wife. I'm doing good, thanks for asking."

I chuckled. In my mind, it came out a breezy carefree sound, but I know in reality, it probably sounded like a nervous grunt.

"No, I was just surprised to see you here helping Jessie instead of Kayla, that's all."

"Look, Tee-Tee, I got an A on my spelling test!" Jessie cried excitedly, shoving her test paper into my hands.

I took the time as I examined her paper to get myself together. It was a damn shame I was this scared of my own husband. Granted I wasn't afraid for my own safety, but that of my brother. My heart was racing too fast and if I didn't get control of myself, I was going to mess this whole thing up.

"Great job, baby!" I told Jessie before giving her a big hug.

However, when two strong arms came around my waist from behind, a squeak of fear escaped my lips before I could catch it.

"Damn, baby, why you so jumpy? I'm just giving you a hug after not seeing you all day," Hitta said from behind me as he tightened his arms, pulling me into his embrace.

I chuckled again and even to my ears it sounded nervous. "You scared me. For a big guy, you move very silently."

Jessie skipped off, completely unaware of the tension in the air.

He gently kissed my ear. "How was your day?"

"G—" I had to clear my throat because it sounded like I had a frog in it. "Good… busy as usual, and yours?"

"Yeah, mine too." He brought his big hand to rest just underneath my breasts, pulling me tighter into his embrace. "What's the matter, Teacup? Why yo' heart beating so fast?"

I don't know if my mind was playing tricks on me or what, but the last of his statement sounded as if it came out a growl.

"Just a little winded from the walk home."

"Why didn't Maddox bring you home?"

"It was such a lovely night, I told him I wanted to walk."

He cupped my waist and turned me in his arms so that I was facing him. He didn't speak right away. Instead, he stood studying me. God, it felt as if he could read everything I was trying to hide. I swallowed trying my best not to fidget under his gaze.

"I told Jessie we could go out for pizza. Grab yo' stuff."

"Tonight?"

"Yeah, tonight…" His gaze sharpened. "Unless you got something else to do."

I shook my head. "No, nothing else to do. Let me go and put the chicken I had taken out of the freezer earlier for dinner away. I'll be right back."

Needless to say, I had not counted on Hitta being home. And now I wish I would have given Westly some money so that he could have gotten himself dinner.

Dang it!

———

Hitta

"His keekin around," Maddox voice came from my cell phone. "'N' he's popped th' snib 'n' is gaun in."

I exhaled… *F**king crack head!*

For the last two days, Angel has been sitting on the fact that her hype ass brother was back in town. She didn't know that I had the inside and outside of the Tea Shop under constant surveillance and that when he first slithered his ass up to her back door, I saw him. I've waited for her to come talk to me so that I could tell her don't even f**king think about welcoming him into our lives.

As soon as she left her shop the first day he showed up after

Summer had sent Maddox on that bogus ass food run, Lannox followed her. He sent pictures to my phone of her hugging and crying for this mutha f**ka like he was her f**king hero. And now look, he was breaking into our f**king crib behind her back.

"He's comin' oot wi' a crakin' size bag. Whit dae yi'll waant me tae dae?"

"Grab his ass and bring him to me!"

———

Angel

I had to bite the bullet yesterday and give Westly a few dollars for food. I wasn't any closer to talking to Hitta about him moving in with us than I was the first day he'd showed up.

I mean, I've tried. Surprisingly for the last two nights, Hitta has been coming home for dinner. I've tried to broach the subject of my brother, telling him about some of his good qualities, but every time I did, it was met with resistance.

"You put too much trust in a crackhead," or and by far, the most disheartening, *"My uncle had to put a bullet in my mother's head. You know why? Because the only thing she cared about was chasing that high."*

So yeah, I was back at square one.

"Hey Angel, we're going to grab some Portello's, you want something?" Carmen and Summer asked as they headed towards the door. It was just after the morning rush and things would be pretty calm for the next few hours until around noon.

I shook my head. "Naw, you guys go ahead."

"Okay, we'll be back shortly."

My thoughts had already gone back to trying to figure out the best way to bring my husband and brother together. A few minutes later, I heard the bell ding, but I didn't look up right away because I was grinding down some fresh cinnamon sticks.

"Wow... you look like you've been through a lot." That voice caused my eyes to fly up.

"Shantell! What are you doing here?" She stood dressed to the nines in a white and black leather coat with the matching hat and bag. Had I not heard her speak, I wouldn't have known it was her. Half of her face was covered by a pair of oversized shades.

She chuckled. "I could pretend I was in the neighborhood, but then I would be lying. The truth is plain and simple. I came to get my man back."

I drew myself up, eyeballing the lone customer who sat over by the window on her laptop, enjoying her tea. Surely Shantell wouldn't try to fight me with a witness here to see it.

"Relax, Angel...I didn't come here to fight you." Her gaze fell on my wedding ring. "Although seeing you with that does make me have violent thoughts."

My protected reflexes caused my hand to cover my small baby bump. She snatched the glasses off her face as she took in my pregnant stomach.

"Oh my God! Are you pregnant?!" She screamed her words, causing my customer to look up.

"Keep your voice down, will you?"

"No! Damn that! You have got to be f**king kidding me! He came inside you!"

My customer packed up her bag and slipped out the door and I don't blame her, I wish I could follow.

"How can I help you, Shantell?"

She held up her hand and stepped back away from the counter. "Give me a f**king minute, okay?! I can't believe this sh*t!"

Seeing me pregnant was really upsetting her. Goodness! I slid my phone over, just in case I had to press the emergency call button, but it seemed as if she got herself together.

She turned back around to face me with a huge fake smile on her face. "I didn't come here for you to help me, I came to help *you*."

I shook my head. "I don't think you can. And even if you could, I don't think I want your help."

She grinned. "Don't be so quick to come to that judgment. You are blind, Angel and you need me to help you see."

"See what?" I snapped, already tired of talking to her.

"You need me to help you see the man you married."

"Wrong... I know who I married. I don't need your help in that department."

"Oh, I beg to differ. Because I'm sure you still believe it was your brother's fault Hitta ended up kicking in your door that night."

I picked up a rag and wiped the counter, pretending she didn't have my complete attention.

"I don't know what you're talking about."

"Sure you do, Angel," she spoke to me in the tone one would speak to a special needs child and I wanted to throw this rag in her face.

"Hitta told you your brother stole money from him and that's why he kicked in your door and got you to agree to be his whore."

I held up the hand my wedding ring was on and twisted my braid. "Ummm, I don't know if you heard, but I'm actually his wife. *You* were his whore."

If looks could kill, I would be dead. She had smoke coming out of her ears.

"Ha ha ha, very funny, but I'm wondering if you'll be laughing if you knew he set your brother up to take that money. He left it in his office, knowing he was going to go for that bait. It was a trap, and you and your stupid crackhead brother fell for it."

That hurt... I had to bite down on my teeth not to show her how much. But then, I remembered this was the same hood rat that lied several times about being pregnant just to try and trap a man.

I shook my head. "I don't believe you."

Her grin made the hairs on the back of my neck stand up. "I figured you would say that." She pulled a tape recorder out of her big purse and pressed play.

"A'richt, boss, 'ere is that cash ye asked fur," Maddox voice came from the device.

"Put it in my top draw. Don't want to hide it too good, his crackhead ass may miss it," Hitta muttered sounding like he was occupied with something else.

"Oh, and don't forget to grab the U-Haul before they close."

She stopped the tape and waited for my response with an evil smirk on her face. I inhaled and congratulated myself. On the outside, I looked cool, calm, and collected. But ohhhh, on the inside, I was cursing like a sailor.

That rotten, dirty liar! I remember asking him about that U-Haul and he brushed it off like it was no big deal. Oh my goodness! He set my brother up and planted that money there, knowing Westly was going to take the bait. I balled up my fists, wanting to punch him!

Evidently, Shantell wasn't finished because she proceeded to pull a big envelope out of her bag. Reaching in it, she pulled out what looked like a newspaper article, sliding it across the counter to me. Still watching her closely, I picked up the article and saw that it was about a Jane Doe's body washing up on the 63rd street beach. Her throat had been slit and her teeth and hands were missing.

"Recognize that description?"

I lowered the paper. "It's Trina."

She nodded. "Very good. Hitta ordered his paid assassins to take her out. Removing the hands and the teeth is their calling card."

She slid several more articles to me, all John Does and all the victims whose hands and teeth had been removed. I stared down at them, shaking my head as I read. There was no way this was true... No way!

"Shantell, this has gone too far. You need to stop lying!" I told her pushing her newspapers back to her.

She smiled, in no way ruffled by my words. "I kind of figured you were going to say that too, but no worries, sweetheart, because I have more." She pulled an iPad out of the envelope and after turning it on, slid it toward me.

"Where did your husband tell you your loving foster father disappeared to?"

I tapped the glass of my counter, contemplating not answering her, but something propelled me to do it.

"He skipped town after murdering my foster mother. The story was in the paper."

She chuckled. "My God, you are so naive. Push play on that video in front of you."

For some reason, my hand shook as I pushed the play button on the screen. Although I couldn't hear what was being said because loud rap music was playing, I could see Stan sitting in a chair in an abandoned car garage. And standing around him was Hitta, the twins, and Wayne.

Hitta was angrily saying something to Stan before he stood and… "Oh my God!" I cried out when he hit Stan so hard his head flew back on his neck before his body slammed to the ground.

"For some strange reason, you're the only person in the world who can't see what kind of man you married," Shantell hissed as I continued to watch the video through horror-stricken eyes.

Maddox and Lannox revived Stan and sat him back up in the chair, but a few minutes later, Hitta hit him again. I have never in my life seen anybody get hit that hard. With the way his head flew back, his neck had to be sprained or fractured.

The twins revived him and sat him back in the chair, but he must have said something to set Hitta off because he began hitting him and didn't stop. The violence he displayed was past anything I could ever imagine. After about the seventh blow, Stan's blood began to splatter on Hitta's shirt.

My hand over my mouth shook badly. He was so violent, y'all. I couldn't believe this. In complete and utter shock, I watched as it took Maddox, Lannox, and Wayne to pull him off of the clearly dead man. I've never seen someone get beaten to death, it was a horrible thing.

"You are so stupid, you convinced yourself that a wild lion was a tamed dog…" she hissed, drawing my attention.

"You married a Chi-town goon. This how niggas like that live! You wasn't made for a man like that. A nice wholesome girl like you *should* have the white picket fence, it's just that the nigga who gave it to you is a natural born killa."

There was so much hate in her eyes it stole my breath. "The father of your child is a mutha f**kan killa!" She repeated, just in case I missed her gut-wrenching words the first time. "How does it make you feel, knowing that will be your child's role model?"

She laughed reminding me of Cruella de Vil. "But wait, baby, I'm not done yet!"

I wanted to beg her to stop. She was ripping my heart out, stepping on it with her red bottom heels. I didn't want to play this game with her anymore. *Why was she doing this to me?*

The next set of pictures she pulled out was those of my mother going into the gym. "Notice the date," she said as she took her time placing each picture on the glass in front of me.

"Did your *husband* tell you he talked to her the night Stan killed her?" I held up my hand, stopping her as my world tilted on its foundation.

"Wait! What?!" I screamed, "My mother is not dead!"

All pretenses that I wasn't fazed by Shantell had flown out of the window and she was loving every bit of it.

"Are you kidding me? He didn't even tell you that the other woman Stan killed was your mother?! So, you don't even know she dead?!" She held her head back and roared with laughter.

"Hell naw! All this time, I've been going crazy believing that he loved you more than me, and he didn't even think enough about you to let you know that your mama was dead! This sh*t is rich!" she said around her laughter.

I stared at her through tears that wouldn't fall. My system was in shock, so much so that I didn't know what to do next. If my body didn't know how to automatically breathe, this would have been the point where I dropped dead. My heart was broken into a million pieces and it hurt worse than anything I've ever felt.

"Okay!" she cried holding up her finger as she tried to get control over her laughter. Reaching up, she dried the tears out of her eyes. "Oh my God! Okay! I got one more thing, I promise…you so pathetic I feel sorry for you!"

Shaking her head, she gave in to the last of her chuckles. When she was done, she cleared her throat.

"Whew girl, you a fool! Anyway… I chose now to come and talk to you because I thought you might want to know that your brother don't have long for this earth."

"What do you mean?" My voice quivered so badly my words were barely legible.

"Well, I just saw Maddox throw him in his truck. My guess is he finna take him back to the gym, probably in the *basement*," she lifted her eyebrows at me as if I should know the significance of what she just said, "where he's going to meet the same fate your dear father Stan met. And then, they're going to make him disappear along with his hands and teeth. No doubt Hitta is going to come tell your silly ass he went to Paris or some sh*t!"

"Get out of my store!" I growled as I took my apron off.

She held up her hands as she gathered her things. "Well, I see how you appreciate—"

"GET OUT MY STORE, B*TCH!!!!"

I walked around the counter seeing red. I was ready to fight if I had to. She must have got the picture because she turned and moseyed on toward the door. When she got to it, she looked at me one more time and burst out laughing again before she left.

I didn't waste another minute; I had to go and try to stop them before they killed my brother. *Dear God, be with me.* I grabbed my coat and locked up the shop. The Heavenly Father must have heard my prayer because coming down the street right then was a—

"Taxi!"

Chapter 23

THERE ARE NONE SO BLIND AS THEM THAT WILL NOT SEE

> *Hear Now This, O Foolish People, and Without Understanding; Which Have Eyes, and See Not; Which Have Ears, and Hear Not:*
>
> *Jeremiah 5:21*

Angel

Surprisingly, I was able to make my way to the basement of the gym without being noticed. There was a section that was open for the public down here and then a section toward the back that was not. Back there was a small barbershop, a kitchen, and the office where all the security cameras and things were.

In order to get past the door to where all of this was, one needed to punch in a four-digit code. Hitta had taught me the code months ago. As soon as I typed it in and opened the door, I could hear my brother crying, begging someone to stop kicking him and several people laughing at him.

For the second time today, I saw red as I ran towards the voices. At this moment, no fear lived in me. I had to protect my brother from these savages, and that's just what I was going to do. As soon as I rounded the corner into the barbershop, I saw Westly balled up on the ground and two of Hitta's goons viciously kicking him.

Hitta sat in one of the barber chairs with a Styrofoam container of food in his lap, laughing as he pointed toward Westly with a chicken wing, telling his men to kick him again.

"Stop!" I screamed throwing myself over my brother, not caring about my own safety. Westly's thin body was shaking so badly it felt like he was going to break.

"Are you okay, West?" I cried when no more kicks came, trying to run my hands over his body to see what all was damaged. He groaned, not able to speak, but he clung to me crying like a baby.

My angry gaze flew up to Hitta, who was sitting there looking like a freaking king looking down at his lowly subjects. The whole time he was eating chicken wings and fries from the restaurant as if seeing a man being beaten on his floor was an everyday occurrence. And what makes it so bad, he never stopped eating.

This bastard!

"What the hell are you doing?!" I screeched, just barely holding onto my temper. I wanted to beat him like his men were just beating West. He wore that evil grin of his that I was coming to hate.

"Naw, shawty," he said pointing some fries with mild sauce on them at me. "The question is what are *you* doing?"

"I'm stopping you and your savages from hurting my brother!"

He chuckled as he continued to eat those freaking chicken wings like this animalistic behavior was normal. I looked around and noticed for the first time that there were quite a few people in the room, several of which were also eating food from greasy white bags and Styrofoam containers. Apparently, someone had made a lunch run to Uncle Remo's so that the onlookers could enjoy a nice meal as they beat the hell out of my brother.

Westly started to push me away. Frowning, I looked down at him.

"You got to get out of here," he whispered, trying to speak around his horribly busted lip that was leaking blood.

"No! Not without you!"

When I turned back to look at Hitta, he was no longer eating, the look of rage that was now on his face almost made my nerves slip.

Almost…

"What the f**k yo' bum ass telling her to get out of here for? Like I'm gon' hurt my own f**king wife! You should have been this worried about her when yo' b*tch ass stole my dough!" he growled.

"And you should take yourself to the nearest police station and turn yourself in!" I hissed, not able to take the hypocrisy.

Hitta looked down at me and blinked before his lips turned up and he began to chuckle. All his lackeys joined him. Well… all except Lannox, who looked at me with sorrowful eyes. He gently shook his head. West balled my jacket up in his hand and tried to push me toward the door.

But it was then as I looked around at all them laughing at me, that it hit me. Shantell was right, I had been lying to myself about the kind of man that Hitta is. No! I take that back! *He's* been lying to me about the kind of man that he is

I stood, even though Westly tried to hold me back. Anger at myself for being so stupid and him for being the world's biggest liar settled over me. Slowly I walked toward his majesty. He went back to eating his food as he watched me approach him through lowered lids. He was so damned cocky! I wanted to wipe that damn grin off his face!

"When were you going to tell me my mother was dead?"

He stopped chewing. "Oh sh*t…" he muttered so low. If I wasn't watching his lips, I wouldn't have heard him.

The look that came into his eyes confirmed everything Shantell had just told me. If hearts could make a sound when they break, then mine would sound like two locomotive trains crashing into each other after going full speed.

Tears came to my eyes. "You knew?" I whispered, feeling too weak from heartache to speak any louder.

His mouth moved, but no words came out. He put his food to the side and stood.

"Angel, I-- let me explain." He tried to reach out to me, but I stepped back hissing at him like a cat.

"Don't...Touch...Me...William!" I bit out through my teeth with flared nostrils.

"You lied to me about Stan. You lied to me about the money Westly had taken. You lied to me about my mother." The tears that were now flowing down my cheeks felt heavier than hundred-pound weights.

"Why?" I cried, just needing him to say something to mend my broken heart. It hurt so badly, y'all, I feared I would drop dead at his feet.

He looked down toward the ground and shook his head. "I f**ked up."

"And now I find you here beating my brother. What were you going to tell me after you killed him? Huh? What were you going to say?"

When he didn't say anything to deny my words, I lost it. One second I was standing there and the next, I was trying to climb Hitta like a tree while punching him and screaming my freaking head off.

"You f**king bastard!" I yelled, using all my might behind each of my blows. He wasn't trying to fight me back or stop me. He just brought up his arms protecting his face in the way boxers do, allowing me to hit him.

"I hate you! I hate you! You ruined my life!"

Someone was trying to pull me from the back, but I only turned and went crazy on them. When I saw that it was Maddox, that only fueled my temper more.

"Calm doon, lassie. Ye hae th' bairn tae think aboot."

I wasn't trying to hear anything he had to say. Shantell said it was he who threw my brother in the back of his car. I kicked, punched, and tried to bite him. I'd lost my mind and I feared it was gone forever.

"Get yo' hands off her," Hitta growled before he pulled me away from Maddox. He wrapped his arms around me, holding mine down by my sides, hugging me from behind.

Maddox stepped back holding up his hands, looking at me as if I was a wildcat or something.

"You got to calm down, Teacup. You gon' hurt the baby," Hitta pleaded with me in my ear. His face was buried in my neck as he continued to hold my arms.

"Let me go!"

His arms tightened. "Only if you promise not to go ape sh*t and start beating me again."

Even though I know he was placating me, it still made me feel better that he was begging me not to beat him. There was no way my little punches were doing anything to him when I'd just witnessed him beat my foster father to death with the strength of an angry silverback gorilla.

"Fine! Let me go!"

He removed his arms, but when he didn't step away from me, I stepped away from him, walking towards Westly.

"Come on, West, we're getting out of here," I grunted as I helped him up off the floor. When nobody stopped me, I thanked God. However, as we took a few steps toward the door with my brother leaning heavily on my shoulder because it looked as if his leg was broken, Hitta's voice came from behind us bringing my steps to a halt.

"Why don't you ask yo' precious Westly, where he was when Maddox grabbed him."

I felt my brother stiffen and groan a bit, he jerked his body toward the door as if to tell me to keep walking, but I didn't move. Instead, I turned back to face Hitta.

"What are you talking about?"

He didn't speak right away. Instead, he studied me. You see, my hate for him just showed through my words and he felt it. I didn't try to hide it either. Once Westly and I got out of here, I was leaving Hitta. There was no way in the world that I would stay with him after this. And I let him see that in my expression too.

"Yo' brother broke into our house," he muttered. There was something off about him, I guess he just now realized that I was done with him.

I was so busy studying his new demeanor that it took a minute for his words to settle into my mind. But when they did, the hate I felt for him only grew.

"God! You can't say anything without lying, can you?" Again, I let my feelings for him show through my hissed words.

His nostrils flared. Some of the bravery I had felt a second ago was starting to recede as loud alarms began to go off in my head.

"You so gullible. You'll believe anything. Yeah, I lied to you to protect yo' stupid ass from that mutha f**ka you got on your arm. Ask his b*tch ass did he or did he not break into our crib and try and f**king rob us!" He angrily turned and snatched a duffle bag out of the chair next to him. And then he walked back and threw it at my feet. When it hit the ground, several things flew out of it. A few of Hitta's chains, some of his watches, and the Chinese golden tea set Hitta had gifted me with for my birthday last month.

I stared down at the things as I shook my head. Yes, I knew my brother was a thief, but he has never stolen from me. Never!

"West, what is this?" I whispered so that only he could hear me. I'd shown him where we lived. I've been racking my brain trying to find a way to convince Hitta to let him come stay with us. He told me he would never steal from me.

God!

I am the world's biggest fool!

"Baby girl, I can—"

"Explain!" I said cutting him off. I couldn't believe this. How much pain can a person take in one day?

Suddenly feeling as if his touch was suffocating me, I stepped back away from him as if he'd burned me. Nearly crashing back to the floor, he managed to grab ahold of the wall and stumble over to a bench sitting heavily on it while still holding his waist. No doubt he had a few cracked ribs, but at this point, I didn't care.

"Angel, I'm sorry—" he began, but I held my hand up.

"I don't want to hear it!" My gaze went from his to Hitta's.

"I want the both of you to stay the f**k away from me!" And then I turned and tried to walk out the door, but Hitta moved so fast he caught me completely off guard. Grabbing my arm, he pulled me to a stop and turned me to face him.

"Who the f**k you think you clowning? You not going no f**king where. This--" he hissed, hitting his chest so hard with his hand it caused me to jump. He hit himself far harder than I had. "Is who the f**k I am! And you better get used to it because I ain't changing! Not for you, not for yo' crackhead ass brother…. nobody!" he growled hitting his chest again.

"And you ain't f**king leaving me. Don't you know by now I will tear these mutha f**kan streets apart with my bare hands until I find you? You mine, Angel! Now and mutha f**kan forever. Take her ass to the house and let her cool the f**k off!" he said shoving me into Lannox's arms.

"Make sure she stay put!" And then he turned to my brother and angrily snatched him off the bench.

"Come here, b*tch! I ain't done with you yet!"

I didn't get a chance to see what happened after that because Lannox was using his body to shield it from my view as he guided me out the door.

During the drive home, it took everything I had in me to hold back my tears. The pain inside of me had all bundled up into a knot in my throat and chest. I was betrayed by both the men I loved, and it hurt more than anything I'd ever felt in my life. Today, I learned that neither of them truly loved me because if they had, they would have made sure my heart never felt this way.

And now I was being forced to stay here with a man I hated.

How had my life come to this?

However, I had no more time to ponder it because Jessie's school bus was pulling up at the house at the same time Lannox brought his truck to a stop. With a forced smile, I thanked Kayla, who was walking toward the house with a few of her friends, telling her that I didn't need her to watch Jess for me today.

As I listened without hearing to Jessie, who excitedly told me about something that happened at school, I somehow managed to hold back those tears that were now a log in my throat, making it hard for me to breathe.

Lannox walked up the stairs of the front porch with us and waited for me to open the door. Jessie talked to the both of us, so my plan of slamming the front door in his face was shot to hell. He followed us in, shutting the door behind him as Jessie continued with her story.

I couldn't pretend that I was alright anymore. "Can you please wait outside. I don't want you in here with us," I told him without looking at him.

Finally sensing something was wrong, Jessie went quiet as she studied me. "What's wrong, Tee-Tee?"

I couldn't speak, if I did, the dam would burst. Plus, how could I explain to my seven-year-old niece that I was broken? Instead, I stood there facing the stairs, waiting to hear Lannox leave my house.

Jessie signed something to him, he signed back and then quietly left.

"Lannox said he'll be outside if you need him."

And that was it… That was all I could take. The dam broke. I hurried upstairs, but by the time I got there, I was blinded with my tears and weeping so badly I was scaring the hell out of Jessie. Too weak from grief to go any farther, I collapsed on my bed and wept into my pillow.

Dear God, help me! I've never felt so much pain in my life. My mother was dead and this whole time my husband knew it and didn't tell me.

He'd killed Stan and Trina!

Oh God! What was I going to tell Jessie?!

"Tee-Tee, why you crying?" she asked crawling into the bed with me rubbing my hair.

I couldn't answer her, because I couldn't stop weeping. My son's father was a killer. *What am I supposed to tell him?*

I don't know how long I lay there crying, but eventually, Jessie crawled underneath my arm, lying on the bed next to me and nodded off. My weeping turned into silent tears that turned into a soul-quivering numbness.

I just lay there holding Jessie, watching as the sun began to set. It was right as my eyes were getting heavy that I smelled elderberries.

"Greatie…" I whispered as a spark of life ignited in my shattered heart.

Quietly, as not to wake Jessie, I eased out of the bed and then hurried down the stairs. Greatie stood at the table pouring a cup of tea for me. Needing to feel her embrace at this moment more than I needed to breathe, I rounded the table and wrapped my arms around her. Instantly, I was flooded by her warmth, but when I felt her arms come around me, the tears that I thought were surely all gone started back with a vengeance.

"There now, child," she soothed as she rubbed her hand down my braids like she used to do when I was a little girl. "It's okay to cry about it."

And I did. I stood there and cried painful tears that ripped my soul apart. I wanted to give up. Of course, I knew I couldn't because of Jessie and my unborn child, but I was so discouraged with mankind I no longer wanted to live amongst them. How could anybody be so cruel and hateful?

"Oh sweetheart, you don't know how many times yo' old Greatie has asked that same question."

I was so used to her knowing my thoughts her words didn't surprise me.

"Here, take a seat and drink yo' tea. Tell Greatie all about it."

I eased down in the chair, feeling too weak to lift my cup of tea. "I hate this world."

I'd cried so much till my voice was barely there, but my Greatie heard me. She nodded as she walked to the oven pulling out a pan of those muffins. Only this time, there was something else added to them, a peculiar spice that I've never seen her add to her muffins.

I frowned a bit. "Is that Sumac?"

She chuckled as she slid another pan inside the oven. "Good nose. Yes, it is."

"Why Sumac? Why not just add lemon?"

"I'll tell you in a minute. For now, tell me what happened."

I exhaled as I stirred my tea and then started at the beginning. "I should have listened to my first impression of him when I walked into that gym for the first time."

I told her about Hitta planting the money for Westly to find and him kicking in my door looking for West. I told her about him forcing me to move in with him and about him forcing me to love him. Had he left me alone and just gone after a woman who wanted him, none of this would have ever happened.

"Why me? Why couldn't he just leave me alone?" I was crying so badly I know my Greatie was having a hard time understanding me. "I'm not that pretty. There's nothing really that special about me."

She took my hand. "Oh, but it is, child. And that man ain't blind, he saw it and he wanted it. He just went about getting it the wrong way." She shook her head. "We do that as humans. We sometimes go about getting things the wrong way."

"He took it too far. He had Trina murdered. He killed Stan." She had a look on her face that said she wasn't too heartbroken by that news.

"Greatie!" I admonished snatching my hand from her.

"Oh, don't Greatie me! You know the world is a better place without those two in it."

"Yeah, but he lied to me. He lied to me about everything. Stan killed my mom and Hitta knew and didn't even tell me."

"Dear Heavenly Father, have mercy," Greatie muttered as she stood from the table to check on her muffins.

"Westly finally came back and like a dummy, I jumped right back into trying to help him, only for him to turn around and break into my house."

Greatie shook her head as she pulled another teacup out of the cabinet and began to plate the muffins. She'd made three pans, way too many for me, her, and Jess. The last time she'd done this, she prepared muffins for Hitta. That thought angered me.

"Are you expecting someone?" I couldn't help the stank in my voice. But I swear if she'd made those muffins for my lying husband, I was going to get up and throw them in the garbage.

She turned around and faced me with her hand on her hip. "Now you get that sass out yo' voice. I know what I'm doing." She pointed at me. "Do you know what you doing?" Dejected, I shook my head.

"Well then, let me do what I'm doing!" she snapped.

I bowed my head, good and disciplined. "If you don't mind me asking, what are you doing?"

She lifted her cup of tea that sat on the counter and took a sip. "I figure you ready to go, right?" I nodded.

"And that priest out there is standing in the way of you leaving, right?"

"Priest?" I asked frowning.

She chuckled. "Oh yes, the mute is of the Zedekian line. He's a priest of the Ancient of Days, one of the deadliest men you'll ever meet. And if we're going to get past him and keep yo' husband from tearing up the streets looking for you, we're going to need some help."

My shoulders slumped. For just a moment, I felt a spark of hope that my Greatie was going to get us away from here. But there was no one who could get me away from Hitta. He was too powerful in both the streets and thanks to Wayne and Kennedy, the system.

I exhaled. "Aww, Greatie… There's nobody that can handle Hitta. Not even the cops could help me now."

She chuckled as she brought the plate of muffins and the spare teacup to the table. "Don't you want to know why I added Sumac in the muffins?"

I lay my head on the table. Suddenly my neck felt too weak to hold it up on my shoulders.

"Why?" I asked her, looking at her through fresh tears.

"Because the Preacher can't resist my elderberry muffins when I make them this way."

Dear God, give me the strength. My grandmother would pick this time to start rambling.

She chuckled patting my hand. "There is only one man that can deal with these slayers, and it's probably because they all came from his loins," she muttered the last of her statement before looking up and smiling just as the back door opened.

"Tabby girl…" That deep powerful voice caused my head to jerk up. "I heard you were looking for me."

"Oh my Go---" My words trailed off as I watched the big dark man duck under my door frame just like Hitta had to do when coming into the kitchen. I couldn't believe what my eyes were telling me I was seeing. This man looked like a bonafide cowboy, so much so he could have stepped right out of an old western on TV.

Except there were a few things about him that set him apart from any cowboy I'd ever seen. His long hair was braided in cornrows that fell to the center of his back. The black hat that he wore cast the top half of his face into shadow, but his piercing dark eyes still managed to stand out as he studied me. Y'all, there was something about this man's eyes that made me feel inferior. Something about his eyes had my mind racing to remember what my Greatie had told me about him the last time she was in my kitchen.

Power exuded from him in waves. As he walked toward us, the black duster he wore opened a bit and I saw that a real sword hung low on his hips. Greatie reached over and put her finger under my chin, pushing it up. I snapped my mouth shut, realizing I'd been sitting here staring at the man as if he was some kind of mystic creature walking through my door.

Heck! That's how it felt…

"Preacher…How are you?" Greatie said, beaming as he leaned over and kissed her cheek.

"I'm good, Tabby girl. Praise Yah! How long has it been?" he asked as he took a seat at the table with us, reaching for one of the muffins at the same time.

Guys, I probably looked like a little kid that had spotted a real-life action hero because I still stared at this man trying to comprehend what I was seeing. And he must be used to folks looking at him this way because he never faltered in putting his muffin on the plate in front of him. He picked up the little knife Greatie had placed there for him, cutting his muffin open and smearing some butter Greatie had softened for him on both halves. Then he picked up one of the halves and took a massive bite out of it, reminding me so much of my husband. In fact, he even favored Hitta as well.

"Shucks, Preacher, it's been a good while. I don't think I've talked to you since our paths crossed in '09 when I made that coat for you."

He reached for another muffin, nodding his head. "I think you may be right. I'm glad you mentioned this coat. I need you to make two more for me, one ruddy like the great king Dawid and the other white like our Master's hair."

She nodded as she stirred her tea. "How soon do you need them?"

He thought for a moment as he chewed. "We have a little time, they're still just boys. It will be years till they become who they're meant to be."

Something in my spirit told me the '09 Greatie mentioned was not 2009. I made eye contact with her.

"'09?"

She chuckled. "1809, I believe. Those coats were in high fashion back then."

The Preacher chuckled nodding his head. "That was a good year."

Okay, so that explained why he looked like a cowboy. Apparently, he was like Greatie and had walked the earth for many years. He must have really enjoyed the wild west days.

"Preacher, I called you because we need yo' help. My daughter here has gotten herself tangled up with one of yours."

"Uh oh," the commanding man muttered.

Greatie nodded. "He's a little rough around the edges and don't quite know how to treat her yet."

When she said he was a little rough around the edges, the Preacher chuckled, shaking his head a bit. His gaze came to me and it took everything in me not to fidget under the weight of it.

"Your son is going to need his father."

I swallowed. I wanted to shake my head and say no, but this wasn't the kind of person you said no to if you guys know what I mean. When he spoke, everything inside of you that was wise encouraged you to listen.

"However, sometimes my children have to lose what they unwisely take for granted as continual in order to know just how much they've been blessed." He'd gone back to buttering his muffins.

Goodness! It was the third one he'd consumed since sitting down at the table. Greatie was right, just like Hitta, he loved her muffins. Seeing this man who reminded me so much of my husband was a little surreal.

"He has a Zedekian priest loyal to him. He's been ordered not to allow her to leave the house."

The Preacher nodded, clearly impressed. "Now, I'm looking forward to meeting this young man, what's his name?"

"Everybody calls him Hitta, but his real name is William," I told him.

He grinned. "Hitta?"

His grin was infectious. I didn't think I would ever smile again, but here I was. "Yeah, Hard Hitta."

"Okay… I see." He signaled toward the stairs with his knife. "Go on, child, pack your bags. You can go. I'll take care of the Zedekite for you and have a little talk with your husband."

I sat there for a moment stunned. Surely, it can't be that easy.

"Go, girl…pack you and Jess a bag. Hurry now, I know the perfect place for y'all to go for a little while," Greatie said, gesturing for me to hurry along.

"That's it?" I asked them both, feeling like I was stuck in the twilight zone. They both nodded at me.

"That's it, and I suggest you hurry. Your husband will be here shortly," the Preacher said before stuffing another half of a muffin in his mouth.

They didn't have to say anymore. I hurried upstairs and woke Jessie.

"Sweetheart, I need you to pack a bag. Get your pajamas and underwear. Pack a few outfits and your toothbrush. Hurry."

"Where we going?" she asked as she rubbed her eyes.

"It's a surprise. Hurry now, go on!" I gave her a little shove out the room before quickly packing me a bag.

When we got back downstairs, the Preacher and Greatie were still sitting at the table catching up on old times. And surprisingly, Lannox stood by the stove helping himself to a muffin and a cup of tea. I froze in fear when I saw him.

He turned to face me and there was a sad smile on his face.

"He says he's sorry you had to witness the things that you did today," the Preacher said before sipping his tea. "He also wants you to think about not leaving his master because Hitta needs you."

I lifted my chin. "I don't care what he needs. I have to think about me now."

Lannox nodded before his gaze went back to the powerful dark man at the table. He just looked at him for a while and then the Preacher nodded.

Oh my God! He was communicating with him the way that he does Maddox.

"He says he prays that you can one day understand why Hitta is the way that he is. He's been created to destroy evil. He'll never hurt the innocent."

"What's your excuse?" I spat my words at Lannox.

He put his hand on his chest, but it was the Preacher who spoke. "I have been made the same way. But I've never killed a man. My brother won't allow it. He won't allow me to have blood on my hands."

Hitta's truck pulled up out front. The sound of loud rap music bled through the front door. My frightened gaze shot to it.

"Lannox, why don't you take Tabby girl and her beautiful grand-daughter to wherever it is they need to go. I'll take care of your master." All this the Preacher said while still sipping his tea. I wanted to warn him that Hitta was really dangerous, but I had a feeling that he could take care of himself.

Lannox nodded and gestured for us to follow him out the back door. Greatie hurried to the Preacher and kissed his cheek.

"Thank you, Ach. I will have those coats for you the next time I see you. Come, child…" she told me as she hurried out the door behind Lannox.

"Thanks again," I muttered to the powerful man as I followed behind her, pulling Jessie with me. However, Jessie had not stopped looking at the Preacher since we came into the kitchen and as I pulled her past him, she still stared. At the last minute, she broke away from me and ran to him hugging him.

"I love you."

He chuckled. "Thank you, baht. I love you too." She nodded and hurried after me.

Before I left, my gaze came to the Preacher's one last time.

"Have faith, daughter."

"About what?"

"That he will become the man you need him to be." I stared at him for a moment before I nodded. As I closed the back door, I heard Hitta's keys in the front.

Chapter 24

CLEANSING

> *There Is A Sacredness In Tears. They Are Not A Mark Of Weakness, But Power. They Speak More Eloquently Than Ten Thousand Tongues. They Are Messengers Of Overwhelming Grief...And Unspeakable Love...*
>
> Washington Irving

Hitta

As soon as I pulled up to the house, I knew my light was gone. I felt it like I felt the hair on my face. This time was different from the last time she left. I'd broken her heart and by default, mine too. Somehow, she'd found out the truth about everything, and now she saw me for the piece of sh*t that I am.

I clutched my head as the pressure built behind my eyes. My temples were beginning to throb and my heart felt like someone had taken a f**king sledgehammer to it.

F**k! I felt like I was getting ready to have a heart attack!

I messed up!

I saw it in her eyes. I messed up bad and I had no idea how to fix it. I've been f**king up since our honeymoon.

I know!

I know!

Y'all out there wondering what the f**k is wrong with me, right? Well, join the party, 'cause I've been wondering the same thing.

Something happened to me on that mountain when the Tea Master berated me. For the first time in a long time, I felt vulnerable; I was in the presence of something more powerful than me. And I ain't gon' bullsh*t y'all, it scared the hell out of me. Angel don't know why I've been staying at the gym longer and I'm too embarrassed to tell her. When I'm not sure of myself and just need to work some sh*t out in my head, I throw myself into a physical regimen and push my body to exhaustion, making myself stronger, faster.

But I know that no matter how hard I work or how strong I get, it will never be enough to be able to stand in the presence of that light without feeling inadequate. And now I'd f**ked up and made Angel hate me.

F**k!!!!

I had no idea how to make this better. She wasn't the type that I could drop a chunk of dough on and make her smile again. I wasn't the type of nigga to do no sappy sh*t like send her a singing telegram or nothing like that to apologize.

I stared at the house that suddenly looked dull, at a complete loss and scared as sh*t to go in. She was gone. She was gone and I wasn't ready for what awaited me on the other side of that door. But even as those thoughts traveled through my mind, I knew I'd reached a point where there was nothing left to do but face it. I'd reached a crossroad, and I had to be a f**king man and face the consequences for my actions.

I wasn't big on praying, but as I put my key in the door, the only thing I could think was, *Please God, don't let her be gone.*

As soon as I opened the door, the smell of those bomb-ass muffins she'd made for me that time filled my nose, bringing a smile to my face. So maybe I wasn't in as much trouble as I thought, but then again, maybe she was trying to poison me.

I heard movement in the kitchen and headed that way. However, when I got there, my steps halted. Sitting at my table was a big black cowboy. I've seen this dude before. He was the same cat I saw talking to Lyon a few times, the only man I'd ever seen my teacher afraid of. It wasn't that he was threatening him or anything, I could just tell that Lyon respected this dude greatly. Plus, when he left the gym one time, Lyon jokingly told the few of us that was there, that the Preacher was probably the only man alive that could kick his ass.

He lifted his head and looked at me with a pair of eyes that made me feel like I was back up on that mountain.

"Who are you?" I muttered, even though I knew.

"Most folks call me the Preacher, but of course, you know that already." As he spoke, he spooned honey into his tea, giving it a good stirring.

"Very rarely can I find tea this good. Only Tabby girl can make it like this."

"Why you in my kitchen?"

"I've come to have a little chat with you, son."

I stepped back into the hallway. I didn't like the way that sh*t sounded. "Angel! Jess!" I called, taking the stairs up two at a time.

I needed to lay eyes on her and know that she was okay. When no one answered me and I didn't see them in their rooms, my heart sped up as the walls began to close around me. I flew back down the steps.

"Where is Angel?!"

He didn't bat an eye at my raised voice. He just lifted his cup and took a sip of his tea, closing his eyes like Angel does to savor it. When he opened them, his ancient gaze pinned me to the spot where I stood.

"Why don't you have a seat?"

I shook my head, about to tell him what I thought about him offering me a seat in my own damn house when suddenly the chair slammed into the back of my legs, forcing me to sit.

"I insist," he muttered before taking another sip of his tea. I stared wide-eyed as the chair then slid back toward the table. Trying not to freak the f**k out, I took several deep breaths. This dude just moved the chair with his mind or some sh*t!

"I remember you now," he told me leaning closer to study me. "You're the warrior with the inferiority complex."

I frowned at him, wondering what would happen if I decked him. He chuckled.

"You wouldn't be the first to have tried, son." Sitting back in his chair, he gestured to the plate of muffins. "Have one."

"Naw," I grumbled.

He shrugged reaching for one. "Suit yourself. You're missing out on some good eating."

"Where is Angel?" I didn't even want to pretend I was happy with him being here. Yeah, I'd seen him before and yeah, a great man that I looked at as a teacher had mad respect for this dude, but I didn't appreciate him telling me I had a f**king inferiority complex. What the f**k did he know about it?

"I know that your lack of belief is the reason you're sitting here alone. There is nothing wrong with being humble, son. In fact, humbleness will carry you a long way. But there is a thin line between humbleness and doubt. At some point, you have to believe that the Ancient of Days knew what he was doing when he chose you."

I sucked in my breath sharply. It felt like I'd just gotten punched in the stomach. How did he know that? He'd just vocalized something that I'd been too afraid to even admit to myself.

"I don't know what you're talking about." My pride forced me to say. I didn't like looking weak in front of no man.

"Sure, you do. Your lack of belief has always stood in your way your whole life. When Lyon told you who you are, you doubted it. You heard a voice say, *This can't be right. He must have me mistaken for someone else. I ain't nothing but a hood nigga.* When Angel told you she loved you and that she was honored to be your wife, you doubted it. You wanted to hurry and get married because you feared she would look and see who she *really* married."

He leaned in closer. "When you realized that you'd been given a gift, you doubted it. You actually felt that the Heavenly Father had made a mistake. What nonsense…"

I folded my hands to keep from tapping them on the table, revealing to this stranger how much his words were affecting me. That was exactly what I said to myself the day Lyon told me I was destined to become this great warrior. And yes, I had doubted that Angel could ever really truly love me and could be a gift just for me.

"Foolishly, you thought that doubting voice that you heard was your own," he continued before he picked up his teacup taking another sip. "You've always taken comfort in that voice that convinced you that you were nothing but a nigga, not seeing it for the enemy that it is. Do you know why?"

I didn't answer him. Between the pounding in my head and heart, and his words that were cutting through my flesh down to my bone, I felt f**king paralyzed.

He chuckled. "Don't worry, I'll tell you why anyway. You took comfort in it because being a nigga came easy. Your fear of trying to become the warrior you were meant to be and failing has held you in bondage. But because you can't contain the fighter in you, you thought to find your escape through boxing, but that wasn't the Ancient of Days' will for you. This is why you have the headaches and it's why you're going to continue to have the headaches until you answer your call, son."

My fingers began to tap on the table. I wanted to tell him to shut up, to just stop... But then, he turned to look at me, once again pinning me to the spot with that gaze that saw too much.

"Do you believe that the voice you're hearing right now is your own?"

I lifted an eyebrow at him. "You mean the voice in *my* head?"

He chuckled. "Yes, the voice in *your* head, the one that's telling you not to listen to me. Do you think that is your own voice?"

"Yeah, it's in my head, ain't it?"

"Well, tell me this. Is it the same voice that was in your head when you told your wife you were not going to change for her?"

His question threw me. Yeah, it was the same voice and it's one of the things that I said but regretted. I don't know why I said that dumb sh*t in the first place.

"Because that voice that sounds so much like your own is actually your *enemy*. Its job is to continue to keep you doubting yourself because it knows the day you realize your value, accept who you are and what you've been put here to do, is the day it has to slither back to its master and tell him it failed in its mission."

"What mission?"

"The mission to keep you believing you are nothing but a nigga and cause you to doubt every time someone tells you that you're so much more. But at last...it's caused you to lose your wife. You couldn't see in yourself what she always saw in you."

I clutched my head. I'd felt the headache coming on earlier, but now it was growing worse. The way the pressure was building behind my eyes told me that this was going to be a bad one. I needed Angel.

"Please... tell me where she is." My plea was quiet, but he heard.

"If you go after her now, she will hate you forever."

I put my head down on the table, needing to close my eyes. "What you want me to do? Just give up? I ain't got it in me." I didn't care that I was growling my words like a f**king animal. I felt like I was dying and even still, I knew with my whole heart and soul that his words were true. If I went after Angel and forced her to come back to me, she would only hate me for it.

I clutched my head, wanting to break some sh*t. I'd messed up and I didn't know how to fix it.

"Why don't you start by fixing yourself."

"How?" I asked without lifting my head that was now beginning to feel like it was going to explode.

"You know what you have to do... *Answer your call, son.*"

I groaned as the pressure in my head got worse. This man talked in a bunch of riddles. What call? No quicker had the thought came to my mind, the answer followed and with it, what felt like a release valve of the pressure in my dome.

The Lyon's Den

I lifted my head to ask him if that was the answer, but he was gone. The only thing that suggested he had been there at all was his empty plate and teacup.

———

Angel

"Ima! What?! You're knocking on doors now?" A very handsome older gentleman said as he opened the door, stepping to the side so that we could enter his beautiful home.

I tried to look everywhere else but at him. He was standing there shirtless in only a pair of sweatpants. And for an older guy, he was ripped.

"Go on now!" Greatie said swatting at him. "Put you a shirt on. This here chile a married woman. She don't need to be seeing yo' goodies."

He chuckled as he headed for the stairs, taking them up two at a time. "Ima's here!" he yelled.

There was maybe a two-second pause before what sounded like a stampede could be heard overhead.

"Watch this," Greatie muttered, just as--

"Ima!"

"Ima, hey!"

"Ima, I got to show you my stitches!"

The kitchen door opened and two children that had to be eight or nine ran from it. Three little boys who all looked to be between the ages of 4 and 6 came running down the stairs and what looked like a sixteen-year-old boy came up from the basement. They all rushed Greatie, trying to hug her all at once.

She chuckled as she accepted all the love the children bestowed on her. It was hard not to share in their joy.

"We haven't seen you in a long time," a beautiful little girl said who had to be Jessie's age, if not a little older.

"Who's this?" her brother asked, coming to a stop in front of Jessie. He looked to be about a year older than the little girl.

"My name Jessica."

I looked down surprised at my niece. This is the first time I ever heard her tell someone her full name. The little boy held out his hand for her to shake.

"My name YermiYah," he told her.

Greatie smiled down at them and then looked at me and winked.

"Come on now, let Ima get through the door," said a very pregnant, beautiful older woman, who looked as if she could be related to Greatie and me as she waddled down the stairs, holding her lower back. I studied her closely because she looked familiar. I'd seen her before, but I just couldn't remember where.

"Hey, Ima..." she huffed when she finally made it to us, leaning in to hug Greatie.

"Hey, baby. I brought you another pair of hands to help out around here for a little while, at least till after you have the baby. This is one of my daughters just like you. I want you guys to take care of each other." The woman's gaze fell on me and she smiled warmly and I saw it. Although she was of a lighter shade than Greatie and me, she definitely favored me enough to be my sister.

"Welcome to our home, little sis!" she gushed, holding out her hands for me. "Noach! Come meet our cousin!" she yelled before pulling me into a hug that surprised me because it was so—so....

Goodness! I was getting ready to cry again. She felt like a blood sister. And as if my arms had a mind of their own, I held her just a little tighter. Surprisingly, she returned the embrace. I wondered if she knew how much I needed the affection.

"I'm so glad you're here, kot. As you can see, I have my hands full around here. The baby is due any day now and I can really use all the help I can get. These children are driving me crazy."

Trying to fight back my tears, I nodded. "I will be happy to help."

"We're going to spend the night here?!" Jessie asked excitedly.

"Absolutely!" The man who I was sure was Noach, answered as he jogged down the stairs now sporting a t-shirt over that very muscled chest of his.

"You guys are family; you can stay as long as you want. We have more than enough room," he continued as he walked toward me and opened his arms. "Shalom, little sista! Welcome to our home."

Unsure of whether or not I should hug him, my gaze went to his beautiful wife. She nodded with a kind smile on her face, nudging me forward a bit. His embrace felt like that of a brother, I could feel their welcome and it was going to be my undoing. I don't know how

Greatie knew that this was what I needed, but this was what I needed. I didn't want to be alone with my thoughts. This house was so busy, it was the perfect distraction.

"Okay, let me introduce you guys to the posse," Noach said, gesturing for the children to line up. He had a big booming voice, the kind of voice that was perfect for giving speeches or lectures. "Starting from the oldest to the youngest. As you know, my name is Noach Hathaway. This is my lovely wife of seventeen wonderful years, Brooklyn." She cheesed, pleased with his compliment. And I knew right off that they were a happy couple.

"Our oldest is Eliyah." The teenage boy held up his hand in a wave

"Next to him at 10 is YermiYah." The little fella that had greeted Jessie waved.

"Next to him at 8 is daddy's little princess, Lyric." Poor baby, she was the only girl.

"And these three knuckleheads," he said grabbing the three youngest boys, bundling them all together, causing them to erupt in giggles.

"Is Joshua, whose 6, James 5, and John, who's the family terror coming in at 4."

"Wow! You guys have quite the team here," I told them, amazed that poor Brooklyn was still standing here in one piece.

I placed my hands on Jessie's shoulders. "This is my niece, Jessica, and my name's Angel. It's a pleasure to meet you guys."

"It looks like you're expecting a new member to your team too," Brooklyn said gesturing toward my stomach.

Greatie chuckled. "Yes, she is. And I figured you can give her some pointers."

"I sure will. As you can see, I'm a pro. Come on, let me show you guys to your room." The children all surrounded us, excited that we were going to be staying with them for a little while. They all talked and asked questions at once. Their energy was amazing. As they bustled us up the stairs, I looked back at Greatie where she still stood by the door.

Thank you... I mouthed to her. With a gentle smile on her face, she nodded.

———

Jessie and I got unpacked and settled into the guest bedroom, then we made our way down to dinner. Let me tell you guys something about eating at the Hathaway's table. It was quite the experience; I can't remember the last time I laughed so much. Between Noach's crazy stories and the children, who all competed with the other to tell the funniest joke, it was the perfect distraction. I didn't think about my husband or my brother once.

But goodness, by the time Noach, Brooklyn, and I got the kitchen cleaned and all the children bedded down, we were beat. She and I sat in her sewing room in front of a nice fire, just unwinding.

"How in the world do you do this every night?"

She chuckled from where she sat in front of the most beautiful sewing machine I'd ever seen.

"By the mercy of the Heavenly Father. I do this every night, morning, and afternoon. Noach drives a truck and sometimes he's gone several days at a time, which leaves me by myself doing this."

"Oh my goodness... You are a super mom."

"Whew, I wish. Poor Noach has had to talk me down from the edge many of days. Eliyah's a lot of help and Lyric. Believe it or not, there is nothing she likes doing more than bossing around her brothers. If she could, she'd even boss around Eliyah."

As she spoke, she threaded the machine and picked up on whatever it was she was sewing before we came. I'd truly never seen anything like it. It was definitely an antique, but not your everyday average antique. It looked like it may at one time belonged to royalty or something. It seemed to be made of pure copper with beautiful swirls that looked a lot like vines carved into it.

"That is a beautiful machine," I told her, mesmerized at watching her graceful hand weave the string while pushing her garment through. She was an artist.

"Thank you. I found it in this very room when I first came here. Back then, this old house was barely standing. Noach had been given the property when he was released from prison and he hired me to help him fix it up. That's how we ended up dating."

"I don't know what it was about this room, but I was drawn to it. Everything was very old and covered in a layer of dust so thick I nearly coughed up a lung as I began cleaning it. And then over there," she pointed to the corner by the beautiful bay window, "buried under a pile of old ratty sheets was this beauty. I couldn't believe my find. They haven't made a sewing machine like this since the early 1800s." Her gaze came to mine. "Guess who I found out was the owner of this machine and this house."

"Who?"

"Our grandmother."

I gasped. "Greatie?"

She nodded. "Yep, I'd become obsessed with getting this thing to work and one day, I came into the room and she was sitting here sewing a garment."

"Did you freak out when you found out she was your great, great, great—"

"Great, great, grandmother," she said finishing my sentence, causing us both to laugh. "You know, I didn't freak out too much because at the time, my heart was like stone. Nothing really could surprise me. Life had already dealt a pretty tragic hand, so anything beyond that was an improvement in my book."

And that was the beginning of the relationship between me and my cousin several times removed. We stayed up all night talking. Her life and mine were so similar it was scary, only the state didn't take her away from her mom when she was little. And where I'd almost been raped by Stan, she was actually raped by one of her mother's lovers.

But alas, I can't go into too many details about her and Noach's tale because it's their story to tell. Look for it, it's out there.

By morning, I'd cried all the tears I had in me. I told her about my marriage and the things that had led up to me and Jessie stowing away in their guest bedroom. And surprisingly, she didn't judge me nor Hitta. She just told me some of the crazy things that she and her husband had gone through on their journey of discovery.

"You take all the time you need to heal, little sista. You are welcome here. If the children get too loud or bug you too much, just let me know and I will make them go downstairs to the basement.

Noach built them a children's haven down there. Everything a young person could want can be found in that basement, chile. It's like a real-life arcade down there."

I shook my head. "No, your children all have beautiful spirits. They're well-mannered. They won't bother me at all. Plus, Jessie is loving it here." And she was. She and Lyric had been glued at the hip since we unpacked our bags in the guest room.

Because Lyric was the only girl with five brothers and another one on the way, you can already imagine that she was a little rough. In fact, she was able to hang toe-to-toe with Jessie. Little did I know at the time, that those two would grow up to be the best of friends. But I'm getting ahead of myself, that's another story for another time.

The rest of my tale is going to be hard enough to get through. Anyhow, the next morning when I woke up, I was unsure of what to do with myself. As you guys can imagine, I didn't get much sleep, thanks to staying up very late chatting with Brooklyn and then the nightmares that made an appearance as soon as I closed my eyes.

What is the irony, that my husband who hurt me and lied to me, is the only man that can chase my nightmares away? What does that even mean? And what does it mean that when I woke up, I missed him like nobody's business? How can I hate him and miss him too?

Ugggh! I was a wreck!

Greatie said that I didn't have to worry about Hitta because if the Preacher said he would handle it, then he would. She said I was free to go to work and move around the city without fear that my husband was going to grab me and force me to come back home.

However, for the first time in my life, I didn't want to go into the Tea Shop, instead, I lay on the loveseat in Brooklyn's sewing room and watched her work. We talked a little, I slept a little, lulled by the gentle hum of her machine.

It's crazy because I'd realized that Greatie said that I was coming here to help Brooklyn in order to save my pride. But the truth was, Greatie had brought me here for Brooklyn to help *me* and that made me so sad. My heart hurt so bad I'd lost the will to do most things.

Noach went on the road for 3 weeks and was off one. It just so happened that this was his off week, so he took Jessie to school for me and picked her up. Watching Brooklyn work was so soothing that I ended up lying on her couch the whole week. I think it was safe to say I had fallen into a depression.

Noach teased me and said I'd fallen prey to this room just like his wife had, and maybe he was right. It was a very soothing place. It reminded me of the Tea Shop; quiet, spacious, comfortable furniture, and it even had a fireplace. Plus, Brooklyn was like the big sister I never had. She was full of good advice and I liked talking to her.

I'd talked to both Carmen and Summer as well. Of course, after I told her what had happened between Hitta and me, she hung up the phone pissed with her uncle and ready to have a chat with him. But they both assured me that they can hold down the Tea Shop while I mourned the death of my mom and whatnot.

By the end of the week, I'd managed to get off Brooklyn's couch and actually help out around the house, especially since Noach had gone back on the road. In order to run from my reality, I submerged myself into helping with the cooking, cleaning, and trying to keep up with the three youngest boys and the three middle children. We'd taken to calling Jessie, Lyric, and young YermiYah the three amigos.

But do you guys know what hurt the most? In all that time, I had not heard from Hitta. And I know what y'all are going to say. If you wanted to hear from him, why the hell did you leave him? The answer to that is complicated. Yeah, I could no longer be with him after the things that had come to light, but I expected him to at least ask about me or at the very least Jessie and the baby. I talked to Carmen nearly every day on the phone. I've even gone into the Tea Shop a few days and nothing…Not, *my uncle asked about you,* or *he wanted to know where you were,* or even, *what did the doctor say at your last doctor's appointment…?* Nothing! And my pride kept me from asking about him.

Maybe he's moved on. Maybe Shantell had been successful and got her man back. Isn't that what she said she'd come to the Tea Shop to do? Yeah, he said he was excited at the idea of becoming a father, but hadn't he proven himself to be a liar?

I told myself I didn't care, I was prepared to raise my son and Jessie on my own anyway. But it didn't take a blind man to see that something was wrong with me. I'd lost my passion for blending teas. Feeling bad that nearly a month had passed and I'd only gone in to work maybe three times, I'd asked Carmen what she thought about buying me out.

"Hell no!" She shook her head as she continued to file away some things in the cabinet.

"What do you mean, hell no?"

She slammed the file cabinet, turning to look at me. "I mean, *heeeelllll* no! This is your dream. You're going through a little slump right now, but troubles don't last always. Take it from me, I know this to be a fact. Storm clouds are hanging over your head, sis. It's hard for you to see the light right now, but that's okay, that's why you have a bomb-ass partner like me. We hold each other down. When you're weak, I'm strong. And when *I'm* weak, *you'll* be strong."

She pulled me into her arms and held me. "Take a few months off. Have the baby and then see how you feel." She shook her head again. "But I'm not letting you quit." And well, what could I say to that? So, I took her advice and took some time off.

Brooklyn went into labor in my sixth month of pregnancy and it was the most beautiful thing I'd seen. Being the big cry baby that I was, I boohooed the whole time. She'd chosen to have a home birth. Her doula was a woman with long beautiful locs named SaafiYah. She'd showed up with another woman with a head full of brown hair named NuriYah and together, the two of them arranged Noach and Brooklyn's bedroom into something that resembled a spa, with a birthing bath and everything. They dimmed the lights and put on soothing music.

Saafiyah knew her herbs and if I was in a better place in my life, I would have loved to talk to her about some of the things that she used with Brooklyn, but I didn't have the will. The spark that came to life in me whenever herbs, roots, or seeds was around, was not there and it hadn't been there for a long time.

Instead, I tried to be helpful and do whatever Saafiyah needed me to do and surprisingly, it wasn't long before she was urging Brooklyn to push. There was a point when I could tell that she was in a lot of pain, but outside of that, she really made it look doable. I've been trying to deal with the fear of not only having a baby for the first time but having him alone.

I was more than positive that having Noach right there by her side, rubbing her hair, telling her how good she was doing, and how proud he was of her, was a big help. That was something I would not have.

Although I felt like I was dying inside, I continued to smile, not wanting to disrupt their special day in any way. They'd been more than kind to me, treating a perfect stranger like family. I'd moped around their place for the last month and now just wasn't the time. So even if it killed me, I was going to be happy for them.

Right after their son, who they named Jahaziel, made his debut in this world, SaafiYah put him in his mama's arms so that she could hold him while his umbilical cord finished pulsating. Noach wrapped his arms around them both and they just sat that way, drawing strength from each other and giving it to their child.

Dear God, help me! To keep from crying, I busied myself helping SaafiYah and Nuriyah clean up. I took a bundle of towels and linen down to the basement and put them in the washing machine and then headed for the porch, desperately needing air.

But as soon as I opened the door, I heard weeping. Stepping out, I saw NuriYah holding her arm to her eyes crying her heart out.

"Are you okay?"

She jumped, wiping at her eyes. "Oh…yeah, I'm good. I just—" She shook her head. "I just, I'm having a hard time right now. That's all."

I sat on the swing chair. "Yeah, I know what you mean. It's hard to be happy for someone when your heart is in so much pain."

"Yeah, it is…" she whispered before she eased down on the bench next to me. I didn't know what had happened to her to cause her tears and neither did I ask. Instead, the two of us just sat there gently swaying on that swing, lost in our own thoughts. We sat like that until Eliyah popped his head out and told us that SaafiYah needed us.

For the next two months, I took over the running of the house for the most part. SaafiYah insisted that Brooklyn stay inside and rest for the whole two months, but by the end of it, she was ready to be out.

That's when I found out that Noach ran community gardens in

several neighborhoods around the city when he was home. And Brooklyn wanted to go out and play in the dirt. I actually was looking forward to it.

Noach's niece had come by the house to babysit for us, so for the first time, we were without children and it felt kind of nice.

"I think I'm ready to start looking for a place soon," I told Brooklyn as we planted onion bulbs in a grow bed. Noach still didn't want her doing anything too strenuous, so he'd shoved some onion seedlings in her hand and instructed her to do a little light planting and absolutely no lifting.

She looked up startled. "But why? I thought you were going to stay till at least after you have the baby."

I shook my head. "I've taken advantage of you guys' kindness enough. It's time for me and Jessie to move—"

"No! You promised that you would stay until after you had the baby."

I lifted an eyebrow at her. "Did I promise, Brooklyn?"

She chuckled. "Yeah, you did. I insist you stay till after. You going to be a first-time mom. You're going to need some help. Remember, I'm the pro…seven children. Stay, let me help you."

I opened my mouth to say something else to her, but right then, NuriYah walked through the little garden gate.

"Look, there's NuriYah."

Brooklyn turned her head to see where I pointed. She was still a good distance away, but I would recognize that brown hair anywhere.

"Oh, HalleluYah! I'm glad she decided to come back to helping Noach with the gardens." A sad look crossed her face.

"Why, what happened to her? I heard her crying on your porch the night you had the baby."

"I've actually known Nuriyah for a long time. I knew her when her name was Butta Baby."

I frowned. "Butta Baby?"

She nodded. "Mmmhhhmmm… Sticky finger extraordinaire. That girl could steal anything. She could take a man's watch right off his wrist without him knowing it. She was famous in our neighborhood.

When she would come around, the fellas would say *It's just like Butta Baby.*"

"Wow! Obviously she's not like that anymore."

"Of course not, that's Lyon's wife."

She said that like I should know who she's talking about. "Lyon?"

"Oh my goodness. You don't know who Lyon is?"

I shook my head. "Girl, we've got to get you to the Lyon's Den. Sometimes Noach, the children, and I go there on the Shabbat to fellowship with them. But listen, they're having a rough time right now. Their son went missing a few months ago and nobody knows where. So, if she seems sad, that's why. Come on, let me introduce you formally to her. I know you guys barely got a chance to talk the night I went into labor, but y'all have a lot in common. She has a beautiful greenhouse upstairs in the Lyon's Den, I bet you would love it there."

Chapter 25

ANSWERING THE CALL AND RECEIVING THE GIFT

> *What can a brother do for me?*
> *(See he can you help you up when you are down)*
> *What can a brother do for me?*
> *(He can know the wrong to make it right)*
> *What can a brother do for me?*
> *(He can be your eyes when you can't see)*
> *What can a brother do for me?*
> *He can help me be the best man I can be...*
>
> Ginuwine, Case, RL, Tyrese

Hitta

As soon as I walked through the doors of the Lyon's Den, something shifted inside of me. I can't prove it, but I swear, the air inside of here was different. It felt as if my lungs expanded and for the first time in a long time, I was able to breathe. The pressure that had been building inside my head since Angel left me released completely.

I exhaled. As I looked around the empty gym, a feeling of nostalgia settled over me, bringing to memory how much I enjoyed coming here as a kid. I remembered that some days, Lyon would close the gym down to the general public and just keep it open for a few people. It looked like today he'd closed it down to everyone because it was completely empty.

Right when I was getting ready to turn around and leave with the mind to come back another day, the sound of weights being shuffled around came from somewhere on the other side of the ring. I debated whether or not to head that way, being a little nervous about seeing my teacher again after all these years.

What would he think of the man I've become? He'll probably be disappointed. That thought made me want to turn around and walk back out the door, but then I heard the Preacher's voice in my head as clear as day.

"That voice that sounds so much like your own is actually your enemy. Its job is to continue to keep you doubting yourself because it knows the day you realize your value, accept who you are, and what you've been put here to do, is the day it has to slither back to its master and tell him it failed in its mission."

Squaring my shoulders, I headed farther into the gym towards the weight area. The hell if I was going to see an enemy and not try to defeat it. When I didn't know it was there, was one thing, but now that the Preacher helped to bring it to my attention, it was a wrap. I wasn't the kind of mutha f**ka that didn't hunt down my enemies and destroy them, even hidden ones that's lived with me so long, I confused it for a friend.

A 250-pound dumbbell flew across the floor. "Garbage… I don't know why they keep ordering this cheap crap." The grumble came from somewhere down by the bottom of the dumbbell rack.

I smiled. Only one man I know could toss a 250-pound f**king dumbbell like it weighs 2-pounds.

"Lyon?"

"Yo!" A head full of brown dreads popped up from where he'd

been sorting through and arranging the dumbbells on the bottom rack. When he turned to look at me over the rack, I was surprised to see that his beard had begun to gray, and there were a few gray strands of hair around the edges of his head.

I smiled. "Oh man, you got old. Never thought I'd see the day."

He laughed as he jumped to his feet, heading towards me. "Yeah, but I can still kick your butt!"

There was no doubt in my mind. Outside of the gray hairs, there was nothing else about him that resembled what a man his age should look like. This bastard was still ripped. And to show y'all just what I was talking about, the mutha f**ka snatched me off my feet into a bear hug that cut my breath completely off.

"Man, it's good to see you, lil Willie!"

I had to tap his shoulder to get him to release me before I passed out. Chuckling, he dropped me back to my feet.

"Don't know body call me that no mo'…" I gasped, trying to catch my breath. This chump rubbed his hand over my head like I was a shawty.

"Ahhh! You'll always be lil Willie to me." Just a bully. That's what this nigga is… a f**king goon. Although he's aged, I see he still hasn't matured that much.

"Come on over here and have a seat. Tell me what's been going on with you, little brotha!" And then the bastard hit my shoulder so hard, I had to close my eyes and swallow a moan to keep from crying out like a little b*tch.

"I see you still soft as butta," he said as we headed towards one of the tables.

I grinned, not taking his bait. Lyon always talked mad sh*t in the gym. "Naw, you must got me confused with another one of yo' students. I'm the one they call Hard Hitta. Just ask a few of them cats that had to get they jaw rewired after stepping in the ring with me."

Chuckling, he nodded as he settled down in one of the chairs. "Yeah, you looked good in the ring, son. I was proud of you."

I had to hold my head down to hide the huge-ass grin on my face. Having Lyon not only call me son but say he was proud of me was a hell of a compliment.

"What's been going on with you?"

I shook my head. "Man…where do I even begin?"

He chuckled as a knowing look came over his face. "Hey, I don't have nothing to do today. Start at the beginning."

And so I did. I told him about how hard life got for me after G pulled me from under his tutelage. I told him how I immersed myself into boxing, trying to escape my reality. Told him about the headaches that forced me to retire and about meeting Angel, getting married, and finding out that I was going to be a father.

"What??? Lil Willie is going to be somebody's daddy???"

"Come on, Lyon man! Don't nobody call me that no mo'. It's *Hitta*." I grinned. "Hard Hitta to be mo' precise."

He held his head back and barked with laughter. "Boy, I'll call you Hard Hitta the day you knock me on my butt…till then, you'll be lil Willie to me."

I shook my head, I guess I'll be lil Willie then, 'cause trying to knock this dude on his ass was an impossibility. It just can't be done. So, I went on and finished telling him about the things that's been going on with me, including losing Angel and getting a visit from the Preacher. Once I started, I was surprised at how the words just poured from me. I guess I'd been needing someone to talk to. I was still talking as the sun started to set in the sky.

At some point, one of his daughters came down with two plates of food that his wife had sent us. I was so engrossed in what I was telling him, I ate without even paying attention to what the f**k I was eating. I don't think I'd ever talked to nobody like this…not even Rome. The whole time he listened, nodding from time to time. And when the words finally stopped, he looked at me and asked one question that threw me for a loop, 'cause I really didn't have the answer.

"So, what do you want to do now?"

I opened my mouth to answer him but shut it when I realized I had no clue. "I was hoping that you was going to tell me."

He chuckled, "Me? How can I tell you, a grown man what step to take next?"

Well, sh*t, I guess he had a point, but damn, I had hoped he would be able to tell me something.

"What you think I should do next?"

He put his hand on his chest. "Oh, you want my opinion?"

Grinning, I nodded. "Do you think I would have sat here and told you all this sh—" I caught myself before cursing, "stuff if I didn't want yo' opinion?"

He chuckled again. "All right, smart ass. I'm guessing you here because of what the Preacher said to you."

I nodded. "You'd be guessing right."

He sat back in his chair and exhaled. "If you want me to train you, son, you have to understand a few things in the beginning. Learning how to physically fight is only about thirty percent of what takes place here. If you accept this, you must be ready to kill the man you were before you walked through those doors today. Life as you knew it is over. There is a point where you won't be able to unsee what I'm going to show you. So, you must be absolutely positive that this is what you want to do."

"Man, I'm ready to do it. I don't care what it takes. I just—I need to get my girl back. I can make it without her, you know?"

He nodded, "Yeah I do. But if you doing this just to get your wife back, you're going to fail."

I frowned. "What you mean? Why else should I be doing this?"

He sat forward, resting his elbows on his knees as he thought of how best to explain this topic to me.

"Little brotha, there is a force that has made it its mission to destroy everything that is light, your Angel, your child, my NuriYah, my children, everything that causes someone's heart to fill with hope, everything that is love. Its darkness spreads like cancer and it won't be satisfied till everything and everybody is filled with it. There are some out there who are light and if not protected, this darkness will destroy them forever.

We..." he gestured between me and him, "were created to fight that evil. You see, its darkness don't affect us like the innocent ones because our hands are already covered in blood. We were created to war. We fight so that the innocent ones can live the best possible life they can in this dark place. We fight for repentance, in hope that when we go and it's time for us to face our Maker, our good will outweigh all the bad that we've done. We fight to become better men."

"But if you're doing this for any other reason than making a connection with your power, that darkness will defeat you, because you have a weakness. When you know that no matter what, you will stand for the Ancient of Days," he looked me square in the eye, "no-matter-what, then you have no weakness because there is nothing standing between you and your power."

He sat back in his chair, shaking his head. "Man, this thing is so much bigger than you and me. And you need to know walking into this that it ain't gon' be easy. Becoming a warrior for the Most High means being obedient to his Word, no matter what."

For the first time, I saw the sadness that was in him. I'd missed it when we first started talking because I was too wrapped up in my own, but there was something going on with him.

"Everything alright?"

He shook his head. "It's just that. For this walk, I had to do the hardest thing I ever had to do in my life."

"What?"

His gaze came to mine and I may have been imagining it, but it looked as if there were tears in his eyes.

"I had to watch my son walk away, not knowing if I'll ever see him again. The only information I have is that it was the will of the Ancient of Days and I have to be alright with that. I comfort my grieving wife every night, telling her that everything is going to be alright."

Wow! I remember lil Dawid, a miniature version of Lyon. The kid had to be like five or six when I was coming here, but he was the business. He was just a shawty and was taking down grown-ass men. He was so raw that he could never train with us or the other boys that were older than him 'cause he would kick our asses, no questions asked. The only way the kid could get even a little work out was to train with his father's men.

"But the truth is," Lyon continued, "I don't know if my boy is going to make it. I don't know if he will survive whatever journey the

Heavenly Father has seen fit to take him on. I just have to have faith and continue to be obedient to what it is I've been told to do."

"What have you been told to do?"

He didn't speak right away. Instead, he turned his head and looked at his hands that were more scarred than mine.

"My orders are to prepare the warriors that He sends my way for the coming battle. And it don't matter what I've lost, I have to carry them out, no matter what."

The last of his words were spoken so low I barely heard them. His pain was real. Although my wife and unborn son were still here in the city, I understood the feeling of loss.

Reaching over, I put my hand on his shoulder. "I'm sorry to hear about yo' boy, but I know he gon' be alright, 'cause the best warrior I know trained him to be. If God is merciful, I pray to be for my boy what you are for yours. I would be honored if you will train me to be the man that the Ancient of Days want me to be so that I too can be obedient and answer my call and raise my son to do the same."

He reached up and grasped my hand in his. "You sure?"

I nodded. "I ain't been mo' sure about nothing like I am about this."

He grinned. "Alright, little brotha, let's do this."

———

"Hey, daddy." My hand froze on the key that I was using to open the gym door; I turned to see Shantell strutting towards me. I exhaled, in no mood for her bullsh*t. Shaking my head, I thought about what Lyon told me right before I left his place.

"Hey, little brotha, be careful of spiritual attacks. They increase when the enemy knows he's close to losing a soul. Stay watchful, he'll use whoever he can to try and keep you from crossing over." If ever there was a servant of the devil, it's definitely Shantell's ass. Don't know what I ever saw in her.

"What you doing here?" I grumbled when she came to a stop right the f**k on me. Crowding my space like a mutha f**ka.

She licked her glossy lips in a way that said she would rather be licking something else as she ran her hand through her long blonde hair, making sure to show me her nails that no doubt cost a grip to get done.

"I was in the neighborhood and thought to stop by and check on you." She purred her words in a way that used to make my d*ck hard, but now, it just irritated the f**k out of me.

I lifted an eyebrow as I turned the key and opened the door. "At 10 o'clock at night?"

She giggled as she ran her hand up my arm, following me into the empty gym. There was no way I was going to be sleeping at my house that no longer felt like a home without Angel and Jessie. So here I am, back on the f**king couch in my office.

Tomorrow, I was going to begin my training at the Lyon's Den and Lyon told me to try and get some rest because I was going to need it. Sh*t... I was screwed. Thanks to Angel, I couldn't sleep without feeling her weight on my back. So now, I was going to have a night of tossing and turning, only to get my ass handed to me tomorrow 'cause I was too tired to keep up.

"Don't you miss me?"

Damn, just that quick I forgot her ass was even here.

"Naw, I'm good. Happily married." I stopped at the counter and picked up the pile of mail that was left for me.

"If you happy, why you here?"

I didn't respond to her as I looked through my mail. But then she walked behind me and rubbed her hand up my stomach to my chest.

"Mmmmm, I sure missed you."

Turning, I frowned down at her. "What the f**k you doing?"

"Come on, daddy, tell me you don't want to have a little fun. Things got to be pretty boring in the bed with little miss goody-two-shoes. Tell me you don't miss your nasty Shanny."

I chuckled. If this sh*t wasn't so pathetic, I would be hollering laughing right now.

"Naw, nasty, I'm good with my wife. Move around."

A look of shock crossed her face before anger. "That's bullsh*t, Hitta and you know it! She can't make you happy like I can. Just look, one little hiccup and she goes running. I've stuck by your side—"

"What you say?" I asked narrowing my eyes at her.

"I've stuck by yo—"

"Before that."

Realizing she'd f**ked up, she took a step back. I turned to face her fully.

"You said one little hiccup and Angel went running. What you know about it?"

She shook her head. "I don't know nothing about it. I just—"

"How you know Angel gone?"

I took another step towards her. This b*tch is the reason Angel left me. Somehow, this sneaky 'ho been spying on me or some sh*t. I've been racking my brain trying to figure out how and the hell Angel found out something that only my men knew. I know damn well neither of them would have betrayed me.

"Everybody knows."

"Bullsh*t! What the f**k did you tell her?"

She started to shake her head, but I reached out and grabbed her by the throat. Her eyes widened as she clutched the front of my shirt. One twist of the wrist and snaky ass was dead.

"What the f**k did you say to her?" I growled.

She closed her eyes and groaned and I realized the b*tch was turned on. "Please, Hitta, just fu--"

The door to the gym opened. "Unc, there you are. I've been looking all over for you," Carmen said, rushing in toward me. The look on her face said she was 10 degrees past pissed with me.

I let Shantell's neck go. "Get the f**k out of my face. You disgust me!"

She backed up, looking at me with crazy eyes as she rubbed her neck. "That's okay. I'm going to make you see that you really love me and not her!" And then she turned and ran out the door.

"Uh uh!" Carmen screeched giving her the stank eyes as she hurried past her and out the door. "What that crazy b*tch want?" she yelled at me, gesturing toward Shantell's retreating back.

I shrugged. "Carmen, I ain't in the mood to hear yo' mouth."

"Too bad! I talked to Angel. What is wrong with you? You gon make her leave you—"

"Carmen!" I yelled. Her lips snapped shut. I''ve never yelled at her before. "Unc f**ked up! I know it! Just—" I shook my head, trying hard to hold onto my sh*t and not lose it.

"Just yell at me tomorrow, okay?"

She swallowed, for the first time seeing how bad this sh*t was messing me up. And then she nodded before locking the door.

"Yeah, alright. You want to watch yo' fight with Brasco the Russian fiasco?"

I wanted to tell her to go away and just leave me to wallow in my misery alone, but it would just be a waste of time. Now that she knew I was hurt, there will be no getting rid of her.

"Yeah, you go ahead and queue it. I need to holla at Maddox real quick." She nodded and headed to my office. I pulled out my phone. I didn't like the look in Shantell's eyes when she left.

Lannox refused to tell me where he'd taken Angel and Jessie, claiming he's doing it to save my marriage. Over the last 10 years, I'd learned to trust his words. I don't know how he knows the stuff that he does, but he does…

He assured me he was keeping a close eye on them, so I ain't really sweating it. I need to get my sh*t together if I ever stood a chance at getting her back. And by me not knowing where they are, I won't be tempted to go and try and talk her into coming back home.

However, we had a little problem with Shantell. I don't know how much she knows or how the hell she got a hold of the information that she did. But by the week's end, I needed answers to my questions. And I needed Lannox to double down his watch on my family because something in that crazy-ass girl's parting words ain't sitting well with me.

Chapter 26

FULL CIRCLE

> *And we know that all matters work together for good to those who love Elohim, to those who are called according to His purpose.*

Romans 8:28

Angel

Do you guys believe in fate? Like... do you ever wonder why certain things play out the way that they do in our lives? I mean... some things that happen can't be coincidence because they're clearly by design. And the design is too intricate for our brains as human beings to comprehend fully. I've always believed in God, but the events that will happen in my life over the next couple of months will seal my belief and cause me to not only believe, but to open that bible my Greatie got me and act on those beliefs.

I know you guys are wondering what the heck am I going on

about, but just hear me out for a moment and then, I'm going to come back and ask you those questions again. Greatie plucked me up from life as I knew it and plopped me down in the midst of complete strangers. But how did she know that these strangers were going to be food for my soul? These strangers would show me a way of life I never knew existed, but would realize I've been being prepared for it since the first day my Greatie showed up to visit me when I was only a baby.

Over the last couple of months, I learned a lot from the Hathaways. Not only are they an awesome and amazingly loving family, they are also a very spiritual family. I watched them all gather and pray with Noach each time he left the house to go on the road and watched Brooklyn pray with her children each morning and every night. I can now bear witness to the saying that the family that prays together, stays together. From them, I learned the power of prayer.

But it was Butta Baby Larou, a.k.a NuriYah who taught me how to love my husband. It was her who showed me the vital responsibilities a woman who is married to a warrior of the Ancient of Days carried. Shantell poked at me and said I was not cut out to handle a man like Hitta and believe it or not, she was right. I *wasn't* ready to handle a man like Hitta, but after spending time with Butta Baby, I was going to be ready. Settle back in your seats and I'll tell you just how this miracle occurred.

You see, Brooklyn was right that day in the community garden when she said NuriYah and I had a lot in common. We were both married to men that ran and owned a gym, and rare plants, herbs, flowers, and seeds were both of our passion, but due to recent unfortunate events, we'd both lost said passion.

That day in the garden, we started discussing her greenhouse and the things she grew in it quite have half-heartedly at first, but Brooklyn didn't give up. She kept prying till NuriYah invited us back to her place to have lunch and take a tour of her famous greenhouse.

I really wasn't in the mood and I could tell Butta Baby wasn't either, but Brooklyn hit us both with the guilt trip, complaining that she'd been shut in the house for two months and that being around NuriYah's plants was just the thing to help her feel refreshed. So, we both caved and pretended to be happy.

Now, when we got to the Lyon's Den and walked through the doors, I felt like I was hit with a new wind. I inhaled sharply and closed my eyes for a brief moment as it washed over me. The feeling that hit me was the same one I got when I took that first sip of Greatie's tea. When I opened my eyes, both Butta and Brooklyn were watching me with knowing grins on their faces.

"Wow! What was that?" I gasped, the sudden rush causing me to feel a little lightheaded.

The grin on Butta's face grew. "I love to see people experience that for the first time. Welcome to the Lyon's Den, sis." Then she took my hand and pulled me through the gym that was bustling with activity.

"I can't wait for you to see their home, it's like a jungle," Brooklyn said as we walked up several flights of stairs.

As soon as NuriYah opened the door to their duplex, I saw exactly what Brooklyn meant. The first thing you see upon entering their place was a beautiful lemon tree in a huge multi-colored flowerpot.

"Beautiful," I whispered as I followed her through her living room into her kitchen. There were plants everywhere along the way. Brooklyn was right, it looked like a jungle in here. I was so taken by them that I didn't see the huge man standing at the kitchen island drinking something thick and green out of a shaker cup till the last minute and he scared the hell out of me.

"Oh!" I squeaked when I turned around from looking at an exotic vine that grew down the length of the hall to find him standing there. He pretended like I scared him too and jumped before chuckling to himself like he was quite used to folks having that response when they first lay eyes on him.

I blinked, shamelessly staring at the man. What the world?! He looked like he'd been sculpted from granite rock. I mean, dang it! I thought Hitta was big, this man made my husband look fragile.

Butta popped his arm. "Behave. Sis, this is my husband, Lyon. Lyon, this is Brooklyn's cousin, Angel."

I put my hand over my mouth, embarrassed to have been caught staring at her husband like he was on exhibit at a museum or something, but goodness, the man didn't look human!

"Wow! I'm so sorry. I didn't mean to—to…" *Stare at your husband with my mouth hanging open because I'd never seen a man so fierce.* That would be just rude.

NuriYah waved away my concern. "No worries, sis, I'm used to it."

Lyon must have been too because he didn't seem to notice me standing here at all scrutinizing him. Instead, he seemed to be thinking hard about something.

"What's wrong with you?" Butta asked him.

"I feel like I just heard the name Angel from somewhere." He thought for another minute before shaking his head. "It'll come back to me. Shalom, little sista, nice to meet you. Shalom B."

Brooklyn grinned. "What's going on, big bro?"

He shook his head. "Not a thing. Congratulations on the new warrior. How many does that make for y'all now, 10?"

She narrowed her eyes at him. "Hahaha...very funny."

He chuckled winking at her. Then he held up a pitcher full of that guck he was drinking. "Can I offer you ladies a cup?" Both Butta and Brooklyn made the yuck face before shaking their heads, my tongue was tied, I'd still not gotten over the initial shock of meeting him. No wonder Brooklyn responded like she did when I told her I'd never seen him.

"Why are you always trying to share that crap with our guests?" NuriYah admonished her husband.

He leaned in and kissed her cheek. "Forgive me for trying to share a healthy and tasty beverage with my lovely wife and her friends. I'm out of here, I know where I'm not wanted." With his pitcher and shaker cup still in hand, he exited the kitchen.

Something shifted in the corner, drawing my attention. A scream of horror froze in my throat when the biggest freaking lion I have ever seen gracefully came to its feet from where it had sat quietly resting in the corner watching us, and regally followed the man out of the kitchen.

Brooklyn collapsed in laughter against the island as she pointed to me. "And I love to see folks face the first time they meet King."

"Brooklyn, dang it! Why didn't you warn her about King?" Butta admonished as she hurried to me and helped me ease down into a chair.

"Oh my God! That was a- that was a…" My system had taken too many shocks within the last ten minutes. Shucks, I'd never came down from the rush of walking through the front door of this place.

Where the heck was I? Nothing here felt real, Butta's husband, his pet freaking lion, and the plants that she was growing that were only supposed to be able to grow in the African jungle.

Needless to say, it took me a little while to get used to things. Luckily, Lyon and his pet had gone back to the gym and I didn't have them imposing on my senses, so that made it a bit easier. Well…that and NuriYah's greenhouse. It was truly a jewel in the heart of the ghetto. It reminded me of the Garfield Park Conservatory, one of my favorite places to go and visit.

When I told Butta that, she got super animated and told me how it was her favorite place and that she had in fact designed her greenhouse after it on a smaller scale. One thing led to another and before either of us knew it, we were involved in an in-depth conversation about an herb that she was growing that only grew in Tibet. I excitedly told her how I'd just come from Tibet and had brought back some seeds for the male plant of this exact herb.

She told me I had to bring her some of the seeds, promising to grow the herb for the Tea Shop if I would. Of course, I was all over that. I wanted to leave and go to the shop and grab the seeds right then but was forced to wait till the next day because Brooklyn had been away from baby Jahaziel for too long and was already missing him.

I came back to the Lyon's Den on the bus the next day by myself with the seeds after I got Jessie to her school bus. Instead of NuriYah showing me around her greenhouse, she followed me as I took a pinch of this, a sprig of that, and a few other items to make her a cup of tea.

"You remind me so much of SaafiYah. When she gets back from the D.R., you guys have to hook up."

"SaafiYah was Brooklyn's doula, right?"

Butta nodded. "Yeah, the Most High has blessed her hands with the herbs as well, but where he's blessed you with the gift to make teas, he blessed her with the gift to make medicines for healing the body."

I sipped my tea, thinking about her words. "Do you think I have a gift from God?"

"Absolutely!" She held up her teacup. "I told you I had a toothache and you went in there and went shopping in my garden and whipped me up a cup of relief. That's exactly what SaafiYah does. She says the plants light up for her."

My hand flew to my mouth as I gasped. Oh my God! That's exactly what happens for me. I never thought about it like that because it's always happened. It's like the ingredients I should use in whatever tea I'm making for whoever I'm making it for stands out. Everything else looks dull. Butta grinned at me nodding.

"See? A gift from on high."

I returned her smile. "I guess you're right. I never looked at it that way."

That day, she and I ended up talking for hours, all the way till it was time for me to go pick up Jessie. Our conversation was so good that she borrowed the keys to her husband's truck to take me to meet Jessie at her bus so that we could keep talking.

When we got back to Brooklyn's, she came in and we ended up in the sewing room, continuing our conversation over another cup of tea while Brooklyn worked on her latest masterpiece. When I tell you that I and NuriYah had so much in common, I mean we really did.

Her mom was a drug addict like mine. Her stepfather figure was a predator that had tried to have an inappropriate relationship with her. Lyon had come into her life much like Hitta had come into mine. Only she'd been the one to try and steal from him, and it was my brother that stole from Hitta. And get this…She'd left her husband for three years after he had mistakenly killed her mom.

Isn't that wild? Hitta didn't kill my mom, but he knew she was dead and didn't say anything to me. It still hurt just as badly. However, Butta went on to tell me about her son Dawid and how she knew that when he was just a baby, he was going to grow up and be a great warrior like his dad. As she talked about her loss, her pain became mine. I wanted to comfort her, but I'd never lost a child, so I didn't know where to begin.

She and Lyon also had two beautiful daughters who she had to continue to live for, but it was taking all the strength she had to do that. I'd met her youngest daughter, Ginayah, who was sixteen. She worked in the greenhouse with her mom and liked to talk herbs with us. I was actually quite impressed with her knowledge.

Butta's older daughter, Anatiyah, who they all called Ty, had not come out of her room much the whole time I was there. There was something wrong with her that the family wasn't talking about and since they didn't volunteer the information, I didn't pry.

But then something happened. Two weeks later, I was doing a little shopping in Butta's greenhouse for the Tea Shop when a loud commotion took place over my head.

"You need to get out of the bathroom! You act like you're the only one that has to use it!" Ginayah yelled.

I couldn't hear Ty's response because it was muffled, but she yelled something back to her sister. Butta was on her knees not too far from me digging up a bulb or something when she paused to look up toward the ceiling.

"Here we go…" she muttered.

"If you had treated Monroe better while he was here, you wouldn't have to mope around like you've lost your best friend. You should have been a better person instead of making everybody's life miserable!" Gina yelled.

There was a loud bang as the bathroom door was thrown open and the sound of running feet across the floor and down the stairs.

"Ma, help me! She trying to kill me!" Gina yelled as she ran around one of NuriYah's garden beds and flew past us and out the door. Right behind her, hot on her tail, was a younger version of Butta Baby. Her long brown braids flew behind her as she leaped over the same box her little sister ran around, displaying incredible athletic ability. Wow! She was simply beautiful. And yes, ready to kill her sister.

NuriYah jumped to her feet and hurried after them. "I'll be right back, sis. Ty, don't you hit that girl!" she yelled before she too disappeared out the door.

Chuckling, I shook my head as I continued to look around the greenhouse for some things that I'd like to try. Against the far wall was a tiny window that was low to the ground. Butta said Lyon put it there so that he could look up and see her from time to time while in the gym. I peeped out of it as I broke off a piece of lavender and popped it in my mouth, but my hand froze midway.

Standing there in the center of the ring facing Lyon was Hitta.

"Wha??" Afraid my eyes were playing tricks on me, I stepped over the grow bed so that I could get a better look and sure enough, my husband and another man stood there listening intently as Lyon explained something to them before hunching low, demonstrating the hold he was teaching them.

I put my hand on my belly as my son chose that exact moment to deliver a big kick. Tears came to my eyes; I couldn't believe what I was seeing.

"Okay, I'm sorry about that," Butta said coming back into the greenhouse. "My eldest daughter is driving us all crazy—" Her words died off. "Sis, you okay?" she asked when she saw I was standing there with tears in my eyes.

I pointed out the little window. "That's my husband."

"What?! Really?" She stepped over the garden bed joining me. "Lil Willie's your husband?" The name she called him caught me off guard at first. Never heard anybody refer to Hitta as *Little* anything, but then I remembered that Hitta said when he was younger, folks called him Willie.

"Wow! What are the odds? He's been coming here training with Lyon for a little over two months now."

My mouth dropped. "Are you kidding me?"

She shook her head with an astonished grin on her face. "No, I kid you not. Your husband has been here this whole time."

I turned back to look at Hitta and my gaze thirstily drank him in. He stood in the center of the ring shirtless, looking so good. I'd missed him so much. I'd told Butta the other day that I believed he'd gone back to his ex, which was why I hadn't heard from him. And here she was telling me that he'd been here this whole time.

"When you say whole time?"

"I mean, he's been here damn near every day for the last two months, including the shabbats. Lyon is training two of them right now, Willie and his friend, Kaleb." She pointed to the other man in the ring. "I feed them lunch every day."

I put my hand on my chest as I watched Kaleb and Hitta face each other and begin to grapple. But Lyon angrily stopped them and yelled at them both before demonstrating the hold he wanted them to do again.

"Girl, I wish you would have told me your husband was Lil Willie. No wonder y'all having a hard time. He's been chosen by the Most High…" She shook her head. "Sis, I could have helped you out a long time ago."

I sat down in the little stool that was there before I fell down. My knees felt weak and it wasn't just because I'd gained an extra thirty pounds either.

"Haven't you wondered why I forgave Lyon for killing my mom?" she asked as she went back to work on those bulbs.

"Yeah, I did, but I didn't want to be nosy…you know."

She chuckled. "It wasn't easy, I'll tell you that. I needed a little help."

"What kind of help?"

She sat back on her heels and looked over at me. "If I told you, you won't believe me."

I gave her the *really* look. "So, you remember how Brooklyn and I told you we were cousins?" She nodded. "Well, we're like cousins five times removed or something like that. And get this… So is Noach, because he's one of Greatie's children too."

"Wait, so Brooklyn and her ish are cousins?" I nodded. Now it was her giving me the *really* look.

So, I went on to explain how it was and after I was finished, she had a look of amazement on her face.

"Wow, so there really are others out there like the Preacher." She laughed. "In that case, me and Lyon are cousins too; we both came from the Preacher's bloodline."

"You know the Preacher? Greatie told me Hitta was one of his children too!"

"Oh yeah…" Then she went on to tell me how she knew the

Preacher and she helped me understand a little more about the mysterious man.

Needless to say, after sharing those odd stories, she felt more comfortable telling me about who helped her to be able to forgive Lyon for killing her mom.

"An angel came to visit me."

Wow! I was not expecting her to say that, but okay, we've started this journey, might as well walk it out.

"He told me that my son was going to need his father. And then he explained to me what a warrior of Yah is."

"What are they?"

She chuckled. "Rough, bossy, hard…" Her gaze came to mine and the smile left her face. "Destroyers of evil."

This was almost exactly what Lannox had told me through the Preacher.

"What does that mean?"

"It mean they kill, sis. They're not like regular people. They're demon slayers, natural born killers. It comes easy to them."

"How are you alright with that?"

"I've never seen Lyon kill anyone who didn't deserve it."

"But your mom?"

"The angel helped me to see that all things worked together for the good for those whose trust is in Yah. My mother had died years before that day. Her body was just a shell being inhabited by foul beings and her time had come. The angel also showed me what would have happened if by some chance she had not died that day. She would have corrupted my children and I would have a whole other set of problems. It's like cause and effect. The Most High removes obstacles from our path before we know they're a problem."

"It's an intricate web, but Yah knows every grain and every detail. Nobody dies unless it is His will and nobody lives unless it is His will. To love a man like your husband and mine is to understand that they are weapons in the hands of the Heavenly Father and have been chosen to clean the earth of some of its most vile evils. That is a hard job that nobody wants to do. But we've," she gestured between me and her, "we've been chosen to be their comfort because even Yah's weapons of war need comfort sometimes. And I've learned to cherish those moments."

She smiled. "Do you know even till this day whenever my husband gets sick, he refuses to feed himself. He likes for me to sit on the bed and spoon feed him."

My mouth dropped... "Noooooo!" No way that fierce mountain of a man liked to be spoon-fed.

She nodded chuckling. "Yes, girl. He is the deadliest man I know, but he can also be the biggest kid. He gets in these moods and he wants to play." Her chuckling turned into laughter. "Sometimes he can be as immature as the children. And... I love that about him."

As she continued to talk, I thought about the way Hitta gets with his headaches. It's true, he did turn into a big baby. And yeah... I did love that about him. In fact, he never showed me the side of him that Stan saw. I didn't even know it existed.

I missed seeing him and Jessie going at it at the PlayStation and him doing something like reaching over and covering her eyes with his big hand, making her lose. She would get so mad at him she would jump up and try to beat him to death and he'd just laugh while teasing her. Then there was the time he decided he was going to teach me how to box because he said I hit like a girl. We went down to the basement and he tried to do just that, but he was such a horny man, we didn't make it far before he was pulling me into the laundry room, locking the door behind us.

Dang, I missed him so much... I know, I'm pathetic, right? Anyway, I asked NuriYah if she didn't mind if I sat there and watched him for a little while.

"Girl naw, take all the time you need. Mi casa es su casa."

"Can you do me a favor and not tell him I'm here? Can you tell Lyon not to mention anything as well?"

She nodded before a devious grin came on her face. "Soooo, you want to spy on him?" She might as well be rubbing her hands together while laughing sinisterly. I see Lyon was not the only immature parent around these parts.

God, I would have loved to have had them for parents. Chuckling, I nodded my head. "Yeah, I guess."

"That sounds like a good idea to me. You can watch Lyon abuse those poor fellas." She shook her head. "I don't know how they put up with it. Anyway, just call me if you need something, I'll be in the kitchen starting dinner."

Now, before y'all get on me and tell me my pathetic level has grown to an all-time high, I just want to say. . . I don't care.

I miss him! And although I have to be strong and not cave in, there are no rules that say I can't do a little spying. Right? Right…

And so, a new hobby for me was born. For the next month and a half, I sat here on this stool and watched my husband. Butta and Lyon were both onboard and they fed me and oh my goodness, NuriYah was always bringing me a plate of some goodness, mac and cheese, fried chicken, sweet potatoes, greens, fried okra…

Even Lyon had gotten in on it. She wasn't lying, he was a big kid. Once while I was here spying, I was completely enthralled by what I was seeing. Hitta was down there sitting at the table studying the Bible with Kaleb. They were so engrossed in their conversation that they didn't even notice that the gym had all but emptied. And I was so engrossed in watching him that I didn't hear or see Lyon come up next to me until he spoke, scaring the heck out of me.

"Boo!"

I cried out, clutching at my chest. "Dang it! Don't do that! You're going to give me a freaking heart attack!"

He was laughing at me so good he had to hold onto the wall to keep from tipping into his wife's lavender bed.

"You shouldn't be so jumpy…" he said around his laughter.

"And you shouldn't be so dang on big!" I'm glad he found the fact that he's scared ten years off my life funny. I didn't find it funny at all. His big cat sat at the door with his mouth open in a way that made it look like he too was laughing at me.

What the world?!

"I'm sorry, I didn't mean to scare you. I made some protein patties and I come to offer you some. My wife said we should make sure we feed you every hour." He held out a plate of what looked like smashed fried poop.

His statement made me laugh though. He made it sound as if I was the family pet. No wonder GinaYah was always offering me another snack and my fat self ate it every time. I eyeballed the plate he held.

"What is it?"

"Protein patties."

I shrugged and reached in and grabbed one. I don't know what was wrong with me. I felt hungry all the time. The baby was due next month, but I felt like I was fifteen months pregnant.

Surprisingly, Lyon's little poop looking patties tasted good. Kind of taste like grainy pancakes.

"You must think I'm a fat pig," I told him as I helped myself to another one of his snacks. He was popping them in his mouth whole, at least I was taking bites.

He shook his head. "Naw, you good. My wife out ate me with each of her pregnancies. It's why she keeps feeding you. She remembers what it was like."

Awww shucks... That brought a smile to my face. The more I got to know Lyon, the more I wondered how I could have been so afraid of him when I first met him. He was kind of goofy in a way. The hardest I laughed in a while was because of him. I'll tell you guys what he did.

It was one day when the gym was empty except for him, Hitta, and a few of his men. They all stood in the ring watching as Lyon instructed Hitta on some fighting technique. He was yelling at him about something or another, but then behind his back, he gestured for me to slide the window open so that I could hear.

"How you gon' get your wife back and you can't land a proper blow?" I heard him yell.

Hitta growled and came at Lyon again, but the older man just moved to the side and shoved him to the floor like he was a little boy.

"Look at you, man. You must don't really want your girl back. You been in here talking crap about doing this to make your wife proud of you. Look at you. You don't want her back."

"I *do* want her back..." Hitta growled jumping up from the floor breathing heavily, reminding me of a little brother that had enough of his older brother picking on him and was ready for vengeance. He was so mad it looked like fire was going to come from his nose. He let out a loud roar and charged Lyon again.

I put my hand over my mouth to stifle a scream when Lyon did a maneuver where he suddenly dipped to the side before grabbing Hitta and bringing him over his head to slam him hard to the ground. And as my poor husband lay there, probably wondering if any of his bones were broken, his teacher stood over him shaking his head.

"I guess you gon' be single."

"No, I'm not!" Hitta yelled up at him from where he still lay on his back.

"Why is that?"

"Because I'm going to get my wife back."

Lyon put his hand to his ear. "What did you say? Your voice was so whiney it was hard to understand."

"I'M GON' GET MY WIFE BACK!" Hitta yelled louder than I ever heard him. He was so angry.

Lyon turned to face me and winked, holding up his thumb. But just then, Hitta jumped to his feet and when Lyon turned around, he hit him with a right hook that would have shattered a normal man's jaw. It took Lyon clean off his feet.

For just a moment, my husband stood there staring down at his teacher in complete shock. Even *he* could not believe what he did. Lyon sat up rubbing his jaw with a grin on his face.

"You sneaky bastard!"

Hitta laughed. "Naw, bro…What's my name?!!!!" he yelled down at him, so full of adrenaline from what he'd done he could barely contain it. "Come on, man! A deal is a deal!"

Still sitting on his butt, Lyon chuckled, looking around as most of his men came closer to the ring, laughing in astonishment. They couldn't believe Hitta had actually landed a blow that took the infamous warrior off his feet.

With a grin on his face, Lyon looked up and muttered something that nobody could hear. Hitta put his hand to his ear.

"What you say? I couldn't hear you!"

"I said!" Lyon spoke louder. "That was a good one, *Hard Hitta*!" My husband was practically jumping up and down he was so geeked.

"But when I get up—" he continued, "you better not be standing here." Then he jumped to his feet and without missing a beat, Hitta turned and jumped out of the ring. I had to hold my hand over my mouth so that they couldn't hear me laughing. I didn't know my husband could run so fast. Lyon chased him around the whole gym before Hitta slipped out the door.

Oh, y'all! I laughed so hard at that, NuriYah feared I was going to go into early labor. Anyway, over these last couple of weeks of spying on my husband, I got to know a side of him I had no clue existed. Every day, he brought his bible to the Lyon's Den with him. And I don't know if he's doing it on purpose or what, but Lyon would talk to him at the table right under the window so that I could hear their conversation clearly. Hitta asked Lyon questions about things he'd read in the Scriptures the night before, which meant he was going home reading it on his own.

And Lyon or another very handsome older gentleman named Solomon would talk to him and Kaleb, teaching them the Way. Lyon told him the Scriptures were a sword that was more deadly than any sword made by the hands of man because it cut coming and going.

But speaking of swords, did you guys know that Hitta knew how to work a sword? I'm talking about the metal kind. Yeah, me either... But he did. Apparently, Lyon had started teaching him when he was only a boy. When his teacher asked him if he remembered how to wield one, he told him a little. Lyon told him to show him before handing him his sword and then he proceeded to wow the heck out of me because for a guy that remembers a little, it looked damn impressive to me. Lyon grabbed another sword and they spent the rest of the day training with them.

Can y'all believe that? Hmmmm... Amazing, right?

Anyway, seeing my husband reading his bible so faithfully inspired me to read mine. Even though he couldn't see me, I wanted to go on this journey with him, so I asked Lyon what exactly he was reading in it. For a minute, he looked at me as if he didn't understand my question.

"Is there a certain topic he's studying?"

Understanding settled over his face. "Naw, little sista. He's allowing the Teacher to guide him. He's started from the beginning, Genesis 1:1."

"The Teacher?" I asked.

He nodded. "When you go home tonight, read John 14:26…Pray that your mind is opened to understand it. And then open your scriptures to the beginning and join your husband in his journey."

I nodded before I dug in my purse for a piece of paper to write down the scripture he told me to read. Then I hugged NuriYah goodbye and took the train to the Tea Shop to get the bible Greatie had given me all those years ago. I felt excited to join my husband in this, even if he didn't know that I was.

While I was at the shop, I took the time to catch up with my girls, Summer and Carmen. Since spending time at the Lyon's Den talking plants with NuriYah, I've been inspired and have come to the shop a few times over the last month or so to trade out herbs and add new things from Nuri's garden.

"Girl, you look like you're ready to pop!" Carmen said as she rubbed my belly before putting her face next to it. "I can't wait to spoil you, lil cuz."

I laughed just as the bell dinged on the door. Looking up, I saw a handsome man in a very nice suit walk through it, my gaze went back to Carmen, but then my eyes flew up again.

"Westly!"

Oh my God! It was Westly, looking like the handsome man I remembered him to be before he got hooked on drugs! His cheeks were fuller and there were no more sores on his face and neck.

Thank you, Heavenly Father!

I haven't seen him looking this healthy in years. Tears came to my eyes as I slowly approached him.

"Wha?!?!?" I was at a loss for words.

He opened his arms. "Hey, baby girl…"

Being careful of my stomach, I threw myself into his arms. For the first time in a long time, he didn't stagger from my weight, although I was thirty plus pounds heavier than the last time we hugged.

Astonished, I stepped back to get a better view of him. I couldn't believe what I was seeing. "Look at you!"

He chuckled. "Look at *you*, when is the baby due?"

"In another three weeks...but wait! Enough about me! What happened to you?" He looked so good... and *sober*.

"I dried out."

"Oh, that's wonderful!" Not being able to help myself because my heart was full, I threw my arms around him again.

"I'm so proud of you!" My words were barely legible because I was crying like a baby. "How long has it been?"

He chuckled. "I haven't touched anything since that night at the gym."

I took his hand and led him over to the couch because a group of customers walked through the door. Over here, we would have a little privacy.

"What happened?" I asked as we sat.

He didn't respond right away, he just shook his head a bit. "Let's just say, your husband beat some sense into me and then put me in rehab."

I clutched his arm. "Hitta did this?!"

He nodded. "Yeah, he did. I thought he was going to kill me that night. He beat me so bad I couldn't stand. When he raised his fist to drop the blow that I knew would kill me, I just started begging for my life. I told him I wanted to live. And he told me to prove it before dropping me off with broken ribs, a sprained ankle, and a fractured wrist to this expensive ass rehab. His parting words to me was that he'd paid a lot of money to know the minute I tried to leave the hospital before they released me and that he will be waiting for me on the outside to finish the job."

"Wow! I'm sorry it was so—"

He shook his head cutting me off. "Naw, Angel, it was just what I needed. Without that added fear, and not being able to move, I would have never gone through with it. It was the hardest thing I've ever done. Although it was a really nice facility, it still felt like a prison. My brother-in-law obviously didn't spare any expense. If my ribs weren't cracked and my foot wasn't in a cast, I would have found a way out of there. But I physically couldn't move." He chuckled. "That joker did a number on me."

Reaching over, he dried away my tears. "He saved my life by forcing me to stay still long enough to get over the hump."

I nodded, but I couldn't speak, because I was overcome with emotion. I was falling in love with my husband all over again, and he didn't even know it. Westly and I talked until it was time for me to meet Jessie at her bus.

"Do you want to see Jessie?" I asked.

He grabbed my hand. "No, not yet. I want to be a hundred percent when I see her again."

I squeezed his hand because his words frightened me. "Where are you going?"

Reaching up, he gently pushed my braid behind my ear. "Your husband's generosity didn't end with rehab and this suit. His assistant found a place for me in Virginia. It's kind of like a halfway house for newly dried out addicts. I've signed up for a year."

"Really?"

He nodded. "They have counselors and job training. It's a safe environment to live until I get stronger, you know."

I nodded. "Yeah! That sounds like an awesome idea."

He leaned in and kissed my head. "I'm sorry for letting you down so many times."

"You didn't," I muttered using my arm to wipe away some of the tears that were spilling from my eyes. Ugggh! I'm such a crybaby!

"You take care of yourself, baby girl." He paused for a moment. "And tell your husband-- Tell him, I said thank you." And then he was gone.

Oh, guys! It took me a minute to get myself together after that. I picked Jessie up from her bus and I boohooed the whole train ride back to Brooklyn's. My poor cousin didn't know what to do because my tears were bittersweet, sweet because my brother was finally clean. This had been a ten-year struggle and finally, he was on the road to recovery. And it was bitter because I had my husband to thank for it.

He'd told me he was not going to change for me, but look, he was changing, and I didn't know what to do. I couldn't just walk back up to him and say let's try and work this out again, because I really want you to be in our lives. We'd gone through too much for that. So now, I had to be satisfied with spying on him from NuriYah's greenhouse, at least that's what I thought at the time.

But then, something happened; the miracles didn't stop. Two weeks later, I took Jessie and Lyric with me to the Lyon's Den. I figured they could hang out with Gina, who seemed to be pretty good with children while I did my spying.

I got my little area all set up and settled in with a nice fruit smoothie that Butta handed to me when I walked in. I've been timing my arrival till right before my husband comes. Today, he wasn't dressed for a workout, which meant it was going to be one of his study days. I was just getting out my bible because I planned on studying right along with him when I heard--

"Unc, it's you!"

I nearly wasted the smoothie as I struggled to right myself after the sound of Jessie's loud voice downstairs in the gym nearly sent me toppling off my little stool.

Chapter 27

SHOW ME WARRIOR

> *Your Word is Love, But You Push Me Away, and Won't Say Why*
> *You Show Me Your Exterior; I Need To See Your Interior*
> *I Need To Be Absolutely Clear With Ya If We Are To Ever Stand A Chance*
> *It's The Last Dance; Don't You See?*
> *Show Me The Warrior You're Born To Be...*

Jill Scott

Angel

"Oh no! Oh no!" I cried when I saw her and Lyric run across the gym toward Hitta.

His head jerked up when he heard her voice. When he saw her racing toward him, he jumped up from his chair and ran toward her.

She leaped in his arms and he nearly crushed her; he was so happy to see her.

"Jess! What you doing here?"

I couldn't hear what she said to him, but my heart nearly stopped when she pointed up toward the window. I dipped back just in time for him to miss me before hurrying out the greenhouse to find Butta in the kitchen.

"Oh my God! You have to help me! He knows! He knows!" I was freaking out.

"Chile, calm down before you go into labor! Who knows what?" She asked, drying her hands on her dishtowel before hurrying to me, clearly worried.

"Hitta! Jessie and Lyric went downstairs!"

"Oh yeah, sorry about that! I meant to warn you that Lyric loves being down there with the warriors. She's like my Ty, it makes sense that she would want to take Jessie down there and show off a bit."

"Butta!" I cried, clutching her arms.

Her eyes widened in amused horror. "What! I said I was sorry!"

"Sorry?! What am I supposed to do now? He's probably on his way up here!" Her gaze settled on something behind me and my heart sank as the hairs on the back of my neck stood.

"He's behind me, isn't he?" I whispered.

She slowly nodded, the sympathetic grin still on her face. "Hey, Willie! How is everything?"

I pressed my lips together, too afraid to turn around. I just wanted the floor to open up and swallow me.

"Real good, Mrs. Nuri. How things with you?" I closed my eyes as that deep voice washed over me. Goodness, I think I missed that baritone the most.

NuriYah nodded her head. "Everything is good. Thank you so much for asking. You are a real sweetheart."

And then came that awkward silence. I just stood there still clutching Butta's arms, staring into her face. Her gaze came to mine and I could see that she was fighting to hold on to her laughter.

"Ummm, I take it you know Angel?"

Hitta chuckled. "Yeah, I know her... How you doing, Teacup?"

I inhaled as Butta and my eyes connected one more time. Still trying to hold on to her laughter, she leaned a little closer.

"I just want to thank you. Having you around has made these days a little easier for me. I've rediscovered my passion for growing things. And it was because of you. Now be a big girl and turn around and greet your man."

Dear God, give me the strength. I turned with a smile on my face. "Good! I'm good…How are you?"

He didn't speak right away. He just stood there letting his eyes rake over me. Feeling self-conscious, I lifted my hand to check and make sure I didn't have a braid that had decided to go rogue or anything, but NuriYah, who still stood behind me grabbed my hand, preventing it.

"You look as cute as a little pregnant button," she muttered so that only I could hear her.

"Wow! You look good." He finally spoke and I exhaled a breath I hadn't been aware of holding. Now don't get me wrong, you guys have to know I'd taken special care of the way I dressed, knowing I was going to be in the same facilities as my husband. But I was still worried because my stomach had gotten considerably bigger since the last time he saw me.

"Tee-Tee, I brought Unc up here to say hi to you. I told him you missed him so much you was sitting in that window, watching him all the time," Jessie said from where she stood next to him holding his hand.

I closed my eyes and groaned just as I heard a choking noise coming from behind me. Because she still stood so close, I could feel NuriYah's body jerking with silent laughter. When I opened my eyes again, Hitta wore a knowing smile on his face.

"Thank you for that, Jessie," I told her through tight lips, still wearing that forced smile. "Why don't you run along and tell Lyric we're getting ready to head out?" She nodded and skipped away, completely clueless to the fact that she had just sold me down the river.

Embarrassed was not descriptive enough to describe how I felt right now. I turned to face Butta and when she saw the agony in my eyes, she blew. She was laughing so hard she had to turn her back to get herself together. When she turned back around, trying to hold her laughter in, she failed miserably because her body kept jerking as those choking noises continued to escape her throat. *If I could just get out of here, I can die on the train.*

"Thank you so much for the smoothie. I will call you when I make it to the house."

Still trying to suppress her laughter, she nodded. "Okay... you be safe out there," she managed to get out before she had to turn around and pretend to be doing something on the counter. Her shaking shoulders told us exactly what she was doing.

When I turned and my gaze fell back on Hitta, he stood looking down at the floor, rubbing his head, trying to suppress his own laughter.

Goodness! I just needed to make it through those doors and I was free. "It was good seeing you again," I told him with as much dignity as I could muster.

"Yeah, it was good to see you too." As I headed toward the door, he fell into step next to me and then Butta Baby Larou decided to drill the final nail in my coffin.

"You guys be safe on that train. Gets kind of dangerous out there when the sun starts to set."

My steps came to a halt as I whipped back around to stare at her. *Why sis?! Why would you say that in front of my overprotective husband that I was desperately trying to escape right now?*

With a devious grin on her face, she waved before making the phone signal by her ear. "Call me!"

"Okay!" I said back with a big fake smile before turning and hurrying down the stairs. I was moving so fast I was practically running.

"Hey, Angel...Angel." Hitta said, catching my arm when I got to the bottom of the stairs. "I was wondering if maybe you'll let me give you a lift."

Okay! Who was this man? And what the heck did he do with my husband? *He was wondering if maybe I'll let him give me a lift?* Not, *hey woman, get in the truck, no way am I letting you take the train by yourself.*

I tucked my braid that had fallen in my face behind my ear. "Ummm…Okay."

WHAT???? Did you just say okay? Are you nuts?!!!

"Come on, girls," I said gesturing for Lyric and Jessie to take my hand. When I turned back toward the ring, I caught Lyon giving Hitta the thumbs up while winking at him. Suddenly I wondered how much of this was coincidence and how much of this was NuriYah and Lyon butting their mischievous noses in my business. But I had no time to ponder it because after we walked out the door, the realization that I was getting ready to be closed in a vehicle with my husband settled on me like a weight, and all of a sudden, I was super nervous.

However, having Jessie and Lyric there, who were taking turns telling Hitta about something or another, made it a little easier. I was able to study him as we walked toward his truck unnoticed.

Goodness, he looked and smelled so good. Both NuriYah and Brooklyn told me that when they got to the end of their pregnancy and wanted to encourage labor, they had some alone time with their husbands—

Oh wow! Where had my mind just gone? *To a place it hasn't been in months and was long overdue for a visit.*

When we got to the truck, Jessie and Lyric climbed in the back. Hitta opened the passenger door for me and a startled chuckle escaped my lips when I saw a step extend from it.

"Oh! You got the step…" I gasped.

He chuckled. "Yeah, but now I wish I hadn't."

"Why?"

"Because now, I don't have the excuse to pick you up and put you in the truck."

That made me laugh. "Lucky for you. You saved your back, I'm so fat—oh!" I cried out when he suddenly scooped me up in his arms. "Goodness!" My hands came to rest on his shoulders and I was reminded about how big and strong they are.

He grinned as he stood there holding me. "You were saying?"

"Ummm…" I shook my head, drowning in his intense gaze. I don't know what the hell I was saying. He took his time and settled me on the seat, the whole time, he held my gaze.

"I see you still short," he muttered without stepping back. His lips were only inches from mine.

I opened my mouth in feigned shock. "You can't call people short anymore."

Biting his bottom lip as he stared at mine, he chuckled. "And why not?"

"It's still politically incorrect." I licked my lips, wondering if he was getting ready to steal a kiss like he did the first time we played out this scene. Although it looked like he was going to do just that, he didn't, instead, he reached over and fastened my seatbelt.

"Forgive me. I don't want to offend." Then he stepped back and shut the door.

What—the—heck?! I turned to look wide-eyed at Jessie and she just shrugged before muttering. "Maybe he changed."

"Yeah, maybe he has."

The drive back to Brooklyn's place was not as awkward as I thought it was going to be. In fact, thanks to Jessie and Lyric, it was quite animated. The two of them competed for Hitta's attention and was hilarious doing it.

I was surprised to see that he didn't know where I lived and needed me to give him directions. When we pulled up, Jessie and Lyric jumped out of the truck and ran into the house. Hitta came around and opened my door before helping me out.

"It was really good seeing you today," he told me as he stared down at me with that gaze that made me feel as if he could to see into my very soul.

"About what Jessie said back at the Lyon Den-" He shook his head cutting me off.

"No worries, Teacup. It's all good."

"Hitta! My man!" Noach's booming voice came as he walked down the stairs toward us.

Hitta turned to look and smiled when he saw him. "Hey shalom, ach!" he said before greeting him with that one-sided hug men did.

"Do you know all this time I didn't know that it was your wife that my wife was hiding here in our guest bedroom?"

"Wait a minute, you guys know each other?"

413

Noach nodded. "Yeah, I've hung out with this young brotha a time or two at the Lyon's Den. I was telling him he one of my all-time favorite fighters. Hey man, you want to stay for dinner?"

Hitta's gaze came to mine. "If it's okay with Angel."

Wow! Who is this man?

I nodded, waving my hand like it was no big deal. "Sure, of course."

"Beautiful!" Noach said wrapping his arm around his shoulder guiding him toward the house. "Man, I can't wait to show you this pair of boxing gloves my granddaddy gave to me. He said Ali gave them to him right after his fight with Joe Frasier."

"What?" Hitta asked.

Noach nodded. "He said they were still wet with his sweat."

I shook my head as I followed them; Noach always has these crazy tales. When we got to the stairs, Hitta's hand surprised me when it suddenly took mine to help me up them.

Whew! Y'all! I've missed my overprotective man.

Anyway, dinner as always was quite the experience with the Hathaways. Noach's stories kept us laughing. Afterward, he stole Hitta away to the basement for a few hours. By the time they came back up, everyone had pretty much retired to their own rooms.

Jessie was bedded down with Lyric, so I took my time showering and moisturizing my skin and hair. I put on my favorite pair of pajamas, which were a pair of pink silk pajama pants with the matching cami that didn't cover my stomach anymore. Then I slid on the matching robe and piled my braids on the top of my hair in a messy bun.

Yeah, I'd planned on giving Mr. Man something to remember me by when Noach called me downstairs to say goodnight to him after they'd finished doing whatever they were doing in the basement.

What I didn't expect was for Noach to knock on my door and tell me I had company before stepping to the side so that Hitta could walk in.

"You guys have a good evening. I'm going to head on in," he said before disappearing out the door, closing it behind him. I had to wonder if Brooklyn and Noach, like Lyon and Butta, had decided to give us a little nudge in the direction they felt we couldn't get to on our own.

For a moment, I was completely at a loss as to what to do. So I sat on my bed, picking up the remote control to the TV as if it was no big deal to have all six foot plus of raw muscle that made up my husband in my small bedroom, looking good and smelling even better.

Whew, chile! Give me the strength! I'm not going to lie, seeing my husband in this state where he seems nervous around me was turning me on big time.

"May I?" he asked gesturing toward the chair next to my bed.

I reached over and removed the throw from it. "Sure."

He eased his big frame down in the chair before exhaling. "That Noach something else, huh?"

Chuckling, I nodded. "Yeah, that he is."

"What you watching?"

"The news…"

He nodded as he looked around my room. Y'all not going to believe this, but he seemed more nervous than me.

"So, do you have any recent sonograms of the baby? The last time I saw one, he was the size of an egg." He chuckled.

"Oh, yeah!" I said excitedly as I got up and reached for them where they were behind him on the dresser.

Now between me and y'all, I could have squeezed around him, so that I wasn't rudely reaching over him like this, bringing his face dangerously close to my breasts, but I didn't. And it just so happened that when I stretched my arms, my robe fell open. My braless breasts, that were squeezed into this cami, had plumped out more since the last time he saw them.

He groaned and I had to bite my lip to keep from smiling as I stepped back, holding the envelope with the sonogram pictures in it.

"Sorry about that," I told him as I loosely retied my robe before easing back down to the bed.

"Naw—" He had to clear his throat. "Naw, it's cool."

I pulled the pics out the envelope, handing them to him. "He's really big. My doctor thinks he's going to be a ten-pounder."

He looked up shocked. "What?"

I nodded. "I'm so scared."

He studied me for a minute before he spoke as if he wasn't sure of himself. "Is it alright if I can be there with you?"

"I would love that actually."

A look of relief washed over his face. "Really?"

"Really."

He studied the pictures for a moment. "Don't be scared, Teacup, everything gonna be okay."

I nearly closed my eyes and moaned. You guys have no idea how good those words felt. I think I definitely missed him telling me that the most.

I cleared my throat. There was something I needed to tell him before we went any further. "Hitta... I wanted to thank you for what you did for Westly."

He nodded before he sat up in the chair, resting his elbows on his knees. This position brought him closer to me.

"Angel... I'm sorry for what I did." He shook his head. "I'm sorry I hurt you. I was so selfish and didn't consider how my actions would affect you. But baby, you got to know I did it all to protect you. That's all I ever wanted to do."

Right then the baby kicked and I gasped, placing my hand on my stomach.

"What's the matter?"

I smiled. "The baby kicked. Here, let me see your hand." I opened my robe and let it slide from my shoulders.

Hush up! I know I'm being fast. But y'all would too if you were in my shoes...so whatever.

I took his big hand and placed it on my stomach just as our son delivered another kick.

"Wow!" he gushed, looking down at my stomach with an amazed smile. "He's strong."

I nodded. "Yeah, he is."

For a few minutes, neither of us said anything. Hitta had gone down to his knees between my spread legs and was now using two hands to rub my stomach. I leaned back on my hands, offering him my belly.

I gasped when he leaned down and gently kissed my stomach. "You're so beautiful, Teacup."

I gently rubbed my hand through his full beard as I looked down at this man that I loved. "You know, I think I figured out what I missed most."

He licked his lips that were only inches away from mine. "Oh yeah? What's that?"

"I miss the feeling of you inside of me, filling me."

Closing his eyes, he groaned as he gently rested his forehead against mine. "Me too, baby. You don't know how much I want to feel yo' heat."

I threw caution to the wind and took his lips in a kiss I'd been dying for since I started spying on him at the Lyon's Den months ago. He was only tentative Hitta for a second before my goon resurfaced and he began devouring my mouth.

When he deepened the kiss I moaned, lying back on the bed. He hungrily followed me, but then he broke the kiss off and I nearly growled at him.

"Is this gon' be alright?"

I pulled his face back down. "Yeah, it's cool." And then I was kissing him, reaching for his shirt.

But he pulled back again and I *did* growl. "I mean, you're so far along. Is it gon' hurt the baby?"

"William!" I hissed, causing his eyes to widen as he looked at me. "Do you want to die?"

With a horrified grin on his face, he shook his head. "Well then, get down here and make love to me!"

He stood and quickly pulled his shirt over his head before kicking off his boots. "Whatever you want, Teacup."

And sure enough, he gave me exactly what I wanted. Twice...

———

My eyes flew open when I felt the warm gush of water between my legs. I moved Hitta's arm to the side and sat up.

"Everything aright?" he grumbled, still asleep.

"I think my water broke."

"What?!" he cried jumping up, but because he was in a strange room and still half asleep, his feet caught in the cover and he ended up tumbling out the bed. A half a second later, his head popped back up.

"What does that mean?" Poor baby was freaking out. "Did I mess something up when I—you know when we—" I grabbed his hand, cutting him off.

"It means it's time."

For a moment, he looked completely lost. "Time?"

I grinned. "Yeah, we're getting ready to have the baby."

"Oh, dear Yah!" He jumped up and frantically searched for his clothes and put them on and then ran out of the room.

Shaking my head, I eased out of the bed and started to get dressed. Brooklyn and I had practiced this. She said when it goes down, it pays to be ready. She'd even helped me pack a bag that was in my closet ready to go.

"Alright, little sista! You ready to do this?" She said coming in the room a few seconds later; Hitta was right behind her. Y'all, my poor husband didn't look like he was going to make it. I've never seen him this way. He was adorable.

"What should I do?" he asked.

"Help me get her to your truck." He nodded before scooping me up in his arms and hurrying to the truck. Brooklyn followed behind us with my bag, saying that she and Noach will meet us at the hospital.

"It's going to be aright, Teacup. We're going to get through this. It's going to be breezy." Hitta repeated several times on the way and I think he was saying it more for himself than me.

I was okay…It wasn't that bad at all. I expected it to be more intense than this.

However, five hours later, it was a completely different story.

"I'm dying!!!" I screamed, squeezing Hitta's hand.

"Arghhh!" He said, trying to pry my hand from around his. "Baby, the grip. It's a bit much…"

"Shut up!" I yelled at him just as another contraction hit. "Arghhh-hhhh!!!!" I screamed, squeezing his hand as more pain than any human body should be able to take shot through me.

He went down to his knees, clutching the hospital bed with his other hand. "Damn! Teacup, how you get so strong?"

"Alright, mama, get ready to give me one last push," my doctor said.

And I did, screaming until my throat was raw. My big strong husband screamed right along with me. Then I felt extreme relief as our son made his entrance into this world.

"You did good, baye…" I heard my husband say as I fought to stay awake. He gently kissed my lips. "You did real good."

———

After Brooklyn and the nurses helped me get cleaned up and settled down with our son nursing at my breast, she and Noach left, promising to bring Jessie back a little later to see the baby after I'd gotten a little rest.

Hitta sat in the chair next to the bed, watching us with a satisfied smile on his face.

"Have you thought about names?" I asked him.

He grinned. "What about Baby Hard Hitta? 'Cause you already know that's what he's going to be." I opened my mouth appalled and he chuckled as he rubbed his finger against the baby's cheek. "I'm just joking. I was thinking about Nehemiyah."

That brought a smile to my face because it warmed my heart. "Nehemiyah…" I repeated, trying it out on my tongue. "I like that."

He smiled. "Yeah?"

I nodded. "Yeah…"

"And so it is," he whispered, gazing down at his son lovingly. "On this day, Nehemiyah was born."

At some point, I nodded off. I woke up to the sound of the nurse quietly showing Hitta how to change the baby's diaper. When she left, he picked his son up in his arms and what I saw next caused tears to come to my eyes. He went down to his knees in front of the hospital window, holding Nehemiyah close to his heart, and then bowed his head and began to pray.

———

The Narrator

Shantell stood looking at herself in her bedroom mirror. She turned to the right admiring the way the blue smock lay on her fit body. She'd started to get the pink ones because they were cuter but didn't not wanting to draw unnecessary attention to herself.

Angel had just given birth to the baby that should have been hers and before the night was over, he would be. Shantell will show Hitta just how much he needed her by being a better mother to his son than his stupid wife could ever be.

She'd left a note to her mother, explaining to her that she was going to have to leave for a while. She didn't tell her why because she didn't want them to be able to trace the missing baby back to her. So, she only told her that she was going to be gone, but if all goes according to plan, she will have a beautiful family when she saw her again.

Then she secured safe passage for her and the baby to get out of town without being detected. The only thing left to do was for her to get past hospital security and make it up to the maternity ward. But thanks to her little disguise, she didn't think she would have a problem.

After taking one last look at herself in the mirror, she turned to head out of the door but froze when she saw Lannox standing there blocking it with his hands stretched over his head as he casually leaned against the door frame.

"Ye know, ah loue whin mah victims mak' mah jab easier, dinnae ye Lannox?"

She gasped when Maddox's big body seemed to suddenly appear next to her before he gently caressed her cheek with his gloved hand. Lannox smiled and slowly nodded his head. Shantell opened her mouth to scream, but the only sound that made it through her throat was that of her vertebrae being snapped in half.

The Epilogue

Angel

1YEAR LATER...

Hitta popped my hand as I tried to fix the handkerchief in his suit jacket. "Baye, gone, please..." He grumbled as his hand flew across the game controller while trying to see around me.

I frowned at the little cloth that didn't want to sit right in his pocket before I went to work on it again.

"Angel, move!" he cried struggling to see around me. "These young thugs trying to run one on me!"

Jessie and Lyric both had a controller and was viciously doing battle with Hitta's avatar on the screen, but I didn't care about any of that. Westly was on his way and I wanted everything to be perfect. It had been a whole year since I've seen my brother and I was so nervous.

I've kept in touch with him over the last year and it sounds like he's doing really well for himself. He has a steady job at an aluminum factory that he's had for a little over nine months. It sounded as if he was also in a relationship because he'd asked if I'd mind if he brought a guest. I was so proud of him.

"Hitta! I don't care about that stupid game," I hissed before I snatched the handkerchief to fold it again.

"Awww, Angel!" he growled just before Jessie and Lyric started jumping around doing a victory dance.

"Loser, loser…" Lyric sang jumping around, sticking her tongue out at him.

"Ain't it time for you to go home? When yo' parents coming to get you? You got to wait on the porch," Hitta growled, tossing the controller angrily to the side. I bit my lip to keep from smiling when I heard the music on the game that indicated someone had died.

"Unc, you suck at this game!" Jessie yelled pointing at him. The whole time he looked up at me with a disappointed look.

"You see what you did?" Ignoring his question, I stuffed the cloth back in his pocket. "Woman!" he snapped, tapping my hand away again. "You bugged me about wearing the suit, now leave me be!"

His astonished gaze went to Greatie. "Can you help a brotha out?"

She chuckled from where she sat in one of the chairs by the fire sewing a shirt she was making for Nehemiyah. "I ain't in it…"

Speaking of Nehemiyah, he was leaning against his father's leg drinking his sippy cup and some of his juice was dripping down on his little suit. I reached for him, but Hitta popped my hand again.

"Don't start harassing my son."

That was it! I put my hand on my hip, getting ready to lay into him, but right then the bell rang.

"Oh wow! They're here!" I screeched before removing the apron from my waist that I had on to protect my dress as I put the finishing touches on dinner.

"Come on, girls," I called as I hurried to the door throwing it open. "Westly!"

He stood looking very handsome in a suit, looking just like the debonair gentleman I remembered from childhood. Standing next to him was a beautiful woman with short locs and a warm smile. When he opened his arms for me, I threw myself in them and nearly cried when I felt muscle.

Thank you so much, Heavenly Father!

"Come on in, guys." I stepped to the side so that they could come in.

"Angel, this is Sybil. Sybil, my baby sister, Angel."

"It is really nice meeting you. I've heard so much about you," she said reaching to shake my hand.

I reached for a hug instead. "We hug around these parts, sis."

"Most definitely," she said before squeezing me in a warm embrace. I liked her already.

"Sybil is one of the organizers at the home. I wouldn't have been able to make it this past year without her." Sybil blushed deeply at Westly words.

I hugged her again. "In that case, let me hug you again, sis, I am deeply in your debt."

"No worries. It was my pleasure." She blushed again when Westly winked at her.

"Come on in, let me introduce you to everyone." I turned to see, Jessie, Lyric, and Hitta, holding Nehemiyah in his arms standing behind me.

"This is Jessie," I said pulling my niece closer. I could tell she didn't want to go because she was very stiff.

Although she acted like it was no big deal that her dad was coming today, I knew it was, because she insisted we invite Lyric over to spend the night, and I know she clung to her best friend whenever she was emotionally stressed about something.

Sensing Jessie's hesitation, Sybil held her hand out for her to shake. "It's nice to finally meet you, Jess. Your dad talks about you all the time."

"Nice to meet you too," Jessie muttered as she shook her hand.

Westly squatted down in front of her. "Hey, baby."

"Hey, dad." She was still muttering, which wasn't a good sign. My worried gaze went to Hitta's. He reached out his free hand, taking mine. That simple act was enough to help me to remain calm and not freak out.

After Westly called last week and told us he was going to be coming to town, Jessie went quiet on us for a few days. Finally, not able to take it anymore, we took her out to her favorite pizza restaurant to loosen her up for a little chat.

It took a little prying, but Hitta was finally able to get out of her what was wrong.

"Are you guys going to give me away now?"

My mouth opened as if I'd been slapped. I reached for her hand. *"Never! What are you talking about?"*

"My dad's coming. Does that mean y'all want me to go and live with him now?"

"Hell no! If he even think about taking you away from us, he gon' have a big problem on his hand." Hitta grumbled.

Jessie's excited gaze shot to his. *"Really? You'll fight for me?"*

"Lil mama, I'll go to war for you. You one of mine! We stay together!" She jumped up from her chair and threw her arms around his neck. He and I shared a *What The Hell* look as he tightened his arms around her.

"Never doubt that, shawty. You belong with us!"

"And this is Jessie's best friend, Lyric," I said to continue the introductions. "My husband, Hitta and our son, Nehemiyah."

Hitta shook hands with Sybil, she told him that one of the newer residents at the home was a huge fan of his and asked her if she would get his autograph for him. He assured her that he would and moved to stand in front of Westly. There was a brief moment where neither of them spoke, they just stood there sizing each other up. These two haven't had the best history. Then Westly grinned big and threw his arm around Hitta's shoulder.

"What's going on, bro!"

I exhaled a breath I hadn't been aware of holding before turning to introduce Greatie, but not surprisingly, she wasn't there.

Mercifully, dinner went over without any more of those awkward moments. Jessie loosened up a bit and started being nicer to her dad after Hitta whispered something in her ear.

Later, after everyone was gone and we got the kids settled into bed, Hitta and I sat in front of the fire playing a game of chess.

"What did you say to Jessie to get her to loosen up?" I asked as I moved my queen, two more moves and I was positive I would have him in Checkmate.

"I told her I didn't care for her dad all that much either, but that we needed to make her Tee-Tee happy so we should at least fake like we do. Then I told her to follow my lead."

My mouth opened. "Hitta!"

He chuckled. "Hey, every man is held accountable for his actions." He put his hand on his chest. "I ran from my responsibility for a long time, the result of which was those headaches. I had to face myself and then defeat myself. Only then was I set free. And HalleluYah, I haven't had a headache in over a year." He held up his finger.

"But in that year's time, I had to repair a lot of things and relationships I damaged in my stupidity. Yo' brother faced himself and defeated himself, now it's on him to repair the relationships he's damaged in his stupidity. Checkmate..."

My gaze flew down to the board. "No way!" I gasped, studying the board.

Y'all, I was still a sore loser. When I saw that he had in fact Checkmated me, I flew out of my chair at him, ready to beat him into the ground. But he was waiting for me, grabbing me out of the air and bringing me to straddle his lap.

"You are such a savage, Teacup..." he whispered as his gazed lowered to my lips.

I licked them before I grinned. "Yeah, but I'm your savage."

"Damn right! Now and forever..."

The End For Now...

Alright y'all, you know how this goes... No pouting. This is not the last time you're going to hear from Hitta and Angel. As a matter of fact, y'all are going to see them again really soon 'cause crazy Carmen will not be silenced any longer. She wants y'all to hear her tale. And you already know, what Carmen wants, Carmen gets. May I present...

Taming the Brat

Taming the Brat

BONUS CHAPTERS!

The Prologue

WAYNE

My feelings for Carmen used to be innocent enough. Although they've never quite been parental, they were definitely that of a mentor looking out for his young pupil…

A pupil who at many times made me want to pull her across my lap and give her the spanking that her mother or uncle should have given her years ago.

Only…

Of late, the thought of spanking her is stimulating a different part of my body than when she was a little girl.

No!

I had to fight those thoughts. She'd just turned nineteen and the last thing she needed was a man ten years her senior perving after her.

Dear God, if she really knew how I felt about her, she'd run far away and never want to see my face again.

I didn't always have to call on a higher power for restraint when dealing with Carmen.

Restraint from what, you ask?

Well, restraint from a couple of things…

One being restraint from strangling her. She has a way of testing the very patience I've always prided myself in like nobody else… including my father, and that was saying a lot because I could not tolerate him at all.

And…

Well…

When I didn't want to strangle her… Of late, I find myself having to pray for restraint from having inappropriate thoughts of her…

Thoughts of tasting her…

Thoughts of ripping off one of those little skimpy gym outfits she's always prancing around in front of me in from her young, supple body and filling her until she begs for me stop because she can't take coming apart for me not one more time.

Yeah, I know… I'm a sick bastard to have these feelings for my employer's young niece. Trust me, nobody has beaten me up about this more than myself.

But like I said, it wasn't always this way. At first, it was so very innocent indeed.

When I got that call from the Department of Children and Family Services the night Williamina, Carmen's mom got locked up for shooting her neighbor in the head, telling me that Hitta had been named Carmen's guardian, I was dumbfounded.

Who in their right mind would leave their female child with Hitta?

I'd gotten the call pretty late; my employer had gone to Venezuela with a little honey dip for the weekend and unsurprisingly, wasn't answering his phone, so the duty to retrieve the brat fell on me. I was a little aggravated because I too was entertaining a honey dip of my own and she'd just told me she had a twin sister who was dying to join us.

Needless to say, when I got down to the police station to see the little fourteen-year-old blue-haired hellion threatening to tear up the station if they didn't release her mom, I was not amused, not even a little bit.

That night, I learned something about Hitta's family; they were all violent as hell. I listened horrified as the officer explained to me what happened.

"The young lady in there threatening to hit Officer Donoghue in the eye says that her mom was simply defending her from the creepy guy next door when she decided to put a bullet in his head."

At the time, I'd been drinking a bottle of water trying to hydrate myself in hopes that it would sober me up a bit, but after hearing his words, I ended up spewing the water back out.

"Excuse me, did you say her mother shot someone in the head?"

With a knowing smirk on his face, he nodded as both of our gazes turned back to the young hellcat who was now yelling at the top of her lungs that she was going to sue for the way she was being treated.

Up until that point, I'd heard Hitta talk about his family, but I'd not really been involved in that part of his life. What he did after hours was not my business, unless of course, my phone rang involving me, like it did that night.

However, I did know that he was very fond of this particular niece and spoiled her something fierce... I knew this because although that was my first time laying eyes on her, I'd orchestrated many purchases for her. Whenever she wanted something new, she called her uncle and he made sure she got it every time.

From what it looked like, he'd created a monster.

After filling out all the paperwork...well, at least all of it that I could, the rest would need Hitta's signature, the officers couldn't wait to dump their little headache on me.

"Who the f*** is this a**hole?" she asked as soon as they brought her out of the interrogation room to where I stood waiting for her.

"Young lady, you really should watch your mouth!" one of the female officers snapped at her.

Carmen rolled her beautiful eyes. "Thank you for your opinion, ma'am...now here's mine, the next time they come through with the box of donuts you pigs love munchin' on, you really should decline." She threw up her hands. "But hey, that's just my opinion."

My mouth dropped. I could not believe she'd just said that.

The officer who told me what had happened turned to look at me with a smirk that clearly said, *good luck.*

"She's all yours…" he muttered as he practically shoved the problem child into my hands.

I shook my head slightly as I tried to come up with a way out of this, but there was no way out and I found myself in possession of a brat.

As we walked out of the station toward my car, I took out my phone and tried Hitta again, praying he picked up. The twins had agreed to wait for me at my place and I needed to get rid of this kid right now, but of course, Hitta's a** did not answer his phone.

When she saw my car she whistled. "Aston Martin…damn, how much is my uncle paying you?"

I looked at her over the top of the car. "That's none of your business. Just get in, put on your seatbelt and don't touch anything."

She pointed at me. "You the help…you can't tell me what to do!"

Like I told you guys before, I am a man that prided myself on my patience. Each time I came in contact with my father and did not wrap my hands around his neck to strangle him until all of the life left his body was a testament to that. I refuse to now allow a fourteen-year-old hellcat with blue hair ruin my pristine reputation.

I walked around the car coming to a stop in front of her short a**. She folded her arms and looked up at me, in no way afraid.

"Let's me and you get a few things clear, brat. I am not your uncle; I am not your friend…in fact, I don't care much for you at all." I opened the passenger door.

"I suggest you get in this f***ing car, zip your lips and put on your f***ing seatbelt like I said."

An evil little smirk came on her face and that's when I realized there was a good chance I was dealing with Satan.

"F*** your car!" she yelled at the top of her lungs. "F*** those crusty a** seatbelts! And f*** your idle a** threats! Ain't nobody scared of you! You don't know me! I'll f*** you up!"

And well folks, for the first time in my life, I lost my cool. By the time I was done, I had my employer's niece tied and gagged in the back seat of my car. And let me tell you something… it was a fight that I might not have won had it not been for the fact that I at the time was a third-degree black belt in Wing Chun and Hapkido.

Apparently, Hitta has been teaching the little hellion how to box, so I actually had to dodge a few swings and just take a few others as I took my belt and tied her hands behind her back before using the strap of my gym bag to tie her feet… And because she was yelling like she was crazy, I took off my tie and stuffed it in her mouth before depositing her in my back seat where I used the seatbelts to secure her.

Yeah, I know it was a bit excessive…and while I was doing it, I was expecting the police to rush out and throw me in jail. However, by the time I was finished, I looked up and saw the two cops that were on Carmen's case standing by the door watching me with satisfied grins on their faces…and would you believe they both gave me a thumbs up?

I got in and turned up the music to drown out her muffled shrieks as I tried to think about the best place to dump this headache.

I couldn't take her to Hitta's place because he and I were supposed to be in Vegas preparing for his fight, at least that's what his girl Shantell thought. The truth was, I'd come back from Vegas alone and Hitta had gone to Venezuela to entertain a beautiful young heiress that had taken one look at him and decided that she had to have some thug passion for the weekend…her words.

Which meant I was stuck with the kid until Hitta got back whether I liked it or not. Reluctantly, I drove towards my place, contemplating for the hundredth time to just quitting. Hell, after this, he may just fire me.

Good riddance!

This was not what I had signed up for…

Believe it or not, my relationship with Hitta had started off a little different.

I was in my fifth year at Morehouse working on my MBA, wanting to get a jumpstart on my career path and join my father's investment firm with my own client list intact, so that the people whose boss I would eventually become, would see that I was going to not only earn my spot at the head of the company, but was also going to pick up where my father left off and grow it even further.

I began to hunt for what we in the field called new money... Or rather people who had just come into wealth. To take new money and grow it to substantial proportions is what put some of the top investment firms on the map, in fact, it's how my father made a name for himself.

At the time, I'd been young and eager to please him. So, when for my birthday, my roommate surprised me with not only tickets to Hitta, who is my all-time favorite fighter fight, but also passes to the after party celebrating his victory, I was thrilled.

I'd already methodically studied Hitta's finances and knew that he would be a perfect first client for me. It had taken a miracle, but I'd finally gotten close enough to him that night at the after party that was taking place in a Vegas night club to proposition him.

Of course, he told me to beat it in that gruff way of his, but I didn't give up and eventually, I got him to agree to a meeting. My first take on him was that he was a brotha from the hood who'd just come into a lot of money and being uneducated, he would eventually be taken advantage of by some of the sharks in the industry until they'd drained him of everything.

So, I'd come to the meeting with that mindset...offering to be his savior of sorts and take his money and grow it while shielding him from the sharks.

Boy!!! Was I surprised when after only thirty minutes of talking to him, I realized he was very educated...And although he didn't graduate high school...or even grad school for that matter, was nobody's dummy.

I had to bring my A-game. What I thought would be an easy client turned out to be a very challenging one. But in the end, he decided to give me a try. I took his money and tripled it. He gave me more to invest...and so on.

Then he brought me another client, his best friend, Rome. Between the two of them, I live quite comfortably. However, after my father did what he did... I'll come back to that in a minute. My plans changed drastically. Everything my father was about left a sour taste in my mouth and I didn't want to have anything to do with it.

For the first time, I found myself without a goal and I felt like I was dangling in the in-between place wherever the hell that is…

The night all that sh*t hit the fan, I found myself drinking my sorrows away, contemplating my life. My boss decided not to let me drink alone and he and Rome had joined me.

"You know, you can always keep me and Hitta on as clients." Rome slurred after maybe about the sixth or seventh round of drinks. "With only two clients, you won't even have to be regulated under SEC. And I guarantee our bread plus your skills will keep you straight. I mean, you may not be Charles Schwab, but you'll be aight."

I grunted… "Maybe, but that would leave me with too much time on my hands." My system was going through a shock. It seemed that my whole life was a lie. Everything I always thought I would be and do was all a lie.

"You know… I could use some more help," Hitta muttered.

I frowned… "How?" He was straight. He was at the height of his career; his investments were doing great… What could he possibly need help with?

"I hate dealing with people. I hate talking to them… I just want to be able to fight and not worry about nothing else!"

I chuckled… "Looks like you went into the wrong career, my friend." Between the three of us, I don't know whose words slurred the worst.

"Yeah, but you can help me."

I lifted an eyebrow. "How?"

"You can be my assistant. You can help me operate in this crazy a** world called fame. Sh*t! You already doing a lot. You might as well get paid for it."

Chuckling again, I shook my head. That was out of the question. Me becoming someone's assistant after my father had spent millions on my education was ludicrous… That would kill him…

"I'll do it!"

Both Hitta and Rome looked at me surprised.

"You will?" They said in unison.

"Yep…I sure will!"

And that's how this all came to be…although working with Hitta sometimes was like working with a big, rough, ornery child, it had still been pretty cool. Traveling the world with a famous boxer came with many adventures, the dream of every young man in his early twenties.

That was until I found myself with the brat tied up in my backseat.

"My uncle is going to kick yo' a**!" she yelled as soon as I untied her hands and removed her gag.

"Do you want to get tied up again?!" The force of my voice got her attention. With wide eyes she shook her head.

"I suggest you shut your flap until your uncle returns." I pointed at her, my finger only inches from her face. "I have no problem with throwing little bratty teenage girls in the garbage can…just try me." She swallowed but wisely kept her mouth shut.

"Welcome back, papi!" the twins cried running for the door a soon as I opened it. I smiled, instantly feeling better.

However, when they saw that I wasn't alone, their steps came to a halt. They were dressed in matching lingerie that highlighted their assets beautifully. And I'm not going to lie, for a moment, all the blood left my head and rushed to other areas of my body.

The brat sucked on her teeth. "Dang, dad! Why do you keep doing this to the family?! Is this why you told mommy to wait in the car, so that you can try and hide your prostitutes?"

"What?! Wait—" I told the girls who stormed towards their coats on the couch.

"Not cool, Wayne!" Melly or Shelly said as she pushed past me to head for the door.

"I'm only twenty-four, I can't have a daughter that old!" I called after them.

"Really, dad? So, now you're denying me? What about my three little sisters? Are you going to deny them too?"

My stunned gaze went to the little hellion. If I didn't know any better, I would have believed her. She even managed a few tears…

As soon as the door slammed shut, she turned it off instantly and an evil grin appeared on her face, but when she saw how angry I was it disappeared.

"You shouldn't be hiring prostitutes anyway…It's against the law."

I had to ball up my fists to resist the urge to follow through on my earlier threat. "They were not prostitutes, you little sh*t!"

She shrugged as she turned to head towards the kitchen… "Could have fooled me. Is there anything to drink in this house of sin?"

So yeah, she and I had a rocky start, but it didn't remain so.

Her mom's trial was pretty hard on her and it took place during one of Hitta's most important fights. Due to all the promoting and engagements that came along with that, he couldn't be there during most of the trial. He paid for his sister one of the best attorneys and sent me in to monitor everything.

It really was a miserable event. Hitta had gotten Carmen and her mom a condo in Chicago's Gold Coast area some years back. Williamina testified that after her daughter hit puberty and started budding out in places, she had caught the attention of their next-door neighbor that both she and Carmen described as a dirty old man in their testimonies.

They said that he on several occasions tried to lure Carmen inside of his apartment. When nothing worked, he grabbed her as she walked past his door and snatched her inside pulling down her halter top to bare her breasts. Thanks to Hitta, who had taught Carmen how to box years ago, the guy ended up with a few bumps and bruises for his efforts.

When she ran home and told her mom, Williamina didn't ask any questions, she grabbed her gun and after knocking on the man's door, shot him in the head.

The prosecutors asked her why she'd decided to take the law into her own hands instead of calling the police like every other law-abiding citizen. The defense attorney attempted to build the case around her being a distressed mother trying to protect her only child. They even went as far as to claim that she had a moment of temporary insanity.

Which is understandable…

However, the jury didn't see it that way. What did her in was the fact that she didn't call the police or report the man on the other occasions he'd harassed Carmen. That and the man she'd shot was a white retired lawmaker, who came from a very prominent Chicago family.

By the time the prosecutors were done, they'd successfully painted the picture of a beacon of society being felled by a black female hooligan. And it didn't matter that Hitta's face was plastered on every television around the world, they threw the book at her.

I worked miracles and called in favors on damn near everyone I knew to keep the story out of the mainstream news...Not just for Hitta, but for Carmen too. She was being dragged through the mud. But in the end, there was nothing I or Hitta could do to help Williamina.

The trial dragged on for months and in that time, Carmen's tough-girl exterior cracked. The day the jury found Williamina guilty on all counts was the toughest. Carmen had asked to stay at my apartment that weekend. She didn't want to go home to Hitta's because she and Shantell weren't quite seeing eye to eye.

I didn't hesitate saying yes. By that time, Carmen had stayed over so much due to the beef between her and Shantell that I'd practically given her the guest bedroom for her own. That night, Hitta sat with his niece for hours trying to comfort her, but she sent him home telling him that she just wanted to be alone.

After I locked up behind him, I collapsed on the couch with my head resting against the back of it, reflecting on everything that had occurred that day. I rubbed my hands down my face...tired. When they lowered, Carmen was standing behind the couch looking down at me, there were huge tears in her beautiful eyes.

"Can you hold me, Wayne?" Her voice was barely over a whisper.

"Sure, sweetheart, come here."

She walked around the couch and surprised me by climbing into my lap. I don't know if it was because she was so petite or what, but after I wrapped her in my arms, it felt like the most natural thing in the world to do.

It was as if she belonged there...

At no point did it feel anything other than innocent.

"I'm scared, Wayne, how am I going to make it out here without my mom?" Her voice quivered as tears rolled down her beautiful face.

"You're going to be okay, brat. I promise. You have your uncle, who loves you so very much… and you have me. I will always keep you safe, sweetheart."

I meant every word…

Okay, so we've reached the point in my tale where I think you guys should know why I hate my father…

During my last year at Morehouse, he left my mother for a younger woman. Now, that in itself was really f***ed up, seeing as to how she stood by him, tirelessly helping him build his image and business for twenty-six years and putting her own dreams and education to the side so that she could be all that he needed her to be.

However, that is not what made my heart grow cold to him. It was the way that he did it. He let his b****of a wife kick my mother out of the house that had been hers for the last twenty years. The bastard had forced her to sign a prenup before they got married, which basically meant she took from the marriage what she brought in.

Being a young grad student when they got married meant that she didn't bring in much. She was so hurt that her husband, who she had thought was her mate for life, had left her that she didn't even care that he and his twat of a wife had snatched everything from under her.

But I cared… And I did all that I could to stop it. I begged my father to do right by my mother.

"Stay out of this, son, you don't understand what's going on," he grumbled as he sat at his fancy desk in his fancy downtown office while my mom was in a hotel crying her eyes out.

"I know that what you're doing is not right. Mom stood by your side, putting all her dreams and aspirations to the side to help you build this company. She deserves half of everything and you know it!"

He looked up at me with amusement in his eyes before he held his head back and roared with laughter.

"Are you kidding me? A part of your mother's job was to stay in shape…and well, you see how well she did that. Like I said, son, stay out of it before you get your feelings hurt."

My mother finally came clean and admitted to me that my father had been cheating on her for several years now. I did notice that she had picked up some weight, but it's my mom, it didn't matter much to me.

She said she'd been doing a lot of depressed eating. Of course, my father told her that was the reason for the divorce. The bastard.

"I'm not going to let you get away with this!"

I'd never talked to my father that way. My words not only surprised me, they surprised him too.

He gave me a look that would have intimidated me a day ago, but now that I'd become my mother's protector because he was too big of a coward to do the right thing, his look no longer moved me. He'd become my enemy.

"Boy, who are you talking to?!" He raised his voice slightly to heighten the effect… It did nothing.

"No, dad! *Man*!!! From this day forward, you will address me as sir! Because now, I am taking care of what you should have!" I pointed at him, angry enough to lay hands on him.

He narrowed his eyes at me. "Now you listen to me, *boy*! I don't care what's going on between me and your mother…I am your father and you will respect me!"

"Like you respected the woman that gave you twenty-six years of her life? If that's the example you're setting, then you got it! I will respect you! I will respect you until my mother receives every dime she's owed!"

I turned to leave his office…But before I walked out the door, I left him with four words that I knew would devastate him.

"Oh, and I quit!"

"Junior!" he called after me. "Junior, what the hell are you talking about?!"

You see, my father had invested in me like any wise man would their future. He'd primed and prepped me to take over where he'd left off. Years of education and training gone!

Shortly after that, I bought my mother a house. She was a wreck, grieving heavily the loss of what she thought she would have forever. The more she cried, the more I set my father's ruination into plan.

He was going to pay what he owed one way or the other.

Meanwhile, my mother's constant grieving was making me

uncomfortable. I didn't know what to say to make her feel better. I didn't know how to get her to get up out of her bed and take back control of her life.

What does one say?

By mistake, I found out the cure for her...

In those days, Hitta and I spent a lot of time in Vegas, an atmosphere that's not all that conducive for a fifteen-year-old girl. We needed to find somewhere to stash Carmen. Sooo... I took her to my mom's.

I figured having someone to look after may pick up her spirits a bit...

What I didn't count on was having to bail Carmen and my mom out of jail a week later.

Yeah! I know... Crazy, right?

The brat convinced my mother that she would feel a whole lot better if she went to my father's place and poured sugar in both his and his new wife, Melissa's gas tanks. When the alarm went off, Melissa came out of the house and caught them in the act.

What did Carmen do then?

Well, she decided to pull all of Mel's hair out while my mother stood on the side and cheered her on. By the time the police got there, the ground was littered with enough fake hair to scare the hell out of my father, who apparently thought that was Mel's real hair. My mother said she will never forget the look of horror on his face when Mel ran out of the house to tell him what happened with only two inches of hair on her head that stuck straight up in the air.

I'd like to tell you that was the last time my mother and Carmen harassed my father and his new wife, but then I'd be lying. Eventually, the bastard got a restraining order against them.

But something amazing was happening, my mom was laughing and cracking jokes again. I came in one day and caught her and Carmen dancing to Al Green in her kitchen. She looked happier than I'd seen her in a long time.

The brat had even managed to convince her that it wasn't too late for her to start a career in interior designing, something she had gone to school for before she married my dad.

Yeah, I got them two out of a lot of trouble, but I didn't mind, because although Carmen was trouble with a capital T, she was good for my mom, who began telling anybody who would listen that she was the daughter she'd never had.

So okay…you're wondering what the hell happened to me and Carmen's relationship to make us the enemies you know us to be today.

And I'll admit… It was all my fault.

You see, because Hitta was always busy, Carmen was always under-foot. If she wasn't at my mom's place, she was at my place. She'd taken an interest in accounting, so quite naturally, I helped her.

From fourteen to seventeen, everything was cool between us. I hadn't notice till Maddox pointed it out that I'd become domesticated.

For all of you out there frowning, I completely understand. When he first told me, I frowned too.

But then he started pointing out a few things that everybody seemed to notice but me and Carmen.

My mom had decided to go back to school for an update…her words, which meant that Carmen was back up in the air and some-body had to look after her. So, although I couldn't really say that I was looking after her, I at least tried to make it back home as much as possible.

In reality, it was she who looked after me.

LOL, allow me to explain…

You see, Carmen is very independent; my mom calls her bossy. I don't know if it's because she lost her mom to prison or what, but she fiercely protects those that she considers hers, my mom, Hitta, and me.

A part of that protection is doing all she can to help that person, even if it's completely taking over their lives and changing things…

For example, she had started helping my mom get her girlish figure back…their words, so she took over preparing meals for all of us because she said we couldn't keep eating restaurant food.

I didn't see anything wrong with that. She did most of the cooking at my place and my mom normally stopped by to either eat or grab a plate on her way from classes since her school wasn't too far from my apartment. And if Hitta was in town, he stopped by to grab food as well. We sort of fell into a pattern.

My place was pretty much the center point of everything, so quite naturally, it was where we congregated. On my way home in the evening, I generally called Carmen to see if she needed me to bring anything in.

Until Maddox pointed it out, I didn't even notice that she'd redecorated...or shall I say, added her touch to my apartment. A piece of furniture here, a painting on the wall there...a rack that better organized my ties because I had hundreds...

Yeah, I was into ties...

I didn't notice her touches because they all made things more comfortable. However, I did notice that my place was more inviting than it had been before she started coming around. She made it feel like home.

The fridge stayed full of the things that I liked; she'd even made my office perfect for when I put in office time. Before that, I generally worked out of the gym.

Until Maddox had pointed it out, I didn't even realize that it had been forever since I brought a woman to my place. If I went out, I always went to my date's place or to a hotel.

And then there was the time shortly after Carmen's 17th birthday, Maddox, Hitta, and I ended up at dinner with our dates and Carmen... Carmen sat between me and Hitta, on the other side of me was my date for the evening.

When our food came, Carmen took the tomatoes off her burger and put them on mine because she knew I liked extra tomatoes on my sandwiches. I took my pickles off and put them on hers because she loved pickles. She poured half of our sweet tea out and added water because we both agreed a long time ago that restaurants made their tea way too sweet.

When she slowed down to about a bite per minute, I knew she was getting full and when she didn't take a bite after two minutes, I knew she was done and ate the rest of her burger... This was something that I've always done over the years. When she was younger, I used to outright steal her food.

For some reason, my date got really pissed and wanted to be taken home. It was later that night when I was talking to Maddox that he pointed out a few things that probably pissed her off. I swear up until then, I hadn't even noticed that I'd f***ing become domesticated.

So, I put an end to it. I stopped making it home all the time and started being away more often. Yeah, it wasn't like being at home and yeah, I was missing my place, but I needed to disrupt whatever the hell it was that seemed to have naturally developed between me and my employer's niece.

My mom was not happy with me, she of course, was worried about Carmen, who was back to staying at the apartment Hitta had gotten for them. Because he was never there, she ended up there by herself a lot.

The tension started rising between us, but then I got word that some pissant boy was sniffing around there when Hitta was away, some boy that word had it, Carmen really liked.

I told myself that what I did was for her protection. She was a seventeen-year-old girl and she didn't need some guy coming around when she was there by herself. If he meant her any good, he would come around when either I or Hitta was there.

So yeah, I paid him a little visit and told him to back the f*** off. I may or may not have threatened bodily harm. I chalked that up to being around Hitta too long; some of his barbaric ways have rubbed off on me...

I told myself many lies, but the truth was, I couldn't stand the idea of some guy touching her or trying to take her comfort. No, I couldn't have it, but I for damn sure didn't want anybody else having it...

Yeah, I know, that's so f***ed up, right?

Carmen came to see me the next day and the sh*t hit the fan. I'd been in my home gym training with my sensei when she barged in.

"Master Pai Mei, can you please excuse us?!" she snapped clearly pissed.

I bowed to my teacher and watched as he left the gym. As soon as he was gone, she ripped into me.

"What the f***, Wayne?! What did you tell John? He won't answer my calls, he canceled our date! When I asked him why, he said to talk to you!"

"Wait! What f***ing date? I don't remember you talking to me or your uncle about a f***ing date!"

"Are you serious?! I'm getting ready to be eighteen—"

"So f***ing what?!" I paused for a second to try and get control over my anger. She'd been spewing that eighteen sh*t and it was driving me nuts.

"You turning eighteen don't mean sh*t!"

She was looking at me as if I'd lost my mind. She had pink hair at the time and was so beautiful it hurt to look at her. I told myself that I didn't desire her and that wasn't why I ran off that douchebag…I told myself it was for her own safety.

"You expect me to be single for the rest of my life?!"

"Yes!" I didn't hesitate to give her my answer. Hell yeah, I knew it was unreasonable, but it was how the f*** I felt.

"Can't you see that's not fair? You have dates all the time…You and my uncle the biggest hoes I know! That's so f***ing hypocritical!"

I shrugged. "No worries, sweetheart! I'm going to make sure you never have that problem."

She was so mad that she was standing there with her little fists balled up, no doubt she wanted to try and take me in a fight. It wouldn't be the first time…my guess is, it wouldn't be the last time. I've had to show her on a few occasions that her little boxing skills could only take her so far.

"I'm telling my uncle on you…" she growled looking so adorable in her anger.

I shrugged again… "Tell him, I don't care. He knows I'm just trying to keep you safe. He put you in my charge a long time ago… I'm just doing my job, baby."

"That's bullsh*t and you know it!"

I smiled… "Maybe it is…but guess what. When it's all said and done, my word stands."

If looks could kill, I would be dead… "I hate you!"

"Don't say that, brat, it's not true."

"I'll show you how true it is…"

And well, that's when the war began. The environment got so tense, Hitta pulled me to the side to have a little chat with me.

"Aye, Bo, let me holla at you for a minute."

At the time, I had been arranging for one of his new fighters to have an interview on WYN news.

"Yeah, boss…what's up?"

"Man, that's what I want to know. What's going on with you and Carmen? She came to me begging me to fire you."

I chuckled as I continued to make the arrangements… "Yeah, I'm not her favorite person."

"She said you won't let her talk to her little boyfriend."

That made me pause and look up at him. "She doesn't have a boyfriend."

It was his turn to chuckle. "That's the problem, she wants one."

I shook my head. "Look, man, you're out of town most of the time. I'm the one that's been handling things with her… Let me do my job. Stay out of it!"

He threw up his hands. "Calm down, buddy… You a little more testy than usual, ain't you?"

I looked away from him going back to what I was doing. "I don't know what you're talking about."

"Sure, you do. You're in love with her, Bo."

I whipped around to stare at my boss with a frown on my face. "I know speaking your mind is your thing, but this is too much…Why would you say something so horrendous?!"

He chuckled again… "Because it's true, *nigga!*"

"It's not. I'm simply looking out for her. Do you know how many punks would love to get their hands on her just because she's your niece? I'm doing what's best for her!"

"You doing what's best for *you*. But I ain't mad at you. I'm not a big fan of her coming home with some random dude. And if I didn't know she love you just as much as you love her, I wouldn't be a big fan of you either."

He stood. "But let me leave you with this. After while, you gon' stop lying to yourself about your feelings for her. I don't want to have to break your arms, so make sure she's past eighteen when you do."

He patted me on my back none to gently. Big bastard nearly made me tip over. "You don't have that long to wait. She'll be eighteen in a few months."

I shook my head. "You got it all wrong."

"Sure, I do." Chuckling, he walked away.

He had it all wrong...

At least that's what I told myself...

Afterword

Note From Edwina Fort

Thank you guys so much for reading Hitta's Tea Maker , please join my <u>mailing list </u>so that you can stay abreast of all the new and fun things we have going...Like the Love Chronicles.

The Love Chronicles are free love stories that are my gift to you for being so awesome! You guys don't want to miss this!

Also, if you enjoyed Hitta's Tea Maker 2, please leave me a comment, letting me know what you think. Your thoughts matter to me and I would looooovvvveeeee the feedback.

The free stories in the Love Chronicles will also answer many questions some of you have about mysterious characters. Those who follow my work, know that there are only 360 degrees of separation. Each story adds another piece to the puzzle.

Be the first to collect all the pieces and solve the riddle....

Happy Reading, family!!!!

P.S. If my stories make an impact on you and they leave you feeling good down on the inside...Please, pay it forward. Go out there and make somebody else's day. It doesn't matter who or how much. You'd be amazed at how far a simple act of kindness can go and how much of an impact it can make on someone's life. Just sow love. We're in desperate need…

JOIN ME

ON SOCIAL MEDIA

www.AuthorEdwinaFort.com

@EdwinaFortFanPage
& @ Edwina Fort

@AuthorEdwinaFort

Stay connected with me by joining my chat group @Edwina's Place Chat With Me on Facebook. This is a set apart place for my genuine fans. Get to know me as I get to know ya'll. You'll also have access to find free stories written by yours truly. So let's chat ya'll...

About the Author

Author Edwina Fort is a writer who writes with a passion and purpose. She was born and raised in Chicago, but now resides in the South. Although she is new to many, this author has been writing for many years and has given her unique style of writing away freely at no cost to those who would receive. Her passion for writing came about at an early age and developed into what it is today based on her experience and life lessons. With her stories, she wants to redefine all that we've been taught to believe and shed light on our truths and potential. Writing is her calling and she wants to share that gift with you through the pages of her work. Each book will take you on a memorable journey you will find hard to forget.